KRYGOR'S HOPE

Braxians 3

REGINE ABEL

CONTENTS

READING ORDER

The Braxians series is part of the Veredian Chronicles universe. While this book can be read as standalone with a complete romance arc and no cliffhanger, to fully enjoy the overarching story, it is recommended to read both series in the following order:

1. Escaping Fate, Veredian Chronicles 1
2. Blind Fate, Veredian Chronicles 2
3. Raising Amalia, Veredian Chronicles 3
4. Anton's Grace, Braxians 2
5. Twist of Fate, Veredian Chronicles 4
6. Ravik's Mercy, Braxians 2
7. Hands of Fate, Veredian Chronicles 5
8. Krygor's Hope, Braxians 3
9. Defying Fate, Veredian Chronicles 6
10. Keran's Dawn, Braxians 4

KRYGOR'S HOPE

For Family. For Honor.

Discarded by her husband who then sells her as a pleasure worker, Hope secretly enters into an Indentured Servant contract with a strip club owner to avoid being given to an unknown master. But she soon realizes that he has not only conned her into endless servitude, he also has nefarious plans involving her child. Desperate, she turns to a broker to find a new buyer for her contract. As soon as she meets the buyer, a Braxian giant named Krygor, with a fearsome face and the body of a god, Hope knows the Goddess has finally answered all of her prayers.

When Krygor comes to Lilith Hive for business and leisure, the last thing he expects is to fall hard for a delicate beauty and feel so paternal towards her teenaged daughter, both in desperate need of his protection. Hope awakens in him feelings he had banished after getting his heart torn to shreds by his first love. But a broken heart quickly becomes the least of his worries when enemies from his past use his females to capture him.

They shouldn't have messed with the most insane of the Braxian Berserkers. They may think they have him at their mercy, but Krygor will bathe in their blood for daring to threaten what's his.

DEDICATION

To anyone who has ever felt like life keeps throwing rotten eggs your way and stacking all the odds against you. To those who keep fighting and standing tall in the face of adversity, when others kick you down or seek to take advantage of you.

To all parents, especially single ones, who sacrifice everything and put themselves second to ensure the happiness of their children. And to all the wonderful adoptive parents who realize that unconditional love for a child has nothing to do with genetics.

You have my deepest respect.

PROLOGUE

HOPE

Roman's dark, penetrating gaze assessed me as I settled nervously in the fancy, black leather-cushioned chair in his office. The salt-and-pepper haired human male possibly held the key to my future and, consequently, to my daughter's safety.

His imposing darkwood desk, adorned with simple straight lines, screamed functional luxury. It ate up half the space of his small office. Considering he didn't lack real estate in the high-end loft that served as both his residence and place of business, I assumed he'd made his office this small to give it an intimate feel. For me, despite the off-white walls meant to make it feel roomier, it just felt like another cage.

"You requested a meeting with me, Ms. Morak," Roman said in a professionally warm voice. "How may I be of assistance?"

I licked my lips nervously and tucked a lock of my long silver-white hair behind my ear.

"Indeed, Mr. Tusk. I—"

"Please, call me Roman," he interrupted gently. "I've been a rogue too long for this kind of formality."

"Roman, then," I said with a nervous smile, "but only if you call me Hope."

"Very well, Hope. How may I help you?"

"I have come to you because your reputation for fair dealing and having your client's best interests at heart is legendary," I said in a deliberately submissive and awed tone. The discreet smile stretching his thin lips and the almost imperceptible way he puffed his chest at the praise told me I'd scored some positive points with him. I needed him on my side at all costs. "I have gotten myself into a serious bind, and I need help to get out of it."

"Are we talking about a debt?" Roman asked in a neutral tone.

"Yes, of sorts," I replied, clasping my hands on my lap.

"Of sorts?" Roman insisted.

"I am an Indentured Servant to Luther Stromland, the owner of Bacchus," I said with a slightly shaky voice. "I need someone to buy my contract, renegotiated with better terms."

"What's the amount of the debt you've enslaved yourself to him for?" Roman asked.

"Two point five million credits," I said almost in a whisper, still overwhelmed by the size of the debt.

"How long have you been serving it?" Roman asked.

"Four years."

Roman's furry brow shot up. "Four years? And you still owe two point five million?"

I nodded, my eyelids blinking rapidly to suppress the tears pricking my eyes.

"What was the original amount of the debt?" he asked, a slight frown creasing his broad forehead, giving his ruggedly handsome square face a slightly intimidating edge.

"Two point five million," I replied, feeling defeated.

His face closed off. He had enough experience to understand I'd been suckered into permanent slavery. The Eastern Quadrant was ruled by contracts, and the party that didn't respect the terms of the one they'd entered into would face dire consequences. Therefore, people were strongly encouraged to hire a professional—be it a lawyer or a broker like Roman—to negotiate the terms on their behalf to avoid getting conned into far more than they intended. But the poor and the desperate were always the ones getting screwed by the predators on the prowl, like I had been.

"The agreement was that I would work for him at Bacchus, food and lodging provided, and that seventy percent of my wages would be withheld to repay my debt," I explained grateful for the absence of condemnation or disdain on his face; only professional curiosity. "With his older girls like me making an average of 120,000 to 160,000 credits per month, I figured it would take a maximum of three years to repay him, less even if I worked overtime."

"First of all, with indentured servitude, the repayment value is never one for one, but usually seventy percent of it. Meaning, according to that same calculation, you should have repaid a little less than one point eight million credits in little under two years," Roman grumbled. "Furthermore, it is illegal for him to prevent you from working or from doing the standard basic weekly hours," Roman added, in a slightly clipped tone.

As floored as I felt at realizing even more how completely Luther had exploited me, Roman's apparent anger on my behalf made my heart soar. His outrage meant he'd possibly go the extra distance to make sure to free me of this nightmare.

"Oh no, he's no fool," I answered bitterly. "I do regular hours like everyone else, some overtime even. But we never agreed what my duties would be. Luther makes sure I only do the less lucrative roles: bartending, stripping, and massages."

"No blowjobs, hand jobs, or full service?" Roman insisted.

"Occasionally the first two, never the last one. Or rather, never with the customers. Luther had included in the contract that he could use me for his pleasure when he sees fit as part of his side benefits. But that doesn't lower my debt in any way," I said angrily.

"But why?" Roman asked, clearly baffled. "Don't get me wrong, you're a beautiful woman, and I can see why he would want you, but that seems a little excessive just to bed you."

"He wants my soon-to-be-twelve-year-old daughter. He wants me to be desperate enough that I will cave in."

Roman recoiled. "He wants to bed your daughter?" he asked with the proper amount of outrage.

I shook my head. "Not him. He has a client who wants a rare virgin for his son's first bedding. Considering how much Luther has been increasing his pressure tactics on me, I'm assuming the time is nearing for when he's supposed to deliver her to him. I will *not* let him have my baby."

"Four years is a mighty long time to plot such an elaborate scheme. What's so special about your daughter to warrant all that?"

I immediately closed off. Even if I'd come here for his assistance, some questions I really didn't care for.

"That's beside the point," I said, my voice slightly more clipped than intended. "The only question that matters is whether you think you can help me find someone willing to buy my contract with better conditions and the promise I will be free in a couple of years or so."

The broker narrowed his eyes at me. For a moment, my heart constricted with the fear I might have rubbed him the wrong way. If he kicked me out of his office, I'd have no one else to turn to.

"You will learn, Hope, that I don't ask questions to pry or out of misplaced curiosity. The more I understand your situation, the better I can help you," Roman replied after a beat, his voice vastly less warm than before. "But you are welcome to your secrets." He gestured at the small open area to the left of his desk. "Please remove your clothes so that I can see what we're working with."

I swallowed hard, feeling inexplicably humiliated. Rising to my feet, my pulse racing with growing apprehension, I removed my coral bandeau top, then slipped down my matching, barely-below-the crotch mini-skirt. That color flattered my lightly tanned complexion, and I had hoped with so much skin exposed, stripping wouldn't have been required. It wasn't uncommon for brokers to ask to 'sample' the goods. Had I been wrong thinking Roman above such slimy practices?

"Lose the thong but keep the heels," Roman said, leaning back in his chair before crossing his legs.

My heart further sank as I peeled off my skin-colored thong, which I'd also hoped would have been sufficient. The curtain of my hair falling before my face as I bent down hid my anger and distress. This wasn't the future that I'd wanted for myself, or that I'd even been destined to. I should have been the lady of a wealthy and influential male on Guldar, not some desperate pleasure worker, enslaved to a ruthless son of a bitch, and seeking a new owner.

How low I have sunk.

Straightening up, I discarded my thong on top of the tiny pile of my clothes on the floor, waiting for him to tell me to bend over his desk or press my palms against the wall, legs spread. Lifting my chin, I stared straight ahead, keeping a neutral expression on my face. As long as he helped me save my daughter, I'd do whatever was necessary.

"Turn around, three-sixty, slowly," Roman said, sounding almost bored.

I proceeded, feeling his burning stare on me. As much as I didn't want him making a move on me, his apparent lack of interest or lecherous expression on his face further fueled my anxiety. Did he think me not attractive enough?

"Are the tits real?" he asked in that same factual, business-like voice, once I completed my full rotation.

"Yes," I said, hating the slight shaking in my voice. "I'm 100% natural, no surgeries, no implants."

"The bare pussy, is that shaved, waxed, or permanent?"

"Permanent," I replied, trying to sound as business-like as he did.

In reality, it was a bit of a lie. Guldans didn't have pubic hair, but he had no reason to suspect I wasn't human.

"Very nice. You're a stunning woman," Roman said, his gaze slowly roaming over me, assessing. "Please answer yes or no to the following questions as to things you would consent to as part of a potential agreement. Bondage?"

"Yes."

"S and M?"

"As long as it doesn't scar or maim me," I said while hating the thought of it.

"Anal?"

"If I must, yes."

"Roleplay?"

"Yes," I said with a shrug. I never understood the appeal, but it was usually rather inoffensive and sometimes even amusing… if not silly. "However, I am more of a submissive. I wouldn't make too convincing of a dominatrix."

"Mmhmm," Roman said absentmindedly, his gaze still assessing me. "Ménage, partner swaps, gangbangs, and orgies?"

I clenched my teeth and fisted my hands, helpless rage burning again like acid in the pit of my stomach. This was all so unfair.

"Look, if it can get me out of this damn contract, I'll chain fuck everything that moves on this space station," I said at last, fighting against the tears that wanted to rise in my eyes. "My ideal buyer would be a single male, jealously possessive, who wouldn't let any other touch me or even stare too intensely at me, strong enough to protect my daughter and me from those who might want to harm us, but gentle enough to never physically hurt me, and not into any kind of freaky kink or fetish. I know this is all wishful thinking, but that's what I would want. Either way, I will submit to whatever will get me free of this contract within the next two years, as long as I can walk away from it mentally and physically sound."

Roman listened dispassionately to my speech, his fingers tapping rhythmically on the top of his desk.

"How's your deepthroat?" he suddenly asked.

"Very good," I said with a shrug.

"Show me," he said flatly, uncrossing his legs.

My heart sank, and I gaped at him for a second. A sense of hurt and betrayal washed over me, even though I had partially expected it. Pinching my lips, I advanced stiffly towards him, kneeled between his parted legs, and reached for the magnetic clasp of his pants. Before my hands could touch it, Roman caught my wrists, startling me. I looked up at him, taken aback by the sad, disappointed look in his eyes as he shook his head at me.

"Oh Hope, what the fuck are you doing?" Roman said in the soft voice a parent would use with a hopeless child.

"What you told me to do," I said, confused and embarrassed.

"Get up, Hope, and get dressed."

Humiliated, I scrambled back to my feet and quickly slipped my barely-there clothes back on, feeling completely lost.

"A broker who demands a free fuck from you just to start scouting on your behalf will screw you with more than just his dick," Roman said in an almost paternal way that finally broke the dam as tears poured down my cheeks. "Sit down, Hope."

As soon as I settled down, he extended a box of tissues to me and gave me a few moments in silence while I tried to regain my composure. And now, mortification joined my long list of miserable emotions.

"I understand that you feel helpless but acting out of desperation will be your continued downfall," Roman continued with the same fatherly tone. "When you act like this, you give people permission to exploit you. And they will, any chance they can. I *want* to help you, Hope, but I cannot lie to you. Your case is a long shot. You are a stunning female, but gorgeous humans are a dime a dozen. And, for this market, you are already considered too old. Most buyers with the criteria you want seek females in their late teens to mid-twenties, the more exotic the better. The majority of men with the credits to buy your contract will want you to consent to questionable fetishes. I would not put you into their hands."

"I will do anything to save my daughter," I pleaded. "Anything. Whatever the cost to me…"

"Hope…" Roman shook his head, looking discouraged.

His broad shoulders slumped, and he bowed his head while thinking. I held my breath, begging the Goddess for help.

"Do you have any other skill that could be of interest?" the broker asked, although his face expressed that he knew better, and slowly nodded when I shook my head. "Honestly, besides Braxians and maybe a couple of the pleasure houses on Jeruna, I can't think of…"

"Braxians are fine. I'm okay with a Braxian master," I said quickly.

"Hope, have you met one in the flesh?" he asked cautiously. "They are massive. Their cocks could kill you and split you in two unless you are given large amounts of Denax before penetration every time. And even then, it can take up to an hour to prepare a human to receive them. Frequent use of Denax will severely affect your health. After two years—"

"I'm not human. I can handle it," I said, interrupting him.

Roman froze, his dark eyes examining my features for the clue he might have missed as to my genetic background. Taking in a deep breath, I clasped my hands on my lap, my grip so tight my nails were digging into my palms.

"I am Guldan," I confessed, holding his gaze unflinchingly. His eyes widened then flicked up to stare at my forehead. "Luther had my horns removed and my pointy ears clipped in order to sneak me off of Guldar among the group of slaves he had just bought from my previous master. It was supposed to be temporary. When sawn off or broken, our horns grow back. But, like with many of his promises, Luther lied. He had my roots cauterized so mine never would. After he removed the prosthetic used to hide the scars, he performed additional esthetic surgery on my forehead to make it seamless."

Roman muttered something under his breath. I couldn't make out the words, but his demeanor said it all.

"What of your daughter? How did he sneak her out?" Roman asked with a clipped voice.

"Siona was quite petite at the time—my baby was a late bloomer," I added with a nervous smile. "He placed her in stasis inside one of their crates. I only consented because we could track her vitals remotely, and because she would only remain inside it for a few hours."

"Two Guldan females, one of them a virgin, outside Guldar," Roman reflected out loud. "You, and especially your daughter, are worth a fortune. No wonder he kept you trapped. But I don't understand why he didn't try to impregnate you."

I tapped my left upper arm with a smirk. "Contraceptive implant. He had mine removed during my surgery, but as it had been close to expiring at the time, I already had a new five-year one that I auto administered. He has no idea I have it. It's still good for a little over a year."

"Smart girl," Roman said with a smile before sobering. "But I admit knowing little about Guldan females. What makes you think you can handle a Braxian?"

"Guldan children are born fully horned," I explained. "Our womb and inner walls are reinforced to resist tears and injury from the sharp tips. They are also very stretchy to allow an easy delivery of our larger babies, horns included. We do not tear, we adjust."

Roman looked at me with new eyes, an impressed but kind smile stretching his thin lips.

"Well then, that changes things. Your secret is safe. I am meeting with a Braxian in a couple of days from now. He's a good man and a good friend. Let me see if I can work something out for you."

We spent the next ten minutes ironing out the final details. By the time I headed back home in the Commons—the affordable section of the space station reserved for customers of low to average wealth and the regular staff of both the Commons and VIP sections—my head was swimming at the thought of a potential new beginning.

As I disabled the multiple locks restricting the access into my humble apartment, I couldn't stop thinking that, in two days, our lives could completely change. No more fear and no more stretching every credit to ensure my baby's safety.

I pushed the door which opened onto a narrow corridor where Tamika—my friend and Siona's babysitter—was standing. She was stunning with her dusty blue skin, elven face with a pointy chin, her large, doll eyes of the deepest blue, and her long silver-white hair almost identical to mine, the petite Avean female was one of the most sought-after females at Bacchus. Like me, she was working off an Indentured Servant contract with Luther. Unlike me, she'd negotiated smartly.

"How did it go?" Tamika asked as sole greeting.

I closed the door behind me and gave her a trembling smile. "Roman is going to try to find me a buyer. He hopes to have some positive news for me in a couple of days."

"Oh Goddess, that's wonderful!" she exclaimed, hugging me fiercely.

"Mama?" Siona said, her soft voice filled with hope.

"Sweetie," I said, letting go of Tamika to pull her into my arms.

She hugged me tightly, and I kissed her forehead between the delicate obsidian horns which started at the top of her forehead, recurved over her head with their sharp points rising back up. They contrasted sharply with the silky curls of her silver-white hair. Cupping her cheeks in my hands, I pulled back to look at her beautiful face. Although my stamp was all over it, her slightly more prominent cheekbones, her emerald green eyes and button nose, and the aura of innocence emanating from her gave my daughter a unique glow that would take anyone's breath away. No wonder they coveted my little gem.

"Everything will be all right," I whispered to her. "Roman will help us. Come what may, I will never let anyone hurt you."

CHAPTER 1
KRYGOR

As we approached the security gate of the Lilith Hive docking bay, the guests on my firstborn's state-of-the-art pleasure barge cowered before us. The fearsome faces of my pilot Yulan and engineer Zartag reflected the same amusement I felt. As Braxians, we towered over most other species by at least a head, sometimes more. Considered as giants, with biceps bigger than a human head, our bodies were naturally built for war. I loved seeing the little people squirm, trembling in their boots, their eyes all but popping out of their heads as we strolled past them.

But then, I was slightly deranged.

I was born in the wrong era, after the Great Wars. As the Leader of a warrior clan, I lusted after blood and battle, the sound of my enemies' screams the sweetest of music, and the feel of their bones crushing beneath my fists an almost orgasmic sensation. I welcomed physical pain, feeding my battle rage with it to inflict it right back to my foes a thousandfold. Too bad the Galactic Council had brought peace to the Eastern Quadrant.

"Welcome to Lilith Hive, Mr. Aldriss!" said one of the guards manning the gate while waving us through with deference. "It is an honor to have you among us."

I grunted in acknowledgment and gave him a slight nod. My crew puffed their chests as the guard also welcomed them with respect. Although I kept a neutral expression on my face, pride filled my heart to bursting as I walked past the security check onto the imposing entrance hub of the entertainment space station. Lilith Hive was one of seven pleasure barges built by my firstborn son, Anton; a half-breed. Back in the day, by Braxian customs, I should have put him down for not being pureblood. Sparing him not only changed the fate of my formerly struggling clan—making it one of the richest and most powerful of Braxia—it also helped change the course of history for our people.

I still couldn't fully grasp how he had managed to achieve all of this when every possible odd had been stacked against him. Lilith Hive was his second largest space station—after his HQ named Venus Hive —and could house nearly five million people. The most wealthy and the common folk from all sentient species of both Quadrants flocked here to enjoy everything that the Hive Network had to offer. Each station offered entertainment in all forms from music concerts to dance shows, casinos to gladiator arenas, fashion and gastronomical, and of course, every possible shade of adult entertainment.

But I wasn't here for pleasure… yet. My son had turned my barren farmlands on Braxia into a gold mine, making me extremely wealthy in my own right. While grateful for how that had changed the fate of my clan, I had made it a point to prove myself worthy of him in return and grow that wealth further.

The chauffeur sent to pick me up by my business contact waved at me while standing by a sleek, oversized hovercar to comfortably accommodate my massive frame. I waved him back before turning to my men.

"You have a two-day leave," I said, smirking at their overjoyed expression. "Anton has given you both free access to every venue on the station. Do not make him regret it." I didn't need to add they'd face my wrath if they did. "If you intend to sleep in one of the local hotels instead of aboard the ship, make sure to give them an early enough warning. Otherwise, enjoy."

"Yes, Clan Leader," both men answered respectfully.

With another grunt, I headed towards the vehicle, nodded at the chauffeur as he babbled some words of greeting, and settled inside without a word. My gaze roamed over the various species strolling down the large walkways alongside the elegant buildings of the VIP venues boasting muted colors and fancy business signs. Humans dominated in numbers, skewing heavily towards a greater female presence. They were beautiful. Unlike any other species, they came in a great variety of heights, sizes, shapes, skin, hair and eye color, and facial traits.

And one of them had given me the only scar I would gladly erase.

Marla… She had been the embodiment of perfection, with the face and the body of a goddess, long, golden hair that had captured the rays of the sun, sinfully plump lips, and breasts made to fit snugly in the palm of my hands. Her throaty voice whispering my name, whispering words of love had been nothing but a siren's song. Like my firstborn, I'd always prided myself in being an excellent judge of character. But she had played me in the most masterful way, before walking away from both me and our son.

I no longer loved her, but my heart continued to mourn the female I had believed her to be—wished her to be. Seeing Anton's happiness with his Grace and Ravik's with his Mercy only reminded me of the gaping hole in my chest and the old scar that never fully healed. To think Anton had planned on sending Mercy to me… She could have been mine. Our Dagna was stunning and fierce, a true goddess among mortals. But while I couldn't deny sharing the collective Braxian infatuation towards the Magnar's woman, I needed a submissive mate, which would never be the case for Mercy.

As carefree and content as I pretended to be, I held the hope that my turn, too, would come when the one female truly made just for me would enter my life. Failing that, I prayed the Ancestors bring us another great war for me to express the excess of emotions filling me by crushing the fools who would stand in my path.

The hovercar stopped in front of a tall building made entirely of reflective, tan-colored glass and a soft golden metal I didn't recognize.

"Thank you," I said to the chauffeur to be more civil than my usual grumpy way.

"My pleasure, Mr. Aldriss," said the young human male with fiery hair and a constellation splattered all over his face.

I suppressed a snort at his obvious joy that I'd acknowledged him enough to actually speak to him. Humans were silly. Stepping out of the vehicle, I entered the sleek building, nodded at the guard manning the entrance, and made my way up in one of the elevators to the penthouse of Roman Tusk. Mercy had initially put me in touch with that human broker. The former mercenary reminded me of William, Anton's right hand. He had already handled a couple of deals for me in the past, finding me strong business partners or buyers for my goods.

The elevator doors opened onto a large seating area, which served as both an entertainment room for guests in the evening and an informal reception waiting area during his business hours. The guard having no doubt informed him of my arrival, Roman stood waiting for me in the center of the room. At fifty-nine years of age—two years my elder—he looked good with his ruggedly handsome features and his tall, broad-shouldered body that he'd kept fit as many former mercenaries were wont to do. Despite being a handful of centimeters short of two meters, the top of Roman's head barely reached my shoulder.

"Greetings, Roman," I said, slapping my fist on my chest in the standard Braxian greeting. "Blessings on your house."

"Hello, my friend," Roman replied, approaching me with his hand extended.

That human practice of shaking hands always baffled me, feeling often unpleasant with their hands being clammy or shaky as they all but feared I would crush it—not that the thought didn't frequently cross my mind. But I went along with it, appreciating his firm, confident grip.

"Come, we have much to discuss," Roman said, leading me to a large couch in his seating area instead of the far too cramped office he loved to bring his customers into.

Without asking, he poured me a large glass of Xelixian wine—for which I'd recently developed a taste—then one for himself before settling in a plush, matching brown leather chair across from me.

"What news have you got for me?" I asked, twirling the bluish liquid in my glass.

"Excellent news," Roman said, flashing his white teeth at me. "Your idea of using your gems as focus crystals for lasers in both weapons and medical equipment was pure genius. I have four buyers in a bidding war. You technically could let them push each other into raising the price and then selling to all of them as I understand you have a near endless supply of the gems?"

"Correct. My son negotiated an exclusive deal for my otherwise worthless crop in exchange for the gems that are equally useless to my client," I said proudly.

"Well then, you keep coming up with such clever ideas, and soon your wealth will rival your son's," Roman said teasingly.

I snorted. That would obviously never happen. Whatever Anton touched all but turned to a mountain of credits. Still, I couldn't wait to show him how I was growing and multiplying his precious gift to me. My son had devoted most of his life to making me proud of him not realizing I'd always been. What would he think if he found out that I, too, wished for him to be proud of me, not for my strength—which was merely due to genetics—but because I could be as smart?

"To success," I said, raising my glass of wine.

"To success," Roman repeated, imitating me.

I took a large sip and purred loudly at the sharp, but lightly fruity taste of the treacherous wine. You could drink it like juice, and then, minutes later, the alcohol would hammer you all of a sudden. Roman laughed, pleased by my approval before taking a sip of his own drink.

Over the following hour, we discussed various other business opportunities and agreed on meeting dates with the potential partners. My original plan on staying for two days ended up being stretched to a full week. Yulan and Zartag wouldn't mind, and I could be tempted into exploring some of the more decadent forms of entertainment Anton's space station had to offer.

As if he'd read my mind, Roman's dark eyes suddenly sparkled with mischief.

"There is one last piece of *business* I want to discuss with you, but later," he said mysteriously, his odd emphasis on 'business' piquing my curiosity. "First, we're going to celebrate your success at Bacchus. I have prepared a very special surprise for you, which should be ready as we speak. We shouldn't delay."

I narrowed my eyes at him. "Is that why you asked me to clear my agenda for the day?"

"Yes," Roman said with a fiendish grin. "You are about to receive the Royal Treatment from a most stunning female; three hours, anything you want."

I snorted and shook my head. "And she'll run for the hills the minute she sees me walk in."

"Wrong. She knows exactly what you are and is quite eager to meet you," Roman retorted smugly. "Spare me the dubious look. I never promise what I can't deliver. And that little gem—who isn't Braxian— does not require Denax."

My brain froze as I gaped at him. Roman burst out laughing at my incredulous look.

"That's impossible!" I exclaimed, this time fully intrigued.

"I never lie. Come on, old friend. It is rude to make a lady wait," Roman added, rising to his feet.

We walked the short distance to Bacchus among the throngs crowding the walkways. Dinner service had just begun in most venues offering meals. Considering the high demand for tables in the VIP section, being even a minute late for one's reservation almost guaranteed it would be passed on to the next person on the waiting list. But carving ourselves a passage through the masses wasn't an issue.

Roman burst out laughing, mumbling something about the way the people moved out of our path being akin to the parting of the sea. When I gave him a blank stare, he shook his head and said dismissively it was some biblical reference from one of the religions on Earth. I shrugged, having nevertheless understood the analogy. Braxia, like most planets of the Eastern Quadrant didn't observe any organized religion. In direct contrast, every planet in the Western Quadrant exclusively worshiped the Goddess, aside from a handful of them—such as Earth—that had either a completely different faith or a mix of various religions.

The tinted double doors of Bacchus opened before us, revealing the warm and luxurious interior of the erotic parlor. Despite the dim lights and the dark floor, the light-colored walls made the place feel intimate rather than gloomy. The diamond-shaped room had three stages, two smaller ones on the sides, and the main one in the center, with a series of tables surrounded by old green Chesterfield chairs. Tall pillars marked the beginning of the invisible sections dividing the three stages by creating a sound field that prevented the music from each stage from overlapping with the one of the other sections. Invisible to the eye, the energy field could be perceived by tiny distortions in the air whenever someone walked through it.

Stunning females of different species were performing artistic and acrobatic erotic dances on the different stages. They weren't the cheap tricks found in the Commons, but true, highly skilled and talented professionals, most with formal dance or gymnastics training.

Knowing my aversion for the standard-height chairs that often proved not only too narrow for my massive frame but so low they made me feel like I was sitting on the floor, Roman led us to a wide, elevated table with cushioned high stools. We'd no sooner settled down than a beautiful Dantorian female with charcoal skin, long ash-colored hair, and slightly glowing stormy eyes walked up to us. Perched on sky-high white stilettos, a sheer, white babydoll dress and barely-existent thong constituted her sole garments. All the other females working in the establishment were dressed in a similar fashion but in various colors and styles.

"Hello, gentlemen," she said with a glowing smile. "I am your waitress, Azoria. What's your pleasure today? Food? Drink? Private entertainment? Or would you like to hear of your options?"

"We will each have a tall glass of your Bacchus Special," Roman said cordially to the female who seemed barely a day over nineteen. "Trust me, you will love it," the broker added when I raised an eyebrow at his presumption in ordering for me. He then turned back to the waitress. "I am shortly meeting with clients for some business discussions in the Pagan Booth. My entertainment requirements were included with the reservation."

"Excellent," Azoria said, her long nails covered in an ivory polish flying over the interface of her small datapad while taking the orders.

"And for my friend here, I have scheduled him an appointment with Hope."

"Oh," she said, slightly taken aback. "For a dance or a massage?"

"For the Royal Treatment," Roman deadpanned.

This time, the Dantorian lost all semblance of stoicism. Mouth gaping, her head jerked towards me, and her horrified gaze roamed over my massive body. I was used to that reaction. Part of me wanted to laugh, but another, deeper part of me licked a wound I refused to acknowledge.

Regaining her composure, an embarrassed expression creeping up on her delicate features, she turned back to Roman.

"With *Hope*?" she insisted.

I frowned at the way she'd said the female's name as if it was a ludicrous idea.

"Yes, with Hope," Roman said, frowning as well.

"Right," Azoria said, clearly not convinced. "I will get your drinks and inform Hope."

She hastened away, her hips swaying sensuously with each of her steps, her legs made infinite by her crazy heels. How in the world females managed to walk, dance, and even run on such perilous footwear always baffled me. Yet, I couldn't deny how beautiful and sexy it made them look.

"What was that about?" I asked Roman.

"The confirmation I was right to get involved," he replied cryptically, his gaze still locked on the Dantorian.

"What the fuck is that supposed to mean?" I asked, getting annoyed.

"In due time my friend, I will tell you everything. For now, I just want you to enjoy yourself."

Azoria busied herself at one of the two bars where the barmaid had already begun preparing our drinks. Then, the holographic curtains hiding a corridor between the left stage and the main stage parted to reveal a tall, tan-skinned female, with silver-blond hair, a nearly non-existent black babydoll split down the middle that exposed her flat belly, and a sheer thong that hinted at the plump lips of her bare pussy.

Shock, fury, then confusion coursed through me in quick succession at the sight of the breathtaking human. I blinked, taking a second look to make sure my eyes weren't tricking me. The female looked around the room, her gaze searching before landing on us. Her eyes slightly widened, and she licked her lips in what I could only interpret as nervousness before approaching us in a sensual strut that had my blood immediately rushing to my groin.

"Is something wrong?" Roman asked, a slight worry in his tone.

"Is that your Hope?" I asked, my gaze still locked on the female continuing her approach.

"Yes," Roman said cautiously. "Is she not to your liking?"

I turned to look at him, a severe expression on my face. "Do you know Marla?" I asked, ignoring his question.

He slightly recoiled, the genuine confusion on his face appeasing the anger that had been rising within me.

"Marla?" he repeated. "I'm afraid not."

"She's the human mother of my firstborn," I replied.

Understanding dawned on him as he cast a worried look towards Hope before looking back at me, his shoulders stiffening with a tension I couldn't quite understand.

"Hope looks like her?"

"They could be sisters," I retorted.

"I can assure you they are not," Roman said forcefully. "Whatever transpired between you and your son's mother, it has nothing to do with Hope. She's a good woman. Don't punish her for the sins of another. Give her a chance."

A chance for what?

Something greater than him gifting me a pleasant fuck with a stunning woman was at play here. But Hope reaching our table kept us from discussing the matter further.

"Hello, Hope," Roman said warmly. "You're breathtaking, as always."

The words immediately made my back stiffen as I suddenly wondered if she'd serviced him before. But the look he cast onto her struck me more as fraternal than as that of a former lover. Although it crossed my mind, I dismissed the notion. For a reason I couldn't explain, I felt certain Roman would never pass off a woman he'd bedded before to me.

"You're too kind, Roman. It is good to see you well and in such *impressive* company," she answered, her eyes demurely cast down in contradiction to the insanely revealing outfit she wore.

Despite her undeniable resemblance with Marla, seen up close, they were clearly not the same person, and unlikely of the same bloodline. Hope's features were softer, her heart-shaped lips fuller, her doe eyes slightly more almond-shaped and wider. Her long eyelashes cast a slight shadow over the mesmerizing deep green of her eyes. Contrasting with Marla who dyed her hair in the sun kissed, golden blond color that had first caught my attention, Hope's silver-blond hair appeared to be natural, including her eyebrows. Although taller and sturdier than Anton's mother had been, the delicate curves of her body made my mouth water. Her perky breasts were smaller, but real, instead of the generous implants Marla had given herself.

"My friend is indeed impressive," Roman said in a teasing voice. "Hope meet Krygor. Krygor, this is the lovely Hope."

"Greetings, Hope," I said, my voice involuntarily taking on a purring tone. Her golden skin erupting in goosebumps gave me the sudden urge to lick every single one of them, one by one. "Roman tells me you want to play with giants."

"I would like to play with *one* giant," she said, boldly taking one step closer to me. Despite the assertiveness with which she spoke, everything about her screamed submissive. And that made the dominant in me even hungrier. "The question is: does that giant want to play with *me*?"

"Who *wouldn't* want to play with you?" I countered, letting my gaze slowly roam over her.

She is far more beautiful than Marla had been.

I immediately chastised myself for the thought, although I did believe it. Roman had been right in his last comment about not punishing her for the sins of another.

Or myself, for that matter.

I could spend a delectable time with this stunning female or let the memory of a bitch who happened to vaguely look like her ruin the moment. But right now, my cock was dying to further make the acquaintance of the delicate beauty.

Hope smiled timidly, the glimmer of relief in her eyes upon hearing my approval of her didn't go unnoticed. She *wanted* me to like her. That both aroused the fuck out of me while also setting off my alarm bells. Unless she was a social climber, what could a breathtaking woman like her possibly want with a beast like me?

Turning sideways, I extended an open palm for her to come around the table to me. Obedient, she complied, stopping directly in front of me between my parted legs. From the corner of my eye, I saw Azoria returning with our drinks. Her curious eyes flicked between Hope and me as I slipped my hands between the parted panels of her black baby-doll to hold her narrow waist. I vaguely heard Roman thank the Dantorian, but my mind was focused on the beauty before me. Hope bit her bottom lip as my thumbs caressed the sides of her flat stomach.

"Tell me, Hope, why do *you* want to play with that *one* giant?" I insisted.

She took a moment to look at me, her green eyes lingering on the bulging muscles of my arms and chest before examining my features. Unlike most other females, she didn't recoil at the sight of my brutish features typical of Braxians. Instead, a certain amount of genuine awe settled on her gorgeous face. Hope raised her hand as if to touch my biceps but caught herself, casting a sheepish look towards me for almost doing so without having first received my consent. I wished she hadn't stopped. And yet, her timid and respectful restraint only turned me on further.

"Because I want to touch the embodiment of true power, of nearly supernatural strength," she said in a breathy voice. "I want to feel it around me... Inside me," she added in a whisper, her face heating. "I want to unleash the passion of hands capable of snapping me like a twig, but that will instead gently bend me to their will. And I want to feel that power come alive beneath my touch, my caresses, and my lips. I want to see the fearsome giant melt for me."

Baring my teeth at her, my palms slipped down the soft, rounded curves on her bare bum and drew her closely against me, her pelvis pressing against my crotch. Hope's lips parted, and she softly gasped, feeling my hard cock through the thin fabric of my pants.

"*Inside* you, little *Vaya*?" I asked, my lips a hair's breadth from hers. "You think you can handle the giant?"

Of all the reactions I had expected from the apparently timid female, her leaning forward and sucking on my bottom lip before giving it a gentle nip had definitely not featured on the list. With a boldness I'd never thought her capable of, Hope slipped her hand between us and gently rubbed my cock over my pants, her eyes darkening. Her lips traced a path along my cheeks up to my ear before nipping my earlobe.

"I *can* and *want* to handle *all* of this giant," Hope whispered in my ear. "I can do for you what only Braxian females can. Better still, I can make you feel things no other female in the entire Eastern Quadrant can."

"That is quite the boast, little *Vaya*," I growled, one hand tightening over one of her butt cheeks, while the other caressed a path up the silky skin of her back beneath her babydoll.

"I do not boast," she said smugly, straightening to stare me in the eye. "Facts are facts."

"Then I shall put it to the test," I said, my voice dipping even deeper with the fire the little minx had ignited in my loins, and my crotch throbbing beneath her touch.

Hope shivered almost imperceptibly. Seeing the little nubs of her nipples hardening through the sheer fabric of her nothing dress, and the maddening scent of her blossoming arousal wafting to me almost had me insane with lust.

"As you wi—"

"Hope! What are you doing?" a tall human male in his late fifties, early sixties, exclaimed in a loud voice just shy of shouting, interrupting her.

I glared at the intruder who was scowling at my female with barely repressed seething rage and something akin to betrayal. Jealousy and bloodthirst surged within me at the dominant and possessive way he stared at her. Hope stiffened, yanking away her hand rubbing my crotch, while the other, slightly trembling, tightening its grip on my waist. The delectable scent of her arousal soured with a sliver of fear. My protective instinct immediately flared, and I snarled at the slightly balding brown-haired male, plain looking but stylishly dressed in an expensive charcoal shirt and black pants.

"As you can see, she's tending to me," I said in a threatening tone.

Hope slightly leaned into me, as if seeking my protection. I drew her even closer to me, daring the male to challenge my claim. I didn't know what rights he had over her, nor did I care. The silver-haired beauty had set my blood on fire, and I would gladly face off against any who would dare attempt to deny me my prize.

The male's head jerked towards me, his eyes widening as he took in my appearance, recognition flashing in his dark blue eyes.

"M... Mr. Aldriss!" the man exclaimed. "Such an honor to have you visiting my humble business. If I had known the big boss' sire was dropping by, I would have ensured you received a proper greeting. My name is Luther, Luther Stromland, the owner of Bacchus."

Realizing the weasel was her boss, not a potential mate—or wannabe mate—dimmed some of my anger... barely. He closed the short distance to our table, his hand extended towards me. I glanced at it, back up at him, then turned to my woman who gaped at me, wide eyed.

"Mr. *Aldriss*?" she repeated in a whisper laced with awe and disbelief.

"Krygor to you," I replied in a gentle voice, my fingers caressing the naked skin of her back in a soothing motion.

Hope licked her lips nervously before giving me a timid smile that made me ache to kiss her. That she hadn't known my identity when she'd been so bold in her attempts at seduction tremendously pleased me. Even merely as Anton's father, people sought to ingratiate themselves to me either to curry favors with my son or to increase their status with him. That it hadn't been the case with her only made me want her more.

"Hope, I will need you on Stage A right after Latena's performance. Then you will have a series of massages to perform," Luther said in a clipped tone after dropping his hand. "Mr. Aldriss, I will have my finest girls come see to your needs and satisfy your wildest fantasies," he added in a syrupy voice that made my fist itch with the urge to punch his throat and crush that annoyingly prominent Adam's apple bulging on his unusually long neck.

"Hello, Luther," Roman intervened in a slightly stern voice before I could give the wretched human a piece of my mind. "I have personally secured Hope's services for a Royal Treatment as a gift to Mr. Aldriss who is both my friend and one of my best clients. Her time is already reserved and paid for in full."

"A Royal Treatment?" Luther sputtered, a horrified look on his face. Once again, he stared at Hope with murder and betrayal in his eyes. "That is out of the question. She's not suitable for such services to Mr. Aldriss. I will refund you and send—"

"What you will do is stop testing my patience," I snarled. "I care not what other females you deem more suitable. If they are so great, send them to your other clients who will thank you for it. I have the female I want, right where I want her. Unless you would rather go perform on that stage?" I asked, turning to Hope.

She firmly shook her head, the intense look in her eyes all but pleading for me not to let her go. The furtive glance Hope cast towards Luther only seemed to increase the fear steadily rising within her.

"But—"

"Mr. Stromland," Roman interrupted before Hope's boss could spew more nonsense that would have made me lose the last shreds of my already frayed patience, "what seems to be the problem? Are you preventing one of your Indentured Servants from providing your more lucrative services to impede her ability to repay her debt?"

"What?! That's preposterous!" Luther exclaimed, his pale skin turning crimson in either outrage or shame at being caught, although I suspected it was a mix of both.

"I would certainly hope not," Roman said in a hard voice. "Although, your insistence on denying her a visibly mutually consensual deal in favor of lesser services raises questions."

"I was merely trying to ensure Mr. Aldriss experiences the best that my house has to offer," Luther snapped back defiantly. "And how do you know she's an Indentured Servant? I certainly do not advertise it anywhere," he asked Roman before casting an accusatory look towards Hope.

"Her collar did," I said rising to my feet, while still holding her tightly against me.

Luther had the good grace to look embarrassed for yet another display of his stupidity. Nevertheless, my gaze flicked towards the sturdy but rather plain collar around Hope's neck. This mark of Luther's ownership on her further fueled my anger.

"Now if you are done meddling in our affairs, Hope and I have places to be." I turned to Roman, ignoring Luther babbling some lame apologies. "I will see you later, my friend."

"Enjoy yourself," Roman said with a naughty smile.

"I intend to," I replied with a predatory smile.

But even as I turned back to my female, I didn't miss the encouraging look Roman gave her. I wasn't half as brilliant as my son, but it didn't take a genius to realize Roman's gift had been motivated by far more than giving me a fun 'roll in the hay' as he loved to put it. That particular human saying made no sense, but then that species as a whole gave me headaches.

Since I'd joined Ravik's Council, learning to interpret people's true desires and motivations had become almost second nature to me; an essential skill to help defend him against those who sought to usurp his throne. I was getting a pretty good idea what Hope, my little *Vaya*, truly wanted. If she proved herself to be half as delectable as she'd let me glimpse earlier and, above all, if her boast proved true, I'd be a fool not to reap the sinful benefits of making her wish come true.

One arm possessively wrapped around her waist, hers around mine, I let Hope guide me through the holographic curtains to the hidden corridor where the elevators to the private suites were located. The smell of her fear receded, taking on the spicier aroma of excitement and anticipation. But it was the scent of her arousal I wanted filling my nose again along with the sound of her raspy voice whispering my name.

As soon as she finished selecting our floor on the lift's interface, I towered over her, invading her personal space, a famished look on my face. She swallowed hard, stepping back until the cabin's wall prevented any further retreat. Pressing my palms against the wall on each side of her head—caging her—I leaned forward, my gaze locked with hers. Hope's breath caught in her throat, yet it wasn't fear that burned in her eyes as they flicked between mine.

"I'm going to do very naughty things to you, Hope," I whispered in an almost threatening voice before claiming, at last, what I'd wanted since she'd sucked on my lower lip.

She immediately responded in kind when my mouth pressed against hers, and her lips willingly parted under my tongue's imperious demand for entry. It invaded her mouth as a conqueror, demanding complete submission. Once more, she complied, her hands timidly caressing my abs. The damn female was intoxicating, perfect in every way. I wanted to drown in the divine nectar from her lips but, too soon, the chime from the lift announced we had reached our destination.

Breaking the kiss, I took a step back, freeing her. Hope bit her bottom lip while giving me a nervous smile, and then, tucking a lock of her silver hair behind her ear, she circled around me to leave the elevator. My female walked ahead to one of the luxury suites on the penthouse level. Her hips swayed with each step. The sensuous curves of her body and the plump globes of her round behind taunted me through the sheer fabric of her dress.

Like a hungry predator, I followed in her wake.

CHAPTER 2
HOPE

Krygor was terrifying: a massive beast of a giant with a fearsome face that should have me cowering in fear. While he undoubtedly intimidated me, he also made my toes curl with excitement. Having grown up on Guldar, I'd naturally developed a taste for big, brawny males as our men tended to be. But this Braxian took it to a whole new level. He could break me with a flick of his hand, and yet, I'd never felt so safe with a male. That Roman had chosen him for me undoubtedly played a role in easing my worries. However, it was the gentle way Krygor handled me that mainly silenced my fears.

When he'd first laid eyes upon me, his shocked, almost angry expression had been both confusing and frightening in that he might not want me. I still couldn't understand what had triggered it. Did I remind him of someone? Either way, I wouldn't stir that potential krillik's nest. Right now, Krygor fiercely lusted after me, and I would fan that flame in the hope he'd keep me.

As much as I had loved him flexing his insane muscles before Luther, my wretched boss would find ways to make me pay for that humiliation, even though he'd brought it upon himself. But even without Krygor talking back to him, Luther would want to punish me for letting another man have what he considered his.

When I first started working for him, Luther had not allowed me to have sex with any of the customers, even though that was the only sure way for me to repay my debt to him in a timely fashion. As I didn't actually want to have random strangers rutting over me, that had suited me just fine. He'd justified this rule by stating that my 'unusual' pussy would give away my identity and risk me getting dragged back to Guldar. But then he'd made sure to cash in as often as possible on the clause allowing him to bed me at no cost to him.

It didn't take long for me to realize that Luther was using me as his exclusive sex toy and considered it cheating or a betrayal for me to even entertain laying with another man. Under different circumstances, his shock at finding out Roman had bought me for a Royal Treatment would have been comical. My master hadn't wanted another male's cock anywhere near me, and yet today, I was going to ride the mother of them all.

I opened the door to the private suite and held it for my 'client' to come in. My inner walls involuntarily contracted as I watched his massive frame walk in, remembering the humongous, rock hard length of his cock as I'd rubbed him over his pants. A part of me wanted to run for the hills at the thought of taking that tree trunk inside of me. And yet, to my dying shame, a part of me tingled with anticipation. Despite my body's natural disposition to stretch and adapt, it would certainly hurt a bit, but then, it would be glorious... I hoped. My gut told me Krygor would be a passionate and generous lover.

And I had a boastful claim to prove.

His gaze roamed over the large room which possessed a gigantic bed, large enough to comfortably accommodate three huge Braxians like him. A massage table—which could convert into a spanking or bondage bench—occupied the right corner of the room. Next to it, hidden doors opened onto shelves and racks holding a variety of sex toys and light BDSM paraphernalia. Bacchus, thankfully, didn't cater to the more hardcore kinks that some more specialized venues did. An imposing hot tub sat on the opposite side of the room, surrounded by holographic walls that could simulate any environment we wished to be in.

"Bacchus Program Hope Giant," I said out loud, as Krygor's gaze turned back to me.

The pale-colored room took on darker shades with a dominance of earth colors, dark greys, black, and burgundy—the Braxians' favorite colors. I'd programmed it as soon as Roman had told me there was a high probability he would get me one of those giants. I'd been apprehensive as most of them had the reputation of being complete assholes to women. But with Krygor, clearly the Goddess had been watching over me. He gave me an approving smile, appearing even a little impressed—although, with his fearsome face, his smile looked like he was already relishing the taste of an enemy's bones as they crunched between his teeth.

His black t-shirt hugged every curve of his bulging muscles like a possessive lover, making my mouth water. I hadn't expected to be attracted to the male Roman would give me, and I wouldn't quite label what Krygor stirred within me that way. But the raw power emanating from him, the animal energy surrounding him, the hungry predatory look with which his dark eyes undressed me, and that godly body of his all did strange things to me. I wanted to caress every curve and crease of his massive muscles, as well as lick every single one of his bulging veins.

Marching up to him with my most seductive strut, I took his hand and rose to my tippy toes to nip at his lips again. His arm wrapped around my waist, and he possessively drew me against him, his chest vibrating with an approving purr. Krygor leaned down to claim my mouth with a dominant way that had my toes curling. I love the controlled way his free hand fisted my hair at my nape, tightly enough to give it a gentle sting and assert his dominance, but deliberately restrained not to cause pain. He tilted my head to the side, his commanding tongue invading my mouth. I gladly submitted, my tongue following his lead while savoring the sweet taste of some fruity wine lingering on his breath.

As his calloused hand began exploring my essentially naked body beneath that flimsy excuse of a dress, I moaned and surrendered myself to him. I loved—too much—the rough feel of his well-used hands and the raw maleness of it against my sensitive skin. But I couldn't let myself indulge in letting him take charge, despite aching to do just that. When he bent me backwards so that his lips could venture down my neck to my chest, I pulled away from him, pushing back against his chest seconds before his lips could close around my erect nipple.

Krygor slightly frowned, pulling back to look at me questioningly.

"You, sir, are far too intoxicating. You're making me lose my head faster than the finest Dantorian wine," I said, rubbing my palm over his broad chest. "You're almost making me forget that *I* am supposed to give *you* the Royal Treatment. But you are way too dressed for that."

Although somewhat displeased to have been interrupted, Krygor grunted a reluctant assent. That I lifted the hem of his skintight shirt with my teeth before slipping my palms underneath it seemed to further meet his approval. Goddess, that man's body was a work of art. As much as his tight clothes had given a glimpse of his carved muscles, seeing them bare as I lifted his shirt took my breath away. My mouth watered, and I couldn't resist licking the sharp creases between his abs. Krygor raised his arms to help me free him of his shirt. But when I stopped to swirl my tongue around his left nipple, he all but ripped his shirt off himself.

"Stop teasing me, female," Krygor growled menacingly.

Chuckling, I peered up at him, feeling no remorse whatsoever. "Sorry," I whispered with a complete lack of honesty.

Krygor grunted, not fooled in the least. It was odd how instantly comfortable I felt with this terrifying giant of a man. Crouching before him, I opened the magnetic clasps of his pants and lowered them while kissing and nipping at the tender flesh around his groin, deliberately avoiding his erect cock.

By the time Krygor had stepped out of his pants and kicked off his boots, he looked on the verge of either strangling me or tossing me on the bed and fucking me into next week. Taking his hand, I led him to the gigantic bed.

"Normally, I would take you to the massage table, but it was made for far less impressive specimens than you," I said teasingly.

"I have no need for massages," Krygor grumbled.

"Yes, you do," I counted. "You sound quite tense."

"Because a certain *Vaya* keeps teasing me," he retorted with false anger. "Keep this up, and I will not be held responsible for losing control."

Vaya... How incredibly flattering that I would remind him of that almost mythical creature. I'd never seen one in the flesh. Although real, some cultures considered them as the messenger of the Goddess. Seeing a *Vaya* was deemed to bring luck, happiness, and prosperity. The beautiful and graceful creature resembled a doe with a snow-white pelt and a long, silver-white mane. Delicate, ivory horns recurved over its head with the tips pointing back up.

Like my black horns used to before they were taken from me.

My throat tightened as it always did whenever thinking of my loss. But now wasn't the time to let such grim thoughts ruin the moment.

"Apologies," I repeated with the same mischievous tone, before pushing him onto the bed. He tried to pull me onto it with him, but I swiftly dodge and chuckled again at his frown. "Scoot to the middle," I ordered while reaching for the bottle of fruit flavored massage oil.

Krygor narrowed his eyes at me. "Someone is being bossy."

I didn't miss the underlying warning in his voice. "Someone is merely ensuring your maximum comfort before she finally gets to touch every inch of that godly body of yours," I deadpanned while climbing onto the bed next to him.

Normally, I should have started massaging his back, but I doubted he would have the patience. And in truth, I doubted I did either. Kneeling by his side, I poured some of the oil in my hand while my gaze roamed with awe over him.

"Enjoying the view, Hope?" Krygor asked teasingly.

And yet, I could have sworn hearing a slight, underlying nervous tension. Was he insecure?

"You are magnificent. The Goddess truly outdid herself when she shaped you," I said genuinely impressed.

His naked body was sheer perfection. Like all Braxians, his face would never be construed as handsome or attractive by any means. They had rough, brutish features, with strong brows that appeared stuck in a permanent scowl, a wide and prominent forehead, a powerful square jaw, and the typical broad and flat nose, reminiscent of that of a lion's. Smiling and gentle expressions only made him look even more terrifying. But that didn't trouble me or turn me off. On my home world, Guldar, handsome males abounded. However, as I'd learned the hard way, external beauty often hid the ugly monster dwelling within.

Leaning forward, I gently kissed his lips. My tongue mingled with his as I began to massage his neck. My fingers lingered on the broad curves of his shoulders, my mouth following in their wake. I took my sweet time, exploring each crease, bump, bulging muscle and vein of his wondrous body. The whole time, Krygor's rough hand caressed my back and the bare curves of my bum.

As I leaned away from him to rub the oil on his stomach and around his pelvic area, Krygor suddenly lifted my leg up, yanking me over him. My yelp of surprise turned into a strangled gasp when he sat me on his face and rubbed his nose against my core. Thankfully, the oil bottle had been closed or it would have spilled all over the bed. Seconds later, Krygor's fingers pushed aside the slim triangle of my thong before his tongue greedily tasted me. I cried out, my stomach contracting violently as he devoured me.

Wishing to reciprocate, I leaned forward to wrap my hands around the massive length of his cock. A slightly darker shade than his sun kissed skin, it felt like silk between my fingers as I gently stroked him. Since his girth would never fit inside my mouth, I licked his length, sucking on the head and grazing it with my teeth. I loved his clean scent and the salty-sweet taste of him on my tongue. His approving grunts and his hips moving in counterpoint of my movements spurred me on.

The pleasure building in the pit of my stomach as he lapped at my core and his calloused thumb rubbed my clit made it increasingly impossible for me to focus on my task. As soon as he sensed me beginning to crest, Krygor accelerated the movement of his thumb, his thick tongue dipping in and out of me. I fell apart with a startled cry, my body seizing violently. Krygor's hands tightened, his fingers digging into the fleshy part of my bum cheeks to hold me in place while he licked and sucked on my little nub. He only relented once I began to come down from my high.

As soon as he released me, I crawled off him. Krygor made as if to sit up, but I pushed him back down. Although still dizzy from my orgasm, I climbed on top of him, face to face, our sexes aligned. My man's predatory expression made my stomach flip flop.

"I want you," Krygor said in a voice so deep with desire it came out as a barely intelligible rumble.

"And so you shall have me," I whispered, rubbing myself against his length to slightly coat it with my essence.

"I must prepare you first," Krygor intervened when I slipped a hand between us.

"Hush," I whispered, interrupting him with a kiss. "I am *always* ready for you. The Goddess made me for you."

It was a bold assertion. And yet, it had been spontaneous and not a calculated hint-hint. Still, as I aligned his cock with my opening, its sheer thickness made me tense with apprehension. What if I actually wasn't able to take him?

I carefully lowered myself onto him. Worry, hopeful anticipation, and a naked hunger played on Krygor's face as slowly, inch by inch, the resistance of my inner walls gave way, stretching to accommodate him. It burned and hurt, despite how wet he'd gotten me. And yet, pleasure still dampened that discomfort as his thick cock rubbed against the sensitive walls of my sex. Unlike other species, Guldan females didn't have a single G-spot, but multiple in the form of rippling ridges covering our inner walls. Even now, halfway in, my ridges contracted around his shaft, greedily drawing it in farther.

Krygor's lips parted, and his eyes widened as they squeezed him from all sides, gently stroking him until he was fully sheathed. I gave him a triumphant smile and, my palms resting on his chest, I leaned forward provocatively.

"I told you I could make you feel things no other female in the entire Eastern Quadrant could," I whispered smugly.

Despite my bravado, relief flooded me now that the burning sensation was quickly fading as my body adjusted to his impossible girth. To further make my point, I ground over him before contracting my pelvic muscles, giving his cock an even stronger squeeze. Krygor hissed with pleasure and bared his teeth in a way that made my stomach do backflips and my nipples harden.

Grabbing my bum cheeks in an almost bruising hold, Krygor sat up, and I wrapped my arms around his neck. Slowly, carefully, he lifted me up then lowered me back down onto his cock, his lips a hair's breadth from mine.

"You did, little *Vaya*, and I'm going to savor every moment of it," he replied before kissing me again.

I moaned in his mouth, each stroke of his cock sending waves of electric pleasure from my core outwards. My fingers fisted in his long, black, wavy hair, I gave myself over to the burning feel of his naked skin rubbing against mine, his calloused hands holding me possessively as he moved me on his shaft, and the conquering way his mouth claimed mine.

"Ancestors!" Krygor whispered, breaking the kiss. "You feel so fucking good."

My heart soared at the awe in his voice made sultrier with pleasure. Turning us around, Krygor put me on my back, his arms slipping under my knees to open me wider. Looking down between us, he watched his cock pumping in and out of me, his face dissolved in an expression of pure pleasure and complete wonder.

"Your pussy was made for my cock," Krygor said with a possessiveness that gave me goosebumps. Leaning forward, he crushed my lips with a kiss while gradually picking up the pace. His mouth moving alongside my cheek to my left ear, he sucked on my earlobe before pressing his lips to my ear. "How much of me can you handle, Hope? How much of your giant's passion can you manage?"

Turning my head to face him, I tightened my hold around his lower back, my nails gently scraping his skin.

"Give me all of you, and take all of me, Krygor. I am yours to do with as you please. Your pleasure is my pleasure. My body was made for you."

A powerful expression I couldn't decipher crossed his brutish features. Instead of the bruising kiss I had expected, Krygor captured my lips with a deep, gentle, almost tender kiss that melted me from the inside out.

And then he unleashed his beast.

My Braxian lover began to move inside me faster, with deeper, more powerful strokes, each one sending sparks of ecstasy through me, until I came undone. My inner walls clamped down on him, and he shouted my name as his seed shot inside me. But that didn't stop him. Even as I writhed in bliss beneath him, Krygor continued to pound into me with near savagery and yet in a controlled fashion.

By the time he finally relented, my giant had released his passion inside me five times and wrested at least six or seven orgasms from me. Turning us around, he lay on his back with me atop him, and his cock still buried deep within my sheath. Heart pounding, skin slick with sweat, I rested my head on his broad chest, cocooned in the powerful embrace of his arms. My body still thrummed with the most intense pleasure I'd ever felt and with an illusion of safety that I eternally wanted to hang on to.

Tightening my arms around him, a single thought played in my mind: keep me.

CHAPTER 3
KRYGOR

Sitting in the hot tub, my female in my lap facing me, and the water bubbling around us, a million questions pulled my mind in every direction. I'd never felt such intense pleasure with any female, and I was already addicted. I'd taken her eight times in our short time together and still wanted more. Although Hope had been an enthusiastic participant, she had to be sore by now or was certainly getting there. Non-Braxian females usually tapped out after round one, assuming they even managed to get through the first one.

But not my Hope.

She was perfect, too perfect. Even the way she looked at me, with tenderness, marvel, and even lust filled the hole in my heart. How many times had I envied my son and Ravik for the way their women looked at them? How I'd hungered to have a female that would gaze upon me with the same genuinely happy and possessive smiles Mercy always cast on Ravik whenever he walked into the room she'd been in.

But it's not real. Hope wants something from you.

It felt so sincere, and yet, how could it be? She didn't know me. We'd met only a few hours ago, and it had been orchestrated by Roman. However, despite being first and foremost a broker, Roman was also my friend. He wouldn't try to screw me over for an easy deal, even if only out of principle. His reputation for honest dealings had been the reason I'd entered into business with him in the first place, which evolved into a deep friendship over the years. But I'd been weak before to a human female who had attracted me almost as strongly as my little *Vaya* did, right before she played me for a fool.

Except, she's not human.

In spite of her fully human appearance—although on the taller side for a seemingly human female—I only knew of one non-Braxian species capable of taking a Braxian without extensive preparation and loads of the muscle dilator and relaxant, Denax. And even then, I would have been clueless about their unusual—but oh so exquisite— ability to have sex with us if not for our Magnar Ravik marrying a Guldan.

So, what the fuck happened to her horns?

"You seem troubled," Hope asked in a soft voice while running the bath sponge over my chest.

"How sore are you?" I asked, ignoring her question.

She chuckled. A delightful blush crept up her cheeks, and her green eyes smoldered. Those instinctive reactions, which Hope had no control over, seemed to substantiate my impression that her responses and attraction to me were genuine. But I didn't trust myself anymore when it came to beautiful females, especially one that resembled Marla so much.

"Never too sore for you," she said, reaching for my cock to put it inside of her.

I wasn't going to fuck her again… yet. We had a few things to discuss. But not having the wondrous feel of her around me as we did so seemed like too much of a wasted opportunity. I was Braxian after all, and we lived in a constant state of arousal. Sure enough, as her warmth enclosed me, I barely held back a moan. Her inner walls natu- rally contracted over me in a gentle caress that felt as if they were undulating around my shaft.

"Do you have any idea how much you please me, Hope?" I asked, my palm holding her pressed against me and my other caressing her hair before settling on her cheek. "How much I enjoy my time with you?"

Her beautiful face melted into a tender smile, and she leaned into my touch. That did funny things to me and made my heart ache with longing at what I feared might be unrealistic expectations. But the sight of her damn collar at the edge of my vision dampened my amorous mood. I *hated* this mark of another male on my female.

"I hope at least half as much as I enjoy being with you," she whispered, her arms tightening possessively around me.

That, too, messed with my head—my fucked-up head.

Tracing her features with two fingers, I moved up the bridge of her straight nose, to the gentle arc of her right eyebrow, before rubbing my fingertips in a slow circle over the area where her left horn should have protruded from her forehead. Hope slightly stiffened, her glimmer of worry flashing through her eyes as mine bore into hers.

"What happened to them?" I asked.

Hope hesitated and, for a moment, the expression on her face clearly broadcast she contemplated lying or at least pretending she had no idea what I was referring to. I couldn't say if my gaze hardening or her own volition had prompted her into not doing so. It would have been a sore mistake on her part. With my trust issues with females, it would have undermined whatever future relationship she and I could have.

Hope swallowed hard then took in a deep breath. "Luther had them removed to help me flee Guldar," she said in a voice laced with worry. "Did Roman—"

"No. Your body told me," I interrupted. "Only one species has females like you," I added, thrusting once inside her to make my meaning clear.

I clenched my teeth at another jolt of pleasure as her walls once more contracted around me. It hadn't been such a brilliant idea after all to try and have a serious conversation with her sex so exquisitely massaging mine. But I'd be damned if I would pull out.

"What's the deal between you two?" I asked, trying to keep the tension out of my voice. "Why is he trying to con—"

A soft chiming sound resounded in the room, and the lights partially dimmed before returning to their normal setting, interrupting me. Hope's crestfallen almost panicked expression set my nerves on edge.

"What was that?" I asked.

"It went so fast," she whispered to herself, before giving me a smile with forced enthusiasm. "It's the twenty-minute warning that our time is almost up."

A possessive anger and jealous rage immediately flared within me. "Meaning what? You will go downstairs to pleasure another male?" I snapped.

Hope slightly recoiled, her lips parting in surprise at my reaction. But instead of the fear I normally would have expected, she seemed pleased by my jealous outburst.

"Once I go back downstairs, Luther will decide what I do next," she said in a soothing voice. "Probably dance on one of the stages or perform a massage."

"I don't want another male touching you, and I sure as fuck don't want you touching anyone but me," I snarled, my arms further tightening around her.

It wasn't a fair demand considering it was her livelihood—not to mention a contractual obligation—but this wasn't about logic or fairness. I was addicted to her, and I didn't share. But history had also taught me not to enter into commitments while thinking with my cock.

"I don't want another male touching me either," she replied softly, her eyes flicking between mine. She licked her lips nervously, her thumb absentmindedly caressing my chest. "But... There might be a way."

I braced, waiting for her to ask me to buy her contract. Chances are, she owed a huge amount which would imply a very long contract. Was I ready to splurge so much on her just because she'd given me the best fuck of my life? Because she made me feel things I longed for but should probably steer clear of to protect myself? Because a part of me wanted her to be what Marla should have been but hadn't?

"If you are here for a few days, you could request my time be reserved exclusively for you for the duration of your stay on Lilith Hive," she said cautiously. "With the Escort Service, the female you choose remains by your side around the clock, unless you require some time alone. You can do and go wherever you want with her, as long as she remains on the space station. So... if you were to retain me as your Escort, I would be yours and only yours for whatever duration you set to the contract."

My heart skipped a beat hearing those words. This would fit my purpose perfectly. With Roman's business proposals, I would remain on Lilith Hive for an entire week; seven days during which I could assess if my apparent infatuation with the silver-haired beauty warranted buying her contract. I caressed her bottom lip with my thumb. Parting them, Hope licked the length of my thumb before sucking it into her mouth. My cock jerked in response, and she deliberately tightened her pelvic muscles to enhance the already divine feel of her around me. This time, I didn't hold back my purr of pleasure.

"So, you would be exclusively mine, twenty-four-seven for the next few days?" I asked, my voice barely more than a whisper as I watched her gently suck on my thumb.

Her hesitation immediately made me tense again. After giving my thumb a gentle nip, she released it and licked her lips in a nervous gesture I was growing familiar with.

"Well, technically, it would be more like twenty-*two*-seven," she corrected.

"Why only twenty-two?" I asked, narrowing my eyes at her.

"Because we must be granted two hours a day for whatever personal matters we wish to attend," she said. Worried by my frown, Hope quickly clarified things further. "Some of us have families. We can't be gone for entire days without making sure they're okay."

My face closed off, and it took every ounce of my willpower not to push her away from me, feeling utterly betrayed.

"You have a family?" I asked, my voice dangerously low.

"Just a daughter," she said, her voice almost pleading. "I'm not mated, and I don't have any partner. Just my baby girl. She's eleven, and she's my world. Everything I do is for her, to make sure she has a better life than I did, and to protect her from those who would exploit her. I never go a single day without spending some time with her. Please, Krygor. Please! Only two hours. Or at least one… one hour. I will go see her when you are having your business meetings. You won't even notice my absence."

My anger immediately melted, my chest filling with a soothing warmth and an even greater attraction for the delicate female. I caressed her face, studying the perfection of her features while she stared at me expectantly, an almost desperate glimmer in her eyes.

"Two hours it is, then," I said in a gentle voice. "A good mother should always put her children first. I will never get in the way of you being a proper nurturer to your daughter."

"Really?" Hope asked in an almost choked voice, joyous tears gathering in her eyes. "You… you accept? You will take me as your Escort?"

"Yes, my little *Vaya*. For the next week, you are entirely mine," I said before starting to thrust in and out of her.

"Krygor," Hope whispered as if in a prayer.

I swallowed the taste of my name on her lips while giving in to the blissful sensation of my woman's body yielding to me. There would be time later for more questions, but for now, I wanted to hear her scream for me. And she did seconds before the ten-minute warning chime went off.

Luther was practically pacing in front of the elevators when the doors opened before us on the ground level.

"You're late," he said to Hope with barely repressed anger. "This is why you can't handle these kinds of services. You're supposed to protect the client from additional fees for being late."

Stepping out of the elevator, my arm tightly wrapped around Hope, I marched up to the insufferable man, towering over him with my most intimidating expression.

"Late fees are not an issue for me," I replied in the dangerously sweet voice my enemies knew to be a sign I was this close from bashing their heads in. "We would have been on time had I listened to Hope, but I was having far too much fun enjoying her."

My hand caressed Hope's bottom in a suggestive way that made no mystery of my meaning. Luther's attempt at maintaining a cool expression failed miserably. Whatever doubt I held that he somehow considered my female his personal property died in that instance. The thought of that weasel touching her had my blood boiling with murderous rage. The sentiment had likely shown on my face as Luther took a fearful step away from me.

"I see," he replied with a clipped tone, dusting invisible lint from his shirt. "Glad you enjoyed her services. But as you are an esteemed customer, we will not charge you the delay," Luther added with a syrupy tone, before turning hard eyes towards Hope. "You are needed on Stage C. You will alternate between the two side stages for the rest of the evening."

"I'm afraid that won't be possible," I said smugly just as Hope was opening her mouth to respond. "As I will remain on Lilith Hive for at least seven more days, I've decided to retain the Escort Services of the delectable little Hope for the duration of my stay, effective immediately."

Luther paled, his bewildered gaze going from Hope to me as he opened and closed his mouth, at a loss for words. "But... but... she has prior engagements!"

"Cancel them. As per standard rules, the current customer has precedence over any newcomer," I said dispassionately. "And longer-term contracts trump any lesser ones," I added, more grateful than ever for having familiarized myself over the years with basic contractual standards, not to mention the years helping Anton run his earlier strip clubs on Braxia before he made it to the big time. "Send the contract to Roman, who will take care of settling the details on my behalf."

"Mr. Aldriss—" Luther started in an argumentative tone before I cut him off.

"Mr. Stromland," I said in a threatening tone. "This is the second time you are trying to cheat one of your Indentured Servants out of a lucrative contract. You are either harassing this woman or you are running a very shady business. Do you also treat your other women in such a fashion? I will make sure to have Anton investigate whether my concerns are founded."

Luther further paled, a glimmer of panic flashing through his blue eyes, and his oversized Adam's apple working overtime. "There is no reason for concern, Mr. Aldriss, I assure you. I might tend to be a little too stuck on my established protocols and role assignments. It's just that Hope's regulars will sorely miss her. Seven days is a *long* time to be away from home."

Hope stiffened against me, the nails of her hand resting on my waist digging slightly into my flesh. The way Luther had said the last sentence reeked of a veiled threat addressed to my woman. More than ever, I realized something greater was currently at play. Whatever the source or the outcome of the little game we were now engaged in, I'd already decided that Stromland would lose, and that he would never get Hope back.

"I'm sure you'll find ways to console them," I said dismissively before turning to my female. "Go change and get your things. We're leaving."

"Okay," she replied breathily, looking up at me with stars in her eyes, as if I was the greatest hero she had ever beheld.

My protective instinct flared, further reinforcing my resolve to free her of the wretch. I didn't consider myself a gratuitously malicious man, but I couldn't help hoping to find dirt on this Luther that would allow me to bring down a world of pain on his scrawny ass. In his presence, every single one of my 'bad news' alarms were going off. Unable to resist the urge to needle him, I gently fisted Hope's hair before giving her a deep and passionate kiss full of promise.

I released her, pleased by her flushed cheeks and darkened eyes. I caressed her bottom lip with my thumb then gestured with my head for her to go on. She smiled, cast a furtive glance towards her boss, and then hastened away.

Turning towards Luther, I held his gaze, mine taunting, daring him to talk back. He pinched his lips and averted his eyes. My smirk broadened as I walked away heading out of the corridor and into the main room of Bacchus. A quick glance at the booths showed Roman no longer occupied one of them, his business having no doubt already concluded. I scanned the room, hoping he was still lurking around. To my relief, I found him sitting at one of the two bars, sipping on a drink similar to the ones he had ordered for us upon our arrival but that I ended up never tasting, too eager to further make Hope's *acquaintance*.

I made a beeline for him, the barmaid's intimidated expression alerting him to my approach. Roman looked around me, no doubt searching for Hope, before examining my features, likely to assess my mental state. I jerked my head sideways, gesturing for him to come away from the bar so that we could speak at a safe distance from prying ears. He immediately complied, and we moved far from any nearby table or patron, but still in a central enough position that I could see Hope coming back out and that she, too, could easily see me.

"You brought me here to buy her contract," I said without preamble in a factual tone.

"Yes," Roman answered in a similar tone.

"What's the deal between Hope and Luther?" I asked, crossing my arms over my chest.

Roman hesitated, a speculative look in his inky eyes, the same color as mine. "Before I answer that, I do not see her. Did she not please you?"

I hated being answered by another question. However, I also knew Roman didn't discuss private information about his clients unless they were relevant to the ongoing deal. If I had decided to pass on her, he wouldn't tell me anything else without her express consent.

"She pleased me very much. Luther will contact you about settling an Escort Service between her and me for the duration of my stay on Lilith Hive," I said, scowling. "Now, my question."

The subtle tension in Roman's shoulders bled out, and he beamed at me, smile wrinkles creasing around his black eyes.

"I am glad to hear it. She's a good woman in an unfortunate situation," he said approvingly. "The chemistry between the two of you was also quite impressive."

"Roman," I said in a menacing tone.

He chuckled at my impatience before sobering. "As you've probably deduced yourself, Luther is a shady fuck. Normally, I would wait until the end of her Escort contract to fill you in on the details, but I believe he might be up to no good, and I don't want you getting blindsided."

My frown upon hearing those words only deepened. Roman gave me a quick rundown of the desperation that had led Hope to his door. By the time he finished his tale, my fingers were twitching with the need to go snap Luther's neck.

"What is the amount of her contract?" I asked just as Hope walked out of the hidden corridor on the opposite side of the room from whence we had gone up to the penthouse.

Wearing a simple short black dress and perched on impossibly high heels, Hope's face lit up when she saw me. She walked with her sensual gait towards us.

"Three million, including my fees," Roman said, also looking at her approaching us.

A pittance compared to the sixteen million Anton had paid for Grace. A tiny scratch to my current wealth, but an insane fortune for the leader of a struggling clan that I had been only a few years ago.

And she was worth every single credit of it.

What I wouldn't have given for Anton's mother to be as devoted to our child as Hope was to hers. For that alone, whatever the future held, I would make sure Hope and her daughter would be safe and cared for.

She walked up to me, and I drew her to my side, passing a possessive arm around her waist. Hope leaned against me, a happy but timid smile on her face. It was endearing considering what we'd been doing for the past three hours.

"I hear you'll be taking care of my friend for the next few days," Roman said gently to Hope.

She nodded shyly, an emotion I could only interpret as gratitude shining on her face as she looked at the broker.

"I'm happy for you," Roman said with a sincerity that moved even me. "He's a good man. Grumpy, especially in the morning, but a good sort nonetheless."

Hope chuckled and looked up at me affectionately. "I can handle grumpy."

"I will show you grumpy," I mumbled teasingly at Roman. "See you tomorrow."

"Have fun," Roman replied, nodding at me before winking at Hope.

She smiled at the broker then we left, my arm around her shoulders and hers around my waist. The heavy stares of the other patrons and of the women working there amused me. I could only imagine how horrified they must be, thinking I'd split poor Hope in half if I bedded her as they all thought her to be human, as I had.

"Let's go to your house so that you can take whatever you need for your stay with me," I said, hailing a hovercar.

They were the only vehicles allowed for public transport on the streets inside the station. However, an underground network provided free public shuttles that allowed patrons to quickly reach the various sections of the massive station.

"Thank you," Hope said. "That's quite thoughtful of you."

While undoubtedly grateful to get some bare necessities and a fresh change of clothes, I was ready to bet that being able to see her daughter first mostly fueled that joy. After we settled in the back of the vehicle —a little too cramped for my liking—Hope gave the driver the directions to her place before turning her luminous eyes towards me. I leaned forward to kiss her, and she melted against me.

The wretched female was turning me into putty in her hands.

"We need to make arrangements for your daughter," I said softly after breaking the kiss.

"I've already contacted my friend Tamika," Hope said. "She will come spend the night at the house with Siona after her work shift."

Hope spoke the words with the same fake enthusiasm she'd used earlier when our time had run out. The current arrangement didn't suit her at all, but she made do with what she had. After closing the privacy window between the driver and us, I turned back to Hope.

"And during the day?" I insisted.

"She'll be in school, and then she'll go straight home and lock herself in until Tamika arrives," she said. "It's what we already do until either Tamika or I can get home to her."

Yes, but Luther made that barely veiled threat tonight.

I grunted my assent before looking out at the changing landscape of the station as we left the VIP section to enter the Commons. The contrast between the two areas was so sharp it made my head spin. Where the VIP section was elegant, with muted colors and discreet signs, everything about the Commons screamed at you, from the psychedelic mishmash of colors, bright and oversized animated signs, and criers outside the establishments calling to the passersby, trying to lure them inside. Where relatively strict dress codes were imposed on the walkways in the VIP section—meaning no S&M attire or naughty bits hanging out—in the Commons, it was pretty much a free for all in the adult entertainment areas. Other neighborhoods that focused on more general arts—such as music concerts, dance, theater, and art galleries—enforced the stricter dress code.

Although Hope resided in the more muted area of the Commons, I still didn't feel comfortable with her living here at all. After telling the driver to wait, I exited the hovercab then walked up to her place; the ground floor apartment of a three-apartment building. Hope unlocked the front door using a bioscan lock then, to my utter shock, she opened it to reveal a second reinforced door with five additional locks on a timer which needed to be unlocked in a randomized sequence each time.

What in the Ancestors' name is this madness?

She gave me a sheepish look over her shoulder as she finished unlocking the second door before stepping inside and inviting me in. Despite the sparse furniture limited to the bare basic required to function, the humble interior was clean and welcoming. I scanned the room, noticing the drawn shades on every window and the utter silence within the house.

After checking that both doors were properly closed, she quickly checked what I assumed to be the two bedrooms and the hygiene room before coming back to the main room that served as both kitchen and family room. Hope cast a nervous look towards me, chewing her bottom lip as if she was trying to make a decision about something important. She gave me a shaky smile before crouching behind the slightly worn leather couch.

"Siona, you can come out. It's Mama," she said loudly at the floor.

My jaw dropped as, seconds later, a group of wooden slats on the floor slid open, revealing a small hidden room, high enough for a child to stand in. It appeared wide enough to contain a small bed and a narrow desk with a bit more room left to walk around. Despite the anger burning like acid in my gut, I kept a neutral expression on my face as a breathtaking, smaller version of my woman climbed out of the chamber. My throat tightened at the expression of pure love on her face as she gazed at her mother. They embraced, Hope pressing a tender kiss between the delicate black horns on her daughter's forehead.

They parted and, as Siona opened her mouth to speak to her mother, her head suddenly jerked towards me, having finally noticed my presence. She recoiled, her jaw dropping in shock, and her eyes widening with fear.

"It's okay, sweetheart," Hope said quickly, caressing her daughter's hair in a soothing gesture. "This is Mama's friend Krygor. He will take me away from Bacchus for a week so that I don't have to deal with Luther."

Siona's head jerked back towards her mother, staring at her in disbelief before looking back at me. Despite her youth and obvious innocence, Siona was no fool. She understood what kind of 'friend' I was to her mother, and with my fearsome face, the poor child had to be traumatized. In spite of that, she forced herself to school her expression.

"Hello, sir," Siona politely said with a slightly trembling voice.

"Hello, Siona," I said with my gentlest voice. "Please call me Krygor." I carefully approached them, and she fearfully pressed herself against her mother. Remaining at a non-threatening distance, I crouched so that I would no longer tower over her. "Do not fear me, little one. I would never hurt a female, least of all Hope's daughter. You remind me of my best friend's son, Garruk, although the boy calls me Uncle Krygor."

Siona slightly recoiled before scrunching her face, slightly offended. I suppressed the smile wanting to stretch my lips.

"I remind you of a boy?" Siona asked.

"Not in your features," I conceded gently. "Anyone can see you are a beautiful little girl. But he has the same silver-blond hair as you and your mother do as well as similar black horns."

"You know other Guldans?" she asked, curiosity taking over her fear.

"Actually, he's a hybrid. The young prince of my home world, Braxia. His mother is half-Guldan and half-Veredian."

"Wow, a prince..." Siona said wistfully.

"Half-Guldan?" Hope exclaimed, looking flabbergasted. "I thought the new Dagna was just Veredian? That's what they said on Guldar about Magnar Ravik's queen."

"Disinformation," I said smugly. "Your Emperor would hate to admit that his plans to enslave my people were thwarted in large part with the help of a Guldan female."

Hope snorted at the thought.

"Is this where you stay after school while waiting for your mother or Tamika to come home?" I gently asked Siona.

The atmosphere slightly tensed again, and she cast a questioning look at her mother.

"Yes," Hope answered in a slightly defensive tone. "It is well ventilated, and she has food and—"

"I do not question that you have accounted for her comfort," I interrupted with a gently chiding tone. Hope's face heated, and she gave me a sheepish look. I caressed her hair in a soothing gesture which earned me a strange assessing look from Siona. "The hovercab is waiting," I reminded her in a gentle voice. "Go pack what you need, and for her as well. Siona can sleep in the guest room in my suite at the hotel. I do not want you stressed and worrying about her welfare."

Hope gaped at me with disbelief, then her emerald eyes misted.

"Oh, Krygor," she breathed out before throwing herself into my arms. "Thank you! Thank you!" she said, pressing her cheek to my chest while holding me tightly.

I chuckled and gently embraced her before kissing the top of her head. Siona stared at her mother and then at me, her reservations towards me giving way to something akin to hope.

"Thank you, si… I mean, thank you, Krygor," Siona said timidly.

"My pleasure, Siona. Now, go on, both of you," I said, gesturing with my head at the bedroom. "Bring the essentials for the next couple of days. We can come get more later."

The two females nodded. Siona retrieved her school bag from the hidden room and resealed it seamlessly. Taking her by the hand, Hope led her daughter to the smaller bedroom first to help her pack. I picked up my com and called the hotel to have them prepare the room for a younger girl in her early teens and set up a proper desk for Siona to do her homework. I then called Yulan and Zartag to confirm our extended stay on Lilith Hive.

But even as I discussed with my men, my eyes remained locked on the now hidden chamber Siona had been holed up in. Such excessive security spoke of a far more complex situation than I had anticipated.

CHAPTER 4
HOPE

The next couple of days were nothing short of a real-life fairy tale. Krygor's penthouse suite at the hotel was three times the size of my entire apartment, and even more luxurious than the mansion of my former fiancé Valdek on Guldar. The staff treated my daughter and me like royalty. We only ate the finest foods instead of the cheapest, basic meals that I could normally afford after sinking most of my meager revenue on defenses around the house for my baby.

Even now, my throat tightened, and my heart filled with gratitude for Krygor letting me bring Siona with us. It had been a gamble which I'd feared might backfire. What if seeing the lengths I needed to go to in order to protect my child had scared him off and made him call off the whole deal? But, as I had suspected, Krygor didn't have a fearful bone in his body. The gentle and protective way he'd interacted with my daughter only further made me melt for the sweet giant.

I shuddered thinking back on all the ways Luther would have made my life a living nightmare had Krygor not kept me as his Escort for the week. But time was slipping away too quickly. I only had today and the next four days to make him want to buy my Indentured Servant contract. We hadn't brought up the subject, and I hadn't had the opportunity to speak with Roman to know if Krygor had discussed it with him. Many a time over the past forty-eight hours, I'd been tempted to just lay it all out in the open before systematically wimping out. I didn't want to come on too strong.

Krygor had often been staring at me pensively, as if attempting to solve an enigma. He had questions, but I couldn't figure out if he was hoping I'd volunteer the answers to them or if he was biding his time for the appropriate moment to ask them. Considering the last two days had been filled with multiple business meetings for him, that he'd prefer spending a quiet, relaxed evening with me—and fucking me senseless—hadn't been surprising.

Today, however, he had a much lighter schedule. We were having lunch at a five-star restaurant after which he would take me to visit the Braxian shop that had recently opened on Lilith Hive as part of his Braxian Councilor duties. Krygor never ceased to blow my mind. Finding out he was the big boss' sire had taken my breath away. I had no idea Roman had planned on matching me with such a powerful male. Then learning that he was not only close friends with his king— well, Magnar as they called that rank on Braxia—but also sat on the Royal Council left me speechless. No wonder he had such a commanding presence.

And he seemed to genuinely like me.

That made me feel all fuzzy inside. Granted, his attraction for me was first and foremost physical. The Braxians' reputation for being in an almost constant state of arousal was legendary. Considering Krygor's voracious sexual appetite, I could confirm its veracity. I didn't mind though: no man had ever made me come so hard, so many times or made me feel so respected and cherished. My giant was wild and savage in his lovemaking. But even when he pounded into me with apparent reckless abandon, I never felt afraid. Krygor always remained in control, always handled me with care, never pushing his roughness beyond what would be safe or comfortable for me.

I was falling hard for my mountain of a man. I wanted to believe he was also falling for me, if only for the way he loved to have me snuggling against him while he watched the news or read a Council report or business proposal. Krygor seemed to simply enjoy my presence and the slightest display of tenderness or affection. The Goddess knew I had plenty of that to give to a good man like him.

The pitter-patter of Siona's steps snapped me out of my musing. Coming out of her room, she beamed at me, dressed in her navy blue school uniform comprised of a sleeveless, just above-the-knee-length simple dress, with short white socks bearing the same school insignia as the one prominently displayed on the left shoulder of the dress. She adjusted her schoolbag on her shoulder while submitting graciously to my inspection.

Even after four years, I continued to pay extra attention to the holographic mask—which was actually a set of rings attached to her horns to make them 'disappear'—to make sure it was properly installed and wouldn't slip or give away my baby's true genetics. As I refused to clip her pointy ears, we had to be ingenious with her hairdos.

By law, Guldan females were not allowed off our home world except to accompany our mate as part of a diplomatic mission abroad. But even then, we were supposed to remain under the constant supervision of a male relative or an appointed male guardian. If the Empire discovered our presence on Lilith Hive, they would do everything in their power to drag us back to Guldar. With Galactic Law now banning all non-consensual slavery—meaning slavery imposed instead of freely entered into via Indentured Servant contracts—my people couldn't force me back home against my will. But that wouldn't stop them from abducting me.

This meant that even should I manage to free myself of Luther, finding a safe place for my daughter and me to live would be another challenge in and of itself.

"You look perfect," I said, kissing the tip of Siona's nose.

She giggled and kissed my cheek. Taking her hand, I led her out of the luxurious suite, and we made our way to the underground public transport hub, which had a stop right outside Lilith Hive's Academy. This had been one of the greatest additions to the Hive Network. After marrying a human who gave him three children, Anton Aldriss had made a number of modifications to his Hives to better support the needs of families, with safe parks where drugs and lewd behavior were forbidden, free healthcare and education for minors, and free breakfast and lunch for students. Without these programs, we never could have made ends meet.

On Guldar, females weren't allowed to pursue a higher education. My daughter would receive everything that I had been denied.

"I like Krygor," Siona said almost wistfully as we rode the escalator back to the surface. "He's nice with you, and you've been smiling a lot lately."

My throat tightened, a sliver of shame washing over me that I'd allowed my baby to see some of the distress that had been choking me for the past few years. The Goddess knew I'd tried to shelter her, but Siona had always been too perceptive. For her own sake, I'd also been forced to warn her of some of the threats lurking around her so she'd beware of overly friendly strangers.

"He's a very good man," I said with a smile which was hopefully not too stiff. "I like him a lot, too."

"And I like staying with him at the hotel," she added, making a face. "Having my own hygiene room and not having to worry about how much hot water I use is amazing."

I burst out laughing, despite the little pain in my heart. Siona loved water and swimming. Our bathtub at home was tiny while the ones in each of the rooms of the suite were massive. The humongous pool on the roof of the hotel would have become Siona's domain if not for her horns.

"I hope he wants us to stay with him for a long time," my daughter said, sobering.

All traces of amusement faded from my face. I stopped walking and cupped Siona's face in my hands.

"Krygor is going back to his home world in a few days," I said gently.

"I know," Siona said, her face taking on a mulish expression. "But we could go with him, if you wanted. I see the way he looks at you like you're the Goddess herself. He likes you! Maybe if you tell him…"

"Hush, child. Hush," I said pressing two fingers to my daughter's lips, distraught by the pleading tone her voice had taken at the end.

"We cannot force someone to want us. I like him very much, and I want to believe he likes me, too. But it has to be his decision if he keeps us or not. Just continue to be your adorable self. No one can resist you," I added, tapping the tip of her nose with my index finger to lighten the mood. "There are still a few more days to go. The Goddess has been good to us by putting him in our path. Keep faith. She will not abandon us."

Siona frowned and pressed her lips together to hold back the arguments that clearly wanted to come out.

"Okay, Mama," she finally said, obediently.

I wanted to hug her and gently rock her in my arms while saying that everything would be all right, but we were in too public a place for me to risk touching her in a way that might cause her hologram to flicker.

"Come on, love. You don't want to be late," I said, taking her hand again.

As I turned around to resume walking the short distance to the Academy, my blood turned to ice at the sight of Luther's lanky frame standing a short distance from the school's gates. Swallowing hard, I kept my head straight, deliberately pretending not to see him as I escorted my daughter the rest of the way. To my relief, Siona didn't notice his presence. She was terrified of him. In the early days of my contract with him, Luther used to come claim his 'side benefits' in the first small apartment I used to share with my daughter. Despite locking Siona in her room so she wouldn't see, Luther had made no effort to be quiet. His grunts, shouts, and the vulgar language he loved to use while rutting over me had severely traumatized her. It had taken some time, but I'd eventually convinced him to hold such encounters at Bacchus to protect my child's innocence.

I waited until Siona had entered the establishment before turning back. Luther hadn't moved from his position, his hard stare locked on me. He turned around without a word and started walking away at a slow pace. Words were unnecessary for me to follow in his wake. My mind raced as to what he would say beyond berating me for 'betraying' him with another man. Surely, he wouldn't dare bring up my daughter again.

We walked past the Academy into a narrow alley where deliveries were performed in the wee hours of the morning while the station was still asleep. Luther circled around the docking platform to hide us from view of any passerby. That further increased my unease. However, as he'd never raised a hand to me, I didn't fear physical abuse. That didn't mean he wouldn't seek to humiliate me by demanding a blow job or to fuck me against the wall.

Not today, you wretched vermin.

"You whoring little slut," Luther hissed, as soon as I turned the corner. "You think yourself smart getting your cunt ruined by that beast? Is *that* what you needed to get off? To be fucked by an animal? You should have told me sooner. I could have arranged that. There are plenty of customers asking for a beautiful piece of ass that's into bestiality."

"If you're done with this disgusting nonsense, please tell me what you want. Krygor expects me soon," I said in a clipped tone, refusing to let him get a rise out of me.

"Krygor expects me soon," he mimicked mockingly. "You think some sweet pussy will make him fall for you? You think he's going to buy your contract?" Luther shook his head, giving me a contemptuous once over. "You were always stupid, but even this is a new height of stupidity from you. Don't you realize who he is? Younger, fresher, far more beautiful females than you throw themselves at him on a daily basis. So what you can take his monster cock? The novelty of your cunt will wear off, and he'll send you right back to your master—to me. Do you think one of the right hands of a king and sire of the owner of the Hive Network would take my leavings as his mate? A whore not good enough to fully service regular customers?"

Every one of his words cut like a knife, echoing each of my fears. But hearing them spoken out loud by another gave them even more weight. Although not as vulgarly put, Roman had also stated I was too old for most buyers. Never mind that I still had twenty-five years of fertility left before me, or that I still had at least eighty to one hundred years still left to live, and that I wouldn't show any real signs of aging for another thirty years. I hadn't told Krygor that Luther regularly used me as a fuck toy. Not only was I too ashamed, but I'd specifically feared he'd be repulsed at the thought of lying with a woman Luther had already thoroughly used. Tears of humiliation pricked my eyes, but I refused to shed them.

"I'm not going to stay here and be your punching bag," I said, proud of my controlled voice. "I am sorry you are displeased by my efforts to repay my debt to you. I may have been stupid entering into that contract without thoroughly reading the clauses, but I'm learning from the best. Good day to you, Luther."

"Not so fast," said a sensual male voice behind me as I began to turn around.

I yelped, nearly jumping out of my skin at the sight of the breath-taking male. The Goddess only knew when he'd managed to sneak up on me. Tall, lithe, with well-defined muscles, his dusty blue skin, silky long black hair, and small horns shaped like a crown gave him away as a Sarenian.

"We just got here, you can't leave already," the Sarenian said in a purring voice that was strangely melodic.

A spicy scent wafted to me, enticing, intoxicating. It took me a second to figure out it wasn't cologne but his pheromones. My blood ran cold as I realized he intended to use his mind control abilities on me. I tried to avert my eyes and flee, but I reacted too late.

"Stay and be silent," the Sarenian commanded, his voice taking on a strange vibration. His midnight blue eyes flashed with a light glow, and I immediately went numb.

Sarenians were a predatory species. While their females were entirely submissive and subservient, the males were true hunters who could release pheromones that enticed their victim. Furthermore, they were able to ensnare and mesmerize their prey with a direct stare and the vibration of their voices. But the worst part was that, while the victim kept control of their thoughts, the Sarenian had full control of their bodies.

"Go to the wall," the Sarenian ordered.

The tears of fear trickled down my face instead of the ones of humiliation I'd held back earlier as I helplessly watched my body comply with his command. My tongue had turned to lead, preventing me from screaming for help.

"You Sarenians are quite efficient. I should hire you to keep misbehaving sluts in line," Luther mumbled, staring at me with malicious glee. "Maybe I should fuck your ass once Faolen is done with you. I know how much you love that," he added with cruelty.

"You will not touch her," Faolen said with a cold voice. "Remember that the Braxian's nose is as sensitive as it is ugly. Even if she showers, he'll scent you on her if you fuck her."

I could have wept with relief upon hearing those words. But that didn't alleviate my fear about what Luther could have possibly meant by his 'once Faolen is done with you' comment.

"As for retaining our services, you couldn't afford us," the Sarenian continued with an obvious contempt that left me confused. "You can barely keep your establishment above water despite the large revenues it generates. You're pathetic. Just be grateful I'm here to clean up your mess. If my client doesn't get the virgin as promised, you will rue the day you failed to honor a contract with a Sarenian."

I stared disbelieving at Luther. Him promising my daughter as a means to repay debts quickly eclipsed the shock of him possibly being in financial difficulties when Bacchus was raking in millions every week. Luther glared at Faolen, his face red with humiliation and anger. The offense cut him all the deeper for being called out in front of me. I opened my mouth to argue with the Sarenian that Siona wasn't his to sell, but no sound came out.

"Do not waste your energy, my Beauty," Faolen said in a soothing voice, cupping my face between his hands.

I grabbed his wrists to tear them away from me.

"Stop. Remain still," the Sarenian ordered with that vibrating tone again.

My arms immediately went limp, falling to my sides. I remained helpless, trapped inside my body while tears continued to blur my vision.

"Hush, Beauty," Faolen said in a gentle voice although he didn't use his power this time. "We will treat you so much better than that idiot who currently owns you."

"What do you mean?" Luther intervened. "Hope isn't part of the deal. You only get the kid. Your Prince pops her cherry, and then you send her back. I have many very wealthy clients impatient to fuck a Guldan female… Especially one that young and that beautiful."

A murderous rage rippled through me, further fueled by my current paralysis. All these years, he'd been biding his time to repay his debt to the Sarenian crown before he could pass my baby around to a bunch of sick perverts…

Over my dead fucking body.

I had no problem going to jail for murder if that meant keeping my baby safe. As the Goddess was my witness, I would kill that son of Gharah.

Faolen slowly turned his head sideways to look at Luther with a predatory look that made me shudder. "You are trying my patience, human," the Sarenian articulated slowly in a low, menacing voice. "The girl will remain on Sarenia for the Hunts of our pre-adult males. She will be well-loved, well cared for, and showered with gifts in exchange for her favors. As for Hope," he continued turning back to look at me, "I look forward to hunting you." He caressed my lips with two fingers before pressing them to his own lips. "I am taking her as repayment for the interests you have accrued and cost to myself for fixing your mess."

"You can't do this!" Luther exclaimed, panic seeping into his voice. "They're—"

"That's enough out of you," Faolen hissed with that vibrating voice, his eyes glowing as he stared at Luther. "You will not speak or complain about this anymore. Hope and Siona are mine. Now leave us and return to your work at Bacchus."

It terrified me watching Luther compelled in this way, forced to comply as helplessly as I was. My gaze followed him until he left my line of sight. I looked back at the Sarenian who was observing me with a gentle, almost tender expression on his gorgeous face.

"Do not cry, my Beauty," he said. "All will be well. You may not think so right now, but once on Sarenia, you will see how much better your life will be. However greedy we may be with our females, we also treat them well and make sure they are sated, happy, and fulfilled. Too bad the Hunt is still a week away. You are ripe. I intend to be the first to capture you and sire an offspring on you. But there will be time to discuss your future later. For now, we've got some business to take care of."

Mind reeling, I couldn't seem to process what was happening until I saw him raise a tool with a sharp point towards my neck. My eyes widened with fear, but I couldn't scream, fight, or pull away, trapped by the compulsion that forced me to remain still.

"Relax, Hope," Faolen said gently. "I will not harm you. I will *never* harm you. I merely need to do some tweaks to your collar."

True to his word, Faolen didn't hurt me but fiddled with my collar for a couple of minutes. I couldn't see what he had done. It felt like he'd swapped a piece or modified the lock at the front which was hidden behind a large decorative gem.

"There. See? No harm," Faolen said, leaning forward to brush his lips against mine. "I cannot wait to have you, little Beauty. In the meantime, I have a task for you to make sure our reunion will go off without a hitch."

Taking on his vibrating voice, Faolen gave me a series of commands that horrified me, especially knowing I wouldn't be able to resist them.

"I'm going to leave you now, my delectable Hope," Faolen said with a seductive smile. "In a few seconds, your collar will chime. When it does, you will forget everything that happened here. You will forget seeing Luther or me, and you will go back about your business as originally planned this morning. And the next time the chime goes off, you will perform the task I have given you then forget all about it once it is completed. Nod if you understand."

Against my will, my head nodded.

"Good girl. Now stop crying and wipe your tears."

Once more, I complied, looking at him with murder in my eyes. But that only made him chuckle.

"I love your feisty spirit, Hope. Courting you will be so much fun. See you soon, my love."

With these last words, the Sarenian walked away. Seconds after he cleared my line of sight, the discreet, but high-pitched sound of a bell resonated from my collar, and my mind immediately went blank.

I blinked, my eyes stinging as if I'd cried or gotten sand into them. I rubbed them, my eyelids feeling oddly humid, and then my surroundings penetrated my foggy mind.

What in the world am I doing in this alley?

Panicked, I looked down at myself for any sign I'd been mugged, robbed, or violated. But nothing felt or looked off aside from the confusion swirling in my head. Shrugging with a sense of unease, I walked out of the alley and headed back to my apartment to pick up a few more things.

CHAPTER 5
KRYGOR

Leaning back against the surprisingly comfortable hotel desk chair—considering very little commercial furniture was scaled to Braxians—I gazed at my son's face through the vidscreen. By Braxian standards, Anton was too pretty and scrawny, even though humans didn't see it that way. As a hybrid, he was certainly much smaller than we purebloods. And yet, my firstborn was my pride and joy. To this day, he craved my approval, but expressing feelings didn't come naturally to my people, least of all me. If he only knew the depth of the love in my heart for him.

"Naya says she misses her Grappa Krygor," Anton said with a teasing smile. "When are you coming back?"

"I'll be on Lilith Hive for a few more days," I replied noncommittally. "Assuming Ravik doesn't order me back to Braxia in a hurry, I'll make a little detour to see your spoiled brat," I added affectionately.

"I'll hold you to it," Anton replied. "Your business on Lilith Hive went well?"

"It did," I said enigmatically. "However, I'm curious about a certain Luther Stromland. What can you tell me about him?"

Anton narrowed his eyes at me. "He runs Bacchus, a highly successful fancy strip club and massage parlor. But I'm not fond of the man. I've been receiving an increasing number of reports about him being involved in shady deals because he's grown highly indebted."

"How can he be indebted with the outrageous prices he charges and when the place is constantly packed?" I asked, taken aback.

"Gambling. He's become addicted to betting on the gladiator battles," Anton answered before tilting his head to the side. "So, you've been to Bacchus. Enjoyed yourself?"

"I did," I replied, slightly annoyed by my son's almost otherworldly ability to read people to which he largely owed his phenomenal success.

"For all his faults, Luther has an uncanny talent for recruiting beautiful females," Anton said.

"And then exploit them," I snarled.

"Meaning?" Anton asked with a frown.

"Maybe I shouldn't generalize as I do not know the situation of the other girls. But he certainly trapped one of the females into a never-ending Indentured Servant contract," I said.

"Who is she?" Anton asked, his voice taking that subtle hard edge that said someone would soon be in trouble.

"Hope Morak," I said, the muscles in my back knotting while my son typed her name into his system.

His eyes widened, and his lips parted in shock as her face no doubt came up on his monitor. Turning back to look at me with a tense expression, Anton studied my features as if they would give him the answer he sought.

"They are not related," I said in a neutral voice.

Anton blinked, heat creeping on his face. My firstborn always took great pride in hiding his emotions. His mother's departure and indifference had also left him with a gaping wound that I was helpless to mend. Hatred surged once more within me for the cold, heartless female who could have been—*should* have been—the one source of comfort our son could have received in the harsh years of his youth on Braxia. I could only thank the Ancestors Anton never knew what horrors she had said about him upon his birth.

Taking a deep breath, I gave him an overview of what had transpired, including Hope's Escort contract to me. Anton listened stoically, asking the occasional question along the way.

"You are fond of her," Anton said matter-of-factly.

"I am," I conceded.

"And her child?"

"She's a good kid. Polite, demure, eager to please, smart, and adores her mother," I replied.

"Why don't you bind them to you?" Anton asked. "Hope is beautiful, submissive, is compatible with a Braxian, clearly has strong maternal instincts, and bears you some affection. What more could you want?"

I snorted at the irony of him throwing back at me the same question I had asked him years ago when Grace had been his Indentured Servant.

"I am seriously considering buying her contract," I said noncommittally, although that decision had in fact already been made.

"If you don't, I will," Anton said in a tone that brooked no argument.

I stiffened and narrowed my eyes at him.

"Relax, Father. I have no designs on her. Grace is the only woman I will ever want," Anton said in the harshest tone I'd ever heard from him. "But no loving mother should struggle and suffer this much just to be able to protect her child."

The underlying hurt at his own mother's contempt resounded loud and clear. Once more, my heart ached for my son. Realizing he was losing his composure, Anton stretched his neck and rolled his broad shoulders, before clasping his hands on the desk before him.

"I will take care of Luther," he said in a business-like voice.

"No," I countered. "Luther is mine."

The shadow of an almost evil smile stretched Anton's lips before he bowed his head in concession.

"Very well. What do you need from me?" my son asked.

"Whatever details you can dig up on his side dealings would be of great interest to me," I answered.

"I'll get William right on it. And Father, remember that my Hives are also *your* Hives. If Luther or anyone else gives you lip or attitude, you have the full power to evict them or shut down their business, contract or not. The penalty for kicking them out is nothing to me."

"Thank you, my son," I answered, my chest filling with affection for this miracle of a boy that had blessed my bloodline.

"I'm afraid I must go. Business never stops," Anton said with an apologetic expression. "I've always wanted a baby sister," Anton continued with a taunting look in his eyes. "I will set up an activity for you and your females in the next couple of days. Enjoy."

I glared at him, which made him chuckle, but didn't argue his comment.

"And, Father, do not let my mother ruin your chances of a happy future like Braxia almost did to me. You are a good man."

Silence hung for a few seconds between us. I snorted again and gave him a smile.

"Goodbye, Anton," I said in a falsely severe tone, when in truth I'd wanted to say: 'I love you, son.'

Anton smiled back, which I hoped meant he'd understood my true meaning.

"Goodbye, Father."

After a pleasant meal with my woman in one of Lilith Hive's overly fancy restaurants, I headed to the Gladiator Arena on the station, Hope's arm possessively hooked around mine. That pleased me... a lot. I loved the way she always publicly claimed me without even seeming to be aware of it.

My little *Vaya* liked touching me, as if to reassure herself of my presence. Unlike my daughter-in-law Grace—who was an exhibitionist and loved attention—Hope didn't flaunt us being together or revel in other people's envy. In fact, she was disturbingly oblivious of her surroundings and anything that wasn't me. While that certainly stroked my ego and catered to my possessive nature, it also concerned me. Once I brought her to Braxia—and there was no question I would—my female would need to develop a greater sense of environmental aware-ness. For all its beauty, Braxia was a harsh world, with everything always eagerly trying to kill you.

"We will only be here for an hour or two," I said to Hope as the large doors of the fighters' entrance parted for us. "This is one of seven arenas operated by Elder Pattel's clan—one on each of my son's seven Hive pleasure barges. Pattel sits with me on Ravik's close Council. He's a good man, still a formidable fighter and hunter for his older age. He had my respect before, as both a clan leader and loyal defender of our Magnar, but he has earned my eternal friendship by protecting my son when Gerwyn, the firstborn of one of our formerly rival clans, tried to kill Anton."

Hope's lips parted in shock, her green eyes widening. "What happened to Gerwyn? Did he flee?"

"He faced the Magnar's justice, and I carried out the sentence," I said with a cruel smile that made my woman shudder.

Ancestors, how I had enjoyed it, too. Gerwyn had personified all the cruelty, narrow-mindedness, and suffering that had been inflicted on my firstborn for the mere sin of being a hybrid. And I had made Gerwyn pay, for both his sins and those of all who had abused, beaten, terrified, and vilified my son from the day he was born. I had a sadistic side that couldn't be denied. For the first time, I had made no effort to keep it in check.

"Pattel is rather displeased with his warriors' recent performances in the Gladiator tournaments," I explained, chasing away the thought of Gerwyn to avoid needlessly traumatizing my woman. "He has asked me to come have a look at their training to assess the source of the problem." I stopped to face her, cupping her face in my hands. "We are a brutal people, Hope. Braxians overflow with testosterone and aggres-sion that we vent by picking fights with each other, sparring in our training rooms, and hunting savage, wild beasts. Do not be alarmed if things get heated or if a brawl ensues. A few bruises, a little blood, and fractured bones won't kill us."

I groaned inwardly at the even greater shock on her face, wishing I could take back the last part that had utterly failed to reassure her.

"Come on, my *Vaya.* All will be well," I said, before gently kissing her lips.

The doors opened onto a long, arched corridor made of dark stone and duralium metals both mined from Braxia. A series of doors on each side gave access to the gladiators' locker rooms and waiting areas. Another corridor at the far end of the right wall gave access to the main building through which patrons entered, including a large reception, souvenir shop, ticket booth, a full bar which also offered light snacks, and a VIP lounge.

But we walked straight ahead to the metal barred door that currently stood open. Hope's eyes flicked this way and that, taking in our surroundings with awe.

"I've never attended a gladiator battle," Hope confessed sheepishly. "Back home, it was deemed inappropriate for a female."

"On Braxia, our females greatly enjoy watching us fight, especially when we beat each other bloody," I said with a taunting glimmer in my eyes. "They say it makes up for all the times they wished they could knock some sense into us."

Hope's flabbergasted expression melted away as she burst out laughing. "Right, I see their point," she said teasingly.

We stepped into the oval arena covered in packed dirt—just like back home—surrounded by bleachers. A few VIP boxes occupied the lower levels of the seating areas for those who liked a close up view of the action, and a few more were located much higher for those who preferred to get a broader view of all that was happening in the large space. Strategically placed giant screens ensured every patron could get a good view of the battle regardless of their position. Above us, a soundproof dome simulated the shimmering silver sky of my home world: the dark planet Braxia.

Hope's wonder quickly turned to worry when she noticed half a dozen Braxians engaged in a rather heated discussion near the center of the arena. I frowned, seeing so few of them present at this time of the day, little equipment out, not a lick of sweat on any of them, and no reddened skin from a few well-placed blows.

"You can go up here to take a seat," I said, opening the hidden door granting access to the bleachers. "The door to the VIP box is unlocked. The seats are more comfortable and there is a mini-bar with cold beverages and snacks if you want."

"Okay," she said with a soft voice.

I cupped her neck with my hands and lifted her chin with my thumbs, trying to ignore the hated feel of Luther's collar beneath my palms. Leaning forward, I captured her lips in a gentle kiss, a tender emotion burning in my chest for the delicate female.

"Go," I said, reluctantly releasing her.

Hope gave me a timid smile then gracefully climbed the few steps up to the fifth row where the lower level VIP boxes were located. My gaze lingered on my woman's beautiful legs exposed by her thigh-length black and blue patterned dress and enhanced by shiny black stilettos. I loved Hope's sense of fashion; sexy but not slutty, revealing just enough to give you a glimpse of her perfection, but sufficiently demure to require your imagination to fill in the blanks and make you ache for more.

"Clan Leader Krygor!" Torog exclaimed, noticing me at last.

Tearing my eyes away from my female, I looked at Pattel's young cousin, firstborn son of his second brother Woltar. Of an age with Anton, Torog had just turned thirty-eight a week ago. But where my son was a true pioneer, constantly challenging himself and pushing the boundaries of success, Torog was content to merely meet expectations, keep the boat afloat, and not make waves. However, putting Torog in charge of the Lilith Hive Arena had been a last-ditch effort by Woltar to whip his son into being a bit more responsible and proactive.

Torog approached, followed by the five other Braxian warriors from various clans. Stopping a few feet in front of me, he slapped his chest with his fist in greeting, imitated seconds later by the others.

"You should have warned me of your imminent visit," Torog said cordially. "We would have welcomed you properly, as deserved by your rank."

His smile quickly faded at my failure to reciprocate the greeting and the stern expression on my face. He swallowed hard before casting an uncertain glance at his companions, who eyed him warily.

"Where are the others?" I asked without preamble.

Torog's broad, flat nose twitched in a nervous response, and he stretched his neck. "It is their day off."

"Their day off?" I repeated in a dangerously soft voice.

Torog shifted uncomfortably but had the courage to hold my gaze. "We cannot spar every day, or the men are too bruised for competition. They need at least one complete day to fully recover."

"Recovering from bruises doesn't mean sitting idle on your ass," I said in a clipped tone. "They could be building their strength weight-lifting, improving their technique through lectures and simulations, increasing their dexterity and flexibility through exercise and stretching, improving their battle focus through meditation, reflex response, and so on. Is any of that even in your program?"

"With all due respect, Clan Leader Krygor," said Hagmar, another of the warriors coming to Torog's rescue, who clearly seemed unable to find an appropriate response, "we have found these techniques to be of no particular benefit to us."

"Of no benefit?" I asked, advancing towards him threateningly. "You have been getting your butts handed to you at an embarrassingly high rate. If you were of my clan, you'd be doing the walk of shame through the compound, and then I'd put you through your paces to show you why, without those benefits, you are pathetic brawlers instead of warriors."

The younger males gasped, outraged expressions descending on their brutish faces.

"Clan Leader K—" Hagmar exclaimed, his face turning red with anger, and his muscles bulging as he fisted his hands.

"What?" I interrupted. "You're offended?" I asked marching up to him and getting in his face. "Your sire and your entire clan should be offended by *your* failure. You got spanked by a scrawny human. You know why? Technique. Go fetch your weapon, *pup,* and see if you can redeem part of your honor against an older man."

I'd put as much contempt as I could muster in the word while gesturing with my head for him to go ahead.

A sliver of worry—if not fear—crossed the young warrior's dark eyes. He cast an uncertain glance at his companions who suddenly all seemed highly interested in the packed dirt beneath our feet, or the detailing of the railings around the bleachers.

"You're still here? Are you too scared, then?" I taunted.

Hagmar growled, then menacingly bared his teeth at me before turning on his heels to go fetch two long staves. He extended one of the staves to me. I looked at the weapon with disdain then stared back at the fool.

"I said to fetch *your* weapon. I don't need one to beat your ass, *pup*," I said, tilting my head to the side.

Growling with rage, he threw away the second staff while the other warriors quickly backed away. Then, holding his weapon with both hands, Hagmar charged me. It would have been laughable if it hadn't been so sad and predictable.

Not allowing the taunts of your opponent to make you lose control constituted the most basic training provided to a young male. In the era of the Great Wars, Braxians were the most feared warriors in the galaxy. This new generation had nothing but weaklings, relying on their greater size and brute force alone to defeat their opponents. This worked in a brawl against most species. Against true tactical enemies, they would be obliterated. And if the prophecies about the Veredians held any truth, then we needed to get our young in shape for the even greater war to come.

Waiting until the last minute, I easily dodged his attack, then flowing with the movement, slammed my elbow in the back of his head. He tumbled forward, managing to stay up with some skill, testifying that he had a proper foundation that simply hadn't been polished due to ego and laziness. Hagmar turned around, waving his staff at me in a flurry. I avoided a few of the blows and blocked the others with my forearms while seeking an opening.

It came quickly enough.

Anticipating his reaction, I pretended to go for a strike. As soon as he defensively raised his staff before him, I grabbed it instead and twisted, forcing him to let go or get his wrists snapped. Shocked to find himself thus disarmed, Hagmar raised his forearms to block my attack, but I brutally struck both of his ankles in quick succession with the staff before spinning around him to smack him a solid one on the rear.

I did say I was going to beat his ass.

To add insult to injury, when Hagmar turned around to face me, his face crimson with outrage, I threw his staff back at him. He instinctively caught it, then gaped at me in confusion. I smirked and gestured with both hands at the younger warrior to come at me again. Infuriated, he charged me once more in the exact same fashion as the first time. Without missing a beat, I yanked the staff right out of his hands, moments from it making contact with my left shoulder. Spinning around again, I smashed the staff twice against his bottom, each blow resounding like a thunderclap.

The pup roared. Using his momentum as he turned around to face me, Hagmar threw a meaty punch that never made contact. The sole of my boot connected solidly with his sternum, sending him flying back. He landed on his ass with a loud thump, slightly winded. I tossed the staff at him, a bored expression on my face as he caught it. A mix of rage, hatred, and humiliation all played on his features.

"I suggest you stay down, *pup*," I said in an icy cold voice. "Unless you want to continue the lesson?"

A part of me was hoping he would. Should he be so foolish, Hagmar would have to sit out the next competition because this time I would not hold back. The crazy part of me that craved the blood and pain of my enemies had been awakened but not yet sated.

Thankfully—for all our sakes—Hagmar wisely chose to remain where he was. After giving him one last disdainful glance, I turned to Torog, who looked completely discomfited.

"You will put together a proper *daily* schedule for *all* the warriors and present it to me tomorrow. No more bullshit days off," I snarled. "You will not bring shame and dishonor to your clans and your Ancestors with your laziness. You were sent here to represent Braxia and earn glory for both yourselves and our people. Start acting accordingly. All entertainment venues on Lilith Hive are now barred to you until you prove to me that you have gotten your shit together. Is that clear?"

While Torog looked at me crestfallen, at least three of the others appeared eager to challenge me.

"You have a problem with it?" I asked making eye contact with each of the three. "Then come at me."

I spread my arms wide, daring them to take on the challenge. But for all their laziness, the young men weren't fools. My reputation for being crazy in combat preceded me. At even odds, I could count on one hand the number of Braxian warriors that I wasn't certain to defeat —number one being the Magnar. Ravik wasn't a man, he was a true beast from the purest of the Braxian bloodlines.

When the pups all averted their eyes, despite their anger seething within, I dropped my arms, took a couple of steps backward before turning around and walking away towards my woman.

My brow creased in a frown at the scared look on her face. My gaze never strayed from her as I circled around the protective barrier to the hidden door in order to climb the bleachers to the VIP box. Hope rose to her feet, eyes wide and hands clasped before her. I hated the scent of her fear and the slight trembling of her body.

"My *Vaya*," I said in a gentle voice, approaching her slowly, carefully as one would a terrified animal. "Why such fear in your eyes? It is me, your Krygor. Your giant."

"I-I know… I'm sorry," Hope said, clearly trying to rein in her fear. "It's… Your eyes…"

I cast them down and took in a deep breath to calm the heat in my blood. Battle always made me a little feral, which gave me the crazy eyes of a serial killer. I held out a hand, palm up. Despite her fear, Hope reached for it without hesitation. I gently closed my hand around her trembling fingers, touched deeper than words could express that she'd still choose to trust me.

"I am a Berserker, Hope," I said softly, carefully drawing her against me, before cupping her cheek with my free hand. "It is a rare Braxian trait passed down in warrior bloodlines. When I go into combat, I gradually build what we call battle rage. It makes me—and those I consider of my clan—stronger, faster, and more resistant to pain. I didn't go berserk right now, but the rush of battle can make me look a little crazy. But know this, I have never raised a hand to a female. Ever. We Braxians have many faults, but we know our strength and how devastating it could be to our females. As the Ancestors are my witness, whatever happens in the future, no matter how angry I could possibly get, one thing I can promise you, on my honor, on my life, is that you will never have to fear physical harm from me. Okay?"

Hope nodded, looking both relieved and embarrassed. "I'm sorry," she said giving me a sheepish smile. "I'm not usually this squeamish. But, wow, you're badass!"

I chuckled and puffed out my chest. "Youth always underestimates experience," I said with false modesty. "Come, my *Vaya*. Let's go home."

CHAPTER 6
HOPE

The four days spent so far with Krygor had been beyond magical. Although he'd 'bought' me as an Escort for a week, my giant treated me more like a committed love interest. We spent almost every waking hour together, especially now that he'd finalized the last bit of business on Lilith Hive, three days earlier than expected. While I loved his undivided attention, with him going so far as to accompany me when I went to pick up Siona from school, the threat of his imminent departure kept growing with each passing hour.

Krygor had still not said anything about my Indentured Servant contract with Luther. Yet, everything about the way he acted and his still very rabid hunger for me all indicated that he had no intention of letting me go anytime soon. So why the mystery? I was going insane with the urge to flat out ask him. At this point, I wasn't beyond begging and groveling. Except, now it was no longer just to protect my daughter—although that remained my number one priority.

My giant had gotten under my skin and into my very life's blood. I was falling hard for him. He was gentle, respectful, and attentive. Best of all, despite Lilith Hive crawling with gorgeous, much younger females of every species, many of whom were vying for the attention of Anton's sire, Krygor only seemed to have eyes for me. He showed absolutely no interest in other females and looked at me like I was the Goddess herself. The sex between us being off the chart was only icing on top. Despite the murderous frenzy in his eyes that had so frightened me at the arena, I'd never felt so safe in my life since meeting Krygor. I wanted this relationship to last forever.

Tomorrow, if he hadn't mentioned his intentions regarding my daughter and me, I would put on my big girl's pants and demand to know where things stood.

For now, however, Krygor had planned a 'family' outing with both Siona and me. This further reinforced my belief—or at least my wishful thinking—that he meant to keep us. I would be devastated if he didn't, not to mention what it would do to my baby. A part of me was wondering if the three of us going there was wise. Siona craved a father figure, and she'd hinted multiple times, without any subtlety, that Krygor perfectly matched the profile. If this outing gave me hope, it would build up her expectations even more.

As with every venue Krygor and I had visited over the past few days, the staff and owner of The Fields of Dreams greeted us like royalty. I didn't quite know how to handle so much fussing over my welfare, having been used to being ignored and treated like less than nothing most of my life. But I loved seeing my baby being treated like the fairy tale princess she'd always been to me. I'd been worried at first about coming to this theme park with Siona for fear it might mess with her holographic mask. But Krygor reassured me that our room would be entirely private. Siona wouldn't have to wear the mask during our stay here if she wished. It made sense considering that some patrons used their space for less than prim and proper activities, if not downright deviant.

The Fields of Dreams constituted of a series of holodecks of all sizes—small for private entertainment to humongous for group activities. They offered a plethora of preset scenarios, although a personalized one could be set up for a steep amount of credits. And ours had been custom made just for us by both Anton and Krygor. It left me speechless and further fueled my hope of a happily ever after for my daughter and me. A beautiful Avean in a skin-tight white dress escorted us to the second floor of the massive, converted warehouse.

"Here you are," the Avean said with a beaming smile, despite the slight wariness in her eyes every time she glanced at Krygor's imposing frame. I understood her fear and yet found it amusing knowing how gentle and cuddly he could be. "As per your request, a meal will be served in the private salon for you and your family. If your simulation lasts longer than expected, the artificial intelligence will inform us, and we'll adjust accordingly. The appropriate holodeck suits have been left for you in the private changing rooms, right inside the chamber. They also contain hygiene rooms should you need to use them. Before I leave, do your mate and daughter require some refreshments?"

My stomach flip-flopped at first hearing her refer to us as Krygor's family and then as his mate and daughter. I had no such designs; it was well known that Braxians rarely married, content to have concubines until they tired of them. But the thought of claiming my gentle giant as my mate and father to my child filled me with a brutal longing that left me reeling.

Krygor didn't rectify the Avean's erroneous assumption and merely cast an inquisitive glance towards Siona and me. I shook my head with a thank you smile.

"No thanks," Siona exclaimed, shaking her head vigorously. "I'm beyond ready to go in," she added, almost hopping on her feet with impatience and excitement.

Krygor snorted before smiling at the Avean. "My females have spoken. In we go."

His females...

A sweet shiver ran down my spine at the possessive way in which he had said it. My arm hooked in his tightened its hold, and I further leaned against him, looking wistfully at his rough features while he thanked the Avean before leading us inside.

We entered an antechamber with a large door ahead that led into the simulation, and a door on each of the side walls leading into the males' changing room on the left, and the females' on the right. I followed Siona into our changing room. Ignoring the six individual booths lining the back wall of the spacious room, she stood next to one of the two long cushioned benches that occupied the central area and stripped out of her clothes at record speed. Chuckling, I imitated my daughter—although at a much more reasonable pace. By the time I'd removed my dress and shoes, Siona had already donned the black sports shorts and cropped top made of a strange fabric with tiny nodes embedded within. She then spent the next minute pressuring me to make haste, which only made me laugh further.

It was so wonderful to see my baby this happy, excited, and care-free. Siona had been under too much stress and fear for such a young age. And we owed this all to Krygor, my gentle giant. He was already waiting for us when we exited our changing room. Clad with nothing but black sports shorts similar to ours, Krygor's mountains of muscles were fully exposed to my greedy eyes. My mouth watered, my nipples hardened, and my inner walls throbbed remembering how incredible he felt inside me, filling me to the brim, his hard body wrapped around me as he unleashed his passion.

Krygor's broad, flat nose flared. His eyes smoldered, and a knowing—if not smug—smile stretched his generous lips. My cheeks heated, but thankfully, Siona had already run ahead to the large doors leading to the simulation. Krygor caressed my lips with his knuckles before taking my hand. As we caught up to my daughter, my hand tightened around my giant's, once more moved by his affectionate ways, but especially by the respectful manner in which he always kept his behavior with me prim and proper in my daughter's presence. It wasn't uncommon for customers to treat us like meat, regardless of whose eyes were watching.

The doors parting made me forget all horniness and wistful thoughts of Krygor. The view before me took my breath away. A bright mid-day sun hung in a shimmering silver sky—similar to the golden one of Guldar. We were standing outside an imposing fortress made of dark stones. Its thick walls seemed able to withstand some serious attacks in a siege or raid situation. The tops of a few tall buildings made of dark and grey stones of varying shades, with a mix of ash-colored woods could be seen towering above the defensive walls. The fortress appeared big enough to contain a small city or a substantial village. Behind it, as far as the eye could see, endless fields of some strange plant I'd never seen before swayed in the light breeze.

But it was the sight before us that held my attention and had me torn between fear and fascination. Two terrifying and yet stunningly mesmerizing beasts stood in the large field ahead. Vaguely reminiscent of horses in their shape, the six-legged creatures had a long, scorpion tail and massive, sharp claws protruding from their hoofed feet. Thick scales covered their muscular bodies as well as their draconic heads. Dagger teeth filled their massive jaws and horns of various sizes rode from the middle of their snouts and up their foreheads. Fan-like appendages sat folded on each side of their faces.

It took me a moment to realize they were a pair male-female as the second beast approached the first one—her smaller stature becoming more obvious. Everything was scaled down on the female who was also more colorful with her dark green scales, than the male with his black and grey ones. Siona's hand slipped into my free one, awe and wariness plastered on her pretty face.

"This is the domain of Clan Aldriss, my compound on Braxia," Krygor said, gesturing proudly at the fortress and the broad expanse surrounding it. "My home," he added with a certain wistfulness that spoke volumes about his love for it. "Behind the compound, you can see my fields of neflium, which is the source of my personal wealth. I know it looks like weeds," he said teasingly at the confused expression on Siona's face, which somewhat echoed the one I felt inside. "And frankly, it is for most species, except the Berulians, a primitive people on the planet Sargaros for whom it is their main food source."

"You're a farmer?" Siona asked, her eyes all but popping from her head.

"Siona!" I said in a chastising tone in response to her stunned but disappointed one.

Thankfully, Krygor burst out laughing. "I am as shocked as you are, little one," he said gently. "I am first and foremost a warrior, as is my entire clan and bloodline. However, with the end of the Great Wars, there is no need for our combat skills. As Clan Leader, I must take care of my people and make sure they are safe, well-fed, and have a roof over their heads. So yes, I farm—or rather, I hire people to do it. These days, I consider myself as more of a businessman, which is why I came to Lilith Hive in the first place."

Krygor took my hand and then extended his free one towards my daughter. She took it without hesitation but stared at their joined hands with awe, her tiny one completely swallowed up by his massive one.

"And these are precious gifts from Magnar Ravik, our king and my friend," Krygor continued, gesturing at the beasts with his chin. "It is a karveli and his karvala. While both are vicious war mounts, they are also the most loyal friends one could have—if they accept you within their pack. The females, while also a serious threat on the battlefield, are mostly used nowadays for racing. Today, we will ride them to the next surprise I have in store for you."

"They look… fearsome," I said nervously.

"The real ones need to be swayed into accepting you," Krygor explained. "If they do, they will lay down their lives to protect you."

"And if they don't?" Siona asked.

"They'll just ignore you in the rudest fashion, and the females will do so with a lot of sass," Krygor replied teasingly. "But today, I've spared you the whole acceptance ritual. These karvelis will be on their best behavior."

As if to confirm his words, the beasts didn't balk or take any kind of threatening stance when we approached them, submitting willingly to our touch—which Krygor was quick to point out the highly intelligent creature would not tolerate in real life without prior consent.

"Karvelis do not accept being saddled or bridled," Krygor said, his dark eyes gleaming with mirth at my dismay. "You have to mount them bareback and hold on to the horns alongside their necks if you don't want to fall off."

Despite my height of 6'1, the back of the karveli reached my eyebrows. I would need a ladder to climb the beast. At least, the back of the karvala reached my shoulders, which was far more reasonable but still intimidating. Her narrower frame also meant I could sit astride her without doing a split. But the male was far too broad.

"Siona will ride with me," Krygor said, as if he'd read my mind. "You will ride the female. We'll go at a slow trot so there's nothing to worry about. I will not let you fall."

I swallowed hard, trying to act brave in front of my daughter—who was clapping her hands with excitement—and the man I was trying to seduce. Krygor lifted me like I weighed nothing to settle me on top of the karvala. I needed to scoot forward a bit to be able to hold onto the creature's horns more efficiently. To my surprise, despite the hard scales covering her, sitting on her back was quite comfortable.

Although she was dying of impatience, Siona watched Krygor mentor me through a short ride on top of the karvala, even encouraging me as I learned how to make her go, stop, turn, and even accelerate. Once confident enough that I wouldn't kill myself, he effortlessly threw Siona up in the air, making her squeal with delight, before catching her. She looked so tiny and fragile in his arms despite being an early teen. He settled her sideways on the mount before deftly climbing behind her. Siona tried a few different positions before settling for legs crossed beneath her and back pressed against Krygor's chest.

Leaning slightly forward, my giant held onto one of the much larger back horns of the karveli and set his mount moving. I followed alongside him, the virtual karvala making things very easy for me, although I suspected in the real world, it wouldn't be that simple. Still, as we traveled through the wide valley on our way to what appeared to be a large river in the distance, I marveled at this foreign world my giant called home.

Like its people, Braxia was a strange mix of harsh brutality and harmonious beauty. Jagged rocks protruded from the soft grass in odd places and angles, threatening the unwary with serious injury. Lush bushes with pretty flowers hid nasty thorns with a toxic coating that could cause severe rashes, fevers, and even death. Centenary trees spread their limbs towards the heavens, offering their dark blue leaves to the rays of the sun, while their roots rummaged through the soil seeking small prey to feast upon.

Krygor wasn't attempting to scare us, but I appreciated the matter-of-fact way in which he told us of some of the more deadly realities of his world. And my baby was lapping it all up. Halfway through the ride, Siona had shifted back to sitting sideways so that she could look up at Krygor while he told anecdotes about his world. The look of wonder and yearning in her eyes clawed at my heart.

Surely, he was showing us his world to see if we would like to stay there?

Too soon, the ride came to an end. I'd been too caught up in his descriptions of his world, including the retelling of an epic battle they'd fought when a pack of joarkals had raided nearby villages. According to him, they were giant, feline-looking creatures but instead of fur, they had some kind of stone scales on their backs and a tail reminiscent of a scorpion. Most weapons couldn't pierce their armor, their true weakness being their softer underbelly.

Everything to make a woman feel safe… After she ran for the hills.

But Krygor had another surprise in store for us. As we reached the shore, large, flat creatures slithered over the water, their silvery-blue color almost blending with it. With heavy splashes all around, they came to the shore and waited. They resembled manta rays with stone-like ridges on their backs and a long pair of vine-looking fins right behind their eyes. Their wings flapped slowly on the shallow water as they pivoted around until their long tail faced us.

"We're going into the water?" Siona asked, wide-eyed.

"Yes," Krygor replied.

She squealed with that crazy high-pitched sound teenagers and young children managed to pull off and clapped her hands in delight. Krygor burst out laughing while looking indulgently at my daughter.

"She thinks she's a siren," I said apologetically to Krygor. "She loves swimming."

Except, she no longer had the opportunity to do so since our departure from Guldar. Entering a pool would mess with her holographic mask, if not flat out damage it. Buying it in the first place had made a huge dent in our already meager funds. I wouldn't be able to afford another any time soon.

"Well then, you should get along perfectly with these creatures," Krygor said, winking at my daughter. "They are reavers," he explained as he dismounted his karveli before helping Siona down. "Have you ever seen surfers?" he asked while assisting me in turn.

"Yes! It's so exciting. Are we going to surf?" Siona exclaimed, jumping in place with excitement.

My stomach knotted with apprehension. I enjoyed swimming, but extreme sports had never featured on my to-do list.

Then again, neither had been riding a karvala.

The ride had indeed been very enjoyable once I'd gotten the hang of it. I could see myself doing this regularly, although I doubted the real creatures would be as docile. And yet, in spite of my apprehension, I was eager to give those reavers a try.

"It's amazing how much freedom your females have," I said out loud. "On Guldar, females would never be allowed these kinds of physical activities."

"They didn't use to," Krygor said teasingly. "Our Dagna changed everything. The poor Magnar is still struggling trying to rein her in. The Queen would have upended all of our more backward customs overnight—which is pretty much most of them. Change takes time, my *Vaya.* But Braxia, despite its dangers, is a much happier and safer place for a female than Guldar will ever be."

And there it was again. The intensity in his gaze, the seriousness of his voice, seemingly hinting at more, as if he was trying to sell me Braxia as a good place to live.

You do not have to convince me. Anywhere you go, I'll gladly follow, if you would have us.

"Normally, their handler summons them with a giant horn," Krygor explained as we approached the creatures. He spoke a word in Braxian that I didn't understand, and our outfits took on the appearance of a wetsuit. "Traditionally, we ride them to hunt large sea predators, or for spear fishing near the reefs. However, our Dagna cleverly realized they make exceptional racing mounts. Being a bit of a speed junky herself, she has made sure females are allowed to ride them. The races have been garnering growing galactic interest, which has further helped our economy, especially for the fishing clans that already have full stables of well-trained reavers. Come, I will show you first how to mount the reavers, and then I will help you each get on your own."

Krygor marched up to the largest of the three creatures wading in the shallow water. He stepped onto its back, just a couple of feet from its tail. Legs spread, feet firmly planted, my giant extended his arms forward, and the vine-like fins at the head of the three-meter long creature lifted and wrapped around his forearms. Krygor gripped them firmly, a mischievous smile playing on his lips as Siona clapped, hooting with excitement. The long tail of the reaver wrapping around his waist made me feel queasy. I didn't mind a bit of bondage as long as it was performed by a sentient being with a clear understanding of safe words. The reaver didn't qualify as such.

"*Fargleh*," Krygor said in Braxian.

The reaver flapped its pectoral fins again as it swam away over the water, quickly picking up speed. Slightly leaning this way and that, and pulling on the vine-like fins, Krygor steered the creature into a figure-eight before coming back to shore.

"That's so awesome!" Siona shouted running up to meet him.

The reaver spun around again before untangling Krygor. He extended a hand towards Siona who eagerly accepted it and allowed him to lead her to the smallest of the three reavers.

"Is it safe for her alone?" I asked, my stomach knotting with anxiety.

"Mama! I can do this. I'm not a baby!" Siona exclaimed, sounding betrayed before casting a worried glance at Krygor for fear he would side with me.

He caressed her hair reassuringly before turning towards me. "It is the safest activity she could perform on Braxia. First, this is a simulation. Should any harm come to any of us, it would immediately end," he said in a gentle tone. "Second, the reavers—both here and in the real world—will never let their passenger get hurt. Their dorsal fins and tail prevent us from falling into the water, even if we let go. Should she lose her footing and be unable to get back up, it will make her lie down onto its back and return her to shore. There is nothing to fear, my *Vaya.*"

My face heated, feeling silly for forgetting we were indeed in a simulation. But then, I'd never set foot in a holodeck for entertainment. They had always been scenarios focused on training me to be the perfect, submissive, and demure mate to a wealthy Guldan.

How low I'd sunk since those days.

Not fazed in the least by the tentacle-like fin of the reaver wrapping around her arms and its tail securing her midsection, my Siona listened religiously to Krygor's instructions before he finally set her free. To my relief, the creature started swimming away at a slow pace, giving my daughter a chance to adapt and learn how to ride it. She burst out laughing, her long, silver-white hair blowing in the wind and her black horns gleaming under the sun as the creature gradually accelerated.

Closing the distance between us, I rested my hands on Krygor's sides, and locked gazes with him.

"Thank you for this," I said in a soft voice filled with all the gratitude that burned bright in my chest. "I can't remember the last time she's been this happy and has had so much fun. You do not owe us any of this, but it means the world to me."

Krygor cupped my face with both hands, his thumbs caressing my cheeks. He examined my features as if I was the most precious treasure in the world, making my toes curl and fanning the flame that had lit in the pit of my stomach.

"Pleasing you pleases me, Hope. You have no idea just how much," Krygor said with an intensity that made me weak in the knees.

Leaning forward, he crushed my lips in a brief but passionate kiss before luring me towards my reaver. Back tensed, I took position and extended my arms, dreading the moment the dorsal fins would bind me. To my surprise, instead of the slimy, slithering sensation I'd expected, the fins were unusually soft, almost spongy as they wrapped around my forearms—although a little cold. The tail circled my waist, right below my navel, with a firm but not choking hold. Siona's joyous squeals in the distance also helped distract me from my discomfort.

"Race you," Krygor said teasingly before giving my bum a gentle caress and ordering my reaver to move.

My stomach lurched as the creature moved and, for a minute, I feared getting struck by a severe bout of motion sickness. It was both uncanny and unnerving to stand on such a wobbly surface. Yet, it quickly became clear that the reaver was paying close attention to me, adjusting its speed and position in a way to help me stabilize. In turn, I began focusing on its responses and the pattern of its movement as it swam over the water. I couldn't say how long the creature and I spent learning each other, but by the time my gaze met Krygor's a couple of meters away from me, we were a good distance from the shore, surfing at dizzying speed.

He gave me a provocative grin, pushed his reaver a little faster. Tapping my foot gently on the back of my creature, I prompted it to accelerate as well. But before we could go all out, my little hellion zipped passed us.

"CATCH ME, YOU SLOWBIES!" Siona shouted.

As one, Krygor and I gave chase.

"**K**rygor is going to keep us forever on Braxia," my daughter said with conviction as I tucked her in bed.

"Siona—" I said, in a warning tone.

"No, Mama," she interrupted with a mulish expression. "I'm not going to be reasonable. I know it. I can feel it in my bones. Why else would he show us his home and his world? Why would he take *me* along for a family outing? Even the hostess thought we were his family, and he didn't correct her. He's going to keep us. He *has* to," Siona repeated forcefully.

I couldn't say if it was more to convince me or herself. Either way, my heart broke for both of us. It also made it clear that the conversation with Krygor needed to happen sooner rather than later before more damage could be done.

"Siona, we already talked about it. Whether or not he keeps us will be the Goddess' will," I said sternly. "Enjoy the good times he is offering us and be grateful for these experiences we would never have had otherwise. Whatever comes afterwards, we will face together, you and me, like we always have in the past."

"I want him to be my Papa," Siona whispered. "I don't want to be scared anymore that bad men will hurt you or take me away."

Tears pricked my eyes. I sat at the edge of her bed and pulled my baby into my arms. I kissed her forehead and gently rocked her, whispering reassuring words. But how could I properly console her when the same fears gnawed at me incessantly?

Siona finally settled down, and I remained by her side until she fell asleep. With a heavy heart, I walked out of her room, carefully closing the door behind me so as not to awaken her. As I padded along the short corridor leading to the common area of the suite, Krygor's rumbling voice reached me. Muffled at first, I quickly realized he was talking on his com.

"…much better than expected. I even have some good news for the Magnar regarding new trade opportunities for Braxia. There's nothing left keeping me here. I want to be home yesterday. Have the ship refueled and fully stocked, ready for departure within forty-eight hours, sooner if possible," Krygor said in a commanding voice that hinted he was likely speaking to one of his two crewmates.

My heart seized in my chest, and my steps faltered.

"There's nothing left keeping me here."

The words felt like a bucket of acid had been poured over me. With a will of their own, my feet continued to carry me forward when I wanted nothing more than to curl up in a corner and cry. Luther's face flashed before my eyes, and my stomach cramped painfully at the thought of the verbal abuse and physical humiliation he would subject me to for having 'betrayed' him. But worse still, a horrible sense of dread descended on me every time I thought of my boss. It went beyond his avowed desire to 'lend' my daughter to some rich perverts. My subconscious knew and felt terrified about something. Something I couldn't name.

"Anton requested I drop by Venus Hive to see his children on the way home," Krygor continued. "So, plan a two-day stop on our itinerary."

With a strength I didn't know I possessed, I schooled my features before entering the room. Krygor's gaze flicked towards me. His eyes instantly smoldered, and a predatory smile stretched his lips.

"I must go," Krygor said to his interlocutor. "Contact me as soon as we're ready."

He listened for a couple more seconds before ending his com then prowled towards me, naked lust written all over his face.

"I'm going to do some very naughty things to you, Hope," Krygor said in a growling voice that sent a shiver down my spine.

For a second, I considered stopping him and demanding answers, but Krygor claimed my mouth with a voracity that made clear he had no interest in deep conversations right now. Slipping his hands beneath my bum, he lifted me up, and my legs automatically wrapped around his waist. He carried me to the bedroom on the opposite side of the living area and kicked the door closed behind us.

For the next eternity, Krygor took me with a passion bordering a feral frenzy. But even as he made my body sing and my throat scream his name, my heart shattered at the thought I might be losing him. I gave him my all that night and prayed it had been enough to sway him —if needed.

Still, in light of his rabid hunger for me, a sliver of hope continued to burn deep within. Tomorrow, at first light, I would confront him. Even if I had to beg and grovel, I would make him keep us.

After wresting a fourth orgasm from me, Krygor gathered me in his arms, holding me close.

"You are mine, Hope," he said possessively in a barely audible whisper.

"And you are mine, Krygor," I replied boldly, snuggling further against him.

His arms tightening around me gave my heart a jolt. Yes, come what may, in the morning, I would make him keep us.

～

A distant chime pulled me out of my deep slumber, and my eyes snapped open. As if going through an out-of-body experience, I watched myself carefully wiggle out of Krygor's embrace and whisper something about needing to use the hygiene room when he tried to prevent me from leaving.

Horrified by memories of Luther and a Sarenian flooding my mind, I tried to turn around to warn Krygor of the twisted plans they had set in motion, but my body kept moving towards his belongings. In the next few minutes, I helplessly watched myself execute the orders that had been imprinted in my mind by Faolen's power. Tears poured down my cheeks to be thus trapped in a body that no longer responded to my will while plotting the demise of the one man to have shown me kindness and given me a glimpse of what a happy life could be for my daughter and me.

My task done, I went to the hygiene room, and forced my bladder to cooperate although I didn't really need to pee. After finishing my nearly non-existent business, I stood before the sink and washed my hands. The chime resonated again. This time, I clearly heard it coming from my collar. I raised a hand to touch it, but halfway through, I stared at my wet fingers, wondering what I had intended to do. Blinking at my reflection in the mirror, I gaped at my cheeks covered in tears. More confused than ever, I dried my hands with a towel before wiping away my tears.

Had I been crying over the uncertainty of my situation with Krygor?

An uneasy feeling lingered as I made my way back to bed. My giant greedily pulled me into his embrace as soon as the mattress dipped beneath me while I climbed back on.

He purred with contentment. "My *Vaya*," he whispered half-asleep.

I snuggled against my giant, but for the next couple of hours, sleep eluded me. Something was wrong, very wrong.

CHAPTER 7
KRYGOR

Roman flipped through the couple of pages of the contract before projecting the terms on the giant screen hanging on the wall of the cramped room he called his office. He knew how much I hated this room, but for the sake of expediency, I sucked it up.

"The debt is three million credits, including my fees," Roman said, casually. "The proposed terms are one year with the standard exclusive Indentured Sex Slave clauses; that means, she's indentured to *you only*. No sharing her or lending her to other men."

I snorted and gave him a disbelieving look as if that was even a remote possibility. Ignoring me, Roman carried on.

"Furthermore, you will pay an allowance of one thousand credits a month to Hope to be spent at her discretion either on herself or on her child, or for her to put away in a savings account as starting money for when she is released from this contract."

It was a wise clause that I hadn't even considered. Without it, she likely would have been left at the mercy of a predator at the end of her contract, stranded with her daughter in the middle of nowhere, with nothing but the clothes on their backs.

"Regardless of that allowance, you will cover all expenses pertaining to their lodging, feeding, and basic standard needs," Roman continued. "Any outings and activities you perform together will be entirely at your expense. Should such activities require specific attires or equipment, the cost will also be borne by you."

I glared at him. "Do I look like the type of male that makes a woman pay when I take her out?"

"You don't look like the type of male that takes a woman out, period," Roman deadpanned, before pursuing his droning, indifferent to my annoyance. "The Appendix lists everything she specifically objects to, and a non-exhaustive list of those she agrees to. Anything not listed in the Appendix but that falls within the category of light to medium kinks will be deemed acceptable. Anything else will need to be formally agreed upon and not automatically implied as agreed to."

I waved a dismissive hand in aggravation. "This isn't necessary. I'm not a freak. I will not make any disturbing demands to my woman."

"I don't doubt it, but a contract is a contract. Better safe than sorry for all parties involved," Roman said matter-of-factly. "Hope learned that the hard way."

That sobered me, and my protective instincts flared up. It still annoyed me to be going through this step, but presenting my *Vaya* with a contract that would give her peace of mind that this time, *this* man, wouldn't take advantage of her justified putting up with this inconvenience—not that it really mattered in the end. I had no intention of ever letting her go; Hope and Siona were mine.

You'd said the same about Marla.

I squashed the uneasy feeling that made my stomach roil. Hope was nothing like Marla who had not only thrown herself at me but also stated early on what she wanted: for me to buy her out of debt as an Indentured Servant. It had been a reckless move considering my tight financial situation at the time. But I'd been too mesmerized by her beauty to think clearly, and she'd immediately sensed what power she would hold over me.

So, what did it mean that Hope—whose situation was far more dire than Marla's had been—still hadn't flat out expressed what she wanted from me? I'd been waiting in vain for her to ask me to buy out her contract, just like she'd proposed me retaining her services as an Escort. Did she have enough of me? Was she eager to move on to something—someone—else? That mere thought made my blood boil with rage. Yet, I couldn't give it any credence. The way she looked at me, touched me, cuddled with me… Hope cared for me, and so did her daughter—*our* daughter. The longing in Siona's eyes and adorable little face as she gazed upon me clawed at my heart. I hadn't missed the hopeful way she'd peered up at me when the Avean had not so 'mistakenly' assumed they were my mate and daughter. In my heart, I'd already claimed them as such.

"Fine," I said at last in a grumbling tone that only made the wretched broker's smirk broaden.

Listening to him go through the list of things Hope would consent to not only had my pants feeling uncomfortably tight, it also made me want to just rush back to the hotel and try out a few of them. Watching the reaver binding my female with its fins and tail had already given me plenty of naughty ideas. The thought of my female bound or shackled, helpless but to submit to my every whim as I ravished her had me squirming in my seat to alleviate the dull throbbing between my legs.

Roman finally ended his endless speech by pointing out the standard rules of an Indentured Servitude contract whereby the owner committed to free his slave in the same physical and mental state he'd received her.

"Are we done yet?" I asked, more distraught by the confined space in his office than I'd ever admit, which only increased my impatience of putting an end to all of this.

"If you are in agreement with all the terms, then you can press your thumb right here, and we'll indeed be done," Roman said, tauntingly.

"I am in agreement except for one clause," I said, leaning back in the far too flimsy chair beneath me, which whined under my weight.

"And that would be?" Roman asked with obvious curiosity.

"The duration," I said in a neutral tone. "Two years, not one."

The broker slightly narrowed his eyes at me, pursing his lips as he carefully chose his response. "For someone of your wealth, one-year for three million is a reasonable duration," Roman argued.

"My wealth is irrelevant," I countered, in the same neutral tone. "The standard is two million per full-time year."

"So then that would mean a year and a half," Roman replied.

"Two years, non-negotiable," I said in a tone that brooked no argument. "After all, I will be looking after her child as well."

My cheeks heated at the lame justification, but I stood my ground. If I had my way, it would have been a ten-year contract. Seeing right through me, Roman snorted and slowly shook his head.

"Two years it is then," he mumbled amending the contract before extending a datapad for me to sign. "Somehow, I suspect the duration will not matter in the end."

I didn't reply, content to hold his gaze for a few moments before signing the contract.

"I'm happy for the three of you," Roman added in a surprisingly soft voice. "She's a good woman, and stunning. Had you been foolish enough to let Hope go, I might have pursued her myself."

He burst out laughing at the menacing look I gave him. If the fool knew how possessive and jealous I was, he wouldn't joke on such matters. Even though I trusted him not to backstab me, his interest in Hope was genuine, maybe more than he was willing to admit to himself. He'd never gone to such lengths to help a 'damsel in distress' as the broker often said when referring to some of the people coming to ask for his help to wiggle their way out of a bad contract.

"If you're done irritating the fuck out of me, please transfer the damn funds so that I can tear the keys of Hope's collar out of that vermin's wretched hands," I grumbled.

"Such hatred!" Roman said teasingly, while typing away on his keyboard to make the transaction.

"It is warranted. Anton has been looking into the bastard," I said through clenched teeth. "He's only scratched the surface so far, but Luther is in deep financial jeopardy and multiplying the shady deals to extricate himself from the mess he's drowning in. There are at least four more of his girls caught in a questionable contract, although Hope's was the worst. Anton is building the case to evict him from the station without owing him the slightest compensation. But Luther has been wise enough to perform his illegal trade off the station, where my son has no jurisdiction."

My com beeped, requesting my authorization for the funds transfer. As soon as I authorized it, I rose to my feet, feeling almost choked in the tiny space.

"Let me out of this damn closet of yours," I snarled. "If you wish to continue doing business with me, you will set up a proper space for us to discuss in the future, or *I* will select our meeting place."

Despite his smile, Roman still looked disturbed about my revelations as he stood up as well before approaching me. "You always have such a sunny disposition," he said, slapping the back of my shoulder. "You just secured your woman for the next couple of years, and you're about to rub it in the face of the bastard you just took her away from. So smile, you old grump."

I harrumphed, not yet willing to let go of my grumpiness—in large part due to my lingering discomfort at having been so confined. I could handle almost anything except being stuck in small spaces or physically restrained. It drove me even more insane than I was.

Roman commed his driver to have him meet us out front of the building. Just as he reached a hand to call the lift, the broker paused then gave me an assessing look. I raised an inquisitive eyebrow.

"I do not mean to pry into your private affairs," the broker said carefully. "But I would be failing in my duties by not reminding you that, although Hope has a contraceptive implant, it is not calibrated for Braxians. Do what you wish with that information."

I flinched. That thought had been at the forefront of my mind since my first time with Hope. With my rabid hunger, I had spilled my seed deep within her too many times to count over the past week. Her blossoming scent also hinted that she was entering her fertile season. The possibility of my seed taking root was high. I couldn't even pretend that it had been fully subconscious on my part. To my shame, I'd done the same with Marla. After a few months with me on Braxia, she'd realized it wasn't the easy life of constant partying she'd hoped for, and that I wasn't swimming in wealth as she'd initially believed. But I'd been so smitten with her, I'd thought getting her pregnant would force her to stay, if only out of love for our child. What a fool I'd been.

And here I am repeating the same mistake.

"Is she aware?" I asked in a thankfully neutral tone, despite the tension stiffening my spine.

"We have not discussed the matter. I had planned on bringing it up at the moment of signing the contract, for which I'd assumed Hope would be present," Roman said.

"She gave you power of attorney," I said defensively. "And I want to surprise her."

"Of course," Roman said in a conciliatory tone, before pressing on the button. "My duty is now done. Let's go say hello to Luther. I can't stay as other duties call me, but I'll be damned if I miss the 'are you fucking kidding me' look on his face when you drop that bomb."

Chuckling, I entered the elevator, already reveling in that man's future dismay.

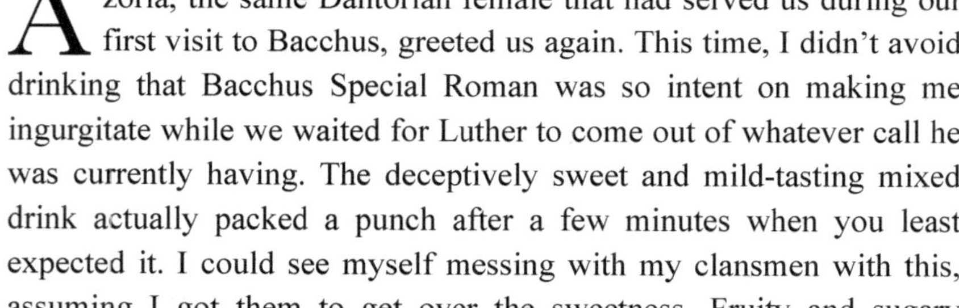

Azoria, the same Dantorian female that had served us during our first visit to Bacchus, greeted us again. This time, I didn't avoid drinking that Bacchus Special Roman was so intent on making me ingurgitate while we waited for Luther to come out of whatever call he was currently having. The deceptively sweet and mild-tasting mixed drink actually packed a punch after a few minutes when you least expected it. I could see myself messing with my clansmen with this, assuming I got them to get over the sweetness. Fruity and sugary drinks weren't deemed manly enough and thus left for the females to enjoy.

I stared without seeing at a pair of females on the main stage performing an erotic dance together, my thoughts locked on my two beauties and the look on their faces once I would announce that they were now mine. Fear and excitement warred within me. I wanted to believe Hope would be genuinely thrilled, that it hadn't been an act, that I hadn't imagined the magic between us...

"I'll call you back," Roman said, ending the conversation he, too, was having on his com, pulling me out of my musing. "He's coming," he added for me, gesturing with his chin towards the hidden passage on the opposite side from the lifts to the suites.

A strained smile played on Luther's lips while he approached us, a wary glimmer in his eyes as they flicked towards Roman. His gaze wandered over my shoulder—probably looking for Hope—before settling on my face. Luther's welcoming expression faded at the sight of the feral grin I gave him. He made no effort to hide his concern as he stopped a couple of feet in front of the same high table we were sitting at.

"Mr. Aldriss? How can I be of service to you today?" Luther asked in a voice filled with tension.

I fished my com out of my pocket, pulled up the funds transfer confirmation showing him as beneficiary, and laid it down onto the table in front of me.

"You can help me by fetching the key to Hope's collar. She no longer needs it," I said smugly, indicating the com with my chin.

From the corner of my eyes, I noticed Roman biting the inside of his cheeks not to laugh at Luther going through the first three stages of grief in a split second. Mouth gaping, the owner of Bacchus stared at my com as if it had grown a head and limbs and was performing an Avean folk dance. He then shook his head, his eyes flicking between Roman and me, appearing to wait for us to tell him it was a joke. When we continued to stoically stare at him, anger rapidly took over his features.

"You can't have her!" he snapped, abandoning any semblance of civility or deference. Teeth clenched, he brutally pushed the com away from him, towards me, as if he found its sight offensive—which he probably did. "Hope's contract is not for sale. She's *mine*. *She* will repay *me*, in whatever form *I* see fit! I don't need your fucking credits. I will have my bank reverse the transaction immediately," he said, fumbling to pull his own com out of his pocket.

"No, you slimy little worm," I said with all the contempt he inspired me, not to mention a sliver of anger he would dare claim my female as his. "I don't give two shits about whether you want to sell her contract or not. I already bought it. See, you may have screwed her over with that barely legal contract you trapped her in, you neglected to include an exclusivity clause."

Rising to my feet, I circled around the table to tower over the human who looked scrawny before me. He cast a scared look at Roman who casually leaned back against the backrest of his chair before tilting his head to the side with curiosity. Luther glanced around the room, which was already quite packed despite the still early hour of the day. I couldn't say if he was looking for help or trying to reassure himself that there were enough witnesses around that I wouldn't dare raise a hand on him.

The fool. Didn't they tell him I was crazy?

"You... You can't buy her because she's already sold to someone else," Luther said swiftly, taking a step backwards. He nervously glanced at the room again, his pale complexion turning chalky with fear.

This time, it was my turn to scan the room. Luther was terrified— not that I cared about his state of mind—but my gut told me the source of that fear was within this room, and that it involved my woman, our daughter, or both. And *that* I deeply cared about. However, with many of the patrons having sensed an unfolding drama, too many of them were looking at us for me to pinpoint one in particular. Well, aside from a Sarenian who—contrary to the other customers who were watching with a certain degree of wariness—appeared tremendously amused by the scene.

"That's a lie," Roman interjected while swirling his drink around the glass. "I checked the public registry before completing the transaction, and then sent the notice of acquisition payment to the Registrar. So, should you refuse to release a Servant that is no longer yours, I will be forced to file complaints for the twelve or so articles of law you will be infringing upon, a few of them criminal in nature. We don't want that, do we?"

Luther's mouth opened and closed a few times, and he appeared on the verge of hyperventilating. Under different circumstances, I might have felt sorry for the man, but his obvious distress pleased me tremendously.

"I will give you another female," Luther pleaded with near desperation in his voice. For a moment, I actually thought he would get down on his knees. "No, two! I will give you two females, younger, fresher, to do with as you please. I can't give you Hope. She—"

"What you will give me is the fucking key I asked for, or I will drag you by that scrawny neck of yours to go fetch it," I hissed, taking another menacing step towards him. "You do not want to test me."

For a split second, Luther appeared to want to continue arguing and pleading. Just as I was wondering if he'd lost his mind, Luther's shoulders slumped in defeat, and he nodded, looking haggard. Turning on his heels, he walked away with the heavy steps of a dead man walking. I cast a look over my shoulder at Roman who was slowly approaching me, his gaze locked on Luther's receding back.

"Is his fear over losing Hope or her daughter?" I asked the broker.

"Both," he said pensively. "Whatever shady deal he was involved in, he's clearly royally fucked. I suggest you keep a close eye on your females," Roman added with a wary tone. "Desperate people do stupid things. And this fellow is beyond desperate."

I nodded slowly, the same thought having crossed my mind. "We're leaving either tonight or first thing tomorrow. Not that it matters all that much. Anton will be kicking him off Lilith Hive in the not too distant future. In the meantime, I trust you to finalize the outstanding deals on my behalf."

"Most certainly," Roman said with a smile. "I want to collect my fees."

I snorted and shook my head at the silly man. His fees were quite steep, but the quality of his services justified it. If he recommended a deal, you could go in blindly knowing you'd make a ton of credits on the other side.

The weight of many stares lingered on me, but my eyes kept turning to the slightly glowing ones of the Sarenian. He didn't stare more intently than anyone else, but there was some major tension between our peoples due to their semi-official alliance with the

Guldans. Luther returning, looking sickly pale, drew my attention away from the disturbingly handsome face of the Sarenian.

"Is there no way I can sway you?" Luther asked in a last-ditch effort. "Whatever you may think of my contract with her, Hope means everything to me. I—"

"Give me the fucking key," I interrupted, not in the least interested in his bullshit change of tactics.

I extended my open palm towards him and, with a pained sigh, Luther dropped the key in my hand with shaky fingers.

"Good day to you, Mr. Stromland," I said, possessively fisting the key—which simply looked like a drop-shaped key fob—before turning on my heels.

Nodding in goodbye to Roman who would shortly be meeting with customers here, I left the parlor, eager to return to the hotel to break the news to my woman.

But I had a little detour to make first.

CHAPTER 8
HOPE

All morning, I'd been rehearsing my speech to Krygor. Well, not so much a speech so much as how I'd ease into the topic of my contract and the many reasons he had to keep Siona and me. But as soon as the door of our hotel suite opened, my mind went completely blank. Mouth dry, heart pounding, I ran a nervous hand through my hair and flattened the non-existent creases on my short, flowy, summer dress.

"Hope?" Krygor called out from the living area.

"Coming!" I replied, casting a sideways glance at myself in the mirror before leaving the bedroom.

The warm and welcoming smile on my face froze at the sight of the breathtaking female by Krygor's side. At least 6'3, copper skin, the face and body of a goddess, with the longest, wavy, dark hair I'd ever seen, I initially thought her human until I noticed the cheetah-like spots alongside her neck, arms and legs.

Oh Goddess, a Veredian!

Under different circumstances, I would have been fawning over the stunning female of the legendary species. They had faced such incredible odds, rising from near extinction and enslavement at the hands of my people, to become the most powerful species in both Quadrants of the known galaxy. But she was everything Roman had warned me people wanting to buy Indentured Servants were looking for: exotically beautiful, young, fresh, and unique. Everything I wasn't.

My heart shattered while my blood turned to acid in my veins. Throat almost too tight to breathe, I blinked to keep at bay the tears prickling my eyes as all my hopes and dreams fell apart around me. I'd truly fallen for my giant, and I'd foolishly believed he had genuine feelings for me. Knowing how devastated Siona would also be further compounded the pain clawing at my heart.

But I wouldn't make a spectacle of myself.

Years of experience wearing the perfect hostess' mask even while dying inside kicked into action. That was the one thing I could thank my Guldan upbringing for. No matter your pain, distress, and misery, it was a female's duty to always put up a happy front in order to never embarrass or indispose a male.

"There she is," Krygor said with the possessive pride and warmth he'd always displayed when looking at me. "Hope, this is Thesala, a friend. Thesala, this is my little *Vaya*, Hope."

Baffled, it took every ounce of my willpower not to show my confusion. Instead, I played along, giving the stunning female a friendly smile.

"Pleased to meet you, Thesala," I said, blown away that my words had come out so cordially—in fact, blown away that any word had managed to come out at all.

"The pleasure is all mine, Hope," the Veredian replied with a gentle, sultry voice that made me feel even more inadequate before such perfection.

"If you would give us a moment, Thesala, I would like to have a word in private with Hope first before we proceed," Krygor said in a kind voice.

The expression on his face when he looked at her was friendly and devoid of the lust and fire that usually burned within them when he gazed upon me. Was I jumping to conclusions too quickly? After all, the Veredians and Braxians had become strong allies since the sister of their military leader had married the Braxian king.

"Of course, no problem," Thesala replied with a smile.

"Make yourself comfortable," Krygor said with a grateful smile, gesturing at the plush leather couches in the living area. "And don't be shy; help yourself to anything in the bar. We'll try to be quick."

Krygor possessively took my hand, which further added to my confusion. Refusing to give myself any false hopes, I docilely followed him as he led me back into the bedroom and closed the door behind us. Letting go of me, he walked to an inconspicuous panel next to the large, wooden dresser and activated a hidden sensor I hadn't even realized existed. The panel slid open revealing a safe. Krygor held his palm up before it, and a pale blue light scanned it before the safe opened. He pulled out a flat and square dark grey box with an elegant brand name printed in swirling maroon letters on top—the traditional Braxian colors. I couldn't read it from where I stood, even after he laid it down on top of the dresser.

"Come to me, Hope," Krygor said in almost a whisper, the intensity of his gaze making me squirm.

Pulse racing, I complied, my knees feeling wobbly. I could barely breathe as I stopped a couple of feet in front of him, my eyes flicking between his. He cupped my face between his hands with infinite care. The tenderness with which he examined my features turned me inside out. Despite the fear gnawing at me, a flimsy flame rekindled on the dying embers of hope deep within me.

Leaning forward, he captured my lips in a slow kiss, devoid of the usual animal passion, but filled with something akin to love that had me melting against him, my hands fisting his shirt with near desperation. Too soon, he released me. I kept on clinging to him, my entire body shaking with a mix of fear and overwhelming emotions from that incredible kiss. No one had ever made me feel more cherished than he just had.

Krygor reached for something in his pants. I stared at his hand trying to see what the dark grey, flat, tear-shaped object between his fingers could be. And then he pressed it to the lock of my collar. My jaw dropped, and my eyes all but popped out of my head when it loosened around my neck. Krygor removed the wretched mark of

Luther's ownership on me and tossed it with disgust into the trash bin.

My hands flew to my liberated neck, rubbing it with disbelief while my mind—which had all but frozen—tried to grasp what that meant. I knew, and yet I didn't dare to believe. As I stared speechlessly at my giant, mouth gaping, he reached out for the luxurious box on the dresser and opened it. Within, a thin, black leather choker with intricate patterns made of leather repoussé technique surrounded the central plated strands of nyrian crystal crushed into fine threads. And in the middle, a large gem matching my eye color had been inserted.

My lips quivered, and my vision blurred with tears of joy as Krygor raised the collar towards me. I stretched my neck and lifted my hair to ease his task while he clasped it on me.

"You will never see Luther again," Krygor said in that deep, rumbling voice I adored. "*I* am the only male you will ever touch and dance for. You are legally mine, and I do not share what's mine."

"You bought my contract," I said in a quivering voice, tears pouring down my face while a grateful grin stretched my lips. "I feared you were going to leave without me… without us."

"I would never leave you behind, my Hope. Have I not told you how much you have pleased me?" Krygor asked, looking somewhat baffled.

"Yes, but… I don't know. I was just so scared," I whispered, placing my hands around his waist and fisting his shirt as if to make sure he wasn't an illusion that would suddenly disappear.

"Do not be scared. You and Siona don't have to be scared anymore. Two years. You are mine for two years," Krygor said possessively. "And no one can buy back your contract from me without your express consent. Roman tried to negotiate a lesser term, but I refused. In fact, I wanted to ask for even more time."

His last words, and the glimmer of vulnerability that flickered in his eyes as he spoke them moved me to my core. It floored me to realize he was as uncertain of my feelings towards him as I'd been about his.

Slipping my fingers through his long, wavy hair, I let my eyes express the depth of the affection I felt for him. "You could have asked for five, ten, or even twenty years, I would have said yes," I said sincerely. "No man has ever been so good to me and my baby. I didn't think it possible to be so happy and feel so safe. You will not regret this, Krygor. I promise to be the best Servant to have ever lived."

"No, my little *Vaya*," Krygor said pulling me into his embrace. "The only promise I will ask of you is to remain the wonderful female you have been since we met."

"That won't be hard," I said, laughing through my tears.

Krygor captured my lips again, this time with a possessiveness laced with his blossoming desire. I pressed myself against him, my core throbbing at the feel of his shaft hardening against my stomach. His mouth plundered mine, one hand fisting my hair, the other holding me tightly against him.

Too soon again, Krygor pulled away from me with a frustrated grunt, obviously reluctant to stop. Eyes smoldering, he gently wiped away my tears with his knuckles, before caressing my new collar with a proud look on his face. It made my belly quiver and my nipples harden. I was his, officially his. I belonged to my gentle giant, my mountain of a man.

"Come," Krygor said, taking my hand again. "I have another surprise for you."

My eyes widened with curiosity, especially in light of the mischievous glint in his eyes. He led me back to the living area where the beautiful Veredian had taken a seat in the fancy, cushioned leather chair and was reading something on her com. Thesala put it away as soon as she saw us coming out and gave me a sympathetic look at the sight of my still overly glistening eyes.

"Thesala is a Veredian Healer," Krygor explained. "Since her ship was traveling through this sector of the Eastern Quadrant, I asked if they wouldn't mind making a little detour through Lilith Hive to help right the wrong that had been done to you. They accepted."

My eyes widened as the meaning of his words sank in, and my head jerked towards Thesala. Even as I stared at her with pleading eyes that she would confirm his words, shock, hope, and disbelief coursed through me. She smiled and slowly approached, stopping less than a meter in front of me. Her eyes went slightly out of focus as she stared at my forehead for a few seconds. Her smile broadened as she refocused on me.

"I see what was done to you," Thesala said in a kind voice. "With your consent, I can restore the symbols of your genetic identity that were taken from you."

The waterworks went wild again as I nodded. "Yes. Please, yes!"

Whatever my feelings about the Guldan culture, my horns and my pointy ears had been an integral part of who I had been. I'd forever felt incomplete since Luther had them permanently removed.

Thesala gestured for me to take a seat in the chair she had previously occupied. My hand tightened around Krygor who still held it. I let him lead me to the chair then, to my surprise, he sat in it first before pulling me onto his lap, holding me safe and cocooned in his muscular arms.

"I'm afraid it will hurt a little and might leave you feeling somewhat weak until you've eaten something," Thesala said apologetically.

"I don't care," I replied in a trembling voice. "Thank you so much!"

Krygor's arms tightened around me, and he gently nuzzled my nape. Thesala raised her palms and set them on each side of my face, her fingertips pressed lightly on my temples. The Veredian's stunning blue eyes went out of focus, and a tingling sensation on my forehead slowly turned hot, then burning. I clenched my teeth at the growing pain which had my skull feeling like it was caught in a vise. Keeping my head up, my hand blindly looked for Krygor's. His settled over the back of mine, his thumb gently caressing my knuckles in a soothing motion.

I hissed at a sharp pain, like a knife cut. A warm liquid trickled down my forehead where the skin had split to let my horns out. Despite the painful sensation of my skin being stretched, I reveled in the steadily increasing long-lost weight of my horns settling on my head again as Thesala's power regrew them to their former glory. The tips of my ears also tingled as their clipped pointy ends were being restored.

I couldn't tell if it had lasted a minute or an hour, but the pain vanished almost instantly, seconds before Thesala removed her hands from me.

"I should have remembered to have a towel handy," Thesala said sheepishly.

"It's okay," I said absentmindedly, raising shaky hands to my forehead.

I likely resembled a victim straight out of some horror movie with the amount of blood that had trickled down my face. But I only cared about the feel of my horns beneath my palms. I burst out laughing and crying at the same time.

"Thank you! Thank you!" I said, running my fingers over the familiar natural patterns along the horns that marked my lineage.

The room spun around me as Krygor stood up, holding me in his arms, and carried me to the hygiene room in our bedroom. He settled me on the counter next to the sink and fetched a washcloth. Through tears of joy, my hands still pawing at my horns in disbelief, I watched with awe as Krygor gently washed my face. On Guldar, no man would have performed such a task for a female as it would have been considered menial work well below them. But looking at my giant, who would have imagined him taking care of his woman in such a delicate and gentle fashion?

"I had prayed to the Goddess for a savior," I whispered as he finished his task. "I never dreamed she would bless me with someone as wonderful as you. You are so much more than I ever thought I deserved. Thank you for keeping me, for making me feel what it's like to be happy, for making me whole again, and for keeping my baby safe."

The same powerful emotion I had glimpsed on Krygor's face earlier settled on his features. This time, he didn't chase it away as he picked me up and held me close. Arms wrapped around his neck and legs around his waist, I locked eyes with my giant, my tongue burning to say words I knew to be too early to voice.

"My people do not observe any religion as your people do," Krygor said in a gentle voice. "But I thank the Ancestors every day for bringing you into my life. You were made for me, Hope. You are mine, and I'm keeping you."

Heart filled to bursting, I buried my face in his neck and reveled in the safety of his arms for a few seconds. Krygor eventually put me back down on my feet, and I took a few moments to stare at my face, mesmerized to see my old self again. We finally went back to the living area where I apologized profusely for making Thesala wait so long. She waved a hand in understanding, complimenting me for my beautiful black horns. After a few more pleasantries, she took her leave with one of their Veredian Warriors who had been waiting for her at the entrance of the hotel to safely escort her back to their ship.

"Pack your things here, and then let's go to your house," Krygor said. "I already have movers waiting outside to take care of whatever you wish to bring. We will not return," he warned.

"Should I go get Siona first?" I asked after a swift glance at the clock.

"Yulan is already on his way to pick her up," Krygor replied smugly. "Come on, woman. I want to leave this place tonight or tomorrow morning at the latest."

I didn't argue, impressed by how he'd thought of everything. It took me no time to pack the few things I'd brought to the hotel for both Siona and me. After a quick ride to the Commons in a hovercab, I was both intimidated and embarrassed by the number of movers standing outside the house. I didn't need that many helpers considering what meager possessions I had. But, more importantly, it shamed me that Krygor Aldriss, Councilor to the Magnar of Braxia and father of the big boss of the Hive Network, should be seen with a female that lived in such poverty.

"There are too many," I said to Krygor in a small voice. "I have nothing worth taking but my clothes and a handful of mementos. I only need four crates, which I can pack myself."

Krygor's dark gaze bore into mine. My cheeks heated as he all but read my mind. He nodded slowly.

"I will bring the crates inside the house, and the men will wait outside until you are done," he said with a smile.

"Thank you," I replied, my cheeks burning with embarrassment.

I sent a message to Tamika informing her of my good fortune before welcoming her to help herself to anything I'd leave behind. It broke my heart not to see her one last time before we left, but she was currently working. However, if Krygor ended up delaying our departure until tomorrow, I might be able to squeeze in a last farewell.

I made quick work of packing everything, amused by Krygor's wish to make himself helpful. But he kept getting in my way, and his efforts at folding anything just required me to redo it anyway. I eventually tasked him to simply follow me around holding the container so that I didn't have to walk back and forth to it. That didn't seem to bother him one bit.

Just as I was finishing packing the last crate, the front door opened, startling me. It took me half a second to realize it was my baby coming home. Krygor immediately walked out of the room ahead of me. I followed in his wake to find her by Yulan's side, looking utterly distraught despite the brave front she tried to put on.

She only had eyes for Krygor. The betrayed expression on her face broke my heart, understanding all too well the thoughts currently crossing her mind.

"You don't want us," she said accusingly to Krygor before I had a chance to say anything.

"Siona!" I exclaimed, mortified.

"No, it's okay," Krygor said, gently squeezing my forearm before approaching Siona and crouching before her. "I very much want both you and your mother. We didn't come here to drop you off but to pick up your things so that you can come live with me on Braxia. I believe you want to ride a reaver and a karvala for real, right?"

She gaped at him, her anger melting to be replaced by shock, disbelief, and then joy in quick succession. "You mean it? You really mean it?"

"I do," Krygor answered in a soft voice.

Siona threw herself into Krygor's arms. He laughed and gently hugged her. My daughter kissed his cheek loudly before burying her face in his neck. He rocked my baby slowly while caressing her silver-blond mane. She finally lifted her head to look at Krygor with adoration before turning towards me with a glowing smile. And then she did a double take, noticing at long last the wondrous gift my giant had given me.

"Your horns…" Siona whispered, eyes bulging. "You have your horns back! And your ears, too!"

"I do," I said, feeling silly for getting emotional again. My man would end up thinking me a crybaby. "Krygor brought a Veredian healer to restore them."

Siona spent the next few minutes fussing over my horns and ears, touching them with awe, and hugging both Krygor and me with an excess of enthusiasm. When she finally calmed down, Yulan and Krygor carried our four half-filled crates outside for the movers to bring to the ship. We settled in the hovercar, my man sandwiched between my daughter and me. As the vehicle took off, taking us towards our new destiny, I cast a final glance at the former home that had protected my baby from those who would have harmed her and thanked the Goddess for all her blessings.

CHAPTER 9
HOPE

Despite being of a smaller size, Krygor's vessel screamed comfort and luxury. Siona loved the private quarters she had all to herself, not to mention the holodeck, which she intended to make intensive use of during the almost ten-day trip to Venus Hive. The thought of meeting Krygor's firstborn and the big boss of the Hive Network had me almost hyperventilating. What if he didn't approve of me?

I hadn't dared mention my worries to Krygor as it would inevitably come across as if I was giving myself far more importance than I officially had as his Servant. Still, after tucking in Siona for the night, my giant didn't rush to ravish me contrary to what he'd said earlier about being impatient to have me. He seemed more intent on us having some serious discussions. Considering he'd stated that we would only be leaving in the morning to give Roman a chance to drop by for a last-minute sync with Krygor, it made me quite anxious. Was he having second thoughts and giving himself a final out to leave us here in the end?

Those irrational and paranoid thoughts wouldn't leave me alone. A man didn't go through all this trouble, going as far as luring a Veredian here to restore me, only to change his mind at the last minute. I should be rejoicing about this giving me time for a last hug with Tamika, but an unexplainable sense of dread kept eating away at me. Something bad was going to happen. I could feel it in my bones. Yet, I kept my mouth shut. What would I have said anyway considering I had no clue what kind of trouble was even involved?

I was sitting in the middle of Krygor's immense bed, crossed legs, naked but for a see-through pink nightgown, when my man returned after his last discussions with his crew. He kicked off his shoes and stripped out of his clothes—which he casually discarded on a chair by the hygiene room—then climbed on top of the bed. The mattress dipped under his weight as he kneeled in front of me. Krygor gently kissed me then rid me of my flimsy dress, which he threw in the general direction of the chair.

Coaxing me onto my back, he lay down on his side next to me, his gaze following his hand as it freely roamed over my naked body. I would never tire of the delectable feel of his rough palms gently caressing my skin, or the awe in his eyes when he looked at me. However, despite the arousal blossoming in the pit of my stomach, I braced for whatever was putting that troubled expression on his face.

Krygor leaned forward, his hand cupping my face as he gave me another tender kiss. His fingers then traced a slow path down my neck, his fingertips caressing my gorgeous new collar. They pursued their journey to my left breast, circling the dark areola with a fleeting touch before streaking down to my stomach where Krygor laid down his palm. He stared at his hand slowly rubbing my flat belly before looking up at me.

"Tell me about yourself, Hope. What series of events led you here, to the Eastern Quadrant so that I should now be blessed to have you in my bed?" Krygor asked with an impenetrable stare.

I chewed my bottom lip, wondering for a second how candid I should be. What man wanted to hear how the vicissitudes of his woman's past had led her from a life of privilege to that of a pleasure worker and Indentured Servant? A part of me feared I would earn his contempt and disgust, but another wanted to be honest as my every instinct told me he would demand no less. If we were to have the future

I was hoping for deep within my soul, we needed to start right. Knowing what a solid contract Roman had negotiated for me also went a long way in alleviating some of my fears.

Taking a deep breath, I took the dive.

"After my father's death, the Goddess sent me on a painful journey through the Eastern Quadrant so that I could meet you," I said softly. "But the pain I endured was worth it for the blessing of the children it gave me and for eventually leading me to you. I would go through it all over again just to get back to right here and now."

Krygor blinked, a look a confusion crossing his features.

"Children?" he asked.

It was my turn to blink, realizing he wasn't aware of my firstborn.

"I have one other child, an adult son named Tevek," I said, sadness seeping back into my voice. "My life had been meant to be quite different than how it turned out. My father was a wealthy tech trader. I was promised to Valdek Farruk, the handsome heir to one of the richest families on Guldar, right behind the Vrok family. They operate some of the top technology labs on my home world. Father had arranged my wedding to Valdek. My virtue had been kept intact for him, and I'd been properly trained to be the perfect wife and lady to manage the domain of a high ranking noble in Kenzenia, Guldar's capital city."

"Why did you flee?" Krygor asked, confused. "That sounds like a comfortable future."

I snorted with derision. "Oh, it would have been. Valdek would have rutted over me for the first two to five years to sire a few heirs, then would have mostly ignored me for the rest of our union, preferring to hunt younger, fresher females, slaves and mistresses while I raised the children. I'd been looking forward to that life once he'd stopped bothering me. But my father made a series of bad investments that ruined everything. We were on the verge of bankruptcy, and Father was pushing to hasten our wedding."

"Hoping Valdek would help redress your financial situation?" Krygor asked.

"Yes. Well, more like to force his hand into it," I said with a shrug. "Guldans are all about success and the survival of the fittest. Had he married me first, my family's financial downfall would have shamed him and lessened his standing. In spite of my father's efforts to hide our dire situation, Valdek got wind of it and stalled the wedding until everything fell apart. And my dearest father, the embodiment of courage and strength that he was, simply took his life rather than fight."

Krygor recoiled in outrage. "He abandoned you and your mother to fend for yourselves after his failure?"

"He'd divorced my mother before selling her a few months after my fifth birthday. She'd become barren after contracting an infectious disease. I believe my father had passed it on to her from his infidelities," I said with bitterness. "Being a child back then, I don't remember much about her except that she had been loving and kind. I'd promised myself to be as good a mother when I grew up."

"And you are," Krygor said tenderly.

I smiled sadly before continuing. "Other wealthy and noble families refused him their daughters, fearing the same fate would befall them, and in turn bring shame to their bloodline. So, that made me his only child—at least the only legitimate one. The Goddess only knows if I have other siblings sired on slaves or pleasure workers," I said, shaking my head with disgust at the way Guldan males treated females in general. "By default, my uncle became my Guardian as Guldan females must belong to a male, be it a blood relative, a spouse, or a master. Since he didn't want to deal with my father's debts, after the creditors collected what assets they could from the bankruptcy, my uncle gave me and our ancestral lands to Valdek."

"So, you did marry him after all?"Krygor asked, taken aback, the sliver of jealousy in his voice plain to hear.

I shook my head. "No, of course not. Valdek would never marry a beggar. My uncle gave me to him as a sex slave. While he would have treated me with a certain level of care as his wife, a slave was merely a tool to be used and abused." My throat tightened remembering the painful days getting punished by Valdek for my father ruining his carefully planned future, as if I had been the one to blame. "In a way, it was luck that he ended up selling me to the right hand of Guldar's most successful slaver."

"How so?" Krygor asked, the tension in his voice hinting at his burgeoning anger.

For a second, I hesitated about continuing my tale, but I wanted the truth out between us. Despite barely knowing him, Krygor was everything I wished for in a man, and I wanted this relationship to start off on solid foundations.

"Valdek developed a lot of high-end technology which Gruuk Vrok —the greatest slaver in Guldan history—used in his breeding compounds," I explained. "Gruuk's right hand, Doruk Sidik, saw me when he came to Kenzenia to negotiate a major contract on behalf of his boss. Valdek had not shared me with anyone. I think he was afraid to let anyone see the scars from the lashings he'd given me."

"WHAT?!" Krygor hissed, his face contracting with rage and his hand fisting the bed covering with such strength I feared it would rip.

"It's okay. It's okay," I said in a soothing voice, caressing his chest gently. "For all his faults, Doruk came with certain benefits, including access to Veredian healers that took away the scars and made me as good as new again." I smiled as Krygor grunted in concession, although his lingering anger was plain to see. I caressed his cheek before continuing. "Doruk wanted me, but he especially wanted my lands. What most people don't know is that Doruk came from very humble beginnings. Gruuk saved his life when he was still just a teenager and put him through his paces, personally training him into becoming his right hand. But despite the wealth and status he had acquired trading Veredians, Doruk wanted the respect and standing that came with owning ancestral lands."

"So, he bought you and your lands?" Krygor asked, still seething, although it came out more like a statement than a question.

I nodded. "In truth, it worked out for the best," I said sincerely. "I was free of Valdek's abuse, and as Doruk spent most of his time in space, he didn't bother me much, and I got to do what I'd been raised to do: run the family estate. Two years later, when I gave birth to my son Tevek, Doruk married me to make our son his legitimate heir. I didn't even know it had happened as the female's permission isn't required, and only found out twenty years later when I gave birth to Siona."

"How did you end up with Luther?" Krygor asked, frowning.

"Gruuk Vrok died," I said with a heavy sigh. "With Gruuk's empire getting dismantled, Doruk came home. While he'd been in space, seeing me only once or twice a year was enough to keep up his interest, but he grew bored of having me underfoot day in and day out for two years straight. With both our children having their legitimate status, he no longer needed me. And with his tremendous wealth, the elite of Guldar sought to form blood alliances with him."

"So, he discarded you," Krygor said, a hard glint in his eyes.

I nodded again, swallowing painfully through the hurt, pain, and shame that seemed to have been passed down from my mother to me. "He had found me a buyer among the slavers that had come home to present their latest 'stock' on offer. Luther had been among those buyers and had haggled to buy me. But he is human, and Guldan females aren't allowed to leave Guldar. So, Doruk rejected his offer and gave me to a Guldan slaver instead who was to collect me three days later."

"Only you? Not Siona?" Krygor insisted, his strong brows creasing.

"Oh Goddess, no!" I said, shaking my head. "Had that been the case, I probably wouldn't have signed such a foolish contract with Luther. My little girl was beautiful and promising to turn into a stunning woman. Doruk already had many suitors lined up for her that would strengthen his status and influence. That's why I had to run away with my baby. That's why I approached Luther."

"*You* went to *him*?" Krygor asked, flabbergasted.

"He never would have dared approach another male's female on Guldar without his express consent. The consequences would have been too dire for him," I said, shivering at the memory. "I'd never been so terrified in my life. If he exposed me, I'd be publicly stoned to death. But the way he'd been looking at me and his bitterness at being denied for being a foreigner convinced me he would at least consider taking me offworld, if only out of spite. There was little time and far too few opportunities to discuss terms. So, of course, I accepted whatever he threw at me, as long as he took both of us away."

"But how did he manage to take you without anyone noticing, or even to perform the surgery?" Krygor asked, confused. "Considering how closely Guldan females are watched, how did they not suspect or catch you?"

"We managed thanks to Luther being clever. In a gesture of gratitude, Luther offered to host an orgy at the house he was renting during his stay, mainly featuring his girls. Not the ones from Bacchus," I clarified quickly. "He runs side deals completely independent of Bacchus involving girls that are often far too young, which I didn't realize at the time. While the men were out enjoying themselves, I went to run errands with my daughter and one of our house slaves. As long as a slave accompanies us, a male supervisor isn't compulsory."

"And you never returned home," Krygor rightfully guessed.

"Correct," I said with a nod. "Luther had us 'abducted' in front of the slave so that she could return home and cry for help."

"And Luther would have been participating in that orgy, with everyone to see he clearly wasn't involved," Krygor astutely deduced.

"Exactly. We remained on Guldar for nearly a week. With the crazy manhunt ongoing, and the spaceports under heavy surveillance, Luther had no difficulty convincing me to let him cut off my horns. Nobody would be questioning one more human slave among his other ones."

"And here we are," Krygor concluded.

"And here we are," I echoed. "My only regret is not knowing what has become of my son. He was away at the Technical Academy when all that mess went down. In my heart, I want to believe he's searching for us, but the Goddess only knows how they've changed him after Doruk took him from me for fear I was making him too soft."

A strange expression crossed Krygor's face as he looked at me.

"What?" I asked, slightly worried.

"You didn't know that the Queen of Braxia, our Dagna, was Guldan. So, you probably aren't aware that she's actually Gruuk Vrok's daughter with his Veredian wife, Maheva."

My jaw dropped, and I gaped at him in disbelief. But that explained everything even more than I'd previously realized. Gruuk Vrok had been praised on Guldar as one of the greatest businessmen of our times. There had been some talks here and there questioning his fierceness, and implying he might have gone soft, but his continued success, wits, and combat prowess against those who thought to duel him for his position of command had proven him to be a role model to emulate.

The Emperor finding out that not only had Gruuk successfully sired a Guldan hybrid with a Veredian but kept it a secret instead of exploiting it must have stung. Then discovering that same hybrid now sat on the Braxian throne, thwarting his efforts to enslave the giant warriors had to be infuriating. He couldn't let that knowledge spread wide. It suddenly made me fear for the safety of the Dagna.

"More still," Krygor continued. "I believe your son reached out to the Veredians not so long ago. And if I'm right, through him, you have earned yourself the undying gratitude of these powerful females."

I stared at him in confusion, eyes bugged, while my heart soared at the news that my son not only lived but was potentially fighting for the right side. "What do you mean?"

"A few months ago, while the Veredians were dealing with some tension between them and the Korletheans, a few Guldan ships tried to sneak in from the rear to attack them both," Krygor explained. "Our friends would have sustained many casualties if not for a certain Tevek Sidik giving them a warning. On top of saving lives, your son gave the Veredians the means to locate all their missing Sisters sold into slavery over the years."

"Oh Goddess!" I exclaimed, pressing my palms to my chest as if to contain it from exploding with love and pride for the son I hadn't seen in far too many years. "Do you know where he is? How I can get in touch with him?"

Krygor shook his head with an apologetic look, and my heart sank. "I do not. As far as I know, he didn't give the Veredians any means to contact him. However, he did mention that he was looking for his mother and little sister. Do not be discouraged, my *Vaya*. I promise you to look into it. Once the Veredians find out you are his missing mother,

I am certain they will do everything in their power to help reunite you, if only as a thank you."

I threw myself into his arms, almost knocking him onto his back, and crushed his lips with a fierce kiss of gratitude. He chuckled, his massive hand behind my back holding me against him. His amusement quickly faded as he demanded entry. My lips parted willingly, submitting to the dominance of his tongue taking possession of what was rightfully his. I moaned and pressed my breasts against his hard, naked chest as my arousal quickly awakened.

To my dismay, Krygor ended the kiss and gently pushed me onto my back the instant my hands began roaming over his godly body. I slightly frowned, wondering why he was stopping us when I could feel his cock hardening against my leg. Eyes locked with mine, Krygor caressed a path up from my wrist before resting his palm on my left upper arm. His thumb pressed onto the contraceptive implant invisible beneath my skin. My mouth went dry, and I swallowed painfully before addressing what I thought might be troubling him.

"It still has over one year remaining on it," I said in a controlled voice. "I will not trap you with an unwanted child."

He snorted and slowly shook his head. "Braxians gladly welcome the children they sire. You cannot 'trap' a Braxian as marriage is optional and not all that frequent. It is *Braxians* who usually attempt to trap foreign females into remaining on Braxia by impregnating them. Although I can never regret the son it gave me, I do not wish to repeat the same mistake."

My eyes widened at his implied meaning. And deep within, his comment stung. Would it be so terrible to sire a child on me?

"Repeat?" I asked.

"I've only ever had one other Indentured Servant before you; a stunning human female named Marla Myers," Krygor said with a sad smile. I held my breath realizing this wasn't the type of confessions he made often. "Like most aspiring performers, she'd secured a gig dancing on the stage of one of the cheap adult clubs on Jeruna. Back then, I had believed her to be the most beautiful female in the world. When she showed interest towards me, I first thought someone had paid her to prank me. How could such perfection be attracted to an ugly beast like me?"

"You're not ugly," I countered genuinely while trying to ignore the pang of jealousy towards some female I didn't know. "You have the fearsome traits of the Braxians. They may not be considered handsome by galactic standards, but that's what makes you unique and incredibly sexy. Everything about you turns me on."

His brutish face melted with tenderness, making him look even more fearsome rather than softer. Still, I loved it.

"My little *Vaya*," he whispered leaning down to give me a far too brief kiss.

I dreaded where his story would go yet couldn't wait to hear more.

"I was only on Jeruna for a couple of days to celebrate me taking over the leadership of my clan," he continued, a distant look in his eyes as he reminisced. "My father's untimely death in a hunting accident had made me the youngest Clan Leader of our bloodline. At nineteen years of age, I'd been a fool entirely controlled by my cock. So, that first night, when Marla flat out asked me to take her back to my quarters, I'd been too eager to agree."

Krygor's gaze refocused on me. He gently brushed a lock of hair away from my face. His gaze roamed over my features before he slowly caressed my left horn. I didn't really want to hear details of his past with the mother of his firstborn, but he wouldn't tell me if it didn't have some importance.

"The first time I saw you inside Bacchus, I thought my eyes were playing tricks on me, and that Marla had resurfaced from my past," Krygor said wistfully. "You could have been sisters."

My stomach dropped, and my blood ran cold. I remembered that shocked, angry look on his face when he'd first seen me. I hadn't understood then, but it all made sense now. Although some things were better left unsaid, I couldn't help but ask.

"Is that why you——?"

"No," Krygor interrupted, a stern look in his eyes. "I despise Marla. When I first thought you were her, and then that you might instead simply be related to her, I almost walked out of Bacchus. I have no fantasies of rekindling the past with Marla. You are more beautiful than she ever was, and that's not anger speaking. Your features are not only more harmonious, but your inner-beauty and your kind heart shine through every cell of your body, making you even more beautiful. I also later discovered Marla had many surgeries to enhance herself. So, never think that you are some kind of replacement. The chemistry between us was instant. Since then, you've continued to please me like no other."

Hearing his words and the sincerity in his voice soothed some of the ache in my chest. The strength of the almost instant attraction between us couldn't be denied. I still remembered thinking how at ease I'd immediately felt with him, and how he should have frightened me instead of turning me on the way he had. I nodded, giving him a soft smile to encourage him to continue.

"The next day, Marla begged me to buy her out of a bad contract she'd entered into with the owner of the club she'd been dancing in," he said, his dark gaze boring into mine. "The owner simply wanted to fuck her for free instead of giving her the exposure he'd promised would help grow her career. Moreover, he'd lied about the type of credits she would make there, trapping her into a much longer contract than originally anticipated."

I stiffened, a cold shiver running down my spine at the uncanny similarities between us. But the contempt in his voice whenever he said her name, and the self-derision with which he spoke told me much about how poorly that story ended.

"It was a foolish thing to do, but I threw away all my savings buying out her contract and even contracting a loan to cover the part missing," Krygor said with such self-loathing my chest constricted for him. "Marla wasn't impressed by my clan's compound. She loved its size and how many people were 'my subjects,' which she wrongly assumed would make them her servants, but she hated that it wasn't posh and fancy, with bling and glitter, like the court of a Dantorian nobleman."

I frowned at such a silly assumption. Even I, who had been forbidden access to any knowledge that didn't involve serving a man on Guldar, knew of the harsh, rough, and functional lifestyle of the Braxians. Biting my bottom lip, I held back the question burning my tongue as to her education level.

"Once she realized that me being a young Clan Leader on Braxia didn't mean I was swimming in credits and that life by my side wouldn't be an endless party, she started pulling away from me and showing her true colors," Krygor said with a bitterness that spoke volumes of the hurt he still felt.

His gaze went out of focus again, and he bared his teeth in a snarl. I couldn't decide if it was aimed at Marla, at himself, or at both.

Krygor snorted, then a sad and disbelieving smile slowly settled on his lips. "I had convinced myself that she was the love of my life. A first love that I was losing for failing to provide her with the lifestyle she deserved."

I couldn't hold back a shocked gasp at such a preposterous statement. He shouldn't be berating himself for failing the entitled bitch but remind her that he had pulled her out of a difficult situation. My expression having no doubt revealed my thoughts, Krygor smiled gently at me and caressed my face.

"Foolish reaction wasn't it?" he asked softly.

I nodded before covering his hand cupping my cheek with my own. His smile broadened then, taking in a deep breath, he sighed heavily.

"I thought with more time, I could show her the beauty of Braxia, despite its harshness, and make her fall in love with me, if only half as much as I loved her. But being human, she couldn't handle my girth without ample Denax," Krygor continued.

I cringed inwardly, less than keen on hearing such details. But I needed to know and understood that my giant wasn't lightly laying himself bare to me.

"For this reason, from the beginning, we had spaced out intercourse to prevent damaging her health by overusing the dilator. But then she increasingly used that as an excuse to deny me altogether. Like a complete idiot, I came up with the clever idea of not touching her *at all* throughout the month except when she entered her fertile period, at which point I would be relentless."

"Oh Goddess," I whispered as understanding dawned on me. "So, she didn't have a contraceptive implant?"

"She did," Krygor said matter-of-factly. "But standard implants do not work against Braxians. The fluid in our semen helps regulate the hormonal levels of a woman to increase the chances of conception. The more I release my seed inside you—including when you swallow me—the more it weakens the effects of your contraceptive."

I froze at his words. A nerve ticked on his temple while he studied my reaction. My head swam at the thought that I might already be pregnant with his child, considering I was entering my fertile period and we'd been going at it at every opportunity. Too many questions fired off in my mind, keeping me from formulating a single one.

"By the third month of our contract, Marla became pregnant with Anton," Krygor continued with a somber expression. "I broke the news to her the day she asked me to put her contract up on the public market in search of a new buyer. Thank the Ancestors, I'd included a clause by which she couldn't sell her contract to another without my consent. She wanted to abort my child, which I of course forbade."

My heart broke for him, imagining the nineteen-year-old boy he'd been—barely a man—bearing the full responsibility of an entire struggling clan on his shoulders while getting his heart ripped to shreds by his first love.

"As my Indentured Servant, she had no choice but to comply. Whatever relationship we'd had died that day. She became nothing more than a breeder for my son—and a resentful one at that," Krygor added with a deep-rooted anger. He looked down at my body before resting his palm on my flat stomach, his thumb gently caressing it in a slow back and forth. "How can a female carry a life within her for months and have nothing but resentment and contempt for it?"

I shook my head, not understanding it either. "I don't know," I said softly, caressing the silky curls of his hair. "I'm sorry."

Not every woman had strong maternal instincts. That wasn't a fault. But I never understood mothers who hated their children or wished them harm. They hadn't asked to be there. Whatever the circumstances under which they were born, they couldn't be blamed for their own existence. I had hated the male who had sired my children, but I loved both my son and daughter with all my heart. The Goddess only knew if I would ever see my oldest son again.

"Don't be," he said with a sad smile. "Marla didn't just resent the idea of being a mother, but she hated how it was messing with her perfect figure. Except, that figure was only 'perfect' thanks to breasts and butt implants, and multiple plastic surgeries. I'm stuck in this strange conundrum where I regret secretly impregnating a female against her will, but grateful for the wonderful son that came of it. Anton changed the face of Braxia and turned things around for my clan. By rights, he shouldn't even exist. For all the stupid mistakes I made in my hopeless pursuit of a cold-hearted female who was never meant for me, knowing what I know today, I would do it all again in a heartbeat."

I nodded slowly. "There is no greater blessing than our children. And the Goddess blessed you above all others for the courage you showed in protecting your child against all odds," I said with fervor. "I know of the old Braxian customs of killing hybrid children, and I've read about Anton's incredible road to success, defying all the odds. I just hadn't realized you were his sire until Luther said so. But you understand, more than anyone, what sacrifices a parent would make for the safety of their child."

"I do," Krygor said. "And your love for your daughter is but one of the many reasons I'm so drawn to you." His gaze flicked to my arm, and he once more touched my upper arm where my implant was located. "And my hunger for you is insatiable. This thing will not prevent my seed from taking root. If you do not wish to conceive—and you *will* in the next few days if you do nothing—see the doctor first thing in the morning before our departure. It will be your last chance."

My breath caught in my throat, and my eyes flicked between his, trying to make certain I wasn't misunderstanding what I could read between the lines.

"You leave that choice up to me?" I asked. "You would risk me bringing a half-Guldan child into your clan."

"I am bringing a Guldan mother and daughter into my clan," he said in a forceful and determined tone that gave me sweet shivers. "I have spent my seed inside you close to a hundred times since we've met, knowing it could take root. So yes, Hope, I am giving you the choice. But know that if and when you conceive, you *will* carry my child to term, and it will stay with me on Braxia."

My stomach fluttered at his words. Krygor had all but admitted that he wanted to sire a child on me. Far from frightening me, the thought made me feel warm and fuzzy inside. That would mean another brother for Siona who was dying for Krygor to become her papa. That would also mean me being able to remain by his side for a long time to come yet.

"And what happens when my contract ends? *I* will never leave my child behind," I said.

"Then you will have to stay on Braxia to raise it with me," Krygor said with an intensity that belied his casual tone.

"What makes you think I will conceive in the next few days?" I asked, my hand absentmindedly caressing the bulging muscles of his biceps.

"You are ripe, my *Vaya*," Krygor said in a growling voice. "Your scent is maddening."

I felt my blood draining from my face upon hearing those words. Something about it had triggered an instant fear and impending sense of doom that I couldn't explain. Krygor immediately sensed my change of mood. His smoldering expression faded, and his face closed off.

"I will not force a child on you," Krygor said in a slightly clipped tone.

I realized then he had misinterpreted my sudden fear. "You cannot impose what is willingly accepted," I said, caressing his cheek, then his lips with my thumb. "You have given me more joy, stability, and safety in the past few days than I've had in my whole life. I want everything from you, Krygor. And you can have everything from me. Everything," I whispered, chasing away the uneasiness that lingered.

CHAPTER 10
KRYGOR

I could smell Hope's underlying fear, lurking beneath the delectable scent of her undeniable arousal. My woman wanted me. Wanted *everything* from me. The sincerity in her voice, on her face, in her eyes wiped away any doubt I still felt. So why the fear?

Hope slipped her fingers through my hair and fisted them. The tender, loving glimmer in her eyes as she gazed upon me like Grace did with Anton broke the defenses I'd erected inside me after Marla. How I had longed to be wanted like this. In that instant, I finally understood beyond any doubt that I'd been so head over heels for Marla because she'd been a pale image of the female that had always been meant to be mine; my Hope, my *Vaya*, my soulmate.

"Then you shall have all of me," I said before capturing my woman's lips.

Hope yielded herself to me in that way that always made me feel like the king of the world. Her sighs in my ears and her hands on me drove me mad with lust. My lips traveled along her jawline to her ear.

"I'm going to fill you with my seed," I whispered, before lifting my head to lock gazes with hers.

Hope shivered against me, and her emerald eyes darkened. My female's consenting smile made something snap inside of me. I crushed her lips again, this time with controlled brutality. I wanted to mark her, brand her as mine forever. Inch by inch, I covered her neck, chest, and breasts with kisses and nips, from gentle to more forceful. When I reached her flat stomach, I rubbed my face all over it, inhaling her spicy scent and already anticipating the lovely aroma she would have once my seed had taken root.

And it would.

I wanted to see her belly swelling with my child and to stand by her as she delivered our newborn just like Ravik had stood by his Mercy when she'd delivered theirs. I wanted to hold my mate and child in my arms as our newborn fed at her teat.

Crouching between her legs, I lifted them over my shoulders before diving in to devour my prize. Hope's strangled cry had my cock jerking in response, eager to take the place of my tongue dipping in and out of my woman. And her inner walls seemed to share the same sentiment as their rippling ridges tried to suck my tongue in deeper.

My mind still reeled at the thought that my *Vaya* could naturally take me—all of me. The way she gripped my cock, stroking and caressing it with her ridges, constantly keeping me on the verge of ecstasy, nearly tempted me to stop feasting in order to slam my cock deep inside of her. But I needed more of her divine nectar on my tongue. I licked and lapped at her, sucking on her little numb before rubbing it with my thumb.

Although Guldan anatomy made it so that females gained far more pleasure from penetration than clitoral stimulation, the selfish part of me wanted to go down on her first. She came too quickly with my cock inside of her, and my own pleasure made me miss parts of her responses to my touches. The sound of her labored breathing, of her sultry voice calling my name and spurring me on, the way her body shivered, and her legs shook as she neared completion had become a drug to me.

Hope's body seized, and her legs slammed shut, holding my head in a vise as if intent on crushing it. I forced them open, lapping furiously at her clit while she writhed in ecstasy. Before she was fully down from her high, I climbed on top of my woman and rammed myself home. Hope's back arched off the bed, and she cried out at the initial burn of my brutal possession. It had hurt me as well, but I enjoyed pain. In the past week, I'd also come to realize my woman enjoyed a bit of roughness, as long as it remained controlled. She loved feeling a bit of danger, feeling fragile and helpless in the brutal—yet loving—embrace of her giant unleashing his passion.

And, by the Ancestors, it would be unleashed.

I started moving slowly in and out of my woman to give her a chance to adjust. The tight grip of her inner walls and their rippling ridges stroked and squeezed me with each movement. I ground my teeth against the burning urge to climax far too soon like some fucking juvenile. Yet, even as I drowned in pleasure, watching the expression of pure ecstasy on my mate's face and feeling her writhe beneath me— her pelvis gyrating in response to my movement—soon threw me into a blissful trance where nothing but the tidal joining of our bodies mattered.

With a startled cry, Hope threw her head back, and her inner walls clamped down on my cock in a painful clutch as she fell over the edge. I roared my release and slammed myself deep inside her as my seed shot into her in a rapturous flow. For a few seconds, I held my mate in a bruising hold, allowing her undulating inner ridges to squeeze my essence from me, before pumping in and out of her until the last drop was spent.

But I wasn't done. Far from it. There would be no rest for my *Vaya* this night. I would wreck her, fill her to the brim, irrevocably brand her as mine and, the Ancestors willing, impregnate her.

I pulled out only long enough to flip Hope onto her stomach.

"On your knees," I said in a voice so thick with desire it barely sounded intelligible to my own ears.

She began to comply, but still shaking from her lingering climax, she failed to move fast enough for my liking. My cock hungered to pound into her. Yanking Hope back by the waist, I pushed myself into her burning sheath with a vigorous thrust. She shouted my name in a needy moan and immediately began to meet me thrust for thrust. Nails fisting the bed covers, lips parted and breathing heavily, Hope turned to look at me over her shoulder with such naked lust that something snapped inside of me.

Reaching forward, I fisted both of her horns around their bases and pulled back. My mate cried out, her movements becoming erratic as her body shook with another violent orgasm. But I didn't stop, pounding into her sweet sex relentlessly, pressing my fingertips around the sensitive roots of her horns, wresting one climax after the other from my woman, filling her each time with my seed.

By the time we both collapsed on the bed, I had lost count of how many orgasms we'd had. I gathered my woman's trembling body in my arms, loving the burning feel of her slick skin against mine and her labored breath fanning my chest. I was still hungry for her. The selfish Braxian part of me could go on for hours—wanted to. But the gentle giant in me, her protector, her mate, took over and sheltered her even from myself.

Two years with my little *Vaya* was not enough. A lifetime would never be enough. I wanted my Hope for all eternity.

Morning found me in a cheerful spirit. While I handled my business with Roman in the small meeting room of my vessel, Tamika had come to bid a last farewell to my woman. She unfortunately had to leave before I could properly make her acquaintance, but it pleased me that Hope and Siona had a chance to say goodbye.

I went back to my quarters to retrieve the data key I'd forgotten to bring for Roman and entered just as my *Vaya* was finishing the removal of her contraceptive implant. The broker didn't buy my explanation about having misplaced the key to justify why it took me over fifteen minutes to return. Then again, Hope's flushed cheeks and lips swollen by my kisses didn't help—not that it bothered me in the least.

The depth of her gratitude as she thanked Roman and bid him farewell moved me to the core, just as it did my friend. In that, too, Hope made me feel like what we had truly meant a great deal to her.

As much as I loved my son's pleasure barges, a hefty pressure I hadn't even realized had been weighing me down lifted as soon as we left Lilith Hive. Even my girls seemed in high spirits. Yulan and Zartag were amused by my Siona's excess of energy. Braxian females were far more subdued—at least in the presence of us males. But having witnessed the antics of our Dagna's wild daughter Lissy, Siona's enthusiastic personality didn't faze them. Zartag gladly assisted my females in setting up a simulation in the much smaller holodeck on board my ship.

I seized the opportunity to sync with my king and give him a heads up on the latest changes in my personal life.

"Emperor Ardrak is trying to undercut us in every market, especially with technology," Ravik said with disgust through the vidscreen. "Why can't the fool understand that no amount of pressure from him will ever get us to align with Guldar?"

"He's getting desperate," I replied with a shrug. "The Galactic Alliance continues to grow in the Eastern Quadrant. Fewer and fewer of the major trading planets are condoning slavery. That leaves the Guldan Emperor in a tough spot. Aside from the Sarenians, he doesn't have any allies of consequence. Ardrak is waging a losing disinformation campaign. His people have no idea that your mate is half Guldan nor that she's the daughter of Gruuk Vrok. While Mercy doesn't leave Braxia often, when she does, she hides nothing of her origins. The media may still mostly refer to her as a Veredian, it's only a matter of time before all of Guldar realizes one of their own—and a female at that—thwarted their plans of enslaving us."

"Is that so?" Ravik said, leaning back in his massive stone chair, a slight frown on his brow. "If not for the risk of exposing my mate and children to even more threats, I would gladly make sure that information leaks to the Guldan population, but we will need to find a different way to spite Ardrak."

"Agreed, especially since I'm bringing more Guldans to live with us," I said nonchalantly, bracing for Ravik to lose it.

"Excuse me?" he asked in that dangerously low voice that usually had all of Braxia shitting their pants.

I took a second to admire my king. The blazing fire in his dark eyes, the permanent scowl of his strong brows further accentuated by his frown, and the snarling expression of his brutish face would justly terrify anyone foolish enough to have provoked him. His bulging muscles, even bigger than mine, threatened to tear up his shirt. Firstborn of the purest of all the bloodlines of our home world, Magnar Ravik was the embodiment of Braxian perfection. He had the giant body of a god, the terrifying face of a feral beast, the strength of an entire legion, and the combat skills that none could rival. Ravik was the only male alive I knew for certain would defeat me. His strength alone would make me want to follow him, but I served my king because I deeply respected the man and his relentless efforts to fight for his beliefs and the prosperity of Braxia.

"I have bought the Indentured Servant contract of a Guldan female who entered into it to flee Guldar," I said matter-of-factly. "She and her juvenile daughter are now both under my protection and will stay with me in my compound."

Ravik's anger faded, his face taking on a neutral expression although his eyes narrowed ever so slightly. He remained quiet for a moment. After years sitting on the Magnar's close Council, I knew to wait quietly while he pondered all the angles and consequences of my revelation.

"Mercy will certainly take umbrage to an enslaved Guldan female," Ravik said at last.

I gave him a stern look. "The Dagna will stay out of my personal business," I said in a hard voice. "Hope is not a slave, and both she and her daughter will have a much better life in my care than the one I just freed them from."

Ravik raised a taunting eyebrow, the shadow of a smile playing at the corner of his mouth. "You are taken with that female," the Magnar deadpanned.

I shifted in my chair, annoyed to be asked such a thing. Although he'd said it as a statement, the underlying question didn't elude me. Except, Braxian males didn't speak of their feelings. It was unbecoming.

"I intend to keep them once the contract ends in two years," I said in the same neutral voice he'd previously used.

Ravik's face softened—or at least, took on that expression that passed as soft for a Braxian.

"I'm happy for you, my friend," he said in a gentle voice. "Few deserve happiness as much as you do. But my mate is still rarer than yours."

I snorted and then chuckled along with him. There had always been a bit of an unspoken competition between us—initiated by him—since the day I'd decided to spare my hybrid son. The silly man had gotten it into his head that he was beneath me for having caved in to the pressure of his father to hurt his own hybrid child. What Ravik failed to accept, even though I'd tried to drill it into him, was that he'd been even younger than me at the time, and that I'd already been the leader of my clan—unlike him. Had my father still been around when I impregnated Marla, there is no question he would have done everything in his power to force an abortion. I wanted to believe that it wouldn't have changed the outcome but was grateful I'd never had to face the horrors Ravik did.

"You are welcome to your female. As beautiful as she is, Mercy is too wild and headstrong for me. I like my woman to be cuddly and submissive," I said smugly.

"You, cuddly?" Ravik said before bursting out laughing.

"You can mock other Braxians' tender sides the day you stop turning into a puddle every time your daughter bats her eyelashes at you," I retorted, not fazed in the least.

A different man I might have punched for challenging my toughness, but we were in the same boat.

Or so I hope.

We discussed a few more matters pertaining to my Council duties, in particular some of the trade opportunities Roman had found for us. I also didn't miss a chance to brag about my new personal business ventures which were promising to further elevate my status and that of my clan's.

"When will you be back?" Ravik asked as we prepared to end the conversation.

"Unless there is an urgent need for me—which doesn't seem to be the case—I will make a short detour by Venus Hive for a day or two to see my firstborn and his family before returning home," I said, both worried and excited at the thought of seeing Anton and presenting Hope and Siona to him. "So, I should be home in about two weeks from now."

"Lilith Hive is way too far," Ravik mumbled. "Try to avoid going there too often."

"Sorry you miss me so much, Magnar. But I'm already taken," I deadpanned.

"Fuck off," Ravik said. "And get your ass home soon."

I burst out laughing as he ended the communication. Once more, I thanked the Ancestors for my son Anton without whom I probably never would have developed such a genuine and close friendship with our king. A quick look at the clock indicated I had enough time to call my son to confirm that we would be coming to see him, and still catch up with my girls in the holodeck before lunch.

However, just as I reached a hand to call him on the vidcom, the system shut down and the lights dimmed. I tapped the button on the intercom, but no response.

"Ella, status?" I asked the ship's artificial intelligence.

"All ship functions performing at optimal efficiency," Ella replied in her monotone, synthetic voice.

"Then what is happening with the lights and the coms?" I insisted, wondering if the A.I. itself was defective.

"Coms are fully functional," Ella responded dispassionately. "However, your access to the coms and all other ship systems are denied."

My brain froze for a second, thinking I must have misheard her. "What do you mean *my* access is *denied*?" I asked in a dangerously low voice.

"The ship is now under the command of Hunter Faolen Velkis. Further instructions will follow shortly," Ella said.

"Who the fuck is Faolen Velkis?" I demanded, my mind racing.

The A.I. didn't respond. Fuming, I attempted to com the bridge. Silence there as well. To my relief, the doors to my quarters opened. I raced to the holodeck first to make sure my girls were all right, only to find them in the hallway with Zartag, looking frightened and confused.

"Krygor, what's going on?" Hope asked, her eyes filled with worry.

"That's what I'm trying to figure out," I said, wrapping an arm around her waist and caressing Siona's hair reassuringly.

Hope gratefully leaned against me. The trusting expression on her face, both stirred my protective instinct and fueled my wariness as I had no clue how the fuck to fend off a hacker's attack. A physical enemy I could crush, but all this technological stuff was Mercy's domain.

"Could this be the same thing the Guldans had done to the Magnar's ship?" I asked Zartag—my engineer—as all four of us headed towards the bridge.

"No," Zartag responded, shaking his head. "Or rather, it's highly doubtful. They had infected his vessel with a virus that had been slowly damaging the ship's system to force them to abandon it. Mercy has upgraded all our vessels to prevent us from falling victim to this again. From what little I've managed to gather so far, whoever is messing with us has merely locked us out of every system, but the ship itself remains whole."

"I need to know who is fucking with us and why," I said in a growl, forcing myself to slow down so that my females could keep up without having to run.

"Do you think… Do you think Luther could be behind this?" Hope asked, a mix of guilt and fear straining her beautiful features.

"Everything is possible, my *Vaya*, although I have a hard time seeing when he could have pulled this off considering I bought back your contract only yesterday, and we came to the ship within a couple of hours after that. It wouldn't have given him enough time to plan and execute this," I said pensively. "This strikes me as something that would have taken a few days to set up."

Despite our issues with Guldar and the random threats from their Emperor Ardrak, the Guldans had not launched any new attacks on us since we'd ousted them from Braxia and Ravik had sent back the broken corpse of Ambassador Lorik.

At last, we reached the bridge. The doors parted to reveal Yulan, his hands flying all over the navigation board, a furious expression on his face as he visibly failed to regain control of the vessel.

"Report," I said to my pilot as soon as I entered the bridge.

"I'm completely locked-out," Yulin said, seething with anger. "The ship is changing course, and I have no clue where the fuck it's heading."

Zartag got onto the copilot's console to attempt to break us free of the pirate's hold, only to curse moments later in the most inappropriate fashion.

"How the fuck did they get in so deeply, and so quickly?" he grumbled. "No one had access to the ship, but this is at least a two-day job, but more like four or five days."

The ship's screen suddenly turned on, displaying a stunning male with dusty blue skin, midnight blue eyes, and long black hair through which peeked the small, crown-shaped horns on his head.

"Actually, it only took me one day," the Sarenian male said.

"You!" I whispered, recognizing the male who had observed me at Bacchus when I'd gone to fetch the key to Hope's collar.

Hope shuddered violently. I tightened my embrace around her waist to comfort her.

"We meet again, Councilor—or do you prefer Clan Leader Aldriss?" the male asked teasingly. "Then again, you Braxians aren't much for formalities. So, I'll call you Krygor, and you can call me Faolen."

"I don't give a shit what you call me or what you're called," I snarled. "What the fuck are you doing to my ship? And what do you want from me?"

"Actually, Krygor, *you* weren't my target *at all*—at least, original-ly," he said in a pretend apologetic voice. "I was only hired to secure the lovely Siona. But then I met her mother, and realized I wanted Hope for myself," he added in a purring voice. "You were gorgeous before, my Beauty, but now that the beast has made you whole again, you're beyond breathtaking. I cannot wait to mate with you after the Hunt."

My head jerked towards Hope who stared at the Sarenian with a horrified look on her face, laced with confusion and a great deal of fear. She pressed herself against me, blinking the way one would when trying to remember something.

"Do you know this male?" I asked between my teeth.

Although subtle, I didn't miss her slight hesitation before vigorously shaking her head. Something didn't add up, but there would be time for me to question her further later.

"I-I don't remember ever meeting this male, and yet, he looks familiar," Hope said, sounding baffled, but sincere.

"All will be explained in due time," Faolen said with a dismissive wave of his hand.

"I don't need any of your damn explanations," I snapped. "You will release my ship at once. My mate isn't for you, and whatever pervert you're working for will *not* get his hands on my daughter."

Siona's small hands tightened around my arm and, like her mother, she pressed herself against my other side.

"Mate? Daughter?" Faolen asked, looking both stunned and amused. "I can see why you would wish to claim them as such. Unfortunately, you became an unexpected addition to my mission. You have made some powerful enemies, Krygor. I have no personal quarrel with you, but business is business. Enjoy my beautiful Hope while you still can. In three days, you will meet your fate."

"Is Sarenia so eager to go to war with Braxia," I asked, in an icy tone.

"Although I am taking you to Sarenia, it isn't a political matter... Well, the main reason I'm bringing you in isn't political. But one of the people who wishes your demise definitely has a political agenda," Faolen conceded. "No one knows where you currently are nor where you are headed. As I disabled your com before you could confirm with your son that you would be visiting him for certain, your Magnar will not begin to worry about your disappearance for at least two weeks. By then, it will be much too late."

"What you are bringing to Sarenia is your own death and destruction," I said, relishing in advance the sound his bones would make as they shattered beneath my fists.

"I am not so foolish as to underestimate you, Krygor. Your physical prowess is legendary," Faolen said, leaning back against his seat. "For this reason, as soon as we're done with this little conversation, you will leave the bridge and not set foot back on it," Faolen added with a hard voice. "You may freely come and go to your quarters, the mess hall, the holodeck, and the training room. I strongly advise you three Braxians make extensive use of the latter—you'll need it. Apologies to your crew that they got dragged into this, but I cannot leave witnesses behind that could jeopardize the welfare of Sarenia."

"You think you can keep me off my own fucking bridge?" Yulan snarled.

"Yes," Faolen said smugly. "I absolutely can. Try to tamper with the ship in any way, and I will punish you. Rest well, eat well, and train well. I will see you in three days."

The Sarenian ended the communication before I could reply. Zartag immediately went back to work on the console.

"Stop," I ordered, my eyes still locked on the black screen before me.

When Faolen had appeared on screen, his first words had been to reply to my engineer's last comment. This meant he had eyes and ears on us. He'd also known about my conversation with Ravik. Although there were no cameras inside any of the private quarters, with some tweaks, the intercom system could be used to eavesdrop on conversations within. However, I doubted he'd used such a primitive method, and simply tapped into my call with the Magnar.

We needed to come up with a solid strategy. But with him spying on us, any of our initiatives would be completely useless.

"All hands, please proceed off the bridge immediately," Ella's voice said, startling me out of my reflections. "Life support on the bridge will no longer be provided in two minutes."

"Son of a krillik," Yulan muttered under his breath.

"Come on," I said in a clipped tone, leading my females off the bridge.

"What if we—" Zartag started saying.

"No," I interrupted, gesturing for him to remain silent before glancing up in the general direction of the camera on the bridge.

His eyes widened in understanding. I fought the urge to smack him across the head for being so slow. As my engineer, he should have been the one to warn me of this risk. Although a genius when it came to tech, Zartag tended to become too absorbed on an individual system rather than looking at the big picture in a crisis situation.

The bridge doors closed behind us, the light on the security lock turning red confirmed we'd been effectively locked out of the bridge.

"I'll meet you both in Yulan's quarters," I said to my men.

They nodded, and I escorted my females back to my own.

"I'm so sorry," Hope said as soon as we entered my room, guilt and despair etched on her face. "I never thought they would come after you, too. If only—"

"Hush, my *Vaya*," I interrupted, drawing her gently into my embrace. "I am glad they caught me with you, because now I can protect you and find a way to get us back home safely. It only spared me the trouble of hunting down whatever location they'd taken you to. You did nothing wrong. No matter how dire the situation may seem right now, we *will* find a way out. I just need you to trust me."

"I do," Hope said fervently. "With all my heart, I do."

"I do, too," Siona said in a small voice.

Letting go of her mother, I crouched in front of the little girl who stared at me with wide eyes filled with fear.

"Do not be afraid, Siona," I said in a soothing voice. "You are mine, now; *my* daughter. I will kill anyone who dares try to harm you. So, you be strong, and hold your head up with pride, no matter what hardships come your way. Do not feed your enemy with your fear. Make them waver with your determination. All right?"

"Yes, Kry… Yes, Papa."

The timid way in which she corrected herself melted my heart. Siona looked warily at me, waiting to see if I would reject her. I smiled with approval, and the tension in her frail shoulders melted. She gazed at me with such joy and wonder that my throat tightened.

"I know you will save us," she said with both conviction and emotion. "I prayed to the Goddess to send me a Papa who would make Mama happy, and who would keep us safe. And she sent you, bigger, stronger, and so much nicer than I hoped, right when we needed you the most. I trust you. And I'm not afraid anymore."

Siona closed the distance between us and threw her arms around my neck before hugging me fiercely. I returned her embrace, caressing her soft hair in a soothing fashion. Feeling the weight of Hope's stare on me, I looked up to find her eyes brimming with tears of gratitude and an emotion I didn't dare name. I rose to my feet with one arm around Siona's shoulders and drew her mother against me. My mate and I exchanged a tender kiss, and then I brushed my lips against my daughter's forehead.

Holding on to my females, I swore to the Ancestors that our enemies would pay... dearly.

CHAPTER 11
HOPE

Three days had gone by since Faolen had taken control of the ship. Krygor, my wonderful giant, had gone out of his way to try to reassure Siona and me that everything would be fine. Yet, I could sense his frustration, anger, and helplessness. He huddled with Yulan and Zartag throughout the day, plotting, scheming, and looking for solutions in vain. Despite the fear gnawing at me, I still believed that somehow, the Goddess and Krygor would see us through. She hadn't gotten us this far only to abandon us now. I just prayed there wouldn't be too great a hardship awaiting us before we got free on the other side.

Therefore, to the best of my ability, I presented him with a positive front, made even easier by Siona. My daughter worshipped Krygor. The fierceness with which she believed he would defeat our enemies and take us home to Braxia was both impressive and inspiring. My throat still tightened at the loving way he had claimed my baby as his. Siona had dreamt of a strong father figure, and he exceeded everything she'd ever wanted—everything *I* had ever wished for. Him claiming her this way implied he'd also claimed me as his mate. It was silly to be so head over heels for a male I barely knew, but my heart told me I'd finally found my soulmate.

I envied the Korletheans' ability to know beyond any doubt when they had found their other half thanks to their psionic powers. But the strong chemistry between us couldn't be denied. Krygor made me happy. So, this new mess only made me angrier. Why couldn't we just be left alone? Had my daughter and I not suffered enough? Was it not finally our time to live the way we wished with the one we wanted? Why the fuck did random men think they had the right to control and use us to their benefit, their pleasure, heedless of our own aspirations?

These thoughts allowed me to get through those three days without going insane. Rather than giving in to the fear that threatened to turn me into a terrified wreck, I clung to my anger, fed off of it, and used it to fuel my determination to live the fairy tale life Krygor had given me a glimpse of.

Whatever it took, we would be free.

However, the Sarenian truly had us at his mercy… at least for now. The couple of times Krygor and his men tried to tamper with the ship, Faolen immediately took punitive measures. The first time, he locked the room the men were in and increased the temperature to sweltering levels until they began showing clear signs of heat stress. The second time, he shutdown life support in the room he'd locked the men in, only reactivating it once they had lost consciousness.

After the men recovered that second time, Faolen warned them that if they tried to pull another stunt, the punishment would be applied ship-wide, therefore affecting Siona and me. My daughter and I had been willing to take that risk, but not the men.

Without access to the bridge and being locked out of the ship's system or any computer—even personal ones—we had no idea of our current position. With each hour ticking, tension in our midst steadily grew until, at long last, the pale, whitish-blue outline of Sarenia appeared through one of the large windows of the mess hall. Another half hour later, Ella's synthetic voice on the intercom relayed Faolen's order for us to gather in the ship's cargo hold.

To my relief, despite his seething anger, Krygor didn't argue and complied. We all followed in his wake. Minutes later, we felt the slight tremor of another ship docking with us. Heart pounding into my throat, I slipped a shaky hand into Krygor's, who gently squeezed it in a reassuring gesture. Siona leaned against him on his right side, while he wrapped a protective arm over her shoulders. Yulan and Zartag flanked us.

As per the ship's artificial intelligence's instructions, we had taken position at the back of the hold. My heart leapt in my chest when its doors opened with a soft hiss revealing Faolen, surrounded by what looked like two dozen Sarenians armed to the teeth. As soon as they entered, Faolen's men fanned around the room, weapons drawn and trained on us—or more precisely on the three Braxians.

My blood ran cold at the sight of our kidnapper in the flesh. I knew this man. I didn't know how, but I most definitely did. Everything about him screamed familiarity and danger. I shuddered and pressed myself against Krygor. My giant let go of my hand to protectively draw me to him, his strong hand resting on my hip. Although I drew strength from him, the minute Faolen would start speaking, every cell in my being screamed that a rift would be created between all of us. It made no sense, but I strongly believed it, and it nearly choked me with fear.

"Krygor Aldriss," Faolen said with that soft, sultry, yet very manly voice that I would have found extremely seductive under different circumstances. "You are even more impressive than in my memory."

"But apparently not enough to stop this foolish plan of yours," Krygor responded with a harsh tone.

"Believe me, Clan Leader, I think my clients are fools to go after you, but it is not my job to question motives. I merely execute the contracts given to me. And you, Councilor, are about to make me very wealthy. I might even consider retiring after this one." His gaze flicked to my daughter, giving her a quick, approving once over before turning towards me. His midnight blue eyes slightly darkened, and a soft, seductive smile stretched his sensual lips. "After all, I will soon go through *drortak*—my final molt—at which point I will settle down with a mate."

The intensity of his stare left no mystery as to his underlying meaning. I shuddered as Krygor's arm tightened possessively around me, and a menacing growl rose from his throat.

"You have much bigger problems to worry about than these two females," Faolen said with an almost apologetic expression. "Whatever your thoughts about Sarenians, and regardless of tensions between our peoples, we treat our females well. They may not think so right now, but Hope and her daughter will be happy with us."

"No, we won't! We want nothing to do with you!" I exclaimed.

"Oh, my Beauty," Faolen said, as one would speak to a naughty child. "Come to me, Hope."

My body seized as he spoke the words with a vibrating voice. In that instant, despite having no memory of hearing it before, I knew beyond any doubt that I had.

Goddess, what did I do? What did he make me do?

Against my will, my feet moved forward. Refusing to let go, Krygor yanked me back against him. I pushed back for him to free me, while shaking my head with a pleading look on my face. Words failed me to tell him that I had no control over this. But a series of blue light dots appearing all over Krygor's body indicated the Sarenians had turned on their tactical aiming lasers.

"Let her go, Braxian. You can't win this one," Faolen said in an almost bored voice. "I would rather not have my men shoot. You will find our stuns are highly unpleasant."

Seething, Krygor let go, murder burning in his eyes. With the stiffness of a machine, I marched to Faolen, calling onto my anger to keep me anchored. The way he looked at me with genuine awe—or at least genuine in appearance—both fueled my anger and confused me. The Sarenian gazed upon me like someone with a serious infatuation. There was a time, I would have wished for such attentions, but not now.

When I stopped a couple of feet before him, Faolen raised a hand towards my face. I jerked my head back in disgust.

"Stop, stay still," he immediately said, compelling me with that vibrating voice I couldn't resist. My anger rose another notch, feeling violated to have my body thus forced to act against my will. "My Beauty," Faolen whispered, his fingers caressing my horns with an air of wonder on his face. "I must thank you, Clan Leader for restoring Hope. She was stunning before, but now she's pure perfection. Do not fear for her. I will love her well."

"I do not want you!" I shouted while my body still remained where it stood.

"In due time, you will, my Beauty," Faolen said, caressing my cheek with his knuckles.

"I will kill you if you touch my mate," Krygor said with a voice so chilling, cold shivers ran down my spine.

"No, Clan Leader, she is soon to be *my* mate," Faolen responded. "As for the delightful little Siona, the Prince is quite eager to make your acquaintance. Somehow, I suspect he might make you his consort."

"She's a child!" I shouted, fighting in vain the compulsion that kept me from clawing at his beautiful face.

"In two weeks, she will be twelve, which means she's come of age," Faolen said with a shrug in that reasonable tone that implied his comment was logical and irrefutable.

"You want to give my daughter to some sick pervert who wants to force himself on a child. No planet but yours deems twelve to be age of consent," I argued with rage.

"That sixteen or eighteen years of age is a nonsensical rule established by adults to control their offspring because you do not have a proper system to raise children," Faolen said, starting to sound slightly annoyed. "Siona has already blossomed, because her body knows she's ready. And the Prince is fifteen, of an age with your daughter. Below the age of twenty-one, we have a three-year age difference cap for matings."

Although I still didn't want my child forced into something she wasn't ready for, and especially not under duress, a huge wave of relief washed over me knowing I'd been mistaken as to the type of male they'd intended for her.

"But—"

"Hush, my Beauty," Faolen gently said with his vibrating voice, interrupting me. "There will be plenty of time for us to discuss the ways of my people—soon to be *your* people—before Siona's Mating Hunt." I watched helplessly as he turned to my daughter before addressing her with his vibrating voice. "Come to me, Siona. Quietly."

His eyes flashed with a soft, bluish glow. Although it hadn't happened to me just now, I recognized the effect. That sealed whatever doubt I still had about having been subjected to his mesmerizing ability before. Of what little I knew about Sarenian, the flash established the binding link between the Sarenian and his target.

Despite her visible will to protest, Siona approached, compelled to obey. For a moment, I feared the hatred in her eyes would stir Faolen's ire, but he merely smiled, seeming more impressed by her spirited nature than irritated.

"I am glad you are not some meek little sheep. The Prince will love you," Faolen said in an amused voice before switching back to his vibrating one. "Go to the docking bay with your mother and get onboard the shuttle. You will wait patiently for me there. You will also not cause any trouble or attempt to flee. Once you've settled in the shuttle, you may speak with each other. Go now, my loves."

Unable to resist the command, I looked at Krygor over my shoulder as we marched stiffly out of the hold. His dark gaze locked with mine. Despite the fury marking his strong features, the contempt and condemnation I'd expected were nowhere to be found in his obsidian eyes. Instead, a possessive and determined glimmer shone bright within them. We were his, and my giant wouldn't stop until he had us safely back by his side. That, too, gave me strength.

I hated that Faolen had separated us and could only surmise he wanted to discuss certain things with Krygor in our absence. What could it possibly be? Who hated Krygor with such passion as to risk the wrath of the entire Braxian empire? Yet, as much as I feared for my man, it reassured me to know Faolen wouldn't harm him, at least for now. He'd had ample opportunities to kill the men without hurting Siona or me when they tampered with the ship. That Faolen hadn't done so confirmed he wanted them alive and in good condition.

When we reached the docking bay, two more Sarenians were standing guard by the hatch leading into their own vessel. Like Faolen and his men, these two males were ridiculously handsome. But then, the Sarenian species as a whole was reputed to be gorgeous. One of them waved us forward, inviting us to enter the hatch into the large shuttle.

To my relief, Siona didn't seem scared, only angry. She took my hand and might as well have been the one leading me in, such was her determination. Once inside, we were taken to the front cabin where we settled into comfortable white leather seats with black accents. The seatbelts automatically wrapped around us. The Sarenian touched a wand-like short device to the buckle of our belts, and the white light on them turned red. I didn't need him to tell me he'd just locked us in. After giving me an appreciative once over, and a curious one to my daughter, the Sarenian left us without a word.

As soon as he was gone, and despite the seatbelts restraining us, Siona leaned over to give me a half-hug and then looked me straight in the eyes with a stubborn expression.

"Don't be scared, Mama. Papa will find a way to free us," she said in a firm voice.

"Yes, sweetheart. He will."

But even as I said those words, I addressed a silent prayer to the Goddess that she make them come true.

It took nearly ten minutes before Faolen and his men joined us on the shuttle. Although I didn't see Krygor and his clansmen, I had no reason to doubt they had been in the back cabin with the other Sarenians. We completed the flight to the surface in silence. For most of its duration, Faolen sat in the copilot's chair, having an intense conversation on his com in his mother tongue. The lack of stress or tension seemed to indicate he was merely coordinating things for our impending arrival.

As soon as we landed, he took Siona and me out of the shuttle and directly into a fancy hovercar that awaited us right next to the landing pad. I twisted my neck in vain to catch a glimpse of Krygor or his men, but no one else had come out of the shuttle by the time our vehicle took off.

"Where are you taking us?" I asked at last, holding Siona close to me.

Faolen, sitting facing us, casually crossed his legs and tilted his head to the side with a gentle smile.

"We're going to your new, temporary home: the Serail of Deleo, our Capital City," Faolen said kindly. "You will be given private quarters in the Atrium, a quiet space reserved for Nymphs such as you both. The Siren Gatina has been assigned to your care and will provide you with mentoring and guidance in preparation for the Hunt."

"Nymphs?" I asked, confused.

"Gatina will explain everything," Faolen replied.

"What are you going to do to Krygor?" I asked, my voice accusing.

Faolen gave me a sad smile. "I'm afraid you will see for yourself what will happen to the Braxian," he said with an apologetic expression. "His fate is not in my hands. But I think Juntel is a fool for pursuing this. You will understand soon enough."

His furtive glance at Siona made it clear he didn't want to go into details in her presence. I almost pressed the issue, but considering what terrible things Sarenians considered normal, the Goddess only knew what he was withholding.

Faolen then launched into a description of our surroundings, pointing out a few landmarks, and sharing anecdotes about them and the city. I considered telling him we weren't here on a fucking sightseeing trip but chose to hold my tongue. Antagonizing him would not benefit us in any way, and I wanted to spare Siona from any additional stress. Under different circumstances, I would have enjoyed discovering this new world that most people knew so little about due to their bad standing with the Galactic Alliance.

I half-listened to him while my gaze roamed over the city. The architecture blended a clever mix of hard and soft lines. White and silver dominated, with black accents and glowing blue swirling ornaments. Most buildings were no more than three stories high, but they spread long and wide. Stunning landscaped gardens surrounded them, with trees, bushes, and tall flowers whose leaves and petals all boasted varying shades of blue from light pastels to bright navies and deep midnight hues. Interspersed among them, bright specks of red and yellow flowers added some drama.

While a majority of males padded along the streets—most of them wearing nothing but sandals and a long, flowy white skirt—a number of females could also be seen, the majority Sarenians with a sprinkle of other species, mainly humans and Aveans. Just like the males, the females were all stunning. They wore sinfully short, sleeveless dresses with plunging necklines that dipped right beneath their navels, giving naughty glimpses of the round curves of their breasts. Each of the females wore an armband on their right upper arm, some of them displaying a glowing gem of varying color, while the band of others had an empty socket where the gem should have been. The armbands themselves came in two colors—at least that I could see—silver and black.

"You will get one, too," Faolen said, as if he'd read my mind, which technically Sarenians couldn't do.

"What is it?" I asked.

"A mating band," he explained casually. "The black one indicates a Temptress. The silver band indicates a Siren. As Nymphs, you both will receive a white one. The gem means you've been claimed and are currently the concubine of a Hunter. The gem's color corresponds to the Hunter's status within our society. It is also shaped according to his house's sigil. But Gatina will be able to give you more details about it."

"Why are there no other teenagers around?" Siona asked, her tone somewhat belligerent.

Faolen smiled, amused by her attitude, before casting a quick glance outside. "They do not hang around this area of the city. They find it too boring and stiff. They are in the Academia areas, in the Palisades and the Woodlands; all sectors where family pods are settled, where the young can run wild, have fun, and burn the excess energy of youth in between their studies. The Capital is for adults."

One building, twice the height of the others loomed in the distance. It looked as if a giant sphere had erupted out of a pyramid that had itself been stabbed with three glowing spears on each side.

"That's the Emperor's Palace," Faolen said. "This dome-shaped building is the Arena. For now, we're going to that flower-shaped one: the Serail."

It indeed reminded me of a flower, with giant, ovoid pods forming each petal and a pointy tipped one standing vertically in the center. Far too soon, the hovercar approached the building, which turned out to have another circular ground floor beneath the 'petals' which I hadn't noticed from a distance. Massive doors leading to the underground parking opened like the giant maw of a beast, swallowing us whole. The driver stopped right in front of a lift. Faolen didn't wait for him to come open the door for us, doing the honors instead.

Once again, I fought the urge to flee. We wouldn't get very far with our current outfits and horns which shouted our uniqueness to the whole world. We entered the lift which flew us up to the twelfth floor of the central tower. The doors parted, revealing a beautiful common room with plenty of seating, from traditional couches and chairs to bean bags and cushions. A couple of giant vidscreens hung on opposing walls of the circular room. A few tables surrounded a decorative fountain in the middle of the room with a small indoor garden, which explained the soothing, flowery scent that had greeted us upon entering the space. A pair of large doors occupied the center of the back wall while a dozen or so regular sized doors were spaced evenly along the circumference of the room.

A stunning Sarenian female, sitting on one of the black leather couches on the left side of the room, unfolded her crossed legs then rose to her feet. The same barely-there white dress the females outside had worn hugged her sexy curves in all the right ways and flattered her dusty blue skin. Cerulean highlights graced the long, curly locks of her shiny black hair. She strutted her way towards us, chest thrust forward, hips swaying, a provocative smile playing on her lips. She barely spared Siona and me a look before her silver eyes locked onto Faolen. I couldn't quite guess her age, but I assumed late twenties.

Our kidnapper seemed more amused by the female's obvious efforts at seduction than actually tempted or aroused.

"Gatina," Faolen said in greeting with that signature sultry voice of his. "You look beautiful as ever."

"You flatter me, Hunter," Gatina said with a throaty voice that matched the smoldering look in her stormy eyes. "And yet, you'll ignore me at the Hunt."

Faolen chuckled. "You are one of the most popular Sirens of Deleo. Hunters in your age bracket do not welcome old-timers like me competing for their females."

The way Gatina pinched her lips hinted that she'd previously heard that argument from him and still didn't take kindly to it.

"The whole point of the Hunt is for the best male to claim his prize," she argued with a pretty pout.

"And the one of your age group will," Faolen said in a sympathetic voice.

"Age no longer matters after the second molt," Gatina persisted.

I fought not to roll my eyes at such a display of lack of self-respect. How many ways did Faolen need to express that he wasn't interested before she got a clue? Desperation, groveling, and naggy unrequited love were *not* sexy. A quick glance at Siona confirmed she was making her 'are you serious' face while staring at Gatina. I discreetly pinched her. Although she schooled her features, Siona visibly bit the inside of her cheeks to keep herself from laughing. That made me want to laugh, too. Once more, I thanked the Goddess for blessing me with such a strong child, even in the face of adversity.

"As I'm about to have my third, it matters to me," Faolen said, a sliver of irritation finally creeping into his voice. "Now be nice and meet Hope and her daughter, Siona: our new Nymphs."

Gatina mumbled words of greeting with obvious reluctance. I didn't sense any animosity from her, only a borderline obsessive infatuation and wounded feelings over his unwavering rejection.

"I trust their quarters are prepared?" Faolen continued.

"Yes, this way," Gatina said in a resigned tone.

We followed her to one of the side doors. It opened onto a fancy room fit for royalty. From the imposing bed dressed in luxurious bedding, to the elegant dressers and embroidered cushioned benches, no expense had been spared. Large windows gave a breathtaking view onto the large landscaped park outside, the busy streets framing it, and the walkways where the local population strolled leisurely.

"This is the Nymph's quarters," Gatina said in a friendly tone. She walked up to an inconspicuous section of wall and waved a hand before it. The hidden panel immediately opened revealing the hygiene room. "Each quarter has its own private hygiene room, although a pool is accessible through the main doors at the back of the common room." She walked up to the dresser and gently tapped the pile of clothes on top. "Please put these clothes on while I go show your mother her quarters."

Siona frowned, an antagonistic expression descending on her features. She opened her mouth to retort but caught herself at the last minute before looking up at me. I almost said no as well, a quick glance at Faolen told me he would compel us with his power if we attempted to resist. Still, I didn't want to give him the impression I was whipped and could be easily bullied. I reached for the dress, unfolded it, and then held it up before me. To my relief, it wasn't the overly revealing outfit I'd feared they'd try to force onto my baby. Although a little short, the dress would fall right above Siona's knees, and the round neck provided a more than respectable and demure cleavage.

I extended it to my daughter with a stiff nod. Her frown deepened, but she didn't argue.

"Gatina will stay with you while I have a quick talk with your mother," Faolen said to my daughter before gesturing for me to exit the room.

Giving him a suspicious look, I hesitated for a second, a million paranoid thoughts crossing my mind. Would Gatina use that to mess with my daughter's mind? Did Faolen want that private time to mess with mine again?

He doesn't need your consent to lure you away.

Helpless anger burned within me at this reminder. I hated this mind-control bullshit with a passion. I needed to figure out a way to make myself impervious to it. Turning to Siona, I gave her an encouraging smile and caressed her left horn before following Faolen out of the room. He took me to the adjacent bedroom, similar in size to the one assigned to my daughter, but with a décor clearly more mature, with deeper colors, simpler lines, and more subdued lighting.

"Thank you for not making things more difficult than they need to be," Faolen said with gratitude.

"I'm not doing it for you," I snarled, allowing my anger to show.

He gave me that insufferable amused smile that made me want to smack him.

"I'm well aware, but thank you, nonetheless. I take no pleasure forcing my will upon you."

"Then don't!" I snapped back. "We've met before, haven't we? What did you do to me? What did you make me do?" Faolen's slightly embarrassed expression further made my stomach knot painfully. My hands fisted by my sides. "Answer me, damn you!"

The Sarenian waved a dismissive hand. "What does it matter? It's done and—"

"I want to know how you fucking used me to trap the only other man to have shown me kindness and treated me with respect," I gritted through my teeth, getting up in his face. "I want to know how you violated me."

"I did *not* violate you!" Faolen exclaimed, a look of outrage—anger even—descending on his far-too-perfect features. That took me aback. "Yes, I did use you, but that avoided bloodshed on all sides. I am a Hunter. My job is to bring back my quarry as smoothly and painlessly as possible."

"Bring back your quarry to be raped and murdered," I retorted bitterly.

"You will not be raped, my Beauty."

"Do NOT call me that. Now show me what the fuck you did!"

I expected him to tell me off and just explain what he'd brought me into this bedroom for. Instead, he sighed heavily and gave me a frustrated look laced with something akin to shame.

"Remember," Faolen said with that vibrating voice I so hated.

And then memories of Luther luring me into the alley and what followed flooded my mind. But the worst were the ones of me getting up in the middle of the night after the chime of my former collar had rung. I'd removed the fake gem Faolen had attached to the collar and connected it to Krygor's com, allowing the Sarenian to hack into it. I sat there helplessly watching as Faolen ripped all the codes and relevant data that he could from the device and established a backdoor access to the ship through the com. After Faolen had—in appearance—disconnected, I'd returned Krygor's device to its place and affixed the gem back into the collar. The chime had once more resounded, leaving me dazed and confused, all memory of my betrayal erased.

I stared at the Sarenian through the tears of rage blurring my vision. "I hate you," I hissed with all the vitriol I could muster.

"No, you don't," Faolen said, lifting his chin in defiance. "You can't."

"Excuse me?" I asked, disbelieving.

"We are Attuned, Hope. You may be angry with me—rightly so—but you can never hate me, just like I could never leave you behind," Faolen said in a soft voice, a tender look descending on his features. "We are meant to be together."

I recoiled, staring at him in horror. "You're insane! I will *never* be with you. I've already given my heart to another. And, anyway, only Korletheans feel this Tuning business."

"Wrong," Faolen said, taking a step closer to me. "Most Veredians can't see a soul's frequency but will clearly feel the tingling sensation at their nape when in the presence of their soulmate. Dantorians also feel the Tuning. And we, Sarenians, can see the wavelengths of a soul. Not as accurately as Korletheans, but clearly enough. I assure you, my Beauty, we are Attuned."

I shuddered and took a couple of steps back, moving away from him, only to have the Sarenian advance to close the distance between us.

"Do not fear me, Hope. You are scared and upset right now, but in due time, all will be well. On my life, on my honor, I promise to make you happy."

"If you want to make me happy, then free us, my daughter, my man, and me!" I said angrily.

Faolen's face closed off. But it was the glimmer of pity in his eyes that worried me. "I am needed elsewhere. Gatina is a bit spoiled, but she has a good heart. Learn all that you can from her. It will make your assimilation to Sarenia a lot easier." Although gentle, his matter-of-fact tone creeped me out even more. "We will meet again in two days. Whatever you may think of your current situation and of me, know that I do want your happiness. The Braxians' fate is out of my hands. Their story will *not* end well. It is best you start making your peace with it. And remember, Hope, I could take your mind from you, but I have not. Truth will be the foundation of our relationship. But, should you ask for it, I will gladly take away your pain."

He means take away my memories of Krygor.

"What are they going to do to him?" I asked in a shakier voice than expected.

Faolen looked out the large windows at the building I'd remembered him calling the Arena. Cold dread washed over me. And yet, a sliver of hope blossomed in my heart. I'd seen my man fight. Despite his massive frame, he moved with the swiftness of a krillik, and his strength struck me as godlike.

"My giant will defeat anyone in the Arena," I said, lifting my chin with defiance. "He will crush their bones and feast on their flesh."

Faolen snorted and raised an amused eyebrow. "Time will tell, my Beauty. And heed my advice; learn all that you can from Gatina."

With a final nod, the Sarenien turned around and left my room, his gait so smooth and graceful he almost appeared to glide. And yet, there was something lethal to it, like contained power and fury that could be unleashed in a heartbeat, devastating everything in its path.

And that predator had set its eyes on its prey: me.

CHAPTER 12
KRYGOR

Sitting on the far too narrow wooden platform that also served as my bed, I strained my ears to listen to the steps approaching down the corridor. The cells where they held us were meant for wild beasts, some of whom we shared the holding area with. Although they clasped our wrists and ankles with magnetic shackles, we weren't currently restrained in our movements. To make sure my men and I didn't join forces to break our way out, they had put us in separate cells with an empty one in-between. I would have expected some vicious predator instead to make sure we didn't try anything.

I had no clear idea of how much time had gone by since they'd brought us onto the surface. Based on the light cycle, we'd been caged here for at least one day, and it was now mid-afternoon. We'd only received two meals yesterday—if the measly portions could even qualify as such. Although, to be fair, they would have likely been deemed generous for most other—scrawnier—species. Still, being in an arena meant an upcoming battle for which I needed to save my energy.

The muffled sound of two voices rose above the three sets of approaching footsteps. I exchanged a glance with my men, one on each side of my holding cell, indicating for them to be on their guard but to remain seated.

My heart skipped a beat as, through the bars of the cells, I caught a first glimpse of the newcomers entering from the right. Shock quickly gave way to a seething rage. While I made no effort to hide the murderous glint in my eyes, I schooled my features into a more neutral and contained expression.

The three males stopped before my cell: two Sarenians and a Guldan. One of the Sarenians, clearly of noble status judging by his traditional black robe made of fancy fabric embroidered with a shimmering blue thread, stood slightly behind the other two. The second Sarenian stared at me with a malicious glee that threw me for a loop. It took me a second to realize the oddness of his gaze stemmed from him having mechanical eyes. The cruel smile on his face spoke of a personal score to settle. And yet, I'd never met that male before. But as confused as his visible hatred made me feel, it was the silver-haired, black-horned, and blue-eyed Guldan Ambassador Hartuk Tellin that retained my attention. The hard glint in his cold gaze left no doubt he intended a painful death for me.

"Councilor Aldriss," Hartuk said in his usual polished and articulate fashion. "It's been a while since our last meeting."

"You mean since we kicked your sorry ass off Braxia," I said dispassionately. "I didn't think you'd be so foolish as to mess with us again."

"In case you haven't noticed," Hartuk said, his voice hardening, "you're in no position to make threats. If you were wise, you'd try to get on my good side and back into the good graces of the Guldan Empire."

"Your good side will be the one I will have crushed into a pulp with my fist," I deadpanned. "And I will fuck your Empire in the ass… no lube."

"Cocky little shit," hissed the Sarenian by his side. His voice sounded strange, unnatural. "As arrogant and self-righteous as that half-breed bastard you sired. I'm going to enjoy hearing you scream."

I narrowed my eyes at him. "What crawled up *your* ass, you scrawny blue rat? I don't believe we've met."

"*You* don't know *me*, but *I* know *everything* about you and that vermin son of yours," the Sarenian replied, his voice filled with venom. "Everything he's done to me, I will do to you a thousandfold. No one will find your remains, except for that thick Braxian cock of yours, which I will send prettily wrapped to that son of a diseased whore you sired."

I stiffened, understanding suddenly dawning on me. My gaze flicked to his crotch, hidden by his fancy robe, then moved back up to his left shoulder. It appeared normal beneath his clothing, but then modern medicine could repair a badly damaged limb. Although I'd never seen the male, I'd heard of the incident back on Venus Hive when a Sarenian had cornered Grace at the opera house and attempted to rape her. From all accounts, Anton had intervened just in time and smashed the male's shoulder.

My son had made a brutal example of that Sarenian. He'd castrated him, burned his retinas, and slashed his vocal cords, ensuring he would never rape another female or use his ability to mesmerize anyone ever again. Afterward, Anton had put the Sarenian on display in a cage at the main junction between the Commons and the VIP sections of Venus Hive, the busiest area of his space station. It had served both as a warning to other patrons, and as a means to further humiliate the male who had dared go after his woman.

I couldn't have been prouder of my son.

"Ah, you were the idiot who couldn't keep his cock in his pants," I said in a conversational tone. "Funny, I would have expected your voice to be higher pitched after getting relieved of your cock and balls. But then, getting your vocal chords slashed would mess with things. No wonder you sound like shit."

"I will fucking kill you!" the Sarenian screeched, his voice finally hitting the high notes I'd imagined. "But before I do, you and all of Sarenia will watch me destroy your Guldan whore's ass in the middle of the Arena, and then fuck that cunt into a pulp."

My blood immediately began to boil upon hearing the threat to my woman. My pulse picked up as the first tingles of battle rage reared their heads. I called upon all my willpower to rein myself in. Going berserk right now would do me no good. Even with my enhanced strength, I wouldn't be able to break through these bars. I needed to bide my time and wait for the right opportunity.

However, I didn't miss the frown of the noble Sarenian at the back, and the severe glance he cast upon his companion at the mention of harming my woman.

"You don't have a cock," I replied to the castrated Sarenian in an icy voice.

He gave me an evil grin. "You'd be surprised what Guldan technology can do these days."

Rising to my feet, I slowly advanced towards the bars of the cell. The nobleman at the back didn't move but the other two men took a couple of steps away to keep out of range from me.

"Anton should have put you out of your misery the first time," I said in a dangerously soft voice. "I will rectify that omission before I leave this rock. See that you stay away from my woman, and I might make your death a little swifter, but it will be just as painful."

"You little—"

"Enough, Juntel," Hartuk snapped, interrupting the Sarenian. "I didn't come here to listen to your ramblings. You can settle your score with the Braxian after I've completed my business with him." Turning back to me, the Guldan Ambassador gave me a hard stare. "You certainly fail at making friends, Clan Leader. It also seems you will bear the punishment for both your mistakes and those of your inner circle. You see, Emperor Ardrak is quite displeased by your people throwing his alliance back in his face. And moreover, he's quite angry at the treatment your Magnar has inflicted upon one of his greatest scientific minds, Ambassador Lorik Zorak."

"That freak was insane," I said in a growl. "He killed the child our Dagna was carrying and would have surgically transformed her into a fucked-up copy of her deceased brother who Lorik was obsessed about. You should thank us for having rid you of that headcase."

"Rik had his issues, but he was nonetheless a Guldan envoy, and a brilliant mind," Hartuk said with a shrug. "As a Braxian, you understand well revenge to restore one's honor. You will be made an example of. You are but the first of a long list of Braxians who will learn their proper place in the greater scheme of things. Your barbaric people will serve the Guldan Empire. Too bad you won't be around to witness it. See you tomorrow in the Arena. I, too, will enjoy your pain."

Without another word, Hartuk and the freak Sarenian called Juntel turned on their heels and walked away. After a few steps, the Guldan Ambassador's stopped to look at the noble Sarenian who had remained in front of my cell.

"I'll catch up," the noble said in a distracted voice, gesturing for his two companions to keep going.

The others hesitated before complying. My eyes narrowed as the noble took a few steps closer, staying just shy of my reach. I realized then that he was much younger than I'd first believed. Tall and muscular—although on the lithe side—he wasn't in his early twenties as I'd initially assumed but appeared to be in his mid to late teens.

"You Braxians are even more impressive in the flesh," the young Sarenian said pensively. "Your presence here is stirring quite a few passions and a great deal of unrest. Tomorrow, half of my people will cheer for your success, while the other will hope for your demise."

"And what do *you* hope for, young pup?" I asked.

The young noble snorted. "Pup… You certainly are irreverent," he said, looking amused rather than offended.

"Prince Zerien! Please step away. It isn't safe!" a male voice exclaimed followed by the pounding of multiple feet running towards us.

My curiosity as to his identity and the reason for his presence here immediately faded, replaced by murderous intent as understanding dawned on me.

"You so much as touch my daughter and no amount of guards, no arenas, and no beasts will keep me from tearing you apart, limb from limb," I said in a low, growling voice.

"Step back, Braxian!" one of the guards that had come to escort the Prince shouted at me, his blaster trained on me. "I said back off!" he yelled.

"Enough," Prince Zerien said in a calm voice. "Clan Leader Aldriss will not do anything silly. I am expected elsewhere, anyway."

His cool demeanor despite my threatening stance commanded a begrudging respect from me, especially in someone so young. Zerien turned and started walking away before stopping after only a couple of steps.

"As for your question," he said, looking at me over his shoulder, "I hope you prevail."

With one final enigmatic smile, the Prince walked away.

~

Morning came quickly. Instead of the regular small meals our guard usually provided for us, they brought highly nutritional energy bars, similar to the ones consumed by gladiators before battle. It made sense as, while spectators enjoyed watching the warriors spill blood all over the Arena, seeing them puking their last meal held no appeal whatsoever.

I chowed down my ration, grateful for the surge of energy the meager portions of the last couple of days had deprived me of. Barely a half-hour later, the shouts and cheers of the crowd above us confirmed the day's festivities—or at least shows—had already begun. From the sounds reaching us, I surmised gladiators were facing off against some roaring beasts, although different from the ones caged in our section of the holding areas. It baffled me that the latter didn't rattle in their cages to try to get at us. You'd almost think they'd recognized us as predators like they were.

Three guards came to fetch my men and me, each one stopping in front of our respective cells. To my annoyance, my guard spoke a command in Sarenian, and my shackles immediately activated, forcing my arms and legs slightly open before lifting me a couple of inches above ground. Helpless, I levitated towards the guard. He turned around to head towards the entrance to the battleground. Although the shackles kept me immobile, they also kept me floating at a safe distance behind him. The other two guards repeated the process with Zartag and Yulan.

Near the gates, a mean looking Guldan stood by a large crate sitting atop a hovercart, waiting for us. By the time we reached the gates, the clamoring had stopped, replaced by a single male voice addressing the audience. I couldn't quite make out his words, but from what little I perceived, he appeared to be announcing us.

The gates parted, giving me a first view of the massive arena, triple the size in length, and double in width of that of the usual gladiator battlegrounds. But then, considering the size of some of the beasts that had been caged around us, it made sense to give them some wiggle room for combat. Oval shaped, with large monitors giving a perfect view to spectators regardless of their seating position, the Arena had seen its fair share of spilt blood as evidenced by the darker patches on the oddly grainy texture of the ground. It seemed hard, but I couldn't tell for sure, levitating as I was.

To my surprise, an almost solemn silence greeted our entrance. My gaze roamed over the people in attendance—mainly Sarenians with the odd humans, Guldans, and Aveans scattered in their midst—before zeroing in on the imperial box. Emperor Nemrox sat on his throne, flanked by two stunning Sarenian females, and surrounded by a few high-ranking officials and guards. On each side of his large box, slightly smaller and lower boxes contained more nobles. But it was the one on the left that held my gaze. Prince Zerien sat in a lesser version of his sire's throne. Beside him, as would a consort, my Siona had settled on a cushioned bench. A couple of meters to her right, the Sarenian Juntel sat next to an empty bench. I assumed it belonged to the Guldan Ambassador Hartuk currently standing by the railing of the balcony, a hovering microphone floating before his face. And further right, my beautiful Hope stared at me with wide eyes, sitting with her back straight next to Faolen. Like with the Emperor's box, a number of other guests and guards filled the back of the Prince's box.

Despite the jealousy burning in my gut at the sight of the Hunter next to my woman, relief flooded me to see both my females unscathed. I pushed the negative sentiment to the back of my mind and focused on my current predicament. As we approached the center of the Arena, three circular panels on the ground opened, and tall metal poles rose from the openings. My guard led me between the two tallest poles located directly in front of the Imperial box while his companions led my men to the shorter poles on each side of my pair.

The Guldan with the hovering crate stopped next to me before opening the container. The sight of the chains and whip within finally put an end to the mystery. With undisguised eagerness, he hooked a chain to my left wrist shackle. I suddenly contracted my biceps. The male recoiled, foolishly thinking I was about to strike him when he knew better that the shackles effectively prevented me from reaching out and snapping his neck.

"Let's see how smug you are when I whip the skin right off your back, you savage," the Guldan hissed in response to my mocking smile.

"Do your worst," I said provokingly. "By the time I leave this arena, your blood will cover me far more than my own."

The sliver of fear in the Guldan's pale green eyes only fueled the pre-battle adrenaline slowly building within me. He mumbled something unintelligible then went to hook the other end of the first chain to the left pole. Repeating the process, he attached a chain to my right wrist and hooked it to the right pole, leaving me with my arms spread wide open. Only then did the guard disable the levitation from my shackles. Planting my feet firmly on the hard, gravelly ground, I braced for what would follow.

Unlike me, my two clansmen weren't stretched for a flogging but had both wrists bound by a single, two-meter long chain to the short pole in front of them. It gave me hope they would be spared my 'punishment.'

"Clan Leader Krygor Aldriss, as a High Councilor of Braxia and representative of Magnar Ravik, you are hereby sentenced to one hundred lashes for the torture and brutal murder of Ambassador Lorik Zorak perpetrated by your King, as well as the assassination of his men by yourself, your clansmen, and other Braxians," Ambassador Hartuk said in the hovering microphone.

Considering Lorik's horrible actions, which had indeed earned him a slow and agonizing death, the sentence was laughable. However, arguing it would be pointless.

"This first part of the sentence will be carried out by Kenor Lorik, Ambassador Lorik's brother to avenge his family's honor, and by Juntel Lenaen, in retribution for the torture, maiming, and humiliation Anton Aldriss has subjected him to," Hartuk continued in the same solemn voice. "For the second part of your sentence, as you had condemned Lorik's men to face a horde of rabid joarkals while weaponless, so will you and your clansmen face off against the most vicious Sarenian wild beast with your bare hands. May the Goddess have mercy on you, for we shall give you none."

Even as he spoke, Juntel rose from his seat and approached the left corner of the box. He climbed a handful of steps only visible on the inner side of the balcony, and then he took a step forward. From where I stood, it looked as if he was walking off the ledge, but he ended up on top of a hovering platform that took him down inside the Arena. I itched with the need to rip his spine right out.

My eyes flicked to my woman who appeared engaged in a heated discussion with Faolen. I didn't need to hear her words. Her body language screamed her outrage at the 'punishment' about to be meted out on me.

If she only knew…

The Guldan—Kenor—picked up a pair of bullwhips from the crate, drawing my attention. He then moved the hovercart carrying the container a little further out of the way while Juntel made his approach. That leather would bite hard and would definitely scar. And yet, no fear entered my heart; only the anticipation of crushing my enemies. I exchanged a glance with my men, silently warning them not to waste their strength trying to break free too early. Despite our tremendous strength, without battle rage, breaking these chains would require us exerting too much energy with no guarantee of success.

Juntel walked in front of me with a sadistic grin. Unlike Kenor, who took position behind me, the Sarenian stopped slightly to my side, clearly wanting to see my face while they carried out their 'sentence.' That suited me just fine. Looking at my prey would get me into berserker mode faster.

I took in a deep breath and allowed my mind to sink into the warrior's trance taught early on to our young, a state of consciousness that kept the warrior focused on the battle at hand instead of pain, on his technique, and both the strong and weaker parts of his body to know what to protect and what to leverage.

The whistling of the whip was followed by a snapping sound of the leather making contact with my flesh and Kenor's voice calling out "one." The sharp sting made me smile. Considering the Guldan's size, I had expected him to put far more muscle into the lashing. This would be a cakewalk. My smirk visibly infuriated Juntel. Shouting "two," the Sarenian lashed at me sideways, striking my lower back, the tip curving around my waist to hit my right rib. My smile broadened at his even weaker blow.

The two males unleashed their fury on me, alternating blows and calling them out loud. I embraced the pain, dampened by the adrenaline and endorphins building within me. A slow chuckle escaped me, gradually turning into full on laughter. It both unnerved and enraged my tormentors, who accelerated the speed of their lashes and attempted to increase the strength. But already, after barely fifteen lashes each, the men were tiring, which only made me laugh harder. It was a deep, powerful laughter, invigorating and liberating, but that sounded completely deranged, even to me.

"That's the best you could do, worms?" I asked at last, my words slurred by the beginning of battle rage descending upon me and the endorphins flooding my system. "I'm going to bathe in your blood."

As I gave myself over to the warrior's bloodlust, I embraced the throbbing pain in my back and along my sides, further fueling my fury. All coherent thoughts fled my mind, replaced by a single thought: obliterate. A deep, rumbling growl rose from my throat. Low at first, the sustained sound grew gradually in volume as my skin heated to feverish levels, my blood boiled, and my muscles bulged with primal energy.

Hands fisting around the chains attached to my wrist shackles, I began to pull with an animalistic roar. A gasp rose from the crowd that had mostly been silent through my 'punishment,' aside from the occasional mumblings.

Startled, Kenor and Juntel temporarily faltered in their lashing. The Sarenian exchanged an uneasy look with the Guldan who I couldn't see behind me.

"You cannot free yourself from your restraints, you freak," Juntel said in a voice that failed to come across as confident and contemptuous as he'd hoped.

The delectable scent of his blossoming fear made my nose twitch and my bloodlust perk up another notch. As the two idiots resumed their 'torture' on me, my own men began screaming under the effort of pulling on their respective chains. As a Berserker, once I'd gone into battle rage, members of my clan—or anyone I deemed as such—would benefit by sharing my enhanced strength and pain tolerance so long as they remained within range of my Berserker aura.

Despite the growing panic on Juntel's face, the Sarenian pursued the lashing, calling out the thirty-sixth blow. And then, with a loud clinking sound, one of the chain links gave way, freeing my right arm. Without missing a beat, I whipped my arm behind me. The chain still attached to my wrist flew out and wrapped around the legs of the Guldan behind me. I yanked hard. With a terrified cry, Kenor fell on his back and stared in horror as the chain quickly dragged him to me.

The crowd erupted in a savage roar, an even mix of shock and excitement that only galvanized me further.

When the Guldan tried to get back on his feet, I backhanded him, reveling in the sound and the feel of his cheekbones crumbling under the strength of the blow. He screeched in agony and fell back down. Stepping on the tip of the chain wrapped around his legs, right beneath his knees, I yanked the chain still attached to my wrist with all the strength I could muster. His bones shattered beneath the metal's tightened grip, eliciting another high-pitched scream from my prey. The divine sound echoed straight to my cock, which hardened as the metallic aroma of metal wafted to me from the open wounds where his leg bones protruded through the skin.

Leaning down, I caught the Guldan by the horns and, pressing my foot to his face, I pulled... hard. Kenor's hands helplessly clawed at my leg and arms while emitting gurgling sounds. And then he went limp as his horns gave way. I stumbled back, blood spraying over me and my former tormentor's mangled face. One horn held in each hand, I turned toward the Sarenian.

Eyes wide with horror, mouth gaping, he slowly backed away from me, his head shaking in denial. I wiped the blood trickling in front of my eyes with the back of my hand, then licked it, my gaze never straying from my prey. The whip slipped out of Juntel's hand, falling to the ground with a soft thump, then he turned around and fled towards the Imperial box.

On instinct, I attempted to pursue my prey, but the wretched chain on my left wrist prevented me from giving chase. But I would taste his blood along with that of the Guldan's I'd just wrecked. Still holding on to the severed horns, I grabbed the remaining chain with both hands. I pulled with all my might, an enraged, drawn-out cry all but tearing my vocal chords until one of the chain's links finally gave. I stumbled back and, flowing with the movement, spun around to dash towards my fleeing target.

Juntel had already reached the wall. Seeing him stepping onto the hovering platform gave me wings as I ran faster than ever before, the roar of the crowd spurring me on. By the time I reached it, the Sarenian was already almost at the top of the wall. Without breaking stride, I jumped as high as possible and, using the horns fisted in my hands as pickaxes, I climbed the wall after him.

Panicked shouts rose from the box as I caught up to my quarry. The sound of chairs toppling over and people scrambling back reached my ears as I reached the edge. Holding myself on top of the stone railing with one hand, I snagged Juntel's ankle with the other before he could jump off the ledge into the box. He screamed and fell forward, almost bashing his head on the floor. Hanging on to the ledge, he screamed for help.

From the corner of my eyes, I saw Faolen stand protectively in front of my woman and Prince Zerien do the same for my daughter. The guards rushed forward, their weapons trained on me, but the Prince lifted his hand in an arresting gesture.

"Juntel is not inside the box," Zerien said in a cold voice. "Until he has completely exited it, all is fair within the Arena."

"My Prince! Mercy!" Juntel cried out.

With a savage grin, I let myself drop down the wall, my weight too great for the Sarenian to keep hanging on. I let go of my prey's ankle right before hitting the ground so that I could lessen the impact of my fall into a roll. Juntel slammed into the ground with a loud thud, the wind knocked out of him.

"What were you saying about fucking my mate?" I asked, my voice so thick and growly the chances of him understanding a single word that came out of my mouth were slim to none.

Half-stunned, Juntel attempted to scramble back onto his feet, but my own coming down brutally onto his lower leg snapped his tibia in two. The Sarenian collapsed, his high-pitched scream like nails on glass due to his messed up vocal chords. Slowly, methodically, I snapped the joints of each of his limbs before lifting him by the neck and bashing the back of his skull against the stone wall of the Arena. It exploded like an overripe melon, splattering blood and gore everywhere.

Dragging him over a couple of meters behind me, I flung him with all my strength to the middle of the Arena. I'd initially considered throwing him into the box, but even through the madness that fogged my mind, the thought his corpse might hurt my mate or daughter kept me from acting.

Turning around, I faced the Emperor's and the Prince's boxes, although my gaze remained locked onto the Guldan Ambassador Hartuk. My men, who had finally managed to break their chains free of the pole restraining them, came to stand on each of my sides.

Without a word, I licked the blood and gore off my hand, then spread my arms wide. A smug grin stretched my lips as I taunted the Ambassador.

Here I am, you son of a krillik. Your move.

CHAPTER 13
HOPE

I stared in awe at my giant… my beast. Covered in blood and gore, Krygor stood defiant under the cheers of the crowd. Instead of fear, disgust, or distress at the sight of such violence perpetrated by my man, pride filled my heart. Strangely, I also felt some kind of bloodlust. It had begun as an odd tingle all over my skin at the same moment Krygor had started emitting that growling sound before pulling at his chains. Even now, energy coursed through me, and a part of me regretted he hadn't prolonged Juntel's execution.

Still, the sight of his back lacerated by the lashes disturbed me. And yet, Krygor seemed oblivious to what had to be excruciatingly painful.

"Interesting spectacle you are offering us, Ambassador," Prince Zerien said in a slightly mocking tone.

The young prince confused me. We had only met him when Gatina and a small contingent of guards had escorted us to the Arena. The way he'd looked at my daughter, like the Goddess herself had appeared before him, threw me for a loop. So far, he'd shown nothing but respect to my child and none of the lurid, sleazy looks or gestures I'd expected. Like all Sarenians, he was stunningly gorgeous. Young, fit, polished, under different circumstances, he matched the type of young male I would have loved my daughter to bring home—at least, based on his behavior so far. But I couldn't forget why we'd been captured in the first place. Nevertheless, he could have saved Juntel but chose to let my mate exact his vengeance. For that alone, the Prince had scored quite a few points with me.

Ambassador Hartuk turned rather stiffly towards Zerien, a controlled expression on his face. He ran a hand over his left black horn before flicking some wavy locks of his shoulder-length silver-white hair.

"Indeed," Hartuk conceded with a nod. "Now you see why, despite their resistance, Braxians must be subdued and brought to our side. When the Great War begins anew, we do not want to fight against them. Hopefully, your sire will see the wisdom in committing to our side to bring these savages into the fold."

Siona bristled at that comment and glared at the Ambassador. Zerien cast a glance in her direction, an amused smile stretching his lips before looking back at Hartuk.

"Or maybe I should convince the Emperor to ally with them instead and be on the winning side of the war," Zerien deadpanned.

Hartuk failed to hide his initial shock at that comment. Regaining his composure, he leveled a cold stare on the younger male. "You would so easily turn on the alliance between our peoples?" the Ambassador asked with an icy tone.

"There is no official alliance between Sarenians and Guldans," Zerien replied with a dismissive wave of his hand. "According to all the prophecies, the Great War will start around the time my father will step down from the throne and my reign will begin. The Veredians have been building formidable alliances, and their technology rivals, if not surpasses, yours."

"But the Veredians will not be the ones ruling the galaxy in the next decade. The Galactic Council will," Hartuk hissed. "They will force you into their way of life, deprive you of your choices and freedoms, and cause the financial collapse of your planet."

"The Braxians have joined the Council and banned slavery on their world," the Prince countered, holding Hartuk's gaze. "If such a 'primitive' species—as you label them—has managed to turn their economy around, then a more advanced race such as ours should be able to prevail as well."

"What are you saying, Prince Zerien?" Hartuk asked in a clipped tone.

"Merely that your little show has given me food for thought," Zerien replied nonchalantly before caressing Siona's cheeks with his knuckles. My daughter stiffened but didn't pull away. "For now, however, the spectators are growing restless. You should proceed with the rest of your plan."

Hartuk harrumphed with a stiff nod then gestured at someone I couldn't see. Some kind of horn blared, and a hush fell over the audience. As the note slowly faded, an eerily expectant silence settled on the Arena. And then, on the left, narrower side of the Arena, the walls slid open with a grinding sound followed by the roar of a beast. Cold shivers ran down my spine, and my skin erupted in goosebumps.

A nightmarish beast slowly came out through the large doors. Well over two meters high and at least five meters long, its body reminded me of a red and black crocodile with a long, club-like tail covered in vicious spikes. A few more spikes rose along its neck and the length of its shoulders. The creature didn't crawl but walked on six legs. The head resembled that of a worm and opened like a flower to reveal a terrifying maw filled with razor-sharp teeth. Two rows of disproportionately tiny eyes lined the sides of its face—although it could have also been its neck. Four thick stinger spikes protruded from its back in an almost perfect square. I'd heard of a Verlenk but never imagined they'd be this dreadful in the flesh.

The beast lifted its head, bobbing it slightly as dogs sometimes did when sniffing the air, although I couldn't see any snout on the creature. My stomach knotted as it continued its slow advance towards Krygor and his men. They had no weapons, and the chains still attached to their magnetic shackles would weigh them down and slow their movements.

"Don't be scared, Mama," Siona said with the same unshakable confidence she'd displayed ever since Krygor had claimed her as his daughter. "Papa will defeat that beast with the same ease he crushed those two idiots."

"Watch your tongue, female," Ambassador Hartuk hissed before I could respond. "Your whore of a mother may have taken you off Guldar, but once the Prince is done fucking your tight cunt, I'll make sure to remind you of a female's place."

"Leave my daughter alone, you piece of shit!" I shouted, jumping to my feet, at the same time the Prince turned to the Ambassador with an outraged expression on his young face.

"You dare?!" Hartuk exclaimed.

As if in slow motion, I saw his hand rushing towards my face to backhand me. Initially paralyzed by shock, I started moving too late, fearing the brutal blow that would no doubt split my lip open, if not knock out one of my teeth. But the impact never came. Moving at lightning speed, Faolen blocked Hartuk's arm before kicking him squarely in the chest, sending him flying back against the stone railing of the box.

Faolen's murderous glare echoed that of every other Sarenian guard surrounding us, and the outraged look of the handful of nearby females. Hartuk's two guards, who had reached for their weapons, hesitated in light of the overwhelming condemnation from their hosts.

"You strike an ally over a female? A slut?" Hartuk asked, disbelieving, while rubbing his chest.

"Disrespect or threaten this woman again—" Faolen said through his teeth.

"Or her daughter," Prince Zerien interjected.

"And you will get far more than a kick to the chest," Faolen concluded.

Hartuk opened his mouth to argue, but Emperor Nemrox rising from his throne to approach our box silenced him.

"Females are created for a male's pleasure and to prolong his bloodline through the pains of pregnancy," the Emperor said in an icy tone that gave me chills. "And in exchange for those precious gifts, a male's duty is to reciprocate that pleasure, protect the females, and provide for them. Raise a hand again to a female on my home world—any female—and I'll chop it off myself and feed it to you raw."

I instinctively knew the Emperor would make Hartuk eat his own hand through compulsion. However horrible that picture was, a sadistic side of me I hadn't known existed actually wished to witness it.

"Emperor—" Ambassador Hartuk said with a shocked expression.

"Silence!" Emperor Nemrox interrupted. "Tread carefully, Ambassador. I am starting to be tempted to side with my heir as to the value of this alliance."

The roar of the beast had all our heads snapping towards the Arena where the three Braxians had begun a lethal dance with the creature. My heart skipped a beat as it charged my giant. Spinning both of his chains joined together, Krygor stood his ground until the last minute. Then just as the Verlenk opened its terrifying maw to swallow him, my man swiped the chains at it. The blow resounded like an explosion. The beast's head violently jerked left, making it stumble out of balance. Zartag and Yulan, moving in sync, rammed it on the side to topple it over.

To my shock, instead of lying helplessly on its side, the Verlenk pushed itself back on its short feet. The four spikes on its back suddenly shot out, attached to tentacle-like appendages, and attempted to spear the men. They scrambled out of the way, while the creature continued to charge them, reeling in its stingers only to launch them at the men again.

With the Braxians scattering in different directions, the Verlenk focused its attack on my giant. It simultaneously attempted to strike Krygor with two of its stingers at once. He dodged the first and knocked the second out of the way. But before he could regain his balance, the other two stingers darted towards him.

"Krygor!" I shouted, jumping to my feet when he fell to the ground onto his back.

He caught the first stinger with both hands, moving his head out of the path of the second in extremis. The Verlenk attempting to retract the stinger my man had caught ended up yanking Krygor off the ground. Hanging on to the base of the stinger, Krygor flew above the beast's head to land onto its back. For a moment, I thought he had lost his mind, but then I realized he stood in the creature's blind spot, preventing it from effectively targeting him with the other three stingers. While the beast lashed at him in vain, Krygor tore the stinger he still held off the tentacle it had been attached to.

The Verlenk screamed in pain and reared on its four back legs. Yulan seized the opportunity to swing his chains at its exposed neck, while Zartag swiped his own at the creature's hind legs. The beast roared again and shot out its three stingers. Krygor caught one, and each of his men did the same, allowing the creature to reel them onto its back like my man had. The Verlenk thrashed about to knock off the men, but they made quick work on tearing off its remaining stingers.

The agonized cries of the beast hurt my ears. A part of me felt sorry for it. And yet, I joined my voice to the encouraging cheers of my daughter and the crowd as the Braxians hung onto the spikes on the creature's back to remain seated atop it and stabbed at the Verlenk's back using its own poisoned stingers. Within seconds, a red foam appeared at the rounded tip of the beast's head. Its movements became jerky while its massive spiked tail frantically swished from side to side. In an apparent desperate last move, the Verlenk lashed at its own back with its tail. The men jumped off just in time for the vicious spikes of the tail to embed themselves into the creature's lower back.

With a drawn-out groan, the Verlenk toppled to the side. Its clawed feet twitched, a shudder coursed through it, and then it went still.

The crowd erupted in a powerful roar of approval as my own soared with gratitude and relief. My feet carried me to the ledge of the box. Eyes locked with mine, Krygor also took a few steps towards me. Even bloodied and covered in gore, my giant was the most magnificent beast I had ever laid eyes upon. In spite of our current predicament, I felt no fear. His Berserker energy continued to course through me, making me strong, invincible. My skin tingled, but it was a different fire that was now setting my body ablaze. A predatory grin stretched his lips—the hungry smile I'd grown to know well in our far too short time together, making my nipples harden and moisture pool between my thighs.

"Your father is a formidable beast," Prince Zerien said to Siona with undisguised admiration.

Although his words echoed the thoughts that had just crossed my mind, the disruption in my lusty trance with my man irritated me.

"He is the best and the strongest," Siona replied, her voice bursting with pride. "And he will destroy anything and anyone who threatens him and his family."

"And yet, that savage won't leave this planet alive," Hartuk said with a condescending tone, clearly displeased by the outcome of his little show.

"No, Ambassador Hartuk," I said in a hard voice, my eyes never straying from my man. "It is *you* who will not make it off Sarenia in one piece if you don't leave in all haste. What he did to those two men will be nothing in comparison to what he'll do to you."

Krygor's arms and legs straightened, once more controlled by the magnetic shackles around them, and his body levitated as a group of six Sarenian guards entered the battleground. The same occurred to his men. My gaze followed them as they were escorted out.

I sat next to Gatina in the imposing hot tub of the Serail's spa, large enough to accommodate a dozen adults. Hamara, another Sarenian, sat across from us. In the deeper pool adjacent to us, a human female named Nadia was performing some water aerobics. Tall, lean, with long, candy pink hair and a few piercings along her left eyebrow and navel, Nadia was a beautiful fifty-two-year-old female, obsessed with maintaining her flawless appearance. I couldn't blame her, considering how breathtaking everyone looked on this planet.

For the hundredth time in the past five minutes, I looked over my shoulder through the glass wall at my daughter lying face down on a massage bed while a female slave was placing hot stones along her spine.

"Seriously, your overprotectiveness of the young one is getting silly," Gatina said with genuine confusion. "She's in a safe environment, and she's grown."

My head snapped towards Gatina, and I glared at her. "She's hardly grown, she's a child!" I exclaimed, annoyed beyond words that they didn't understand something so simple. I turned to Nadia who was running in place with water up to her shoulders. "Your people understand well that you're not an adult at twelve years of age."

Nadia stopped running although she kept walking in place. "Adulthood and age of sexual consent are two very different things," the human said. "Children are becoming sexually active at younger and younger ages. Aside from some highly conservative colonies, a majority of humans have their first sexual encounters in their early teen years, meaning around your daughter's age."

"But it is of their own free will and with someone of their choosing," I countered. "And even then, it is discouraged. They do not have the maturity to deal with the consequences. What if they get pregnant? Can you imagine children raising children?"

"It would be a disaster, which is why it doesn't happen here," Gatina explained patiently. "All of your species are trying to fight the natural order of things by imposing all kinds of laws and rules. Our bodies know when they are ready for coupling, and that's when we blossom into puberty. There's also a reason we get horny during our fertile cycles. But unlike the rest of the galaxy, instead of shaming, denying, or controlling, we embrace our normal and natural desires."

"And then you end up with a bunch of teenaged mothers," I replied in a cold voice.

"Yes," Gatina said with a dismissive shrug. "I had my first child a few weeks shy of my thirteenth birthday and gave birth to my ninth one five months ago."

"You have nine children!" I exclaimed, my eyes all but popping out of my head.

"I have eleven," Hamara said smugly while Gatina nodded with an amused smile.

My head turned towards Nadia who burst out laughing.

"Nope, not me. I have no use and no patience for children. I just like to fuck," Nadia said with a lecherous expression on her face. "Give it to me hard, give it to me soft, missionary, gangbang, anal, you name it, just give it to me. I can never get enough cock, especially not when it's attached to those ridiculously hot and sexy Sarenians. They are the best lovers any woman could want. They will not leave you alone until you've come at least five times. Even now, I wish one of them would fuck me into next week. I'm what the Sarenians call a Temptress: a single, willing female, either no longer fertile or taking contraceptives—although back home they call me a nymphomaniac."

My face heated at the crude language, and the unrepentant smile on her face left me speechless, which had the other two females giggling.

"Nadia isn't the only foreigner to have come to Sarenia specifically to find sexual fulfillment without the judging and shaming of their own worlds," Gatina explained. "Hamara and I are what we call Sirens: single, willing females that are still fertile. As you may have noticed, our males outnumber us four to one. The Serail system was put in place to avoid the bloodshed that used to occur because of men fighting over females, especially for a chance to keep their bloodlines going."

"With the Hunt, it is all about the survival of the fittest," Hamara said. "The best male catches first the most coveted females. Any female he manages to catch, he fills with his seed and then moves on to the next. The more females he inseminates, the greater the chances one of them will bear him an offspring."

"Although, another could catch that same female during the Hunt, and spill his seed inside her as well. So, if she does conceive, it may not be the child of the first Hunter," Gatina specified.

"True," Hamara conceded. "However, some Hunters will want to increase the chances of conceiving with a specific female. Therefore, if he manages to catch her, he will insert his gem in her armband. That effectively eliminates her from the Hunt. For the next month, she will live with him, and he will bed her daily to try to impregnate her. It is a great honor to be so chosen," Hamara insisted at the sight of my horrified expression.

I examined the faces of all three women, shocked that they would consider it natural and normal to basically be used as sex toys and broodmares by their males.

"And what of those children they keep conceiving on you?" I asked, speechless. "Hamara, you say you have eleven, and Gatina nine. And yet, I've been here three days and haven't seen a single child here or any of you leave to go care for them."

"Oh, fuck no!" Gatina exclaimed with a horrified expression. "I'm still too young to deal with that kind of responsibility. I wouldn't trust myself with one child, forget nine."

"I'd be even worse," Hamara confessed without the slightest remorse. "Like Nadia, I do not have a single maternal cell in my body. I would make a lousy mother, but I take pride birthing beautiful children for our greatest bloodlines and for proper parents to raise."

"You birth children that you abandon?" I asked, my voice barely higher than a whisper from shock.

"I realize this sounds horrifying to you, especially seeing how protective you are of your daughter," Gatina said in a surprisingly understanding voice. "Like I said earlier, we approach sexuality and reproduction very differently from the rest of the galaxy. Children shouldn't raise children. No teenager is capable of properly raising a baby. But even a twenty or thirty-year-old lacks the proper maturity for parenthood. Those are our true formative years, when we define who we are and what we want in life."

"Those are also our prime years physically and reproductively, when we want to be carefree, have fun, and enjoy the wilder things in life," Hamara continued. "We can't do that with a bunch of toddlers demanding attention and to be taught everything. Which is why we have Matriarchs and Patriarchs. On Sarenia, you cannot be a parent before the age of fifty. Between studies, our youth is to have fun and reproduce. Once we reach true maturity between fifty and sixty and go through *drortak*—our final molt—we begin our social duties. While I lack maternal instinct to raise children, I have a great scientific mind. I will work in our research labs, train and mentor young graduates, and help teachers keep their scientific materials up to date."

"But… Do you at least get to pick which parent raises your child?" I asked, bewildered.

"No," Gatina said with a shrug. "It can take years for us to know if our offspring survived long enough to achieve its first molt."

I gaped at her, almost rendered speechless by such indifference. "What do you mean?"

"We are amphibian," Gatina explained, while kicking her feet underwater. "Our pregnancies last only three months after which we will lay our tadpole in a large body of water. It will fend for itself and hunt for its own food for four months. If it survives the predators in the river, the tadpole will have grown arms and developed legs beneath the sheath of its tail, which it will shed during the first molt. At that point, the child will leave the water and climb the hill of the Tenyema River's shore. It is fairly steep and slippery. If the child hasn't gained enough strength, it will die trying or get snagged by birds of prey hunting the region."

The three females burst out laughing at my renewed expression of horror. The Guldan Empire also heavily relied on the concept of survival of the fittest, but this struck me as extreme. Granted, many animal species had similar natural selection mechanisms, but I couldn't understand it coming from an advanced sentient species such as the Sarenians.

"If it's any consolation to you, not that many who complete their first molt actually die," Hamara said. "We do control the predator population in the area to give our offspring a chance. The children who reach the plateau are taken to the adoption center where parents and child mutually choose each other. There are always more eager parents than there are available children."

"However barbaric our ways may sound to you, our children are loved and very well taken care of," Gatina said, this time with a serious tone that drastically contrasted with her previous almost cavalier indifference. "Not everyone is meant to be a parent. Having the ability to reproduce doesn't automatically make you qualified to raise the next generation of children. There is no child abuse on Sarenia. No orphans or starving children. The titles of Patriarch and Matriarch are earned by the best among us. While I just want to have fun at the moment, twenty years from now, I hope to receive that honor. We are a species of predators. Our males have violent instincts. With their pheromones and compulsion abilities, they could wreak havoc and throw our world into complete chaos without a proper upbringing from parents wise enough to do so."

"And despite that, the occasional failure occurs," Hamara said in a somber tone. "Juntel is a prime example, and one of the reasons Sarenians get such a bad reputation abroad."

"Your species gets a bad reputation because your males use compulsion not only to violate non-consenting females but to force them to give birth to the offspring that might result from it," I said with a hiss. "You are reviled because you think it's okay to rape a child because your prince wants to deflower an exotic virgin."

The faces of the three females closed off, all friendly demeanor evaporated. Under the current circumstances, I should probably be more careful with my words, but I couldn't be quiet about such outrage while listening to them bullshitting me into painting this as perfectly normal.

"First off, your daughter will not be raped," Gatina said in an icy voice. "While she has been bought as a gift by Juntel to ingratiate himself to our future Emperor, the Prince *never* requested such a thing. However, Siona isn't only Attuned to Prince Zerien, she's his soulmate. We can all see that their souls vibrate in perfect harmony."

I rolled my eyes. "How convenient. She's Attuned to your Prince like I'm Attuned to Faolen," I said with heavy sarcasm.

Hamara gave me a look that clearly stated I was trying her patience. "You *are* Attuned to Faolen, but he is not your soulmate. Your giant is. Had you not met the Braxian first, you would have been swept off your feet by Faolen. Your souls vibrate at an extremely close frequency, but you are in perfect harmony with the Braxian."

"Second," Gatina continued as if Hamara hadn't intervened, "you are just parroting the rumors being spread about us. Our males do not go around raping and impregnating random females. A handful of degenerates like Juntel did, and that sufficed for the entire Quadrant to give us that label. Yes, we are predators, and beautiful, compatible females stir our males' basest instincts, but the majority do not act on it. In fact, most of our people do not leave Sarenia."

"You know, I find you quite hypocritical," Nadia said, giving me a hard look that made me squirm. "You're sitting here all high and mighty, criticizing a culture you know nothing about, but you've been here three days now. Have you been raped? Has anyone even groped you or copped a feel?"

I shifted uncomfortably and shook my head.

"Earlier today, your own Ambassador raised a hand to strike you just because you said something he didn't like," Nadia continued with a harsh tone. "Who stood up in your defense? Every single Sarenian male, including the Emperor himself. Tell me, Hope, aside from your Braxian, how have men been treating you back on your home world? How about your previous boss? How much respect has any of them shown you? How many of them have made love to you instead of just using you as a fuck hole?"

My cheeks burned with humiliation at the truth of her words. While I still disagreed with my circumstances, Siona and I had indeed been treated with kindness and consideration by all the local males we'd met.

"Nymphomaniacs like me tend to end up in nasty situations, which often result in us getting hurt badly," Nadia said, a haunted look crossing her light brown eyes. "Here, I am safe. No matter how wild and crazy things get, Sarenians will always make sure I am unharmed, and that I have enjoyed myself. So, don't you fucking dare sit here talking down about an entire species and acting like you're better than the rest of us, because you're not. When it comes to the way females are treated, Guldans are the assholes of the galaxy."

With those words, Nadia hoisted herself out of the pool, grabbed her towel lying on a nearby bench, and stormed out. Hamara and Gatina each gave me a look both hurt and disappointed before rising to their feet and slowly walking out of the pool room.

I sat alone in the warm water bubbling around me, feeling lost, confused, and angry. I understood the logic of their words, and I recognized the error of judging without knowing. But while I respected their right to live according to their own rules, I didn't ask to be here. I was their prisoner, not their guest, and they were torturing my man. Until they'd given us back our freedom, whatever qualities they may possess, I didn't care.

CHAPTER 14
KRYGOR

The delicate hands of the female slave applying the medicated cream on my back moved quickly and efficiently. Although my magnetic shackles held me once again immobilized, it surprised me they would bring a female in my cell seeing how protective they were of them. Then again, the Emperor and his heir struck me as perceptive enough to know I would never raise a hand to a female.

"To what do I owe such illustrious company in such lackluster accommodations?" I asked sarcastically to the father and son—who looked more like siblings.

"I find myself in an awkward situation," Emperor Nemrox said.

He was sitting inside my cell on a cushioned bench placed a couple of meters in front of me, to the obvious dismay of his guards. Upon their arrival, the guards had wanted to set the benches for the Emperor and his son on the safe side of my bars, but their liege had insisted on coming in. I couldn't decide if they were recklessly stupid, overly confident, or trying to establish a relationship of trust. I figured it was likely a mix of all of the above.

"Is that so?" I asked, swallowing back a purr from the soothing effects of the salve kicking in.

Although I possessed a very high pain threshold, once my

Berserker battle rage wore off and my endorphins level returned to normal, the discomfort from my lacerated back had made its presence known a little too strongly.

"Like the Guldans and the Braxians, my people are strong believers in the survival of the fittest. We admire strength and scorn weakness," Nemrox said, nonchalantly crossing his legs beneath his fancy, embroidered dark robe.

The sleeveless garment with a very low V-shaped collar hid nothing of his sinewy muscles. His son, dressed in a similar fashion, but in a shimmering grey fabric with silver embroidery, stood next to the bench. Although more lithe compared to the Braxian bulky physique, the boy's broad shoulders and well-defined muscles already promised he'd grow into a strong male.

"Your performance in the Arena has greatly impressed," Nemrox continued.

"Greatly," Prince Zerien echoed.

"The people feel you've earned your freedom," the Emperor said in a neutral voice belied by the intensity of the gaze he leveled on me.

"But Hartuk disagrees," I intervened.

"Precisely," Nemrox said with a slight nod. "Which puts me in a bit of a predicament. If I free you, my people will rejoice, but your people will attack us in retaliation once they hear what befell you, and the Guldans will be pissed, which will jeopardize our budding alliance. If I execute you, my people will grumble, and my son's soulmate—your daughter Siona—will never forgive us harming you."

I stiffened at those words. "Soulmate?" I asked in a slightly menacing voice.

Zerien clasped his hands behind his back and lifted his chin defiantly, his gaze boring into mine. "Siona and I aren't just Attuned, we are in perfect harmony. She is my lifemate."

"You can't be certain of that," I challenged.

"He can," Nemrox countered. "We see souls almost as accurately as Korletheans do. My son and your daughter *are* soulmates."

"Then sounds like you're screwed," I said mockingly to Zerien. "My daughter wants nothing to do with Guldans after the abuse she and her mother have endured at their hands. Siona is Braxian now. You want her, you will need to revisit who you ally with."

"We'd always contemplated an alliance with Braxians," Nemrox conceded. "Even more so after your prowess in the Arena. But your people have not only bowed to the Galactic Council, you're now also in bed with the Korletheans."

The contempt in his voice, reflected on the faces of his son and guards, took me aback. Before I could answer, the slave stepped away from me and cast a questioning look towards the Emperor. He nodded and, with a surprisingly gentle smile, gestured with his head for her to go. She smiled back, curtsied, then left the cell between the guards parting to make way for her.

"Braxia bows to no one," I said in a clipped voice and narrowed my eyes at him. "And what's your quarrel with the Korletheans? Afraid they'll grow even prettier than you now that they are mating with Veredians?" I added tauntingly.

Nemrox, Zerien, and their four guards all snorted with disdain as if I'd said something outrageous.

"No species will ever rival our beauty," the Emperor said smugly with a dismissive wave of his hand, before becoming serious again. "But Braxia has *indeed* bowed to the Galactic Council. I understand how dire your people's situation had been, and how the embargo over your continued practice of slavery had put your home world on the verge of bankruptcy. I do not blame you or your Magnar for taking the measures to turn your fate around—and you have done remarkably well—but you are now forced to follow more and more of the 'new' rules being introduced regularly by the Council. First, it was the ban on slavery other than Indentured Services. Now, they are attempting to regulate the type of contracts that can be entered into, their duration, rates, and acceptable refund methods. The Galactic Council started off as a good idea with great intentions. But they are growing drunk with power and the need to control the galaxy. They are already talking about tariffs for intergalactic trades. Where does it end?"

"It ends when they cross a line we are no longer in agreement with," I said with conviction.

The same topic had surfaced numerous times of late in our own Council. Our people chafed easily whenever others would impose rules and restrictions upon them, which was why each clan governed itself however they saw fit within the confines of their respective compounds.

"And where will that leave you, Clan Leader?" Zerien asked in a soft voice. "Out of the Alliance again, shunned by its members at the edict of the Galactic Council, and struggling to find trade partners to keep your economy growing. What will happen to your bond with the Veredians and Xelixians who both happen to be the main peacekeepers of the Galactic Alliance?"

"The bond between our three species is deep, blood deep," I countered. "Our rulers are blood-related. Like you, our species do not play with family. And that includes the Korletheans who sired the majority of the new Veredian generation."

The Emperor's face immediately closed at those words, his features taking on a savage expression. "The Korletheans are not family. They are snakes," Nemrox hissed. "The truth of their misdeeds will soon be exposed."

I recoiled at the vehemence of his tone, and the contempt in his voice.

"Tell me, Clan Leader, do you recall at which point in your history the first mention of a Berserker was recorded and what triggered it?" Nemrox asked.

I shook my head. "Legends only claim that in a time of great hardship, some of the Warrior clans with the purest bloodlines began displaying tremendous power in battle and spurring their clans into victory."

"The same way the Veredians began showing greater psionic abilities, that the Geminate trait began appearing among Xelixians twins, that Dantorians began displaying empathic abilities, and that Sarenians began to perform mind control," Zerien said. "All unexplained new talents that seemed to appear overnight within all of those species."

"What are you saying?" I asked, although I already knew the answer.

"That the Korletheans have fucked with all of our species in an effort to enhance their own," Nemrox said in a hard voice. "My people were always Hunters, but we were peaceful. They have turned us into predators. They are the cause we mostly live in isolation to avoid incidents like the one between Juntel and your son's mate that make the galaxy believe us to be monsters. They are the reason millions of Veredians and Xelixians have died. And they are the reason your people now have the Berserker trait. Braxians and Dantorians came out on top of this mess. The rest of us got fucked."

I hadn't known any of this, and yet, none of it shocked me.

"You aren't surprised," Zerien said, perceptive as ever.

"Since our allies have found the cure to the Veredian reproductive issues and the Xelixians' Taint, a growing number of speculations have been pointing at potential Korlethean interference," I conceded. "The truth has a way of always coming out. Once it does, we will handle it as families always have, no matter how painful—keeping in mind that whatever was done occurred centuries before the current generation was born."

Nemrox harrumphed in concession. He suddenly spoke a few words in Sarenian. Startled, I felt my magnetic shackles activate, levitating me from my standing position to the wide wooden bench that also served me as a cot to sleep on. A soft cushion had been added following the battle in the Arena. After I was lowered into a seating position, the Emperor spoke another command which disabled the restraints on my wrists, giving me free use of my hands. But the shackles around my ankles kept my feet stuck to the floor. If I attempted to charge the Emperor or the Prince, I would faceplant in a most spectacular fashion.

I nodded in gratitude, realizing this visit represented far more than sharing his hesitations about how to handle my case. Contrary to our previous beliefs, the alliance between the Sarenians and the Guldans was far from being set in stone. Nemrox may not have planned my capture by Juntel and Hartuk, but he was definitely seizing the opportunity to test the waters for potential alternative alliances… a chance to isolate the Guldans that I couldn't let slip by.

"Fair enough," Nemrox said. "We will observe with great interest how this all pans out once the truth is out in the open. To be candid, yours is the only species we would really rather not go to war against."

"Is that so?" I asked, raising a dubious eyebrow.

"Indeed," Zerien said with that disturbing maturity he always displayed.

In many ways, the Prince reminded me of the young man Ravik had been at that age, although my king had been raised by a psychopathic father, not the seemingly wise and thoughtful Emperor Nemrox.

"You're the only species completely immune to our compulsion," Zerien said matter-of-factly. "Only the most powerful psionics among the Korletheans can resist us. That is how we were able to drive them out of our home world."

"Hmmm," I said, my gaze narrowing at them. "That means you could technically make the Guldans your bitches if you so chose."

Nemrox's predatory smile tickled me the right way, while also giving me pause. The potential damage they could wreak among their enemies, getting them to sabotage themselves from within, was both intriguing and terrifying.

"Who says we aren't already?" the Emperor asked. The teasing tone he used made it difficult to know if he was playing or actually meant it. My gut said it was a mix of both. "But this brings us back to my predicament. Since you have been bought as a slave, I cannot simply free you as one of those who paid for your capture is still alive. However, I am allowed to grant you the Warrior's Boon, which can either be a merciful death, a single weapon in the Arena, or—in the case that concerns you—a chance to run a Blood Hunt."

"Which is?" I asked, already liking the sound of it.

"You will be launched into the forest in a random location with no weapons, no tools, and no supplies," Zerien said. "Any Hunter, Sarenian, or Guldan wishing to participate will hunt you with the same constraints. If you manage to reach the Monolith of Marras on the other side, you will be free to go home. If you get captured, the person who does will have the choice between executing you or keeping you permanently as their slave."

"I will beat your Hunt," I said with a confidence that no doubt came across as arrogance, but I didn't care. "And when I do, I will leave with *both* of my females."

Zerien's eyes locked with mine in challenge. I held his gaze, impressed by the unflinching way in which he sustained mine.

Nemrox chuckled, his gaze flicking between the two of us. "The females, too, will be running a hunt: the Mating Hunt. Whoever reaches a female first owns her either for a quick romp, right there and then, or for a month; winner's choice."

"The females will run in the same Hunt?" I asked, my heart soaring at the thought of all the skulls I would bash in before snagging my girls and running them to our freedom.

"Not exactly," Nemrox conceded. "Normally, the Mating Hunt and the Blood Hunt occur on different days. This time, I will make an exception and run them simultaneously."

The way the Emperor spoke the words made it crystal clear he was doing me a special favor. This, more than anything else before, confirmed he was trying to pave the way to a potential alliance between our peoples instead.

"However, they are held in different parkours," Zerien cautioned, flicking his long, bluish hair over his shoulder. "The women run through the Gardens—the east side of the river. The terrain is flat and unencumbered, and the woods are safe. You will run through the Gauntlet on the west side of the river. The terrain is uneven, with treacherous vines eager to trip you, poisonous plants, and wild beasts determined to feast on your flesh. But the finish line is the same. Should Hope and Siona reach the Monolith without getting claimed, they will be free to leave."

"I will cross that river and make sure *both* of my females get to the Monolith with me." My gaze bore deep into the young prince's eyes, a warning in my voice. "I will crush *anyone* who stands in my way."

"Siona is my soulmate," Zerien snarled. "I will fight for her to my last breath."

"You may fight for her when she comes of age," I snapped back, although impressed by the strength of the boy and the genuine feelings he seemed to bear Siona. "Until then, she will be raised on Braxia."

Zerien glared at me, his lips twisting into a snarl while the tips of his descending fangs peeked out. I could smell his anger and see the predator lurking within his silver-blue eyes identical to his sire's. The Emperor stared intensely at his son, as did the guards. His words as to his people's struggle with their nature finally sank in. Although no one said a word, they kept watch, ready to intervene. The metallic smell of blood reached me seconds before I noticed the blue drops pooling at the edges of Zerien's fisted hands. The boy swallowed painfully and slowly opened his hands, as the vicious tips of his claws receded. Raising his palms to his face, he deliberately licked the blood of each, his darkened eyes never straying from mine.

The shadow of a proud smile stretched the Emperor's lips, while tension bled from his shoulders and those of his guards. The storm had passed. Turning away from me, Zerien faced the wall, teeth clenched, a nerve ticking at his temple.

"She will return to me at sixteen," Zerien begrudgingly said at last.

"Eighteen," I countered in a tone that brooked no argument.

Zerien's head snapped towards me, his anger coming back with a vengeance. He took one menacing step towards me that had his sire straighten and the guards stand at the ready.

"Sixteen is the galactic age of consent," Zerien snarled.

"Of *sexual* consent," I corrected in an appeasing tone. "Eighteen is the age for formal bonds and marriage. If you wish to date her, you may come stay on Braxia. But if you wish to claim her as your bride, you will wait until she's eighteen."

The boy stared at me with growing resentment, but still he showed restraint that further increased my esteem for him.

"And then she comes back here with me," Zerien said.

"And then you get to court her for a week in a neutral terrain," I said cautiously. "And she will choose whether she wishes to formally enter into a relationship with you."

"One month on Venus Hive, no meddling or interference from you, her mother, or anyone else," Zerien replied through his teeth.

I hesitated, knowing pushing him any further wouldn't benefit anyone. I didn't need to see souls or auras like the Korletheans—and apparently the Sarenians—to know this young man would fight even gods to be with my daughter. In a way, it warmed my heart to know she would be truly loved and protected. But it also worried me that we were currently on opposing sides of the building conflict.

"Agreed," I conceded at last with a stiff nod.

Zerien stared at me for a few seconds longer before turning around and taking a seat on the cushioned bench next to his sire, to the relief of the guards.

"You know, you are mighty cocky and demanding for a prisoner in shackles," the Emperor mused out loud. "We could simply kill you and keep your females."

I snorted and nodded slowly. "You could," I conceded. "But only keeping me alive and my females safe has a chance to avert an open war between our peoples. As we speak, my firstborn and my king are zeroing in on Sarenia. My son was investigating the shady deals Luther Stromland—the human who sold my mate's daughter to that vermin Juntel—was involved in. By now, they will know the biggest deal came from Sarenia, and failing to reach me to update me about his findings will have tipped him off. So, yes, I'm cocky. But even without that, whenever my family is concerned, especially my child, I do not compromise."

"Fair enough, but you still need to survive the Hunt," Nemrox reminded me. "The Guldan Ambassador will do everything in his power to make sure you don't."

"I do not fear the Guldan," I said with a dismissive shrug. "I'm looking forward to seeing him on the field. We have a score to settle."

The Emperor chuckled. "Feel free to maim him, but do not kill him," Nemrox demanded. "I have plans for him."

The hardness of his tone erased any doubt the Sarenians had nefarious plans already in motion involving the Guldans. An uneasy feeling settled in the pit of my stomach. How much were they also playing me? I believed myself a great judge of character, but that hadn't prevented Marla from utterly fooling me.

No. You 'allowed' yourself to be fooled.

"How do I trust you will keep your word on everything we've just discussed when you are openly plotting against your current allies?" I asked in a stern voice.

"We aren't allies," Zerien said smugly. "That will be *my* decision to make when my reign begins. My father is laying the foundations for a potential alliance while ensuring we have the proper safety measures to avoid a potential betrayal like they attempted with your people."

I chuckled, further impressed. "So, then you do intend to join the Galactic Alliance despite your reservation."

"No," Zerien said with an intense stare. "I intend to make the Braxians, the Veredians, and the Xelixians leave it, and join us instead."

"Then it is the Guldans you've already decided to cast aside," I said.

Zerien's smile, mysterious and taunting, contained a wisdom far beyond his years. In that instant, the image of the young Vahleryon Praghan, the prophesized Great General who would lead the alliance into the Great War, flashed before me. Like him, Zerien was an old soul.

"The only thing I have already decided, High Council Aldriss, is that when the Great War comes, I will be on the winning side, and that victory will mean freedom for my people and the preservation of our way of life," the young prince said calmly before rising to his feet. "So, see that you win your Blood Hunt. I need you to ensure my Siona will be raised to be as fierce, as strong, and as ruthless a queen as your Dagna for when she reigns by my side. May your Ancestors fight with you."

After a slight bow of his head, the Prince turned around and walked out of my cell, accompanied by one of the guards. The Emperor rose to his feet, an unreadable smile playing on his lips.

"Remarkable young male," I said, genuinely impressed.

The Emperor puffed out his chest, his smile broadening. "The strongest of my offspring. He found me through our blood bond a few weeks before his fifth name day when most children only find their sires between the ages of nine and twelve. He will make a formidable ruler for our people... and a great ally." The way he said those last words left little room for interpretation. "I like you, Krygor Aldriss. When the Great War comes, I hope we will be on the same side."

With a similar bow of his head in farewell, the Emperor turned to leave my cell.

"Emperor Nemrox," I called out before he left. He looked at me over his shoulder. "I would see my mate and child."

He hesitated, a slight frown marring his forehead. The intense stare of his guards seemed to indicate my request was not only unusual, but that their rules would have implied his immediate refusal. Nemrox pursed his lips and gave me an assessing look.

"Thirty minutes, not a second more," the Sarenian ruler said at last. "See that you use that time wisely before the Hunts."

I snorted, once more awed by his perceptiveness. "Thank you. I most certainly will."

"Good man," Nemrox replied. "May your enemies tremble before you."

With those last words, the Emperor left, accompanied by one guard. The other two swiftly removed the benches from my cell, locked the door, and then deactivate the shackles around my ankles that kept me rooted in place. I walked up to the bars and made eye contact with my men. They approached their bars so that we could begin to strategize.

Yes, tomorrow, my enemies would tremble before me.

CHAPTER 15
HOPE

Some sort of frenzy had taken over the Serail that had nothing to do with the upcoming Hunt. Although the women had been thrilled to know it had been moved up to tomorrow, something else was going on. A few of them had received a private message, and immediately rushed out of the common room to enter their private quarters. Seconds later, the other females had gone to prepare some kind of feast and arrange the common room and private areas.

Baffled, Siona and I exchanged a confused look, uncertain what to do.

"Gatina!" I called out as she was storming past me, "What's going on?"

"We have special visitors coming," she replied without slowing down.

More confused than ever, Siona and I decided to stay out of the way and watched with awe at the bustling of activity.

"They're here!" Gatina shouted about five minutes later.

Excited squeals answered her. Within seconds, the females who had gone into their private quarters came back out, looking like complete nervous wrecks. Tough, confident, sassy Hamara appeared on the verge of a nervous breakdown. She'd changed out of her usual *very*

192

revealing outfits into a sexy but proper dress that hugged her curves in the right way without giving glimpses of her naughty bits. The word 'lady' came to mind as she ran a nervous hand through her long hair.

I opened my mouth to ask her what was going on with her, but the chime of the elevator drew my attention. The other females who had received a private message had also changed into more demure outfits and gathered near the lifts.

As soon as the doors parted from both elevators, the mystery evaporated. My throat tightened at the sight of two dozen children pouring out from each cabin. Nine adult Sarenian males and three females accompanied them. They were older than any other Sarenian I'd met so far, and also looked different. The crown-shaped horns on their heads were longer, and three rows of gills graced each side of their necks. To my shock, what I'd assumed to be light-blue, iridescent capes on their backs actually appeared to be some kind of flowy fins.

"They are the Patriarchs and Matriarchs of three different pods," Gatina said softly next to me, startling me.

"Three?" I asked, confused. "But there are twelve of them."

"Three females, nine males," Gatina said with a mischievous glimmer in her eyes. "Do the math."

My jaw dropped, and my head jerked back towards the older adults. Sure enough, it quickly became apparent that a group of three males gravitated around a specific female and their clutch of children. The latter left their 'parents' to scatter through the room towards the females that had received messages. Seeing Hamara fiercely embrace two young boys before covering their faces with kisses turned me upside down.

"The lack of females to males doesn't disappear once we reach full maturity," Gatina said softly. "Over the years, we grow close to some of the Hunters. In the last decade before our final molt, many pods will begin to form. This is when you see the highest frequency of Hunters claiming the female they caught for a full month to assess their compatibility in cohabiting."

The 'parents' were standing at a respectful distance to allow the mothers a few minutes with their children. They would then approach when the mother turned to greet them. It was fascinating watching the 'parents' give something akin to a report about the children's progress and random little tidbits about them, from their favorite foods, to special talents, and bad habits.

But the most striking thing to me was how harmonious and joyful the whole process appeared to be. I had expected some kind of resentment from the children at being 'abandoned' by their mothers. And yet, I found none. In fact, their eyes were filled with love as they basked in the attention of the mothers who gazed, in turn, upon their offspring with pride.

"Are those fins on their backs?" Siona asked, her eyes wide with awe.

"Yes, although they also serve as wings," Gatina explained. "In the early days after their first molt, the babies spend half of their time on land and the other underwater. While we can all breathe through our skin when submerged, if the body of water we're in doesn't have enough oxygen, we could drown. By gaining gills and fins during their final molt, Patriarchs and Matriarchs are better suited to accompany the children and give them assistance during that transition phase."

"You guys can fly?!" Siona exclaimed, as stunned as I was.

Gatina laughed, amused by our expressions. "Yes and no. We do not fly like birds, but we can ride the air currents, and therefore glide over short or long distances. But that normally requires us launching from some kind of elevation."

Hamara waved us over, a huge grin on her face. We approached, Siona buzzing with excitement, and me feeling mightily intimidated, if not embarrassed, remembering how judgmental I had previously been of their culture.

"Hope, Siona, meet my third son, Mares. He is nine and top of his class in sciences. He wants to be a biochemist," Hamara said, puffing out her chest with pride. "And this is my fifth son, Volias. He's six, but already displaying tremendous physical skills and dexterity. He wants to become an Imperial Guard."

"I will be the First Guard to Emperor Zerien when he ascends," the stunning boy said with his high-pitched young voice.

"Work hard and you will, my love," Hamara said. She then waved at the Matriarch and three Patriarchs standing nearby. "These are his parents. They are currently raising five other children, including my two boys. It's always a blessing when blood siblings end up under the same roof."

"And I believe I've found my sire," Mares said, puffing out his own chest. "I felt the tug of the blood bond when we flew past the Palace."

"That's wonderful, sweetheart!" Hamara exclaimed, before casting an inquisitive look at the Matriarch.

"Kinan will take Mares on a walk through the Palace after our visit here," the Matriarch said, indicating one of her mates with the wave of a hand.

"Wonderful, thank you," Hamara said with a grateful smile.

"Matriarch Leona and her pod have raised some of the finest members of our society," Gatina said with undisguised awe. "I hope my own pod will be as successful."

"You flatter me, Siren Gatina," Leona said, blushing prettily under the approving gaze of her mates. "Just be thorough in the selection of your life partners. A strong pod makes all the difference."

The chime of the elevator ringing drew our attention again. Stunned expressions descended on everyone's faces at the sight of two Imperial Guards coming out of the lift. They scanned the room, looking for someone, until their eyes landed on me. My stomach lurched, and Siona pressed herself against me, her body tensing.

The lack of alarm from the other females somewhat reassured me as they looked on with curiosity.

"Nymph Hope, Nymph Siona, you have been granted a thirty-minute visit with the Braxian prisoner Krygor," one of the guards said. "Please, follow us."

"Oh, Goddess!" I exclaimed, my heart soaring in my chest.

"Papa!" Siona whispered with excitement.

Mumbling some mostly unintelligible apology to the other females and the visitors, I promptly followed the guards down the elevator into the underground parking lot from where we hopped onto a shuttle to the Arena. A brutal rainstorm raged outside. It wasn't terrible enough to ground all shuttles, but it would beyond dampen any desire for naughty plays outside—pun intended. If it could continue into the morning, the Sarenians would be forced to cancel the Hunt. If nothing else, that would give my man a bit more time to heal from the savage whipping he received.

It took every ounce of my willpower not to yell at the guards to get a move on while they leisurely strutted their way down the wide corridor of the holding area. It was much nicer and cleaner than I'd expected, despite the glaring lack of comforts. The large cells all appeared empty aside from the three Braxians. We passed in front of Yulan's cell first. He nodded at me then winked at Siona. Seeing him looking well and in such high spirit reassured me. The cell adjacent to his sat empty but, through the bars, I caught a glimpse of my beloved giant's massive frame.

Pushing past the guards, I ran to his cell and hung onto the bars, my lips silently forming his name. His brutish face softened in that frightening way it always did whenever he gazed upon me. The tender smile that stretched his lips would have sent most people running for the hills, but it made me melt from the inside out.

"Papa!" Siona exclaimed, after coming to stand next to me.

"Stay where you are," one of the guards said to Krygor who hadn't moved from the back of his cell.

He spoke a command in Sarenian and a red light lit on the shackles around my man's ankles, no doubt rooting him in place. After forcing my daughter and me to take a step back, the second guard opened the cell's door. I all but shoved him out of the way to rush to my giant and throw myself into his arms.

The sound of his soft chuckle, the feel of his powerful arms closing around me, and the heat of his hard body against mine turned me into a complete mess. I swallowed the tears of joy that threatened to surface and crushed his lips with a desperate kiss. Krygor immediately took over in that commanding way that made my toes curl and my knees wobble. And yet, despite the passion between us, lust didn't fuel the fierce and frenzied way in which we kissed. The depth of our feelings, joy at being reunited, and the fear of the last few days were stamped all over the way our tongues and our bodies clung to each other's.

The sound of the door closing snapped us out of our trance. Breaking the kiss, Krygor cupped my face in his hands and looked at me as if I were the most precious of gifts before pressing his forehead to mine.

"You have thirty minutes," the aggravating guard said while deactivating the shackles, although his voice was apologetic.

Letting go of me with obvious reluctance, he turned to Siona who was staring up at him with needy eyes. I felt slightly ashamed for my selfishness in hogging Krygor. He crouched in front of her and opened his arms. Watching my baby throw herself at him and cling to him with the energy of despair successfully undid me.

After a few moments, Siona pulled back to look at Krygor.

"You showed them," she said with a fierce pride while gazing at his fearsome face. "I knew you would crush them. You're the strongest warrior in the galaxy."

Krygor chuckled and caressed my daughter's left horn. "Actually, I believe Magnar Ravik is the strongest warrior in the galaxy, but I wouldn't mind claiming second place. I am glad you approved of my performance."

"You were amazing!" she exclaimed.

He had indeed been. But while pride also filled my heart, worry gnawed at me at the sight of the lash wounds covering his back. The angry welts and split skin had thankfully been treated, reducing the risks of infection. Still, the pain had to be excruciating.

"I am fine, my mate," Krygor said in a soft voice, having noticed me staring at his exposed back. "The healing salve is doing wonders and, like most Braxians, I have a very high pain threshold. I've sustained far worse injuries while sparring with my people."

The lightness of his tone, the absence of stiffness in his movement, and the lack of any sign of pain or discomfort slightly lessened my worries, but I still wished a doctor would tend to him. Better yet, I wished Thesala—the Veredian healer who had restored my horns—could fully mend him.

"But how are the two of you?" he asked, rising to his feet. "Have you been harmed or mistreated in any way?"

"No," Siona and I responded at the same time.

"We have been treated with the utmost respect and consideration," I continued. "No one has behaved in any inappropriate manner towards us. The Sarenians… aren't quite what I expected."

Without a word, Krygor stared intensely at me, then at Siona. I frowned, taken aback by his odd behavior. And then it dawned on me.

"I obviously cannot swear to it, but I am certain no one messed with our minds," I said in a soft voice. "I remember all too well the discomfort, the impending sense of doom I'd felt on Lilith Hive when Faolen had mind controlled me. I didn't know what was going on, but my every instinct screamed something was off. I feel no such thing right now," I added with conviction.

"Me neither," Siona said. "Everyone has been kind to me, even the Prince."

Krygor's gaze weighed heavily on my daughter, examining closely her features. "You like Prince Zerien?" he asked in a neutral voice.

Siona's cheeks took on a crimson color that gave her away. She scrunched her face and shrugged her shoulder dismissively. "He's treated me nicely."

"He claims to be your soulmate," Krygor insisted.

The redness in Siona's face cranked up a notch, making her look as if her cheeks would soon burst into flames. "I'm too young for a soulmate, right now," my daughter mumbled, clearly eager for a change of topic.

"Agreed," Krygor said.

Drawing us to him, my mate sat down on the cushioned wooden plank that also served as his bed. He settled Siona on his lap then wrapped an arm around my waist. I snuggled against him, hating that our time together would soon come to an end.

"I've spoken with the Emperor and the Prince," my mate said in a serious tone. "They are giving us an opportunity to regain our freedom and go home. We must not let it slip through our fingers. Therefore, you must both be strong and focused."

Krygor spent the next few minutes informing us of the simultaneous Hunts the Emperor had setup for the occasion. Although he didn't say it out loud, I could read between the lines that it would not be an easy journey for him. Still, I had seen what a formidable warrior he was. Nothing could stand in his way, especially not with his men by his side. It gave me hope that we could actually make it, that we would be free.

Morning came quickly. It was both too soon and yet not soon enough. In the next few hours, Siona, Krygor, and I could be on our way to Braxia. To my dismay, the terrible storm had abated, and a beautiful sun shone over the city. It had been a foolish hope, anyway, as the rain would have merely delayed the inevitable.

In preparation for the Hunt, my daughter and I were given simple short dresses, comfy shoes, a small pouch with energy bars, water, and a distress flare. In theory, we would be caught long before needing the food that was given to us. However, in very rare instances, some females had avoided capture for nearly half a day. I wanted to believe that Krygor would find a way to us long before that. Still, I appreciated the care they showed their females.

To my surprise, hundreds of women were herded to the launchpad a short distance from the Serail. We were granted a thirty-minute head start on the men. However, I was dismayed to realize that each female was being launched individually inside some sort of bubble transport. The glass spheres, equipped with a single bench, could only fit a single person. Once we entered, one of the guards would close the door and the sphere would immediately begin to hover. Seconds later, it would fly away at high speed towards the forest surrounding the city.

I had hoped that Siona and I would travel together in the same sphere. Unfortunately, she was sent away first. I followed the path of her bubble as closely as possible to get a sense of where she was, and how I would get to her. Relief flooded me to find her sphere headed close to the river, which we'd agreed to follow while heading towards the Monolith. However, to my further dismay, my bubble ended up being shot in the opposite direction from my daughter's. Under different circumstances, I would have reveled at the breathtaking view flying over the city gave me. Seizing the opportunity, I surveyed the land for potential landmarks while enjoying this bird's eye view.

My heart sank at the sight of the very wide river between the Garden and the Gauntlet. Worse still, the high cliff of the plateau where Krygor would run would impede his ability to get to our side of the river. The great distance prevented me from getting a glimpse of my mate and his men, or of the Hunters who would be tracking them down. But soon, too soon, my bubble began its descent. I could see many others landing a short distance from me. I hoped the Hunters would chase after those very willing females and leave us be.

The sphere settled smoothly in the middle of a small clearing, if it could actually qualify as such. Tall trees surrounded the area, making it impossible to see my destination. However, thanks to the little trip in the sphere, I had a good sense of which direction I needed to travel in. The glass door of the bubble automatically opened as soon as it stopped moving. Without hesitation, I started running northeast of my current position. I took on a slow but steady pace while building into my second wind. As an exotic dancer, fitness and stamina had been essential to my 'career.' I didn't fear a long run, but I also did not want to wear myself out too early on. It would be at least a couple of hours to reach my destination assuming nothing got in our way and that I managed to find my daughter quickly.

Although they called it the Garden, this truly was a forest, but a peaceful one. Once again, had the situation been different, I could have seen myself jogging through its beauty in my daily routine. The tall trees, the lush bushes and greenery, the colorful plants that filled the air with sweet floral scents, the lively chirping of the birds hiding in the high branches, and the adorable, small wildlife scurrying about made it an enchanting path to tread.

The sound of voices ahead startled me. For a second, my stomach knotted with a sliver of panic. For some silly reason, the thought that the Hunters had already caught up to me flitted through my mind.

However, not only were the voices feminine, but the males would also come from behind, their starting point being a lot closer to the city than our drop points. Although I slowed down a little, I did not veer from my current path. Soon, the two females came into view. Standing by a tall tree with large, drooping, dark blue leaves, the women whose names I did not recall appeared to be weaving flower crowns while making idle conversation. They paused to look at me when I entered their line of sight.

"I'd invite you to join us," said one of the women with an amused smile, "but I know you have places to be."

The other female chuckled and gave me an encouraging smile. "We're not running for another thirty minutes at least. No point wearing ourselves out before the chase has truly begun. Plus, we want to save energy for the real fun," she added with a naughty glimmer in her eyes. "The Monolith is that way," she continued, pointing in its general direction. "You still have plenty of time. We intend to keep those Hunters quite busy."

The lurid expression on her face left no mystery as to what she meant. Her companion launched into a peal of laughter. I shook my head, both envious of their laid-back demeanor and amused by their odd culture. While it would never be for me, I appreciated that it worked for them. In truth, I could see the appeal of being chased by a sexy man you wanted to capture you and give you a memorable tumble in the bushes. The thought of my giant hunting me down, pinning me against a tree, and pounding into me with that glorious cock of his had butterflies swirling in the pit of my stomach.

But now was not the time to fantasize over my mate. I kept pushing, controlling my breathing, straining my ears for the sound of the river nearby. In the following twenty minutes or so, I encountered a handful of other females, a few of whom were also running, or rather traipsing about while casually increasing the distance between the city and them. Like the first two females, they were preserving their strength for when the males were closer.

I couldn't say how much time had passed, but since the last female I had met, a loud horn had resonated in the distance; this signal meant the Hunters were finally on the prowl. It distressed me that with my bubble launching after hers, Siona would have no way of knowing in which direction I'd be coming from, nor the fact that I had a far longer distance to travel only to reach the river. However, we had been clear that in her case, she would keep heading for the Monolith.

Minutes later, the trees finally gave way to tall grasses leading to the shores along the river. Looking across it at the edges of the tall cliff of the Gauntlet, I searched in vain for a glimpse of my giant. Plowing ahead, I kept my eyes peeled for any signs of my daughter. But I was soon distracted by a strange keening sound emanating from a short distance ahead. At first, I assumed it to be the rustling of wind through the leaves, an exotic bird or small animal, or merely the singing of the river. But soon, it became clear whoever, or whatever, was making that sound was in distress. Knowing this side of a river was safe of any dangerous wildlife, I didn't hesitate to move towards the sound. It didn't hurt that it also came in the same direction I was already headed.

The closer I got, the faster I moved. The desperation and the weakening sound indicated that being would not last much longer. Moving to the edge of the water, I noticed a series of broken branches stuck in the rocks lining the shore. The sound emanated from them. Treading carefully, I stretched my neck to get a better look through the branches and brambles. At first, I thought some kind of small animal had gotten trapped, and then I saw a child's face.

A panicked cry tore out of my throat as I rushed to the rescue. Pulse racing from both the sustained effort I had performed since exiting my bubble and out of fear for the child, I carefully lifted the branches, my task rendered more difficult by the current that kept pushing them against the rocks, effectively forming a cage trapping the young tadpole.

The child—a boy—his skin a very pale dusty blue, appeared to have been in the midst of his first molt when he became entangled in the branches that then dragged him to this location due to the force of the current. Judging by his weakened state, he must have been trapped there awhile. I carefully pulled him out before cradling him into my arms. The child looked at me with exhaustion, gratitude, and something akin to pleading.

The way his arms flopped down whenever he tried to reach for my face further displayed his weakness. Reaching into my satchel, I pulled out one of the energy bars that had been provided to me. The little boy stared at me with glassy eyes, his little mouth gaping, revealing tiny pointy teeth that had barely begun to protrude out of his gums. I doubted he would be able to chew the bar. Therefore, I bit out a piece, chewed it just enough to soften it, and then fed a small portion to the child. Despite his low energy, the boy chewed greedily before swallowing, his mouth reopening immediately for more. Without hesitation, I repeated the process until I had fed him an entire bar.

His pale blue skin seemed to darken slightly, taking on a healthier hue thanks to his returning strength. For a moment, I wondered if I should feed him a second bar. However, the boy seemed to have other ideas in mind. Clinging to me he began to wiggle in the oddest fashion. it took me a moment to realize but he was trying to free his legs of the thick skin that had bound them as a tadpole tail. I almost helped him but held back at the last minute. For such species, that kind of effort allowed them to develop their muscles in the proper fashion. I was about to put him back into the water by the shore to ease his molting process when a sudden sound behind me had my head jerking around.

I froze at the sight of Faolen slowly approaching me. The wistful, almost heartbroken, look in his eyes took my breath away.

"You were truly born to be a Matriarch," he said, closing the distance between us.

I eyed him warily as he crouched down next to me. He caressed the head of the little boy, and then told me to hang on. Getting back up, he ran towards a nearby tree and climbed up it with the dizzying dexterity of a feline. He reached for something I couldn't see on the trunk, before deftly jumping back down. The Sarenian jogged back to me, while scraping with his claws at what look like a piece of tree bark. Kneeling back next to me, Faolen leaned over and fed the white paste he had removed from the inner part of the bark to the child.

"The sap of Nejon trees is very sweet and will provide him with enough energy to complete his journey," Faolen explained in a soft voice. "Normally, the shores would be scouted by the Matriarchs and Patriarchs to make sure no tadpole was stuck this way. This often occurs following a major storm like the one we had last night."

The boy devoured the three portions of sap my companion gave him before resuming to wiggle out of his molt. Within seconds, the translucent skin came off. The child gave us an ecstatic smile then raised his palm, fingers spread, towards us.

Faolen shook his head with an apologetic expression. "No, little one. We are not your parents. You must go back to the river and finish your journey. You will find your pod ahead."

I realized it had been some kind of joining or bonding gesture. Although I doubted the infant understood the words Faolen had spoken, I believed he understood we wouldn't adopt him. Taking the child from my arms, Faolen took a few steps into the river and gently placed the boy in the water at a safe enough distance from the shore and the rocks.

"Go on, little one. Strengthen your leg muscles and find your way home. Safe journey."

Faolen stared at the youngling as he swam downriver towards his destination, towards the parents that awaited him. I rose to my feet as the Hunter waded out of the water to join me.

"I would have raised many such as he with you," Faolen said with a pained look on his face. "However many you wanted... I could have made you very happy."

I smiled apologetically and gently caressed his cheek.

"Although I hate that you kidnapped us, you are a good man, Faolen," I said in a soft voice. "One day, you will find your true mate. But I've already found my soulmate, and it is Krygor."

"I know," he replied with a resigned tone. He extended a hand towards me. I instinctively took it. "Come on. Let's go find your daughter. I would rather not have your beast spill my brothers' blood should they be silly enough to pursue her."

Chuckling softly, I let him lead the way.

CHAPTER 16
KRYGOR

The bubble transport in which they had us travel into the forest was barely big enough to accommodate our large frames. My men and I departed almost simultaneously, each of us in a different direction. Mine was closest to the center while Zartag flew farther west from us. He would have a much longer journey to catch up with us. Thankfully, both my men were experienced fighters and hunters. I didn't know what creatures dwelled within this forest, but my home world had savage beasts of its own which could rival any other. Yulan's sphere flew further ahead than mine and closer to the river. Unfortunately, my sphere began its descent far too early through the thick woods, blocking my men from sight.

Thick vines and gnarly roots covered the uneven terrain, making it difficult to travel the forest. The trees, with their thick trunks and sprawling branches, rose endlessly towards the sky. The rays of the sun struggled to pierce through the tightly knit canopy. It would be a long race to the river. Weaponless, and deprived of any tool, I avoided making unnecessary noise in any area that looked suitable for animals to make their lairs. I preferred not to find, out if at all possible, what creatures haunted these woods. At least, the Hunters tracking us had the same restrictions we did.

The Sarenians considered the Blood Hunt as a trial for the most talented among them to prove their worth. Deaths often occurred during these hunts that didn't necessarily have sentient beings as prey, as was currently the case. But the creatures didn't worry me as much as the Guldan Ambassador who had every reason to make sure my men and I never reached the Monolith. The risk of retaliation from my people against his was way too high. He had counted on my death in the Arena shortly after our arrival. I also could not count on him not to play dirty, especially not after their betrayal on my home world. The need to win at all costs tended to reveal the worst side of people.

Unlike the females doing their Hunt in the Garden, we only had a ten-minute head start on our pursuers. As we had a much longer distance to travel and on a harsher terrain, our bubbles were launched before the women's Hunt began. It gave me hope that I could reach my mate before any fool could make a move on her. But it also meant that I needed to make haste so that my enemies, who probably already knew the terrain, wouldn't catch up to me before I could reach the river.

I kept my eyes peeled for anything that could be used as a weapon but came up empty. The almost eerie silence in the forest made me uneasy. It was far too quiet. For a moment, I wondered if maybe I was heading in the wrong direction. The broad and thick leaves of the trees blocking out the sun made it harder for me to get a proper sense of direction. And yet, I felt confident I had not been turned around.

And then I heard a loud squeal of a beast. Correction, make that a couple of them… at least. I froze, wondering if I should start moving in a different direction. But the way they screamed implied more that they were fleeing from something rather than being the ones giving chase. With my captain, Yulan, having landed in that general area, I couldn't dismiss the fact that he might be the one chasing away some wild beast while trying to reach our rendezvous point.

I rushed towards the screams that kept moving northwest, careful not to trip or twist my ankle on the gnarly roots covering the ground. But just as I ran past a thick outcropping of rocks beyond yet another giant tree, my heart lurched. I crouched down for cover at the sight of a couple of Guldans focused on throwing what looked like rocks wrapped in some kind of leaf. They were running, oblivious to my presence, trying to keep up with their quarry. It took me a second to realize they were hurting the squealing beasts.

Further ahead, a savage roar rose through the forest—Yulan's war cry—the sound muffled by the distance and carried by the wind. I cursed inwardly at the cowards' tactics, using wildlife to eliminate us rather than facing us head on. Then again, the scrawny bastards would not have stood a chance against us. I couldn't hasten to my captain's side to help him fight the creatures. Taking out the Guldans took priority as we would otherwise be in too vulnerable a position.

Sneaking up behind the first one proved quite challenging despite the large trees behind which I could take cover. The uneven terrain and the speed at which he ran required for me to be extra careful not to give myself away. Although they didn't appear to have any weapons, I didn't put it past them to break the rules to win at all costs. Cutting diagonally along the path he was following, I hid behind a large trunk and grabbed him as he passed by. I yanked him onto the opposite side of the tree, breaking line of sight with his partner and slapped my hand over his mouth before he could scream. To my dismay, I noticed the presence of two more Guldans on top of the second one I had already seen.

Wasting no time, I snapped my first victim's neck. A quick look at him confirmed he had no weapons; surprising. Throwing caution to the wind, I rushed towards the second Guldan who was too focused on the beast to see me coming. I grabbed him by the throat and bashed his face in with my fist without stopping my race towards the third one. Hearing the panicked yelp of his companion, the third male tried to flee towards the fourth one, foolishly thinking that their joint forces would give them a chance to prevail against me.

I didn't have to chase long; the uneven terrain threw the third Guldan onto the ground, cracking his head hard against a root so thick and ancient it almost looked like it had turned to stone. Dazed, the fool scrambled to get back up, but he never got a chance. Careful not to meet a similar fate, I rushed to him and jumped, landing with both feet at the base of his nape. His shoulders and spine collapsed under my weight and the force of the impact. The crunching sound mixed with the gurgling breath that whooshed out of him further fueled my blood-lust. A violent spasm coursed through him, and then he went still.

The last Gulden threw a wrapped rock at me and then dashed towards the beasts that surrounded Yulan and shouted threateningly. At first, that struck me as odd. But then I realized he was hoping they would turn on me. One of them indeed pulled away from my captain to face the incoming menace. The Guldan waited until the last minute to throw his last covered stone at the creature. Whatever that leaf was, it appeared to be repulsive to the beast.

As my prey had intended, the beast veered in my direction. However, the fool had waited too long. In its momentum, the creature failed to completely miss him. Resembling a giant crab with massive tusks, the beast stumbled on the uneven terrain while attempting to make a sharp turn. One of its long legs, which ended as a spear, violently struck him on the side, sending him flying straight into a tree. He struck it sideways at an odd angle, breaking his spine. His shout of agony stopped abruptly as he lost consciousness—or maybe even died. Either way, I would not waste any more time on him. The way his broken body crumpled to the ground, he wouldn't be getting up any time soon.

Eliminating the weaponless Guldans had been the easy part. The three beasts, at a height with us, were getting into each other's way while attempting to get at my clansman. For the first time, I was grateful for the narrow space the forest afforded us. Yulan was doing a great job of staying just out of reach of their potentially fatal blows. Repeatedly using the large tree trunks as cover, he would circle around them, then dash at a leg of one of the creatures to knock it out from under them before taking cover again.

I joined the dance, knowing it couldn't last eternally. In the distance, I could hear the rumbling of the river. From my flight in the bubble, I already knew we were on an elevated plateau. If we could get the creatures to the ledge and knock them over, they would not survive the fall. Yulan appeared to have come to the same conclusion. We coordinated our efforts, making slow progress to lure them where we wanted. But as we drew closer to the edge, the trees thinned, presenting us with a new challenge.

For the next few minutes—which felt like an eternity—we tried in vain to come up with a solution. Just as despair was beginning to set in, sudden movement in the branches overhead startled me. While dodging the incoming attack from one of the creatures, I warned my clansman of the presence of Sarenian Hunters in the trees.

"Do not kill the Crawmaws!" one of the Hunters shouted. "They must be returned to their mother before she goes on a rampage."

Jumping down the tree on top of one of them, the Sarenian bashed the head of the beast with a branch covered in leaves similar to the ones that had wrapped the rocks. The creature shrieked and tried to knock him off. The Sarenian managed to hang on a few moments, and then the creature violently rearing sent him flying off. To my shock, wing-like fins spread from his back, and he glided instead to a nearby tree. He clung to a branch, settling on it with impressive dexterity. A few more of his people took turns repeating similar behavior with the three Crawmaws, driving them away from the ledge and deeper into the forest.

Confused, Yulan and I stayed out of their way. But it was already too late. A furious roar in the distance resonated through the forest. The three young creatures rushed towards the sound, having no doubt recognized the call of their mother. If those were the young, I shuddered at the thought of what the adult version would be like.

As soon as the young Crawmaws left our vicinity, the Sarenians all scrambled up the trees using their claws, scattering evenly in a circular fashion as if laying a trap. The ground shook as the adult Crawmaw made her approach. Realizing we were about to be fucked, Yulan and I reached for the lowest but thickest branches we could reach and pulled with all our might to try and get ourselves some sort of weapon. Taking cover behind a tree, we waited, heart pounding, for the beast to reach us.

A quick glimpse into the trees revealed the presence of about six to eight Sarenians. To my surprise, they were all clawing off pieces of bark the size of a blade and pressing their fangs to it. It took me a second to realize they were coating it with whatever venom they possessed.

"Bash the face in," said one of the Sarenians to me. "Do not let the head come out. We will take care of the rest."

That comment confused me. Technically, the Crawmaw did not have a head. Just like a crab, it had spaced out eyeballs on each side of the gaping hole that served as its mouth—or so I thought. Still, I had no reason to challenge the Hunter's comment. Even though they had come out here to hunt us, the Sarenians understood the angry mother represented the greatest threat to us all. We would settle our differences afterwards. Strangely enough, I would not have joined forces with the Guldans in a similar situation.

As soon as the beast entered the trap area, the Sarenians took turns jumping off the tree onto its back in a perfectly choreographed dance. I rushed out from behind my cover to bash in the face with my makeshift weapon. On closer inspection, I realized what the Sarenian had meant about the head. It wasn't a mouth per se that gaped between the spaced-out eyeballs, but the opening through which the actual head would come out like a turtle. And even that did not quite qualify as a head. It looked more like a trunk from whence the Crawmaw could shoot thick, long, black darts that were more than likely covered in poison.

I barely managed to dodge out of the way before it fired three of them in quick succession. The trunk-like appendage could stretch over nearly two meters and move in all directions, allowing it to fire even at a target behind or above her.

"Control the fucking head," a couple of the Sarenians shouted.

Unlike with the children, the Hunters weren't striking the mother with branches of those plants that had repulsed her young. Instead, they were stabbing the joints of her articulations with the bark coated with whatever venom they had put on it. Despite the confined quarters in which we fought, the adult Crawmaw still managed to fling her legs left and right, striking violently at the surrounding trees, attempting to impale us with the viciously sharp tips of her legs, and firing those damn darts every time we failed to bash her 'face' in.

Yulan and I were kiting the creature around the narrow circle where our temporary allies were helping us battle. I couldn't say at which specific time Zartag finally joined us, but between the three of us, we effectively managed to prevent the Crawmaw from rearing its head. Like we had done with the children, we rammed into its legs to get her off balance while striking at its face. The Sarenians reminded me of an army of ants—although flying bugs would probably be more accurate—as they continued to dive onto the beast's back, stab its joints, and then glide off—for those who possessed those strange wings—or jump off if they didn't. It was disturbing watching the wingless ones jump off and climb a tree in a blink with the dexterity of a cat only to immediately backflip onto the creature again to stab another joint. They moved in a constant motion that would have been a mesmerizing ballet were we not fighting for our lives.

The creature seemed all but invulnerable aside from the fleshy part well-hidden in between the articulations. It took me a while to understand the purpose of that attack from the Sarenians. For the first twenty minutes—at least—of the fight, the Crawmaw seemed mostly unaffected by that tactic. On our end, we couldn't find a single section of its body that could be vulnerable enough to any blow we could give it without a traditional weapon. The shell covering every inch of its body might as well have been titanium it was that hard and impenetrable. However, as time went by and the number of pieces of bark embedded in the joints increased, the beast's movements became increasingly stiff and jerky.

It shamed me to admit that without the Hunters' help we more than likely could not have defeated the creature on our own. But with our joint efforts, the beast eventually found itself immobilized. Yulan, Zartag, and I charged the Crawmaw simultaneously from the same angle, toppling it over. Its legs jerked in a vain effort to try and get back up. Without missing a beat, I rushed back to its face. This time, I didn't prevent the head—or rather the trunk—from coming out and grabbed it with both hands. Putting a foot on its face between the eyes, I prepared to pull and tear out the trunk, but the alarmed shouts of the Hunters stopped me.

"You do not kill a mother," one of the Sarenians said in a stern voice. "Her young would die. They never should have been used as bait to begin with. The punishment you exacted on the Guldans is well-deserved. Our venom will wear off in half an hour or so. No other creature in this forest will be able to harm her in the meantime."

But even as he spoke those words, his fellow Hunters all descended from their trees, surrounding us. I carefully let go of the trunk. To my surprise, it didn't swiftly re-enter the shell as it previously did but hung limply where I had left it. I realized then that the Crawmaw hadn't simply toppled over from the stiffness caused by having too many pieces of bark embedded in her joints, but because the poison had effectively paralyzed her.

My men and I closed ranks, making sure none of the Hunters could get the drop on us. It didn't go unnoticed, eliciting amused smiles from the Sarenians.

"We have just hunted together," said the male who had kept me from killing the creature. "I can no longer hunt you as prey. I will not try to spill your blood this day. Good luck on the rest of your journey."

The seven other Hunters each made a similar comment, some of them content to nod their heads before turning around and leaving. We didn't know who else might still be tracking us in the Gauntlet but didn't intend to stick around to find out. It also would not be wise to waste time while the poison wore off. More importantly, it worried me not to have seen the Ambassador among the Guldans who attacked us.

With a nod of our own, my men and I spun on our heels and headed for the cliff, which we followed looking for a path down to the river. After racing along the ledge for a good fifteen minutes, movement on the other shore drew my attention. Uncertain at first due to the distance, I finally recognized the shape of the horns gracing the head of the female standing by the water. Then the Sarenian male by her side extended her a hand. Seeing her take it willingly and follow him as he led her away ignited a rabid fury within me. As battle rage set my blood on fire, I picked up the pace, ready to obliterate any who would dare get in my way.

This time, I was the one on the hunt.

CHAPTER 17
HOPE

Faolen and I made good time marching north towards the Monolith and hopefully towards my daughter. He seemed impressed by my ability to keep up a steady pace. Then again, few people understood the level of fitness required to perform on stage day in and day out and how much strength was actually required for pole dancing.

Faolen turned out to be a rather pleasant companion as we hastened along the shore. He regaled me with a series of anecdotes and stories about his home world. It was fascinating learning how he grew up in a large pod with eleven other siblings before finding his sire at the age of ten. Like him, his father was a great Hunter. Despite that, he remained with his pod until the age of fifteen.

"Why didn't you join him sooner?" I asked.

"Because he was too young to be a proper mentor," Faolen said with a smile. "The Prince is one of the rare exceptions. As the heir, he needs to be groomed early on to take on the important responsibilities that will befall him. As soon as he found his sire, he moved from his original pod to a new one permanently in residence at the Palace."

"He seems surprisingly mature for his age," I said pensively.

"He is an old soul," Faolen said with a nod. "An ancient prophecy spoke of the rise of the young Prince. Since our falling out with the Korletheans, we are now blind to any new foretelling that could be of relevance. In many ways, it is for the best. Knowing the future has a way of depriving one of their freedom of choice. However, with the Great War looming on the horizon, knowledge is power."

"I have heard rumors of that Great War," I said with a frown. "It disturbs me that everyone takes it as something inevitable. Instead of all of you preparing for a bloody battle, why not work towards a solution to prevent it?"

"Because it is a prophecy, not the vision of an Oracle that could be averted. Prophecies are inevitable," Faolen replied. "If—"

The sound of footsteps to our left drew our attention. The Hunter they belonged to had made no effort to be discreet, clearly wanting to announce his presence. Faolen immediately took a protective stance in front of me and bared his fangs at the newcomer. The Sarenian gave me an appreciative once over before smirking at my companion. He advanced by a few steps, his demeanor provocative, and then stopped.

"Relax, brother," the intruder said with a taunting glimmer in his eyes. "No matter how delectable your catch is, there is no pleasure to be had with a non-consenting female… unless as part of consensual role playing. As for you, my brother, I suggest you find yourself another mate. Word out there is that her Braxian easily defeated a Crawmaw without weapons. Only a fool would risk his wrath. The Garden is filled with sweet peaches eager to be caught and devoured. Off to hunt I go. Safe travels to you both."

I gaped at the male's receding back while Faolen's shoulders relaxed. He turned to look at me, a bemused smile stretching his lips.

"A Crawmaw?" I asked, curious but relieved to hear my giant was doing well.

"A nasty critter that roams the Gauntlet," Faolen replied.

I chewed my bottom lip and gave my companion a sideways glance.

"Would you find me strange if I said that, despite my relief this didn't turn into battle, my ego is slightly offended that he didn't even try to fight for me?" I said with a sheepish grin.

Faolen burst out laughing and shook his head at me. "Females, whatever the species, you're all just as strange and illogical. Come on, my Beauty. The sun is already high in the sky."

"So, without the existence of my mate, what would have happened if I had been reluctant regardless to be captured in this Hunt? Would any of the other Hunters have simply walked away like this one just did?" I asked with genuine curiosity.

"More than likely. Again, contrary to the rumors being spread about us, the Hunt is about ensuring we maintain our population level through selective reproduction. But it's also a game about pleasure that caters to our predatory instincts. Still, our protective instincts towards our females are far stronger than our need to conquer. We can be ruthless killers to our enemies, but we never harm females."

"If the female was mesmerized, you could convince her that she was enjoying herself, couldn't you?" I asked.

"I have compelled you before as you well recall. Your subconscious is aware something isn't right. The more you disapprove of the command given to you, the more uneasy you will feel," Faolen explained. "In the long term, it can have severe psychological effects on the subject. We use compulsion on the females to enhance their pleasure, and the excitement of the chase. Because they are already willing, it makes for a wonderful experience. The opposite is not true."

"I see," I said, nodding slowly.

"But even if I had been ruthless and forced myself on you, in the end I would have still lost you," Faolen said, sobering. "Luther has been arrested on Lilith Hive. According to the latest reports I've seen, Anton and the Head of security of the Magnar have been bombarding Krygor's ship with messages. By now, they know he's missing, and they're hunting for him."

"The Braxians are on their way here?" I asked, hope blossoming in my heart.

"Not yet," the Sarenian replied. "They cannot track his ship here, but it's only a matter of time before they figure out his location. If Luther doesn't spill his guts first, some of his records will lead them to

Sarenia. The Emperor will want to avoid entering into a war at this point in time."

"But what—"

Faolen's head jerked left, his ears perking up while he appeared to strain to listen to something. Shutting up immediately, I, too, tried to listen. Weak at first, the clear sound of battle reached me in the distance. Without a word, we both broke into a run. I instinctively knew it involved my daughter somehow.

Sure enough, a few hundred meters ahead, partially hidden by the trees lining the shore, the Prince was engaged in a fierce battle with a Guldan. Ambassador Hartuk, another Guldan, two Imperial guards, and my daughter were bearing witness.

"Siona!" I shouted.

Her head jerked towards me. Recognition and then joy lit up her beautiful face. She shouted my name and ran to me. She threw herself into my arms, and I hugged her fiercely, relieved to find my baby safe and sound. The shouts and grunts of the two men battling recalled our attention. Weaponless as well, they fought with a viciousness that left me baffled. From all accounts, the Mating Hunt very rarely ended with deaths. The men would rough each other up fighting over the same female, but the best man would get her, the loser conceding with nothing more than a few minor physical bruises and a major one to his ego. But, in this instance, the Guldan was clearly out for blood.

"Isn't he much too old?" I asked with a frown while staring at the Prince's opponent. "I thought the Hunter had to be within a three-year age gap from the female? This male is clearly more than double, if not triple, her age."

"He's allowed to fight for her," Faolen said with a tensed voice. "But he's not allowed to mate with her. In accordance with our laws, he could claim her for a month during which he might choose to court her, even though he cannot obtain her favors. It is a tactic sometimes used by males coveting a specific female for their pod—or for the pod of a friend or sibling unable to win her during that Hunt—to make sure another is unable to court her in the meantime."

"He cannot win her," I said with a sliver of dread. "Guldans are abusive to their females. Ambassador Hartuk is a well-known fanatic when it comes to the place of females in society. We have fled our home world, which is a grievous offense to our people. He would seize this opportunity to brainwash my child."

"Do not fear, my Beauty," Faolen said in a soothing voice. "The Prince is already a seasoned warrior. In the unlikely event he should lose, I will challenge the Guldan for your daughter."

Indeed, Zerien moved with a grace and confidence far beyond his years. He appeared to be combining a variety of hand-to-hand combat styles and techniques. Without a doubt, he was making efficient use of his claws, if only judging by the number of bleeding cuts on his opponent. His shorter height and lither constitution seemed to play in the Prince's favor. The bulkier Guldan could strike with more power but moved at a slower speed. It pleased me to no end to watch Zerien backhand him with such force his teeth had to have rattled in his head, followed by a vicious roundhouse kick behind the knees of his opponent, almost knocking him off his feet.

Increasingly, I got the distinct impression that Zerien wasn't simply trying to defeat his challenger but was also attempting to humiliate him. The Prince had not hidden his lukewarm feelings towards the Ambassador and his followers. It actually confused me that Hartuk challenged the Prince's claim since my daughter had specifically been bought for him as a gift for his fifteenth name day. For the sake of diplomacy alone, Hartuk shouldn't be causing any waves. But part of me was starting to think he flat out wanted to eliminate the Prince.

While Faolen's promise to intervene should Zerien be defeated had partially soothed my concerns, my relief was short-lived. The Ambassador turned his hateful eyes towards me. The cruelty and contempt that shone within twisted my innards. With a gesture of his head, Hartuk directed the other Guldan by his side to challenge Faolen for me. My blood ran cold as my companion accepted.

As the second man approached, a familiar scent wafted to me, turning my blood to ice. Molgar, a hallucinogenic mushroom often used on my home world as a recreational drug, was also known to rob the user of rational thinking and control. Combined with an excess of adrenaline, it could turn the user into a rabid beast. It finally dawned on me that the Ambassador did not want his men to win the fights. He intended for them to lose after both the Prince and Faolen had been exposed to a sufficient number of spores that they would become a threat to my daughter and me. What better victory for the Ambassador than for the two males who had humiliated him for threatening me in the box to end up raping and brutalizing my daughter and me during the Hunt? Even now, I could see the Prince's eyes turning glassy. We could not be around them by the time the drug fully took effect.

Grabbing my daughter's hand, I started running. The Imperial Guards hesitated, as if wanting to give chase. But their duty remained the protection of the Prince. We were still a long way from the Monolith. With luck, my giant would find us soon. I still could not see him on the other side, but at least the river was narrowing a little, and the cliff of the plateau had significantly lowered. It remained too high for Krygor and his men to jump down from it. With a little luck, they might find a path down to the shore.

Siona easily kept up with me. In truth, I believed she was taking it easy on me and that, on her own, she could have fled even faster. But whatever distance I thought we were putting between us and the men soon proved null. The sound of footsteps on the dried leaves resonated behind us in hot pursuit. Panicked, I pushed my daughter to run even faster, telling her to go all out even if that meant leaving me. As I feared, she stubbornly refused to abandon me.

One glance over my shoulder revealed something even more frightening. It wasn't the drugged Prince or Faolen chasing us, but the Ambassador himself. The malicious look on his face made me shudder. Technically, he couldn't hurt us. However, I didn't want him claiming me or my daughter and hauling us back to the city before my giant could rescue us. If he did, all would be lost.

Hartuk rushed me, tackling me to the ground. I tried to fight him off, but he turned me around onto my back, sat on top of me and, with one hand, pinned both my wrists above my head. Siona screamed for him to get off me, to leave me alone, but he, of course, ignored her. Reaching for his belt with his free hand, the Ambassador withdrew some sort of gem which I recognized as the claiming symbol he would insert in my arm band. That would mark me as his for the next thirty days. While he couldn't touch my daughter, he and I were within a similar age range, meaning I would be fair game. After the humiliation Krygor had subjected him to in the rena, Hartuk would take an extensive revenge on me. I knew his type all too well after years of abuse at their hands on my home world.

My efforts to buck him off failed miserably. With a war cry, Siona threw herself at him to try and knock him off. But the Ambassador resisted before shoving her forcefully away with one hand. The way she fell, I feared she had seriously injured herself. But not my baby. Siona got right back onto her feet and, with a near frightening determination, she fumbled with her sack and pulled out the distress flare that had been given to her. My eyes widened in understanding. I just needed to keep the bastard on top of me from laying his claim before Siona could fire the flare.

As he attempted to insert the gem, I kept struggling to make it difficult and even tried to bite him. Just as he lifted his hand to backhand me, Siona launched the flare at his back at close range. It brutally struck him with a sizzling sound. Hartuk shouted in pain, immediately releasing me to tear off his clothes that were burning on his back. He threw himself off me, rolling on the ground to put out the fire. But my baby was not done with him. Grabbing any rock she could, Siona began pummeling him with them. Still screaming in pain, the skin of his back bubbling from the burn—the stench of crisped flesh stinging my nose—Hartuk scrambled to his feet, covering his face with his arms as he rushed my daughter.

In that instant, something feral came over me. I ran to intercept, ramming into him from the side. The momentum sent him careening into a nearby tree. He fell to his knees, seeming somewhat stunned from the impact. That didn't stop me. Following him, half stumbling, half running, I threw myself at him, kicking, clawing, and pulling out his hair. Siona ran away, looking on the ground for anything she could use as a weapon. With one powerful shove, the Ambassador sent me tumbling a few meters backwards. My bare knees collided brutally with the forest's floor, rocks and dirt scraping them and stabbing the palms of my hands. Pain radiated from my injuries, but I ignored it: a thirst for blood had taken over my senses. My skin tingled, and my blood boiled. A single desire occupied my mind: to see him bleed.

My eyes caught sight of a broken branch lying a couple of meters away. I scrambled forward to grab it. Even as I rose back to my feet, the Ambassador was also trying to get up; but he never did. With a well-aimed throw, Siona struck the back of Hartuk's head with a massive rock. Stunned, the Guldan fell back down on all fours, head bowed and trickling blood.

With a savage cry, I ran and kicked the bleeding side of his face with all my might. He fell over onto his side, and I kicked him again, this time in the lower stomach. He doubled over, winded.

"Leave us the fuck alone!" I shouted, letting go of all the rage, the anger, and the helplessness I accumulated over years and years of abuse. I brought down the wooden branch hard onto his hip. His strangled, half-choked cry awakened something savage and primal inside of me. "We're not property, not objects for you to use for your pleasure, you piece of shit." And down came the branch again, this time striking the forearm he'd weakly raised to protect himself. "Never again!" And another blow, this time near his pelvis. "No man will ever hurt me or my daughter again!"

The sound of his fingers breaking under the blow only increased my lust for blood. I pummeled him relentlessly, no longer paying attention where the branch fell. All I cared about was the divine sound of wood meeting flesh, his screams of agony, the force of the impact resonating through my arms, stinging my palms, and fueling my rage. In the distance, the soft voice of my daughter spoke words my brain couldn't process. And then, a powerful hand stopped mine, which was raised above my head, ready to bring down more pain on to the bastard that embodied everything that was wrong with this fucked up world we lived in. I tried to fight back, but another strong arm with bulging muscles wrapped around my waist immobilizing me against a hard, familiar body.

"Enough, my mate," said a beloved voice. "Peace, my love. Peace."

The words penetrated my skull, but their meaning eluded me. It didn't matter, though. My giant was here. We were safe now. All fight bled out of me, my arms suddenly feeling heavy, and weariness seeping into me. I let him take the stick from me and leaned back into his embrace. Blinking, the red haze falling from my eyes, I gazed around the small clearing in which we stood. My daughter stared at me with bulging eyes, a strange mix of awe and fright gleaming in her eyes. A short distance to the left, Prince Zerien and Faolen stood by, observing the scene. One look at them clearly indicated the effects of the drugs had started kicking in. The Imperial guards watched them closely, ready to intervene. For a second, I wondered what had become of their challengers. But that, too, didn't matter anymore.

Looking down at the Ambassador at my feet, my breath caught in my throat. I had beaten him into a bloody pulp. I had no idea such savagery dwelled within me. And yet, I felt no remorse, only feral satisfaction at his pain.

Krygor gently pushed me behind him. I complied, startled to notice the presence of his two clansmen also standing nearby. He gazed upon Hartuk with contempt and cruelty.

"I would have taken great pleasure in wrecking you, but I promised not to take your life… this day. It is poetic justice that the female you sought to mistreat should have put you into such a state," Krygor said in a voice so deep and rumbling it was barely intelligible.

I understood then that my mate was under battle rage and that the whole bloody madness that had taken over me had likely stemmed from his Berserker aura. Without another word, Krygor bent down, took each of the Ambassador's legs in turn, and snapped them right below the knee. Instead of the horror such violence should have inspired in me, I smiled; Hartuk's screams the most soothing music to my ears.

Stepping away from the mess on the ground, Krygor extended a hand towards my daughter. Without hesitation, Siona ran to us and took it. My giant turned to the Sarenians, who continued to look on impassively.

"I would have brought my mate to you at the Monolith, but I no longer trust myself," Prince Zerien said in a slurred voice. "You have won your Hunt, Braxian. No one else will challenge you on your way to the extraction point. We will see you at the Palace."

With these words, the Prince turned around and started heading back towards the city. One of his guards removed a flare similar to the one that had been given to us and sent out the signal. Krygor slipped an arm around my waist and, holding my daughter's hand, he led the way to the Monolith, his men closing the march.

CHAPTER 18
KRYGOR

As soon as our shuttle landed in the city by the Palace, I demanded to be taken to my ship. The Emperor suggested that we take the day to recover from our ordeal, and for his personal physician to attend to my injuries. I told him that as much as I appreciated the offer, I couldn't see the back of this rock soon enough. That comment seemed to amuse him more than offend him.

Regardless, it took a good hour to get the ship ready, properly stocked, and for my females to say their farewells to the other females of the Serail. However strange it felt to me, Hope had formed some genuine bonds of friendship with at least a couple of them. She still didn't understand—or rather couldn't quite relate—to their culture, but she appreciated that their differences worked for their world and brought them happiness.

By the time we gathered at the launchpad, the sun had already begun its decline on the horizon. Surprisingly, we received a royal sendoff, with many Sarenian nobles, the Imperial Council, and the Imperial Guard all in attendance. The young prince held my daughter's hands while softly speaking to her. Either he was an excellent actor, or the depth of his feelings for her were genuine. As much as I hated admitting to it, I believed the latter to be true. But it was her response that mattered to me most; and my little Siona was clearly quite taken with him.

The Hunter, Faolen, also attended our departure. Wisely, he remained at a distance although his longing gaze never strayed from my woman. In a way, I pitied him. I couldn't imagine being in his shoes watching my Hope turn to another male. No doubt blood would be spilled.

"This is it then," said Emperor Nemrox. "I guess I should thank you for keeping your female from turning Ambassador Hartuk into a complete pile of mush. It would have been awkward having to explain to Emperor Ardrak that his representative had been obliterated by a Guldan female."

The taunting glimmer his eyes made me smirk and reminded me, once again, that the alliance between their species wasn't as strong as the Guldans had led us to believe while attempting to sway us into joining with them.

"Despite the hardships you faced, I hope you will not hold too much of a grudge towards my people," Nemrox continued. "Your presence here, although short, has made clear it had been a mistake not to open the channels of communication sooner. I believe it would greatly serve both our peoples to maintain the dialogue going forward." His gaze flicked to his son still engaged in a whispered conversation with Siona. "We have more than just our empires that seem meant to be united."

I slowly nodded and smiled noncommittally at his less than subtle meaning. "There indeed seems to be some interesting times ahead," I replied in a neutral tone. "I will keep in mind that so far you have kept your word regarding releasing us. But one of yours hijacked my ship once. Who knows if another of yours hasn't hacked it further while we were detained in those cages?"

The Emperor stiffened, looking mildly offended at that remark. "Your ship was hacked by a Hunter to capture you and your females without violence; a wise and effective choice on his part. You are being released by my edict. All viruses have been removed from your ship." A sudden gust of wind blew the Emperor's long hair in his face.

Nemrox flicked the offending locks over his shoulder with a certain level of annoyance. "You will also note that, while we were readying your ship, my head of security has sent a message to both your son Anton and Magnar Ravik informing them of your imminent return. They have sent a small fleet to meet you along the way."

"Then we should probably get going soon," I said in a taunting tone. "We wouldn't want that fleet to come too close to your home world."

"Indeed," Nemrox replied in a neutral tone.

"Until we meet again, then," I said, slapping my chest with my fist in the traditional Braxian greeting.

"Until we meet again," the Emperor echoed, with a slight bow of his head. He turned to my woman who had just given a last hug goodbye to Gatina and was walking towards us. "Take good care of the Councilor, Madam," Nemrox said to her in that incredibly soft and gentle voice he always used with women, regardless of their station. "I suspect he will play a major role in the future that awaits all of us."

"I certainly intend to," Hope responded as she stopped by my side.

I slipped a possessive arm around her waist and drew her against me. She leaned into me with a soft smile, then allowed me to lead her towards Siona.

"Remember your promise to me for I will not forget mine to you," the Prince said gently to Siona. He then turned to me with that same serious and mature expression that never ceased to amaze me. "I will trust you to keep my mate safe until the day I finally get to reunite with her. In the meantime, may you have a pleasant journey home."

"Farewell, young prince," I said before boarding my vessel with my females by my side.

Yulan and Zartag, already aboard the ship, made quick work of getting us airborne. After seeing that my females were comfortably settled in, I went back to the bridge to first send a video confirmation both to my King and my three sons that we were on our way. Not knowing whether to trust the Emperor about any viruses that might not have been cleaned from my ship, I kept the communication neutral and non-committal. Ravik knew me well enough to read between the lines.

Along with my crew, we spent the next couple of hours running full ship diagnostics and checking for any form of viruses, backdoors, or suspicious subroutines in the system that could make us vulnerable to hijacking or eavesdropping.

By the time I returned to my quarters, Hope had already tucked Siona in for the night. Although still a little early, the ordeals of the day had taken their toll on the young girl. Even I felt somewhat bone weary. But any thought of sleep fled right out of my mind the minute I entered my room to find my woman dressed in nothing but a translucent, short white nightgown that hid little of her delectable curves, and the perky nubs of her erect nipples. Blood rushed to my groin, and a hungry growl rose in my throat.

My female gracefully descended from the bed where she had been sitting with her legs crossed beneath her. She slowly strutted her stuff towards me, the panels of the open front, sleeveless top she wore parting with each of her steps, giving me tantalizing glimpses of her belly button. The scent of her blossoming arousal made my nose twitch and my cock jerk in my pants. Stopping in front of me, my female slipped her hands under my shirt, caressing my abs upwards all the way to my chest. Her thumbs circled my nipples before her nails clawed their way down my stomach, the exquisite burn drawing another groan from me.

My hands reached for the perfect globes of her ass left exposed by the three flimsy strings that served as her so-called thong. But before I could get a proper grip, Hope dropped to her knees, her delicate fingers deftly opening the magnetic clasp of my pants. My abdominal muscles knotted in anticipation as she freed my cock from its confines. The burning feel of her hands on my length stroking me ignited a blazing flame in the pit of my stomach. My fingers closed around the beautiful horns gracing her forehead as the inferno of her mouth closed around the head of my shaft. She sucked me slowly, teasingly, and licked at my slit while her hands squeezed and caressed me at an increasing pace. I pressed my thumbs at the sensitive base of her horns. She moaned, immediately responding to their erogenous quality, and the scent of her musk rose another notch, making my mouth water.

But as much as I loved the feel of her hands and mouth on me, I wanted to be buried deep inside her, the rippling ridges of her sheath squeezing me from all sides, the heat of her body pressed against mine, her labored breath fanning against my shoulder, and those sexy as fuck moans she emitted while I pounded into her filling my ears. I swiftly removed my shirt, ignoring the sting of the fabric pulling at the wounds from my lashing. Then, holding onto my female's horns again, I pulled up, forcing her onto her feet.

She gasped and gave me a surprised look. One hand still fisting her left horn, I slipped my other one between her legs while crushing her lips with a possessive kiss. I growled in approval at feeling her slick, hot, and wet for me. In a single brutal move, I snapped the flimsy string of her thong before rubbing the engorged little nub between her legs. She moaned against my lips as my tongue invaded her mouth. My female all but melted against me as I plundered her mouth, savoring her sweet taste, and reveling in her trusting submission to my dominance.

Without breaking the kiss, I lifted her up with my hands on her ass. Hope immediately wrapped her legs around my waist. I rubbed my throbbing cock against her core, her shivers of pleasure making me painfully hard and aching with the need to possess her. It took all my willpower to gently impale her on my cock. Hope gasped against my lips as I pushed myself deeper and deeper into the tight grip of her sex. I hissed with bliss as her ridges tightened around me, sucking me in farther, and undulating around me in the most exquisite caress. I could never have enough of this, of her. She was my drug, my addiction, my everything.

As she adjusted to me, I gave up holding back, surrendering at last to the rabid hunger that had plagued me for the eternity we'd been separated while being detained in that damn cell. I held her up, my hips pumping upwards, in and out of her in a frenzy. Fire coursed through my veins, further fueled by the throaty moans of my female and the searing feel of her feverish skin against mine. Hope's nails dug into my wounded back as she began to crest. The pain only turned me on even more, awakening the beast, transforming blood rage into unbridled lust.

Closing the short distance to the nearby wall, I pinned my female against it and then thrust into her brutally. Hope shouted my name as she came apart, her inner walls convulsing around me with greed as my seed shot out inside her. I roared in ecstasy as my essence poured out blissfully but continued to thrust in and out of her until I hardened again. My *Vaya* chanted my name as I wrested two more orgasms from her before relenting.

Eyes locked with my woman's, my cock still buried deep within her, I slowly walked to the hygiene room and reluctantly pulled out of her before settling her on the counter. I ran us a warm bath in the large tub scaled to my Braxian dimensions. Carrying her in, I sat down and placed her in front of me, her back to my chest. Taking my sweet time, I washed every inch of her, slowly, reverently, like the goddess she was to me. Hope turned around, a strange glimmer in her eyes. For a moment, she appeared to want to say something, but then held back at the last minute. It disappointed me, and yet, it didn't matter. My heart already knew the words that had burned her lips. My *Vaya*'s eyes told me everything I needed to know.

Without a word, Hope reciprocated, washing me carefully, as if she feared to break me. It was odd, and yet I couldn't recall any female touching me with such tenderness and affection. Something within me shifted, and I further melted for the delicate female who had captured my heart. As soon as she finished, Hope moved closer to me and, in a fashion similar to our very first time together, my woman grabbed my cock and put it inside her before hugging me and burying her face in my neck. I closed my arms around her, a profound emotion choking me. I had never been loved this way by anyone. This was no longer about sex, it was about us, my *Vaya* and me, being one soul, one body, joined for eternity.

"You are mine, Hope. And I am yours," I whispered in her hair, not caring that emotion made my voice unsteady. "You are my heart, my mate, and the very air I breathe. I love you."

Hope's arms tightened around me, and her slender body trembled against mine. After a moment, she pulled back and stared at me with an expression on her beautiful face that I could not put into words. All I knew was that, for as long as I drew breath, I would fight the entire galaxy itself so that she would always look at me this way.

"My giant," Hope whispered with a trembling voice. "My magnificent Krygor, I didn't know what life was, except for pain, hardship, and despair until you taught me that happiness was possible. You are my heart and my soul. I love you beyond words, and I can never thank the Goddess enough that she would take pity on one such as me and bless me with one such as you. You are beyond anything I could have ever dreamt of. Anything."

I captured my woman's lips in a slow and tender kiss in which we expressed our love and devotion. Rising out of the water, I took my time drying her and then letting her dry me in return. I carried her to our bed and spent the next eternity showing her how much I worshipped her. It was gentle and tender, devoid of the feral hunger that had animated me earlier. By the time we fell asleep in each other's arms, we were bound for life, body and soul.

CHAPTER 19
HOPE

My heart was attempting to pound its way out of my chest as a tall human male named William led us to the elevator simply labeled 'One' in luminous letters inside the HQ of Venus Hive. In the nearly two weeks it took us to travel halfway across the Quadrant from Sarenia to Anton's main space station, my nervousness at meeting my mate's firstborn son steadily escalated. Where Siona couldn't have been more excited, I felt faint with worry.

It didn't help that we had arrived so late in the evening. By the time we had landed, my baby had already been struggling to keep her eyes open. I stood nervously next to my mate as the lift flew up to the penthouse. Siona leaned against me, half dozing, while William and Krygor made small talk. Despite the size of the cabin, my man all but filled it up. Even William, with his non-negligible size, appeared tiny next to my giant.

The lift came to a smooth stop, a high-pitched chime resonating before the doors parted. A stunning human female, perched on the highest heels I had ever seen and dressed in an elegant sarong expertly wrapped around her perfect body, stood next to Anton. Her delicate hand held his massive one. I had seen pictures of Grace, her performances as a singer having earned her galaxy-wide admiration. At first,

I had assumed her fame was owed to her marriage to the big boss of the Hive Network. However, the first time I heard her sensuous, throaty voice, I had been sold. She was more beautiful in person than I had expected. To my surprise, she appeared shy and yet welcoming, nothing like the entitled bitch one often unfairly assumed the wife of one of the most powerful men in the galaxy would be.

And Anton was indeed one of the most powerful men in the Eastern Quadrant. With his wealth, he could wreck the entire economy of major cities and even lesser planets. His reputation of being a shrewd but ruthless businessman preceded him. He was known to have an almost magical ability to read people, to understand what drove them down to their deepest desires, and to manipulate them into getting exactly what he wanted. Whenever you did business with him, no matter how beneficial it was to you, it was always ten times more beneficial to him. But right now, I would be the one facing his scrutiny; a test I couldn't afford to fail.

He was his father's spitting image, but a smaller version—although small was a relative term where Braxians were concerned, even a hybrid. Anton would still be deemed a giant compared to humans, but small compared to purebloods.

"Thank you, William," Anton said with a friendly smile to his right hand and head of security.

William nodded, went back into the elevator, and left. Anton's dark eyes, the same intensity as his father's, glided over me, pausing on my face. My stomach knotted at the reminder that I looked a great deal like his mother; the mother he hated. The Goddess only knew to what extent it would impact whatever relationship he and I could have in the future.

His gaze moved down to my daughter, who was blinking furiously to keep her eyes open, looking mightily embarrassed and nervous that her tiredness might come across as rudeness. An almost imperceptible smile stretched his lips before he looked at his father. Like my giant, Anton's face became almost terrifying when he smiled. And yet, my heart melted at the love and pride that lit up his eyes upon seeing his father.

"Krygor!" Grace exclaimed. "You're here at last. I should scold you for scaring us like this. Naya won't stop demanding to know when she will see her Grappa Krygor."

Krygor chuckled. "Apologies," he replied not sounding remorseful in the least.

"Right," mumbled Grace with false displeasure. "And these two lovely ladies must be Hope and Siona, correct? I am Grace, and I married scary-big-guy junior."

That made me laugh, and I instantly liked her. Krygor had told me she was a sweet lady, but I had not expected this almost youthful innocence that emanated from her.

"Hello, Grace," I said with a friendly smile. "Thank you for welcoming us in your home at such a late hour. We had meant to arrive much sooner, but this one ended up having never ending meetings with the fleet that had met us halfway."

I cast a severe look at my mate, to which he responded with a shameless grin.

"My father is well-known to be almost as hopeless a workaholic as I am," Anton said in a teasing voice. "Welcome to my home, Hope, and you, Siona. Father has spoken highly of you both. I want to hear all the details about that foolish Guldan Ambassador. But that will have to wait. The little one seems to be in dire need of a restful place to lie down."

"I'm so sorry," said Siona, looking mortified. "I don't mean to be rude."

"Nonsense, sweetheart," Grace said. "My own three children are long gone into la la land. I can't wait for you to meet them in the morning. My daughter, Naya, will be crazy about you. I hope you won't mind if she gets a little grabby with your horns," Grace added sheepishly. "My youngest one is a little obsessed with them. She's relentless with the Magnar's children."

"I don't mind," Siona said, a charming blush creeping up her cheeks.

"Come on, honey," Grace said, extending a hand towards my daughter. "I will show you to your room."

I smiled with gratitude at the younger woman. She winked at me, gently took Siona's hand, and led her down the hallway on the opposite side of the luxurious seating area that sprawled in front of us, three steps down from the elevator's doors. Seconds later, the elevator chimed again. Startled, I turned around to see William bringing in our bags on a hovercart. I felt silly for having already forgotten them. With a final nod, the human male left, bidding us goodnight.

"Please make yourself comfortable," Anton said, gesturing at both of us to take a seat on the dark leather couches in his spacious living area. "Father, I count on you to offer Hope a drink while I take your bags to your room."

"Thank you, my son," Krygor replied.

My giant led me to the three-cushion couch which faced a wall decorated with a large portrait of the family. A series of smaller pictures depicting their three children in various activities surrounded it.

"They are beautiful," I said, looking at the adorable and exotic faces of the little ones.

They were the perfect mix of their parents, with their mother's beauty and a cute, smaller version of their father's broad, flat nose and prominent forehead. Although their Braxian heritage couldn't be denied, their features were refined and not as brutish as a pureblood or even a hybrid.

"Too pretty," Krygor mumbled while pouring us both a drink. "It's fine for females, but males should be fearsome."

I couldn't help but laugh at his grumpy expression. It was so odd to have spent the past few days with a species that took great pride in its tremendous beauty, and now be with another that sought the exact opposite. For a Braxian, the more brutish the features, the purer the bloodline, and therefore, the more fearsome and stronger the warrior. It had been hilarious watching my giant curse up a storm when the Veredian healer from the small fleet that had met us on our way back from Sarenia had proven a little overzealous in tending his wounds from the lashing, also mending old wounds and battle scars he had taken great pride in.

And yet, as I sat here waiting for his son's return, tension painfully stiffened my back and shoulders. Krygor approached me with a glass filled with an amber liquid that I wasn't familiar with. I gratefully took it from him and drank deeply, before coughing like a novice at the burn. My mate laughed as he sat next to me, a commiserating look on his face.

"Relax, my love. Everything is fine. Don't worry so much. My son is just as nervous as you are; he, too, wants to earn your approval," Krygor said in a soft voice. "He knows how important this is to me, how important you, Siona, and all my sons are to me. Family is everything."

"I know but..."

Anton's return prevented me from continuing. Grace had joined him. He sat on a chair across from us before pulling his mate onto his lap. She cuddled against him, and the love between them moved me deeply.

"Your daughter went out like a light," Grace said. "I promised you would come to wish her goodnight. She said thank you, closed her eyes, and off she was into dreamland."

"I'm not surprised," I replied sheepishly. "It's a long and somewhat complicated story, but she has decided she will be the Empress of Sarenia. And as such, she must be a fierce warrior. Krygor made the mistake of showing her the training program the Dagna has set up for Braxian females. My baby now spends her entire days in the holodeck going through the various modules over, and over, and over again."

Grace burst out laughing, while her mate simply smiled, a knowing expression in his eyes. The next thirty minutes flew by with us having friendly conversations. However, taking mercy on us, the younger couple sent us to bed, looking forward to spending more time with us in the morning. According to Krygor, Anton and Grace were night owls who could stay up till the wee hours of the morning going to one of the local clubs—a boast I intended to put to the test at least once before we left Venus Hive.

I checked in on my baby who had been given an impressively large room all to herself. I kissed her forehead and caressed one of her horns before letting my mate take us to our room. Cuddling up against him, I let sleep take me away, my heart soaring with the hope of a joyful new beginning.

Morning found me fully refreshed. Although I knew the rooms to be properly soundproofed, I refused to play naughty with Krygor, to his utter dismay and annoyance. He didn't understand why it would be a problem for his son and wife to know we'd been going at it. It wasn't like they didn't have a clear idea of what we've been up to during our two-week flight from Sarenia and even before that. It was silly, but I couldn't help it. Once I got more comfortable with them, maybe it wouldn't feel so awkward. And yet, somehow, I believed I would always feel self-conscious about it.

We ate breakfast with the kind of joy and excitement I had always craved. Between Anton's three children, my daughter, and us four adults, this was truly the family spirit that had been denied to me and my children our whole lives. Gavin—Anton's oldest son who had recently turned nine—had an impressive maturity to him. When Siona brought up the Sarenian Prince, Gavin mentioned he, too, had already found his soulmate: a young girl named Zhara who lived in the Western Quadrant. That spurred on another discussion at the end of which I realized my newfound extended family was far more powerful than I ever imagined.

As we finished breakfast, Anton received a com message from William informing him that Roman had arrived. Krygor then explained that he had business with both him and his son. I rejoiced at the thought of seeing the broker again. I owed him a lot.

Just as we were heading to Anton's office where Roman waited for us, it was Krygor's turn to receive a com, this time from his king. He apologized and went to take it in our room for some privacy. While Grace looked after the children, I followed Anton to his office. Roman rose to his feet as soon as I entered, a warm smile on his face.

"I hear things have been quite exciting for you lately," Roman said in a teasing tone. "Trouble seems to follow you everywhere."

"So it seems indeed," I replied slightly discouraged. "But, hopefully, this was the last of it. Trouble would truly have to be a vindictive bitch to follow me all the way inside a Braxian compound."

The two men chuckled, and Anton gestured for me to take a seat in a fancy, collection-item chair made of red leather, which stood right across from his massive dark wood desk. That struck me as odd. Roman, still standing next to the minibar on the right side of the room, nodded encouragingly at me to proceed. Not wanting to make waves, I complied and settled in the incredibly comfortable, and luxurious Empire chair.

Anton circled around his desk to take a seat in the imposing chair behind it. His dark gaze lost all the warmth—correction: the pretend warmth—he had been displaying since my arrival. The man sitting before me was no longer the son of my mate, but the ruthless businessman who had built the greatest adult entertainment empire in both the Western and Eastern Quadrants. A wave of unease washed over me, and I cast an inquisitive glance at the broker. His face was unreadable, which only heightened my discomfort.

"Trouble indeed has followed you your entire life. It was quite an unexpected twist of fate that my father should have come to Lilith Hive when he did. The perfect timing to meet with the one female that could have almost passed for my mother's sibling," Anton said matter-of-factly.

My stomach dropped, and I clasped my hands nervously on my lap to keep them from shaking. There it was, the conversation I had so dreaded since first learning of my resemblance to his mother. In that instant, I realized Krygor being called away at this time had probably been deliberately orchestrated for me to get cornered here by these two men. But why Roman? Why would he turn on me? I felt totally betrayed and fought the urge to just get up and walk out of the room. But I would not run away and hide. I had found my Prince Charming, and I would fight for him tooth and nail. No one, not even my mate's firstborn, would take away what I had searched for my entire life. Krygor and I deserved this happiness. We had earned it.

"It is truly uncanny," Anton continued, tilting his head to the side as he examined my features.

"So, it may be," I said in a clipped tone. "But she's not me, nor am I her. As you can see," I added waving at my horns, "we're not even the same species. And I am pureblood."

"That you are," Anton replied. "And yet, you came to my father the same way she did, as an Indentured Servant."

Once more, his tone was factual, devoid of any emotion and, thankfully, any contempt. Still, I felt slighted, offended, and even humiliated despite the truth of his words. It was the comparison to his mother that hurt, the implication that I could be as cold and calculating as she had been. I bit my tongue not to point out that his own mate had come to him through indentured servitude. I lifted my chin defiantly and waited for him to finish his thought, both fearful and eager to see where this was headed.

"I love my father, Ms. Morak. I owe him my life in far more ways than you can even begin to imagine. I would do anything to protect him. Anything." This time, a hard glint shone in his eyes.

"That is understandable," I replied noncommittally. "Your father loves you very much as well. You are his greatest pride."

An emotion I couldn't define flickered through his brutish features, vanishing so quickly I wondered if I hadn't imagined it.

"He is mine as well" Anton said. "Therefore, I would like to make you a proposal."

My blood turned to ice. The feeling of dread that had hung over my head since this whole conversation had begun now came to the forefront with a vengeance. I cast another glance towards Roman who averted his eyes with something akin to guilt and shame.

"You may speak your offer," I said stiffly, "but I strongly suspect that it will not interest me."

"My father bought your contract for three million credits, with the agreement to pay you an allowance of a thousand credits per month for two years at which point you will be free," Anton said calmly while he tapped a few commands on his datapad which he then turned towards me. "I'm offering to pay off your contract and, instead of the 24,000 credits you would receive at the end of it, I will give you three million credits, deposited directly to your account and free for you to use however you see fit, if you and your daughter leave Venus Hive today and never come back. You are never to contact my father again for anything. My head of security, William, already has transport on standby to take you and your child to the sanctuary planet Haven, here in the Eastern Quadrant, where you will both be safe from anyone who might want to hunt you. Alternatively, the Veredians have agreed to offer you asylum on their home world if you prefer."

I felt the blood drain from my face as I gaped at him, disbelieving. I turned to look at Roman, hoping for him to tell me this was just some kind of a sick joke. The embarrassed expression on his face crushed the last illusion I still held. The pain that clawed at my heart went deeper than the humiliation I felt at my mate's son thinking he could so easily buy me. It was the dream of my perfect family crumbling around me, the knowledge that Krygor would be utterly devastated by his son's ruthless—if not cruel—behavior.

Worse still, the possibility that my giant might be in on it cut me to the core. I understood that he had been terribly hurt, but how could we have any future if he didn't trust me? Was that a test?

"I will pretend you never made such a disrespectful offer," I said in the iciest tone. "In fact, I will pretend none of this ever happened."

"Fine. Twenty million credits," Anton countered in a sharp, hard voice, his black eyes never wavering from mine. "Same conditions."

I froze, my brain unable to even comprehend that anyone could so casually throw away such unfathomable sums. Speechless, I stared at the man I had hoped to call 'son' just like his sire had adopted my daughter as his.

"It is an honest offer, Hope," Roman said in a soft voice, snapping me out of my daze. "I have reviewed the contract. You know I have your best interest at heart."

"My best interest?" I hissed. "You think my best interest is to walk away from the one man who has ever shown me kindness and respect? Who has ever made me feel like I was worth something? That I wasn't just some fuck toy or exchange currency for men to advance their personal affairs? The only man who has made my daughter and me feel safe and showed us what it was like to be happy?"

I turned back to look at Anton, holding back none of the anger burning inside of me. He lifted his chin and held my gaze unflinchingly. I fought the urge to get up from his damn fancy chair and reach over his desk to smack him a good one in the face.

"I don't give a fuck about your wealth or how much of it you can throw around," I snarled. "Your father loves me and, newsflash, I love him with all my heart. No amount of credits can ever buy what we have. How dare you try to destroy his happiness? You're allowed to have it but not him? I thought you, of all people, would rejoice for him."

"One hundred million," Anton said impassively, almost sounding bored, as if he hadn't heard a single word I had said.

At that instant, my heart broke. Whatever I could say wouldn't matter. He had judged and condemned me before I even arrived here. It hurt all the more that I didn't know where I'd gone wrong or if there was anything I could have done to bring about a different outcome.

"If I hadn't shared similar facial traits to your mother, would you be acting the same way?" I asked in a soft voice, musing out loud.

"That's irrelevant," Anton said with a dismissive wave of his hand. "Do we have a deal? One hundred million credits deposited within the next few minutes into your account, and you leave with your daughter within the hour with the explicit promise never to contact my father again."

"Fuck you," I said calmly, in a conversational tone. "Fuck you and your offer. You can throw at me all the wealth in the world, my answer will always be the same. No amount of credits will ever be worth what I have found with Krygor."

"Hope—"

"Fuck you, too, Roman," I snapped, interrupting him. "If you want to make yourself useful, you can draw a new contract for this fool," I said, gesturing with my head at Anton. "Since we'll be here for a full week, please draft the equivalent of a prenuptial agreement by which I confirm that should I ever leave Krygor, whatever the reason, I forfeit any rights to his wealth, leaving only with whatever I brought into the relationship, and the twenty-four thousand credits agreed upon in the original contract. That's the only 'agreement' I'll happily sign." Rising to my feet, I leveled both men with a look filled with contempt. "I do not require your love or your respect, but I will not let you ruin my mate's happiness. For his sake, not yours, I will pretend that none of this shitshow just happened. But be warned, you say anything unbecoming to my daughter in any way, shape, or form, and all of your millions will never be enough to protect you from what I'll do to you."

I turned on my heels so abruptly that the fancy chair almost toppled over. As I stormed towards the door, the scraping of Anton's chair resonated behind me.

"WAIT!" he shouted.

I ignored him.

"Please."

Something in his voice stopped me dead in my tracks. I turned around, baffled, only to have the wind knocked out of me at the sight of the vulnerable expression on the brutish face of one of the most intimidating men in the Eastern Quadrant. Lips parted in shock, I stood frozen as he slowly approached me, like one would a frightened animal —or, in this case, a vicious one. Eyes widening, too shocked to react, I watched him stop before me and raise his massive hands to gently cup my cheeks. My fingers instinctively closed around his wrists. The tender look on his face, so similar to his father's, took my breath away.

"I am so glad he has found you at last. Father has searched for you his whole life," Anton said in a soft, gentle voice. "He fell for her because she was a pale version of the one that had truly been meant for him. But it had always been about finding you, Hope. You are far more beautiful than she ever was, or ever could be, both inside and out. I wish *you* had been my mother. Marla would have never fought for me —and in fact never has; not like you did and continue to do for your daughter… my sister. Forgive my previous cruelty, but I needed to be sure. I do not give my heart easily. But when I do, it is unconditional. Welcome into our family."

My throat was too tight to speak a single word. When Anton leaned forward to press a soft kiss on my forehead, tears pricked my eyes and a shiver ran through me. My hands, still wrapped around his wrists, tightened their grip, and I exhaled a shuddering breath.

The sound of the door opening startled me. Anton slowly straightened and gently released my face from his hold.

"What the fuck is going on here?" said the thundering voice of my giant behind me.

I turned around to see him standing just inside the door, a deep frown creasing his already strong brow, making him look even more menacing than usual. His eyes flicked between us, a suspicious expression on his fearsome face. My mind raced to answer, not wanting to create a conflict between father and son, especially not now that Anton and I just had this breakthrough.

"I just offered to repay Hope's contract and give her one hundred million credits to leave you and walk away," Anton said casually.

My head jerked towards him, my mouth gaping in shock. Roman's choked gasp behind Anton was muffled by Krygor's powerful voice.

"WHAT?!" Krygor shouted.

The anger on his face and the look of betrayal as he stared at his son with murder in his eyes was terrifying. I instinctively took a protective stance in front of Anton and raised my palms in an appeasing gesture before me as I looked at my mate.

"It wasn't like that," I said in a soothing voice. "Well, not quite like that."

"It was exactly like that," Anton countered. "I do not keep secrets from my sire."

I looked at him over my shoulder in disbelief. What the fuck was he thinking? Why was he attempting to further provoke his father?

"And she told me to shove it," Anton continued.

"Actually," Roman intervened, "*fuck you* were her exact words."

Krygor's confused gaze cycled through each of us in turn, clearly taken aback by the absurd situation he'd just walked into.

"I already waived her contract," Krygor said through his teeth. "I've already set her free."

My head jerked towards my mate, flabbergasted. At this rate, I'd soon be getting a whiplash.

"I know, but she didn't, which made it easier to attempt to bribe her," Anton confessed. "However, she wasn't even remotely tempted. Heck, I would have even offered three hundred million credits, not that it would have swayed her. She genuinely loves you."

"I know that," Krygor said, both upset and baffled by his son's behavior—although hurt dominated. He extended a hand towards me, and I willingly went to him. "As I love her, too. Why would you try to drive her away from me? She is not your mother. She is nothing like Marla. I may have shown poor judgment all those years ago, but I am no longer a fool. Hope is my soulmate."

"I know that now, beyond any doubt," Anton said sheepishly. "I wish nothing but your happiness, Father. You are everything to me. I am sorry if what I did hurt you, but I will never apologize for attempting to protect you, our family, and yes, myself as well."

"As you should," I said softly. I extended a hand towards Anton, the same way my giant had done with me. Anton came willingly, taking my hand in his much bigger one. I smiled at him before turning to Krygor. "I am his mother, now," I corrected gently. "The same way you have become my Siona's father. I do not just take you as my life partner, but everything that comes with you: your three sons, your clan, Braxia, and anything else that matters to you and that has helped define the man who has captured my heart."

"My *Vaya*," Krygor whispered.

He leaned forward and gently kissed my lips, but I could feel him restraining himself not to show even more emotion. Straightening, he gazed at his son's face and then gently held him by the nape.

"We're family," Krygor said.

Anton glanced at me and smiled. "Yes, we all are."

"You know that I love you, right? That you are my greatest pride and joy?" Krygor asked his son. A powerful emotion crossed Anton's face. He swallowed hard, blinked quickly, while nodding his head. "Good," Krygor continued. "Now, attempt to bribe my mate again, and I will put you across my knees."

We burst out laughing, and I found myself squished into a three-way hug. My heart filled with love for my two giants.

Our stay on Venus Hive flew by way too quickly. By the time we left, Grace steadily called me Mom, and Anton called me Mother. As I'd later on found out, Grace had been left at an orphanage as an infant and never fully recovered from her sentiment of abandonment. Family and a sense of belonging meant a great deal to her. I could relate. With my own messed-up childhood, the much too early loss of my mother, and then being sold and used as currency, had left far deeper wounds than I had realized. To thus be claimed soothed old scars I'd too often denied.

Their children calling me Nana did something weird to me—something weirdly wonderful. Siona was crazy about her new big brother Anton. Beside the fact he doted on her, she was missing Tevek terribly —my firstborn son. The Goddess only knew when we would be reunited. At least, the Veredians had promised to keep hunting for him.

Our arrival on Braxia turned out to be another surreal experience. I'd thought the Sarenian sendoff had been impressive with the Prince, the Emperor and so many noble houses, but it paled in comparison to the Braxian greeting. Their Dagna alone—the Veredian-Guldan hybrid called Mercy—could have stolen the show all by herself. She was tall, stunning, with a you-better-not-fuck-with-me aura that commanded respect. But to have her standing next to Magnar Ravik—the most fearsome beast I had ever seen—and surrounded by his army of giants, including two dozen guards riding real karvelis, was enough to have me weak in the knees.

The Magnar and his queen approached us with a savage grin on his face. He gave my mate a brutal embrace and slapping his back with such strength it resounded loudly. The Dagna followed, and only then did I notice the two young Braxian-Veredian-Guldan hybrids shadowing her: the firstborn young twins of the royal couple. Siona gasped in awe at their sight. Far more intimidated than I'd ever admit, I smiled with what I hoped would come across as confidence to the most gorgeous Guldan female I had ever beheld. The softness of her expression as she returned my smile turned me upside down.

"Hello, my sister," said Mercy in a soft, sensuous voice. "Welcome to your new home."

"Thank you, Dagna," I said, relieved that my voice came out firm and confident despite my being utterly star struck.

"Please, call me Mercy," she said, with a dismissive gesture of the hand. "You'll find that Braxians aren't formal. And I fully intend to call you Hope. It is good to see that more of us have escaped the chains of Guldar. I will want to know everything about you, about that lovely daughter of yours, and how in the world you managed to tame that crazy beast."

Krygor chuckled and pulled me against him with a possessive grin. "With all due respect, *Dagna,* I'm not crazy, just borderline insane… sometimes. And I would rather you do not corrupt my mate with your strange ideas. My daughter has already grown obsessed enough with those wretched combat training programs of yours."

Mercy's brows shot up, and her head jerked towards Siona. "You love combat?" she asked my daughter.

"Absolutely!" my baby exclaimed, staring at the Dagna with undisguised awe. "We're not allowed to do things like that on Guldar, but now I definitely want to learn more."

"You and I, my dear, are going to get along beautifully," Mercy said with a mischievous glimmer in her eyes.

The Magnar rolled his eyes and moaned as if in pain. "And another daughter ruined," he grumbled with false despair.

"Hush, my beast," Mercy said, playfully elbowing him, before giving me a resigned look. "You will also find that Braxians like to shout, roar, and flex their muscles, thinking they're intimidating someone. But deep down, they're all big, fluffy teddy bears."

Outraged scoffs resounded all around from the massive giants surrounding us.

"Come," Mercy said, slipping an arm under her 'beast's' arm to lead us inside the imposing walls of their compound. "The feast awaits."

We followed in their wake, a silly grin plastered on my face.

"Welcome home, my beautiful Hope," Krygor whispered in my ear.

CHAPTER 20
KRYGOR

Sitting at the table of Ravik's private council chamber, I let my gaze roam over my fellow Councilors—including Ravik's heir, Keran—each of them eyeing me with the same eagerness. I could no longer sit in this room without being reminded of Mercy all but raping the Magnar while under the effect of her mating heat. A part of me regretted that my Hope didn't have that purely Veredian trait—not that she wasn't naturally wild and unbridled.

I quickly chased away the naughty images of my mate popping into my head. The last thing I needed was to get distracted by a raging hard on while discussing the serious matters that I had to share with my king.

I spent the next half hour or so going through a detailed report of everything that had transpired from the moment Faolen had taken control of my ship. The fleet that had met us after our liberation had run a battery of tests on my vessel, and the most powerful virus scans in Mercy's arsenal. Nothing had been found, as per the Emperor's promise. So far, it did look like there had been no foul play.

"I still think we should retaliate," said Raylor Caldes. "They have captured and tortured one of the Magnar's High Council. Not responding makes us weak."

I smiled at the irony that the man who had hated me—and probably still did—for executing his firstborn son in the slowest, most excruciating fashion for the wrongs against my own firstborn, would now be advocating for avenging my honor.

"A fair point," replied Keran, pensively. "At the same time, Emperor Nemrox could have disposed of you and of your ship long before we reached you."

"You have stated the facts of what happened," Ravik said, "but what is your sense of the actual situation there? I would have expected you to come in here demanding blood. And yet, you seem disturbingly calm and peaceful."

"I do want blood," I said with a predatory smile. "I will be spilling it shortly when I go pay a visit to the special friend my son had delivered to my dungeon. But I do believe it would be unwise to enter into a war with Sarenia at this point in time."

"Why?" Fenton asked with a frown.

Along with Elder Pattel, Fenton was one of the more moderate members of our Council, and both were part of Ravik's inner circle of trusted friends and allies.

"Because I believe there's far more going on than meets the eye," I said in a somber tone. "The one thing that struck me was how easy everything turned out to be."

"How so?" Ravik asked.

"The whipping was real, as was the Verlenk they unleashed in the Arena," I said pensively. "They had not expected us to free ourselves of our chains. But then, offworlders always underestimate the power of a Berserker. However, the minute the tide turned in our favor, they adjusted their plan in real time. The Prince is as big a player as his sire. It was uncanny how much decisional power was left to the boy."

"The same boy who covets your adopted daughter," Boros said, his pale brown eyes narrowing. "Is that why you suggest avoiding a war with them? An alliance of your houses could bring great power to your clan and to Braxia as a whole."

I liked the Clan Leader Boros Grumar. He had come a long way from being on Ravik's list of the Fifteen to be executed to now sitting on his Council as one of the voices that spoke truth to power honestly instead of the political games others liked to play.

I pursed my lips, pondering my words carefully before I spoke. "It could be both a great benefit and a recipe for disaster. I do not relish the thought of my daughter so far away, living amidst an entire species with the power to mind control her."

"Mercy is already hard at work to develop some sort of technology or method to make the Veredians and our allies immune to the Sarenians' compulsion without impeding their own psionic abilities," Ravik said. "There are still many years left before the Great War. We will be ready."

"I am relieved to hear it," I replied. "But many other things troubled me. The Emperor and his son made it a point to prove to me on multiple occasions that the relationship between them and the Guldans is lukewarm at best. He has hinted they are currently planting moles or sleeping agents within the ranks of the Guldan Empire.

"Isn't that a good sign of them wanting a genuine alliance with us?" Raylor asked.

I rubbed my chin pensively then shook my head slowly. "I do not know that we can trust them. It felt to me that they were trying too hard. You see, after I killed Ambassador Lorik's brother and then Juntel—that fool who had attempted to force himself on my daughter-in-law—everything became too easy."

"I still can't believe the idiot sought revenge on you for the punishment Mercy and I exacted on that insane son of a bitch," Ravik muttered. "But what do you mean by too easy?"

"They gave me a way out through the Blood Hunt," I said, my eyes going out of focus as I revisited the events in my mind. "A way out that ensured both my clansmen and my females would leave Sarenia with me, unscathed. Having seen us battle the beast in their Arena, they knew we could handle what creatures lurked in their Gauntlet. Except, it turned out we couldn't. We were not prepared or qualified to defeat a Crawmaw. And yet, conveniently enough, an elite group of Sarenian Hunters showed up just at the right moment to help us ensure victory.

And then, while they had us surrounded and outnumbered, they merely walked away."

"That is indeed unusual," said Fenton. "They wanted you to succeed while giving you the illusion that you were earning your way out."

"Exactly. And the same happened when I found my females. They had conveniently been escorted by the Prince and the Hunter who had captured us to begin with." I refocused on the men around the table, puffing out my chest with pride. "You should have seen my mate and daughter beating the living daylights out of that pompous Ambassador Hartuk. I almost didn't stop my woman from killing him."

"Why did you?" Keran asked with genuine curiosity.

"The Emperor made me promise that I would only maim him, not kill him," I replied matter-of-factly.

Startled gasps resounded around the table as my fellow Councilors all stared at me in disbelief; a sentiment I understood all too well.

"Nemrox wanted to earn my trust and keep the peace between our peoples," I continued. "Until we know more, we should keep open the communication channels between us. Either way, I do not trust them, even though I genuinely believe that the Prince actually is my daughter's soulmate. But this whole thing feels too much like a setup. Nemrox knew that I would find myself in a position to kill the Ambassador and made sure I wouldn't. How could he be so sure unless he had planned it? How do I even know that Hartuk's actions were his own and not compelled by the Sarenians? After all, it made no sense for him to challenge the Prince's claim to Siona during the Hunt when he's courting an alliance with them. It made even less sense for him to act so brutally against my mate to subdue her after he'd been sternly warned against the consequences of harming females in any way."

"You said that compulsion makes the victim uneasy," Fenton argued. "They do not know what is bothering them, only that something isn't right. Under the circumstances, Hartuk would have known or at least guessed that the Sarenians were messing with him."

I shook my head slowly. "Not necessarily. In fact, in this instance, it completely makes sense that the Ambassador would not have realized he was under any compulsion if they were in fact controlling him. The unease stems from being coerced into doing something that goes against the victim's normal will. But Hartuk wanted to hurt my mate and to spite the Prince after the disrespect they both showed him. He also wanted to hurt me by taking ownership of my woman and abusing her. So no, he wouldn't have resisted being incentivized to do those specific things."

"Following that logic, we can't even know if the Ambassador was truly the one behind ordering your capture along with your mate," said Raylor. "The Emperor could have been behind the whole thing from the start and only mind-fucked Hartuk into thinking it had been his idea to begin with."

"That thought crossed my mind," I said, nodding in concession. "But I do believe the idea originated from Juntel, who mentioned it to the Ambassador, who in turn decided to pitch in for my capture. When Juntel ordered the purchase of my daughter for the Prince, he had no idea that I would eventually be brought into the deal by Roman. He merely saw it as an opportunity to get revenge on my son. The Emperor then seized the chance to turn the events to his advantage."

"I don't like any of those mind fucks and will manipulations," Boros said in a growl. "This is messy business. Are we sure we want to deal with these people?"

"It's even messier than you realize," I said. "The truth is, I don't know that anything that happened on Sarenia, if anything of what I've seen of their people and their culture is real at all. That does not sit well with me."

"Why would you doubt it?" Ravik asked. "We're immune to negative psionic powers. Your mind was your own throughout your stay there, unless you were drugged."

"I was not drugged that I'm aware of," I replied crossing my legs as I pondered further. "But it is quite possible everything we experienced was orchestrated to give us a specific image of their people; a positive image straying from the negative one that has been spread about them, and that would make it enticing to consider an alliance with them."

"That would seem extremely difficult to pull off in the short time between your capture and your arrival on Sarenia with so many moving parts," Keran argued. "How could you ensure that someone in such a large population wouldn't give away the plot?"

"That's just it," I replied staring intently at my future king. "Who we got to see and where we got to go were strictly controlled. I only had direct contact with the Prince, the Emperor, their guards, and the two idiots that set up the whole thing to begin with. Hope and Siona were kept inside the Serail, under the constant supervision of a couple of their females. Those females spent their entire time trying to sell them the beauties of their home world and the upsides of their culture. Conveniently enough, a strong emphasis was put on how well females are treated on their planet, and how their entire society revolves around the protection and nurturing of offspring."

"The exact type of topic that would resonate with your mate," Fenton replied, understanding dawning on him.

"Now you understand my reservations," I said. "For this reason, I do believe we need to grow closer to them. We must be able to spend time on their home world with the ability to move freely in order to understand who they truly are or if this was all just a show."

The men muttered their agreement. How we went about it, though, would be a completely different discussion, especially appointing the perfect candidate with the right diplomatic inclinations and the right analytic mind to see through whatever schemes or deceptions might be thrown his way.

"But there's something else you should be aware of," I said, leaning against the backrest of my chair. "The Emperor had a lot to say about the Korletheans, none of it positive. If what they are implying is true, our four-way alliance may not survive."

"One less player only means the remaining ones grow closer," Keran said calmly. "I have no particular affection or dislike of the Korletheans. There is some shady business going on with them and the way their people are currently divided. They are no threat to us. We are immune to their psionic powers unless we allow it. The Veredians are the ones we must remain allied to at all cost. *They* will rule the galaxy. All others are expendable."

"No, son," Ravik said. "The Xelixians cannot be eliminated from the equation. They are too tightly integrated with the Veredians and married to their leadership. However, the Korletheans *might* be expendable, even though they fathered many of the Veredians."

"So, do we further fuel that fire by sharing those revelations with the Veredians?" Raylor asked.

"And thus, do the Sarenians' dirty work for them?" Boros challenged.

Ravik stared at Boros for a long time. His words had hit a nerve. I had felt that the Emperor had been playing a game, but it took this comment for it to really sink in. I hated feeling used.

I snorted slowly shook my head, feeling stupid for not having seen it sooner. "I feel used and yet, they have been up front with me about what they wanted. Prince Zerien flat out said he wanted Braxians, Veredians, and Xelixians to leave the Galactic Alliance and join them. This is the first seed of dissent that would eliminate the part of the alliance they don't want."

"Do it," Keran said. We all turned to look at him, surprised. "If this alliance is meant to be, we will all need to trust each other. That means secrets will need to be exposed. We do not have that many years before the Great War. If we are to have a fallout, let it be now so that, should there be any chance of mending the rift, we will have a long enough runway to do so. And if it cannot be mended, then we might as well cut out the cancer now rather than let it fester."

Ravik smiled with a glimmer of pride that I understood too well. I didn't know how much longer Ravik would hold the throne before passing it on to his son, but it warmed my heart that his heir was a man that I would proudly follow as I had followed him.

"So, it shall be done," the Magnar said. "As for Sarenia, we will keep the communications open, but do not trust them. And regarding Guldar, as much as I would like to confront them, your abduction was an opportunistic attack by the Ambassador, whom you've already punished. We cannot lay it at the feet of Emperor Ardrak. But let's try to get eyes on Hartuk and find out what the Sarenians are getting him to do."

With everyone in agreement, we moved on to other important matters that took far too long to settle for my liking. Even though it had been swift considering the complexity of some of the cases, I was dying to go say hello to someone. When Ravik finally released us, the men chuckled watching me all but bolt out of the room. Despite their amusement, I didn't miss the glimmer of unease in some of their eyes. I had no qualms being who I was and enjoying the things I did. But when it came to dealing with my enemies, especially those who wronged my family, I took extra pleasure giving in to my most primal urges.

The journey back to my compound took an eternity. I commed my mate to let her know I would be late. Thankfully, she was busy with the other females doing whatever females did. I had bloodlust in my veins and didn't care much for her to see me like this. And as much as I had enjoyed her demolishing Hartuk in that forest, I didn't want my blood rage aura to drive her to violence again. My mate was a nurturer, not a killer.

I walked through the streets of my compound, nodding at my clansmen rushing to and fro to handle whatever business they were up to. Pride filled my heart at the sight of the modern dark stone buildings lining the streets, the high spirit of my people when barely a decade ago we'd been shunned by the other clans, teetering on the verge of bankruptcy and starvation. And with my recent successful deals on Lilith Hive, even greater prosperity would come to my people.

The clash of swords, war cries, and grunts of battle greeted me as I strolled by the battlegrounds around the back of my fortress. Dheran, my second-born and my heir, was sparring against two of my clansmen while the others were all training one-on-one. That, too, filled me with pride. Originally, it had saddened me that, even had I chosen to ignore the outrage from my people at the thought of a half-breed leading the clan, Anton could have never inherited the role from me. Braxia was a brutal world ruled by the strongest of each bloodline. Despite my first-born's strength and intelligence, as a hybrid, he would never stand a chance against the mass and power of the purebloods. In the end, it turned out for the best. Anton lived and breathed business, while Dheran embodied the very spirit of Braxia—of *modern* Braxia. He would make our Ancestors proud and lead us into a glorious new era after I stepped down.

Walking past the barracks and into the underground prison, I made eye contact with Sorek, the guard in attendance. He nodded in greeting and swallowed hard as I kept walking towards the back lift into the dungeon. Sorek knew I was not to be disturbed. With each step bringing me closer to my victim, my blood heated up a notch. My fingers twitched with anticipation during the short ride down the lift. The doors parted onto a short hallway at the end of which a reinforced, soundproof door opened with a simple wave of my hand before the biometric scanner.

My guest of honor stiffened, his head jerking up at the grinding sound of the door. I could have made it quiet, but the sadistic side of me liked the fear that sound instilled in the victims within, knowing their tormentor had returned.

He attempted to get up from his kneeling position, but his magnetic shackles kept him down on all fours.

"Hello, Luther," I said in a sickly-sweet voice, the acrid scent of his fear giving me a hard on.

My pulse picked up, and my head swam from all the adrenaline flooding my system.

"Please. Please," Luther begged, his lips dry from the beginnings of dehydration.

A necessary evil to avoid the unpleasant messes the subjects tended to make once the fun began if they had anything to eat or drink prior to my ministrations.

"No need to beg me," I said in a teasing tone. "You're about to get my undivided attention for the next little while… Or rather, the next *long* while. You see, I do not appreciate when people mess with what's mine. Not only did you ignore my warning to stay away from my woman, you had a fucking Sarenian mess with her mind, and you planned very bad things for my daughter."

I voiced a command in Braxian, which activated the magnetic shackles on his wrists and ankles, forcing him into a standing position, arms above his head and legs parted. He shivered, looking like a giant maggot in his pale nudity. Lips quivering, eyes pleading, he watched me with dread as I closed the distance between us and started slowly circling around him like a predator preparing to pounce on its prey. My footsteps resonated loudly on the metal grids covering the floor. It had been designed specifically for the blood and gore to drain neatly while I worked on my latest canvas.

"Even after buying that shady contract you had conned Hope into," I continued in a conversational tone, "I would have let you get away with your wrongdoings against her and the fact that you had trapped my woman without a chance of earning her freedom. And you know why? Because, however foul, your scheme allowed me to meet her. What I do not forgive is the stress and trauma you put my females through by sending a Hunter after them."

"Mr. Aldriss, please—"

"Quiet," I said in the same neutral tone.

"Please, I—"

I backhanded him with more force than I had intended, having forgotten how fragile a constitution humans possessed. Blood exploded from his mouth. I couldn't say for sure if I'd broken a few teeth or fractured the bones of his cheek, but the crooked angle of his lips indicated clearly that I'd dislocated his jaw. I cursed myself inwardly for my carelessness. I had extremely unpleasant plans for the man, and one-shot killing him with a broken neck did not feature in said plans.

"I said quiet, Luther," I repeated in a soft but slightly disappointed tone.

Obviously, that request could no longer be fully obeyed the way he was whimpering and moaning in pain. Such a weakling. If that sufficed to already have him in agony, how would he react once I really went to town on him?

"You see, your punishment is going to be greater than what I had first intended after you had us kidnapped," I said passively while going to fetch the hover-tray containing all my tools. Luther twisted his neck to look at me over his shoulder, sheer terror twisting his features. "My son sent me a detailed report of the activities you've been performing in order to supplement your revenues. The way you abused a lot of the females you conned into signing contracts with you was already questionable, but the minute you began dealing in underaged trading, your fate was sealed."

I returned with the tray, stopping in front of him. Pausing for a moment, I allowed him to feast his eyes on the instruments of his impending torture neatly laid out on the tray. Luther opened his mouth to plead again. A single stern look from me silenced him. But that, too, wouldn't last very long. I picked up a wand-looking device and waived it before his eyes.

"This is a cauterizing scalpel," I explained in the same casual tone. "Normally, I don't use it because I love the sight of blood dripping from the many cuts on my canvas. But I do not want you bleeding to death. At least, not yet."

"Please, please!" Luther slurred, his dislocated jaw making it harder for him to properly form words. "I didn't hurt her."

Ignoring him, I looked down at the limp, shriveled appendage that he called a cock. It would never cease to amaze me how tiny an adult human's genitals were. Luther's would barely be big enough for a thirteen-year-old Braxian. Words were unnecessary for him to understand what was about to happen. He began struggling and pulling against his restraints, screeching for help that would never come. It was the sweetest music to my ears. A part of me, deep down, understood such response to a sentient being's distress was disturbed, and yet, I felt no remorse for reveling in it. With another verbal command, I ordered the shackles to stretch him further, thus restraining his movements. After all, I wanted to cut off his dick, not eviscerate him.

"That's for using my woman as your personal sex toy. You were never worthy of her," I whispered, my face inches from his.

The strident sound of his scream failed to bury the sizzling sound of his flesh burning as the scalpel effortlessly sliced through it. Little plumes of smoke rose from the wound instantly cauterized. The somewhat nauseating stench did not turn me off in the least. His severed appendage flopped to the floor with a soft, fleshy thud. Luther's screams faded into silence as he lost consciousness.

That was fine. We had time for him to come back around.

While waiting for him to regain consciousness, I used a marker to delineate the sections from waist to neck that I would be flaying. Switching to a laser scalpel—wondrous for the precision of the cut and the limited bleeding it provoked—and a pair of tweezers to hold the skin, I gave in to my sinful pleasure.

Three hours later, I put my tools down next to the large bowl filled with strips of skin. Luther's screams had dwindled to no more than unintelligible grunts and pained moans, his voice having broken within the first hour. Walking over to the sink, I slowly washed my hands, impressed with how cleanly I had worked. Then, without a word, I exited the dungeon.

Sorek didn't need any instructions from me. In the morning, all that remained of Luther would be fed to the karvelis.

EPILOGUE
HOPE

Settling in my new home in Krygor's compound went smoothly. Strangely enough, meeting Krygor's other two sons didn't stress me out as much as meeting Anton had. But then, they still had their mothers who looked nothing like me. I had feared that they might resent my presence, as it had robbed them of a chance of being with their children's sire. To my relief, Dheran's and Gorav's mothers didn't live in Krygor's compound. Those females each came from different warrior clans. They had been my mate's concubines decades ago, for the specific purpose of giving him pureblood heirs then had returned to their respective clans after fulfilling their duties.

As I soon discovered, contrary to my home world, there was no such thing as an illegitimate child. In fact, very few Braxians actually married. Procreation was mostly a business arrangement between bloodlines and clans. To my surprise, unless specified otherwise, the sire always kept the offspring by default to become part of his clan. The mother usually only stayed for the first couple of years to breast-feed the child if the purpose had been purely reproduction and no romantic involvement existed between the pair.

Dheran—Krygor's second born son and heir as future leader of Clan Aldriss—was as impressive a beast as his father. I hadn't known what to expect in terms of a welcome, but definitely not the warm and rather teasing one he gave me. Whenever I looked at Gorav—his youngest—the word antsy came to mind. He, too, was just as tall, broad shouldered, and muscular as his father, but seemed unable to sit still. However, it was the way both sons melted for my daughter that truly won me over. Then again, they had grown familiar with handling young female relatives thanks to their niece Naya—Anton's youngest child—and their Magnar's daughter Lissy. Between Gorav being permanently assigned as the Dagna's bodyguard and the closeness between the royal family and their clan, they were all but an extended family as well.

At first, I had been worried that the rest of the clan would reject me. I had feared to be useless and maybe even in the way of whoever was running the compound. Instead, the females welcomed me with open arms. Things had radically changed on Braxia in the past few years since their new Dagna's arrival. With the abolition of slavery and females' increasing emancipation, every clan had been redefining the rules and lifestyle within their respective compounds. Without a wife or consort within the Aldriss Compound, the place was a real mess; the type of mess I'd been raised to handle as the lady of a wealthy man's estate.

As much as my people were hated here on Braxia, Mercy had made Guldan females popular. I wholeheartedly embraced my new role as wife to Clan Leader and High Council Aldriss. With my mate's blessing, I turned the functional, but somewhat cold compound, into a home. The clansmen mumbled a little at first when I requested some modifications to the layout of certain rooms to make things easier, such as a straighter path from the kitchen to the main hall so that the staff serving food didn't have to travel through narrow corridors and perform inconvenient detours because that's how it had always been done.

Discovering the underground trade market the women had set up delighted me beyond words. I had known of the Braxian shops in the Hive Network owned by Anton, but I had not realized it had originated from traditional craft passed down from mother to daughter. Taking part in developing our own clan's line of products was exhilarating. As a foreigner, one who had lived not only on Guldar, but especially on Lilith Hive among the rich clientele, who was familiar with the type of exotic trades and trinkets that could appeal to potential customers made me incredibly sought after by the other females of other clans always seeking to pick my brain. It became a game I genuinely enjoyed, giving them just enough tidbits to make them curious and give them ideas, while keeping the juicier stuff for my own clan.

I never found out what became of Luther. Rumor had it he'd actually been brought here to Braxia. Once, I asked Krygor about him. His response, the hard, wild glimmer in his eyes—almost feral—told me all I needed to know. His answer was simply that my daughter and I would never have to worry about him again. I felt no pity for whatever fate had befallen him. Even though he had helped me off my home world, he'd lost any right to sympathy on my part; not for entrapping me in an endless contract, but for seeking to take advantage of my daughter.

Siona was blossoming in this new environment. Although Braxia had its problems with gender inequalities, Mercy and the Magnar were steadily helping mentalities evolve. But more importantly, each compound was run almost as an independent city or state. As my giant simply didn't give a shit about what anyone thought of how he ran his, he allowed us to do pretty much whatever made us happy, as long as it didn't endanger us or the clan in whole or in part.

I was happy, truly happy. Despite his busy schedule, Krygor always made time for us. Siona and I each received our own karvala, courtesy of the Magnar, after the magnificent females chose us. Watching my adrenaline-junky of a daughter riding a real reaver also freaked me out, but I had promised myself that the day we were free, no one would tell her she cannot do something she cares about as long as she approached it in a responsible way. And my baby *was* responsible.

Something had changed after our abduction to Sarenia. I didn't quite know what it was, whether the shock from our adventures, meeting the Prince, fighting the Ambassador, or getting a better under-standing of the political stakes that were already at play and that would shape our future. All I knew was that my daughter had become Mercy's and Krygor's shadows, learning everything from them, from combat, to politics, to the technological rivalries among the main players.

Krygor had told me about his agreement with Prince Zerien. It bothered me that her future should be set by third parties. And yet, I had seen and felt the chemistry between them. Still, I was grateful that my mate had been wise enough to only consent to courting at the end of which my daughter would respond in the way she saw fit—which included the right to walk away if she so chose. Anything less would have been met with my categorical refusal. Nevertheless, Zerien kept proving his interest by sending regular vidcoms to my daughter, relating random tidbits about his day or random events taking place on his home world. I allowed it but kept a close eye on it to make sure he wasn't brainwashing her into anything.

But this was neither here nor there. For now, I had a much different conversation to have with my mate. This morning, halfway through my meeting with some of the wives and concubines from neighboring clans, my guests had suddenly gone still, their noses twitching and their eyes widening as they stared at me. It had been incredibly disturbing and unsettling. And then Thala, the decades-long concubine of Clan Leader Fenton—one of the High Councils of the Magnar and a good friend of my mate's—recovered from her shock and congratulated me; my daughter had blossomed.

That comment left me even more confused. Siona had already entered womanhood weeks prior. Considering she wasn't even in the room at the time, being at school, that remark made even less sense. And then all eyes lowered to my stomach and understanding dawned on me. The Braxian's ability to smell pregnancy, down to the gender of an at least one-month-old fetus, blew me away.

I was a complete nervous wreck by the time my mate arrived home. Despite his sons rejoicing at the news, having scented my baby as I approached before I could even speak a word, I worried at Krygor's reaction. It was illogical, but I couldn't help it.

I stood in the Great Hall as the entrance doors of the fortress opened to let him in. Siona stood a few steps away from me, framed by her big brothers, Dheran and Gorav. The rest of the clan members, both males and females who dwelled within the fortress—not the individual dwellings within the walls or surrounding the compound—had also gathered in the Hall. A part of me wished for privacy when revealing the news to my giant. Unfortunately, he would know the minute he walked in, and his people wanted to be here to congratulate him.

As soon as he entered, Krygor's steps faltered at the sight of such a welcoming party, unusual on a regular day. His gaze locked with mine. The expression on my face must have given away my nervousness as his eyes narrowed, instantly suspicious. Within three steps towards me, Krygor froze, shock plastered all over his face. I held my breath, waiting to hear what he would say. But not a word came out.

Too many emotions flickered through his features for me to latch onto a single one. Approaching me carefully, his gaze never straying from mine, Krygor stopped right in front of me and rested his massive hands on my hips. His thumbs gently caressed the sides of my still flat stomach. My lips quivered as I gave him a shaky smile. A powerful emotion took over his fearsome face before he returned my smile. All tension bled out of me, and my mate kneeled in front of me to press his nose to my stomach and inhaled deeply. An approving growl rose from his throat, the most beautiful purring sound I had ever heard as my fingers slipped through his silky, wavy black hair.

His arms closed around my thighs, and when I least expected it, he lifted me up while rising to his feet with a victorious roar. I squealed in surprise, my hands fisting in his hair with fear before bursting out laughing. The voices of his clan mates rose in a powerful clamor of celebration. As he spun me around, covering my stomach with kisses, I addressed a silent prayer of gratitude to the Goddess.

We were home. We were safe. We were loved.

THE END.

THE VEREDIAN CHRONICLES
Escaping Fate
Blind Fate
Raising Amalia
Twist of Fate
Hands of Fate
Defying Fate

BRAXIANS
Anton's Grace
Ravik's Mercy
Krygor's Hope
Keran's Dawn

XIAN WARRIORS
Doom
Legion
Raven
Bane
Chaos
Varnog
Reaper
Wrath
Xenon
Nevrik
Rogue

PRIME MATING AGENCY
I Married A Lizardman
I Married A Naga
I Married A Birdman
I Married A Minotaur

I Married Wonjin
I Married A Merman
I Married A Dragon
I Married A Beast
I Married A Dryad

THE MIST
The Mistwalker
The Nightmare

DARK TALES
Bluebeard's Curse
The Hunchback

BLOOD MAIDENS OF KARTHIA
Claiming Thalia

VALOS OF SONHADRA
Unfrozen
Iced

EMPATHS OF LYRIA
An Alien For Christmas

THE SHADOW REALMS
Dark Swan

OTHER
True As Steel
Alien Awakening
Heart of Stone

ABOUT REGINE

USA Today bestselling author Regine Abel is a fantasy, paranormal and sci-fi junkie. Anything with a bit of magic, a touch of the unusual, and a lot of romance will have her jumping for joy. Hot alien warriors meeting no-nonsense, kick-ass heroines give her warm fuzzies.

Before devoting herself as a full-time writer, Regine had surrendered to the other passion in her life: video games! As a professional Game Designer and Creative Director, her previous career had led her from her home in Canada to the US and various countries in Europe and Asia.

Facebook

https://www.facebook.com/regine.abel.author/

Website

https://regineabel.com

Regine's Rebels Reader Group

https://www.facebook.com/groups/ReginesRebels/

Newsletter

http://smarturl.it/RA_Newsletter

Goodreads

http://smarturl.it/RA_Goodreads

Bookbub

https://www.bookbub.com/profile/regine-abel

Amazon

http://smarturl.it/AuthorAMS